Rave Re~ ... ~~ ..~ ~~.~~.

Divorced, Desperate and Deceived

"The fun—and action—never stops in the enchanting *Divorced, Desperate and Deceived*. Christie Craig's prose practically sparkles with liveliness and charm in the exciting conclusion to her stunning Divorced, Desperate and Delicious Club trilogy."

—Joyfully Reviewed

Gotcha!

"The mystery and romance plots fit seamlessly into a witty and fast-paced novel that's easy to read and satisfying to the heart."

—*Publishers Weekly*

Divorced, Desperate and Dating

"I was simply delighted by this breezy, snappy, goodtime story . . . This book is sure to brighten your day."

—Beyond Her Book Blog, *Publishers Weekly*

Weddings Can be Murder

"A story that twines emotions and feelings with sizzle and steam, all wrapped around bits of humor . . . *Weddings Can Be Murder* combines passionate and intense characters with a plot that's well-balanced and fast moving. It's edgy and fun."

—Once Upon a Romance

Divorced, Desperate and Delicious

"This is an entertaining fast-moving mystery and romance peopled with interesting, likable characters, as well as warm cuddly animals. The main romance, as well as the secondary ones, are delightful, and the suspense is well done. This is an all-around enticing and fun story to read."

—RT Book Reviews

Shut Up and Kiss Me

"Craig stays focused on playfulness and sexual tension, and hits all the high notes en route to happily ever after."

—*Publishers Weekly*

Other Books by Christie Craig

Divorced, Desperate and Delicious
Weddings Can Be Murder
Divorced, Desperate and Dating
Gotcha!
Divorced, Desperate and Deceived
Shut Up and Kiss Me
Hotter in Texas Series

For more information: www.Christie-Craig.com

Books by Christie Craig writing as C. C. Hunter

Shadow Falls Series (Young Adult)
Turned at Dark (Free download!)
Born at Midnight
Awake at Dawn

Taken at Dusk (available April 2012)

For more information: www.CCHunterBooks.com

Murder, Mayhem and Mama

Christie Craig

Murder, Mayhem and Mama
Christie Craig
Material excerpted from *Blame It on Texas* copyright © 2012 by Christie Craig. Printed with the permission of Grand Central Publishing, Hachette Book Group. All rights reserved.
Material excerpted from *Born at Midnight* copyright © 2011 by Christie Craig. Printed with the permission of St. Martin's Press. All rights reserved.
Copyright 2011 © by Christie Craig
Cover design and illustration by Janet Holmes

ISBN: 978-0-9838902-6-3

Acknowledgments

To my agent Kim Lionetti of BookEnds, whose support and guidance is just what this writer needs. Thanks for helping me whip this book into shape. To Faye Hughes, my first reader, who isn't afraid of my scary first drafts. Thanks for the help, but mostly thanks for the friendship. To Susan Muller, Teri Thackston and Suzan Harden: thank ya'll for the support, the friendship, the critiques, and a heck of a lot of laughter. You will never know how much you mean to me. To Jody Payne, a woman whose courage and strength inspires me, whose writing support and friendship is invaluable.

To Rosa Brand, AK A R. M. Brand, whose brilliance as a graphic artist stuns me. Thanks for your support, for your fabulous videos and for the newfound friendship. Thanks to Kathleen Adey for the editing, and support with publicity; you make meeting my deadlines an easier task.

There's always a person in your life who you know helped make you who you are. A person who, without them, you wouldn't have taken the same journey. A person who didn't just make a difference in your life, they were the springboard to all you've achieved. Thank you hubby, Steve Craig, for all you have done to help me become the person and the writer I am. Thank you for the love, for the years, and for the endless laughter you share with me. We make a hell of a team, don't you think?

Prologue

"Do you want to die, old man?" One of the four ski-masked men jammed the cold barrel of a gun against Farley Goldstein's throat.

Farley stared into the dark eyes peering out of the mask. Between jolts of panic, he remembered asking himself that very question this morning. Did he want to die?

"Open the safe or I'm gonna blow your head off." The armed stranger latched onto a handful of Farley's starched shirt.

The gunman slammed Farley against the wall. He slid to the floor, pain vibrating through his head. As lights exploded behind his eyelids, fear clawed at his chest—not fear of death, but fear of dying.

The flashes hadn't stopped when the biggest assailant stepped forward. "Easy. He knows we're serious. Don't you, ol' man?"

Farley nodded, but he couldn't seem to talk. The shattering of glass echoed as the other two men swung baseball bats against the locked display cases filled with the most expensive pieces of jewelry. Twisting his wedding ring around his knuckle, Farley thought about his wife's ring that he always carried in his shirt pocket.

The meaner guy with fat fingers crouched down and screamed, "Open the effing safe!"

When the assailant slammed Farley against the wall the second time, his hearing aid squealed. The whiteness that seemed to come from his brain exploded again. He stared into the sheet of light. The shapes started taking form. Fat Finger's lips were moving, but Farley didn't hear the words.

Then he saw *her*. She appeared out of nowhere. Like a . . .

"Wow." She stood looking at the case of diamond rings. Farley reached up to touch the ring nestled over his heart. Beth, his wife, had come to take him home. Oh, how he'd missed her these last few years. But his image cleared, and he realized the redhead wasn't Beth.

The woman looked up at him. "I like the chocolate diamond. I've always been a chocoholic."

Holding a cigarette, she turned and focused the big fellow and frowned. "Weasel." She blew smoke in his face. "They say second-hand smoke can kill you. I hope they're right."

The big guy waved a hand in front of his face and looked around the room in an odd way.

"You're not going to hurt my girl." After a second, the woman turned to meet Farley's eyes again. "I may not look like I can take him on—" she waved her cigarette in the air, "—but nothing pisses a mama off more than some nitwit going after her kid. I'll neuter his butt when he's sleeping. He'll wake up and be a nutless wonder." She moved closer to Farley, walking in her high heels, her hips swayed, and the bracelets dangling on her wrist jingled as she moved.

Farley just stared. Something wet oozed down his brow, sweat or blood, he didn't know which. "Who are you?" She didn't belong with these guys.

"Who do you think I am?" Fat Fingers screamed.

The woman knelt and touched Farley's hand. Oddly, the attacker didn't even look at her. Her touch sent a wave of warmth through him. "Just a 'not ready.' I have someone's balls to collect before I . . . dive into the light, do my last tango, or make the big leap into the hereafter. Or whatever it is they call it." She smiled.

"You're dead?" he asked.

"Say what?" one of his attackers asked.

"Yup. Kind of sucks, doesn't it?" answered the woman. Pursing her lips, she spoke around her cigarette. "But I heard when I cross over, it'll be different. And don't worry, your sweet Beth's waiting on you. But first, I need a favor. Open the safe and then . . ."

Farley listened and then opened his eyes. Had he fallen asleep? The woman was gone. Had he been dreaming? Only imagined her? Was she an angel? But what kind of angel smoked and talked about cutting men's balls off? He watched as one of the other men lunged forward.

A different guy swung a bat and hit the wall over Farley's head. "Let me talk to the old geezer."

The sheetrock above Farley's head crunched. White particles, appearing almost like snow, rained down on his face. Dragging a deep breath into his tired lungs, he smelled cigarette smoke. While he couldn't see the odd woman anymore, he felt her presence. And for some reason he didn't feel so alone. He blinked and tried to remember what she needed him to do.

The baseball bat crashed into the wall again.

Oddly enough, he wasn't afraid anymore.

Chapter One

"Cali Anne, your alarm went off twenty minutes ago, and that naked weasel in bed with you cut it off."

"Thanks, Mom." Cali McKay rolled over in bed. She buried her nose deeper into her lavender-scented pillow and tried to ignore the roar and grind of Hopeful, Texas' Monday morning traffic filtering through her bedroom window. Sleep offered escape. Escape from—

"Did you hear me?"

The four-finger touch against Cali's back sent panic shooting through her sleep-dazed mind. She popped up on her hands and knees, air hitching in her throat. Gasping, she stared over her shoulder. Nothing. No Mom. Of course, no Mom.

"What is it?" a masculine voice asked.

She looked at the weasel—er, Stan—stretched out next to her. His black hair lay scattered across his brow.

"Just a dream." Still positioned as if offering horsey rides, she saw Stan's gaze zero in on the scooped neckline of her nightshirt. Her girls were no doubt making an appearance.

His violet eyes went from casual-sleepy to wanna-get-laid in a nanosecond. She flipped over and plopped on her butt.

"Bad dream?" he asked as if guesstimating his odds for getting lucky.

And from the smirk in his eyes he had the odds all wrong.

"Not happening." She adjusted the nightshirt to non-cleavage level, and blinked at the red-illuminated numbers of the clock. "Crap, I needed to be up twenty minutes ago."

"Kids love it when their teachers are late." He inched closer as if he hadn't heard her not-happening comment. His calf hair crinkled against her knee, and his tongue flicked inside her ear. A move that had even her liver shriveling up and screaming yuck.

She really needed to tell him she didn't like that. But telling men what she liked and didn't like in the sex department was like asking a new boss for a raise, or telling a stranger he had a blob of spinach in his teeth. It just didn't feel right.

"Can't be late." She leaned out of tongue range.

"Then skip work." He caught the hem of her nightgown and finger-walked his way up. Past the knee, past the thigh . . .

"No." She grabbed his wrist and jack-knifed out of the bed. "Do you know how long it's been since we had sex?"

Halfway to the bathroom, she pivoted, stared, and decided the relationship was too new to be having this conversation. That meant it was also too new for her to be waking up with him. He'd been here for three weeks now. She couldn't remember for sure how long he'd told her it was going to take for his new apartment to become available. But three weeks was too long, wasn't it? Or had that been a lie?

Oh, goodness, she hated early morning epiphanies.

"It's been forever since we've done it," he snapped.

She blinked. "Four days. We did it last Thursday." Before the call from the hospice nurse.

"And that doesn't seem like forever to you?" He yanked off the blanket. Naked and aroused, he stood up. And at six foot plus, a lot of man stood there, too. His penis jutted out and bounced. Once. Twice.

How could men do that? Just prance around, penis bobbing, with no concern whatsoever? A man's privates were not eye friendly. Well, not when you were late for work and sex held about as much appeal as a pap smear.

Stan groaned. "It isn't normal." His Mr. Wiggly lost some of its oomph.

She tipped her chin up, swearing not to look at it again, and anger stirred inside her. Anger at Stan. Anger at herself for letting this thing with Stan get so out of control. Why hadn't she already asked him about his apartment? Oh, yeah. She'd been too busy dealing with her dying mother.

Then came the anger at her mother for refusing the last sessions of chemo. And that was the anger that hurt the most. The chemo would have given her another few months.

Stan continued to stare. "Why don't you want to have sex?"

Maybe because funerals are not an aphrodisiac? She bit down on her trembling lip. Crying in front of him felt wrong, but she'd had sex with him. What did that say about the relationship? When had crying become more intimate than sex? What did that say about the sex they'd had? Not a good sign. "It's been a bad week," she said with sarcasm.

"For Christ's sake, Cali. *She* died. You didn't."

His callous words burrowed so deep she stumbled back. The baseball bat he'd left leaning against the wall banged to the floor. She watched it roll under the bed. Was a four-day reprieve from sex too much to ask when one's mother died? She didn't have the handbook to know. Didn't want to know. All she wanted was a shower and to get away from the naked weasel and the—she looked one more time— limp penis in front of her.

~

Detective Brit Lowell stared at the dog-eared file amongst the other litter on his desk. Until the mold was scraped off Hopeful's Homicide Division's ceiling, the entire unit had temporarily moved into the main precinct. Brit slung a Styrofoam cup into the metal trash can. They had cases to solve and higher-ups were worried about a freaking fungus. Right now, he'd take his chair and his office—with the mold—over being stuffed in this broom closet.

"Go home, Lowell," someone said as he passed an office door.

The grit that lined his eyes reminded him he'd been here too long. He hadn't adapted to the graveyard shift. It might help if he went home and slept during the day. He seldom did. Go home or sleep.

He curved his shoulders back in the pitiful desk chair. Then, knuckle-locking his fingers behind his neck, he tried to work out the kinks. The kinks hung on. The stress had hunkered down in his shoulders for the long haul. As had the grief.

Damn, he missed Keith. Partners on the force for two years, they'd seldom agreed on anything except that they each would have taken a bullet for the other. But Brit hadn't been there when the bullets were fired.

"Hey." John Quarles, his new partner, freshly transferred from another unit, walked into the office and tossed one file on the desk while he clutched another two.

"What's this?" Brit reached for the file, his chair squeaking like an injured bird.

"The jewelry store heist got promoted to homicide." Quarles dropped into a chair and rolled closer. Too close. Brit could smell what his partner had eaten for lunch, and it wasn't particularly appetizing.

"The old man who owned the place died," Quarles added.

Brit heel-skidded his chair back and tried to remember the buzz he'd heard about the case. He shuffled through a few crime-scene photos and remembered the owner of the store had been knocked around with a baseball bat. "I thought he was okay."

"Doctors thought so, too." Quarles ran his fingers through his blond hair. "They stitched him up and sent him home. His daughter found him later."

"Prints at the crime scene?"

"Come on, do we ever get it that easy?"

"I could use some easy," Brit said.

"And if she was gorgeous and female, I'd fight you for her." Quarles grinned. "But, the vic gave great details of the robbery. He even called the distributor and asked for images of the stolen jewelry, so, we'll have something to show the pawn shops." Quarles rolled closer.

Brit leaned back. Quarles didn't seem to appreciate personal space. Right now, Brit needed a lot of space. And it wasn't just because of Quarles' fondness for chili-fries, or the fact that he'd fight Brit for some gorgeous girl. Which, frankly, Brit was about as much in the mood for as he was chili-fries.

Quarles dropped the other files on the desk. "I did find two other jewelry store robberies. Same MO. Four men, ski masks. One in Austin, the other in Dallas."

"So our guys move around, eh?"

"Yeah." Obvious pride at his findings brightened the man's green eyes.

"Any leads?" Brit flipped open the other files. More photos, a few written reports. Unfortunately, the only case Brit gave a rat's ass about now had Keith's name stamped on it.

"Nope."

It figured. "Any chance we can pass this over to Smith and Tates?" The smell of yesterday's coffee assaulted Brit's nose; he picked up another half-empty cup and tossed it. It landed with a dead thud in the trash can.

"Nope. Sergeant gave it to me personally."

A clattering noise exploded down the hall.

"Get your freaking hands off me you pervert! What's wrong? You gotta tiny dick or something?" The woman's tone, more so than her words, made a man want to cover his dick, small or not, and it brought Brit's head up in a flash. He knew that tone. More important, he knew the woman—Rina Newman, a local prostitute.

Rina, wearing red and very little of it, jolted to a stop in his doorway. Brit's gaze moved over her. The part of his male psyche that hadn't had sex in seven weeks appreciated her hourglass form and exposed cleavage, but the appreciation fizzled out before anything below the belt reacted.

Brit started to turn his chair to face the wall, hoping to do it before Rina spotted him.

His hope was futile when she suddenly swung around. "Detective Lowell, make them take the cuffs off!"

Having worked in the sex crime division before homicide, he knew most of the girls. They all had a sad story to tell. Thanks to his mother, he had grown immune to sad stories.

"What'd you do, Rina?" He crossed his arms.

"Soliciting drugs," Officer Pratt offered and latched a hand around her arm. "Come on."

"Lowell! You told me if I talked, you'd do me a favor," she yelled over her shoulder as Pratt attempted to walk her away.

"Wait." Brit leaned forward. The chair squeaked again, begging for WD-40.

Rina swung around and grabbed on the door as Pratt tried to drag her away. "Work with me on this."

Hope ricocheted through Brit's chest. He'd gone on a rampage after Keith's murder, offering his right arm for information. He couldn't remember if he'd approached Rina, but maybe he had.

"Work with you on what?" Hope tightened his chest.

"Your partner's death. Tell them to get these damn cuffs off me, and I'll sing like a horny parakeet."

Brit jerked up so fast his chair pitched back. Quarles did the same. They exchanged a quick glance and then both turned to Pratt. "Uncuff her," they said in unison.

Pratt frowned. "She might go after your boys; she went after mine."

"I'll protect my boys," Brit insisted, but he saw Quarles take a step back.

~

That evening, after joining Tanya Craft, a co-worker for a glass of wine, Cali lingered at the bottom of the stairs at her white-stuccoed apartment building. A November breeze, scented with Chinese food from a nearby restaurant, seeped through her light-weight sweater.

She forced herself to take one step closer to the inevitable argument that awaited her upstairs. But oh, she hated arguing. Plain and simple, she sucked at it.

Making it to the second level, she counted the white painted doors as she passed, dreading facing Stan. Her neighbor popped her head out of apartment 211. A true miniature, the wrinkled woman reminded Cali of a raisin, a sweet raisin, with an accent.

"Wait here." Mrs. Gomez ducked back into her apartment, and returned with a plastic bowl. "Paella. The best you'll ever taste." Her faded brown eyes grew sympathetic. "That kind man of yours, he help me with my groceries and tell me about your mother. You are a good girl. You never use bad language like apartment 209. I hear bad words from there. I sorry about your mother."

Cali's chest ached. Why couldn't she hear condolences without wanting to sob?

"Thank you." Another breeze, this one scented with teriyaki, gave her a chill and she pulled her sweater closer. The sweet woman touched Cali's arm, then disappeared into her apartment.

With a bowl in one hand, Cali fumbled with her keys with the other. She pushed open her door, braced for the inevitable. Silence greeted her. No Stan. No arguing. Relief blossomed.

She put the plastic dish in the fridge to party with the other dozen bowls. What was it about a death that made people want to feed you? Had she missed the scientific study that proved overweight people didn't feel as much grief? She stared at the stacked bowls that her mother's friends had supplied, and considered eating her way through the refrigerator. Anything to stop the grief.

"*Any other family?*" Cali remembered the funeral director asking. "*Aunts, uncles? Surely there's some family.*"

"*No. Just me.*"

Unable to stomach the idea of food, she wandered back to her living room. She dropped on her beige leather sofa and freed her hair from the banana clip. *Just me.* She opened and closed the banana clip. Squeeze. Release. Squeeze. Release.

Spotting the blinking of her message machine, she hit the play button. The voice bounced out of the recorder. "Stan. It's Nolan. We've got a fucking problem."

"Mrs. Gomez won't like you if you cuss." Cali let the banana clip snap shut again. She'd only met Stan's band member buddies once. Not her type of crowd.

Next, she listened to Mom's lawyer telling her he'd scheduled their appointment for Wednesday. Then the hospice nurse, Betty Long, needing Cali to sign papers.

Cali looked around the too-quiet apartment. Stan's callous words echoed in her head. *She died, you didn't.* He might help old ladies with their groceries, but he could be a jerk.

An hour later, freshly showered, she sat on the edge of the tub and painted her toenails a cherry red. Pretty feet had been her mother's cure-all for the blues. Wearing only a towel and cotton between her toes, she heel-walked to her bed and collapsed on the mattress. Then she waited—waited for the mood-altering effect of pretty feet to kick in. "This is supposed to work, right, Mom?" Mom didn't answer.

~

"He thinks Tanya is a lesbian," Mom said.

Somewhere in the recesses of her brain, Cali knew this was a dream. She didn't care. She needed to hear her mother's voice.

Suddenly, the dream went visual, and her mom sat on the end of her bed. She wore one of the navy business suits that she'd always worn to the real estate office. Her hair, kept red with Nice & Easy's help, bounced around her face. She looked good. Healthy, not like the twig of a woman who'd died in Cali's arms last week.

Cali blinked. "Who thinks Tanya is a lesbian?"

"That guy living with you."

"He's not living with me. Just staying until his apartment is available."

"And how long has that been?" Her mom's brow arched. "I know why you never introduced me. You knew I wouldn't like him."

Regret stirred in Cali's stomach. "You were sick and—"

"Doesn't matter." Gold bracelets jingled down her mother's wrist as she raised a cigarette to her lips. "He reminds you of somebody we used to know, doesn't he?"

"Who?"

Smoke rings floated up and faded into the air as her mother spoke. "You know who."

Cali didn't know, but didn't care. She studied the cigarette. "You quit five years ago."

"Yeah, but bad habits die hard."

Even asleep, Cali marveled at the absurdity of the dream. Mom smoking and talking about lesbians.

"You know why he thinks Tanya is a lesbian?" her mom asked.

"What do you know about lesbians?"

"Betty, my hospice nurse. She's a lesbian. Did you know there are tools that they strap on? A fake . . . you know what. Oh, damn, I'm dead, I can say penis, can't I?" Her mom's laughter hugged Cali's heart. It didn't matter that her mom spoke about fake penises, or that this was just a dream. It felt good to see her without the pain shadowing her eyes.

"Betty has a partner. Been together for years." Her mom took a long, pleasurable drag on her cigarette. "The reason the weasel thinks Tanya's a lesbian is because she didn't respond to his flirting at the funeral. He thinks any woman who doesn't go weak-kneed for him is gay."

"He didn't flirt with Tanya." Cali squeezed her pillow a little tighter.

"Ask her." Her mom looked over her shoulder. "You'd better get dressed. He's coming home, and you know what he'll think if he sees you in bed naked."

The sound of her front door opening knee-jerked her from the dream. She leapt up, naked, and darted to the dresser. Tugging a nightshirt on, she expected Stan to walk in. Instead, she heard the TV click on. She fell against the dresser, trying to shake off the dream. She'd heard the door while sleeping. Mom hadn't woken her up. Nor had she sat at the foot of the bed. Just a dream. Right?

Heavy footsteps thudded down the hall. Then the bedroom door swung open. He tossed her extra set of keys on the dresser. They clanked against the mirror.

"You want to talk about this?" His words came out slurred. He'd been drinking.

Now wasn't the time to talk. "It's late."

"So no sex tonight either, huh?"

His bullying tone had her clenching her toes, and she realized she still had cotton between them. "We'll talk tomorrow." When she'd tell him he had to move out.

"Fine. But you may want to take a shower. This room reeks of a bar." He slammed the door.

Cali inhaled a deep gulp of Marlboro-scented air. She recalled the dream of her mom smoking. Hands shaking, she walked over to the chair where she'd left her clothes. She lifted them to her nose. No cigarette smoke.

The door swung back open and whacked against the wall. She jerked around, her nose buried in the blouse.

"Got you something. Not that you'll give a damn!" Stan tossed a small, shiny object on the bed. It picked up the light from the hall and glittered. The door slammed again.

~

The next day after school, Cali parked in front of the Arts R Us store and hurried across the parking lot to meet Tanya, who waited by the entrance.

Tanya was looking for a few art supplies and Cali was there for one thing: procrastination. And who knew, maybe between the acrylics and oils, she'd find a tube of liquid courage. She hated conflict. And telling Stan he needed to find his own place had conflict warnings stamped all over it.

She met Tanya and they hurried in to escape the cold wind. When Cali pushed the door, her sweater sleeve pulled up.

"Hot damn!" Tanya grabbed Cali's wrist and eyed the tennis bracelet with diamond-filled, flower-shaped studs linked together. "Is this new?"

"Yeah." Unlike Tanya, Cali wasn't the bling-bling type. But when she'd found Stan MIA this morning, she'd felt guilty for not even thanking him for the present, so she wore it. Not that it changed anything. She was still asking him to move out, because frankly, she'd never asked him to move in.

"Is it real?" Tanya gawked at the bracelet.

"No," she said. "Cubic Zirconia, I'm sure."

Tanya twisted the bracelet around Cali's wrist. "Looks real."

"I doubt it," she said.

Thanksgiving hadn't come and gone and already Santa and red-nosed reindeer displays stared back at her as Tanya collected a shopping basket. Cali's chest grew heavy with thoughts of the holidays. Alone.

"You want to grab a salad later?" Tanya leaned onto the basket handle and kicked up her feet like a teenager.

"No. I need to go home and slay a dragon."

"What dragon?" Tanya reached for a paintbrush.

"My boyfriend. We've known each other less than three months. His roommate asked him to move out, so he's crashing at my place until his new apartment becomes available. But it's been almost a month and he hasn't once mentioned the apartment again."

Tanya scowled. "I hate moochers."

"He chipped in a little money to help out, but . . . I used to like him. He's nice to old people. A month ago, I thought we had something, but now . . . maybe I'm just losing it." The words vibrated through her head. God, she didn't want to admit that either. So what if she had dreams in which her dead mother talked about lesbians? She felt Tanya's gaze. "I'm dealing with my mama's death, and he wonders why I'm not in an amorous mood."

"It hasn't even been a week since the funeral." Tanya stared at the tip of the paintbrush. "I think he's a jerk. Especially if the bracelet is a fake."

She thought about her dream, her mom's accusation of Stan flirting, and almost asked if Tanya had met Stan at the funeral. But that was silly.

"I've got a boyfriend crisis myself." Tanya dropped the paintbrush into the basket. "His name is Eric—blond, a little short, but a nice ass." She grinned. "I'm an ass woman."

Cali smiled at Tanya's bluntness. "So what's the crisis?"

Tanya let out an exaggerated huff. "This will be our third date. And you know what happens on the third date."

"I hold out to the fifth," Cali teased.

Tanya's brows wiggled. "You wouldn't with his ass."

Cali laughed. Something about hanging with Tanya made Cali feel normal. She hadn't felt normal in a long time.

"The gallery that sells my earrings sold six sets this week. If I don't replace them, they'll give the space to someone else. So I've got to decide if it's a jewelry or a sex weekend."

"You can't do both?" Cali asked.

"Nah, I'm an all or nothing kind of girl. It's screw the jewelry—or Eric."

Cali hadn't touched a canvas since her mom's cancer. "Couldn't you have sex on Saturday, and do jewelry on Sunday?" She ran a finger over the tubes of colors, nostalgic for left-behind dreams.

"But if it's good sex, I'll want more on Sunday." Tanya picked up a tube of ice-blue acrylic. "What's your thing?"

"Watercolors," Cali said. "But I haven't painted in a while."

Tanya laughed. "I meant with men. I'm an ass woman. What are you?"

"Oh." She chuckled. "I don't know. I guess—"

"Shoulders." Tanya leaned into the buggy. "Stan has nice shoulders."

The question spilled out. "Did you two meet at the funeral?"

"Yeah." Her friend turned back to the paint. "You should start painting again." She grabbed a pack of watercolors. "Art therapy. My treat."

"No." Cali reshelved the paint. "I'm not in the mood." The words sounded so familiar that she pressed her hand to her forehead. "God, have I said that enough lately."

Tanya arched a brow. "So are you breaking up with him, or just telling him to get his own place?"

Cali hesitated. "I don't know. Before my mama died I thought I liked him. Now . . ."

"Sounds like you're breaking up." Tanya eyed the bracelet. "Hide the jewelry before you toss his ass out."

Cali frowned. *Silent Night* played in the background, and Cali wondered how silent her night would be once she got home to Stan. Something told her Stan wouldn't go quietly.

Chapter Two

Thirty minutes later, Cali parked her Honda beside Stan's white truck. She climbed the steps to her apartment and opened the door.

Stan stood up from the computer desk in the corner of the room. "Hey." He moved closer. "I was hoping you'd get here before I left. I got you set up so you can pay your credit card online."

Cali took a step back. "We need to talk."

He kept coming. "You look tired."

"I am tired, but—"

"Do you want me to grab you a beer? I picked some up this afternoon."

"No." Her gaze slid to his chest. Stan did have nice shoulders. Is that what she'd seen in him? Had she even noticed them until now?

He caught her hand and twirled the jewelry around. "You like it?"

"Yes, but I can't keep it." She started to take it off.

"Of course, you can." He dipped in for a kiss. She wiggled away.

"We've got to talk, Stan." She tossed her purse on the sofa. It landed off-key on his guitar, which sat beside his packed bags. So Stan was leaving? Confusing emotions bumped around her chest. She'd been going to break up with him. But right now, one thought surfaced. Just me. Alone.

"You got your apartment?" she asked, unsure if she was relieved or . . .

"No. Just a gig in Austin. I'll be home Sunday."

Home. This wasn't his home. "I think . . ."

He moved in again. "Tell me you love me."

She shook her head. "I'm sorry. I—"

"Come on. We're good together." His hands moved to her breasts.

He twisted her nipples as if they were turn-on switches. Another thing she didn't like, but hadn't told him. Nipple twisting, ear licking, and that thing he did with her navel. The longer she stayed with Stan, the longer her list got. And she wasn't even a list person.

She attempted to step back, but he held her there, and continued his nipple assault.

"Stop!" She pushed her hands against his chest. "I don't love you."

He released her, but his nostrils flared, and something flickered in his violet eyes. Something not so pleasant. She inhaled, seeking calm, but the air tasted like cigarette smoke.

Had he started smoking?

"So you'll take my gifts, but won't put out?" His gaze cut to the bracelet on her wrist.

"That's why I can't keep it." She tried to get it off, but the dang thing wouldn't release.

"How long do I have to go without?" he snapped.

She raised her gaze. Anger brightened his eyes. "It's over. Leave." She used her teacher's voice, then darted into the kitchen and tried again to get the dang bracelet off. It wouldn't give. She waited to hear the door slam. It didn't. She swung around. His large frame loomed in the doorway. Her breath caught.

Panic cat-walked her spine, and she'd never been clearer about what she wanted. Or rather, about what she didn't want. She didn't want the Cubic Zirconia bracelet. She didn't want Stan. Earlier, when she'd seen his bags, she'd mourned being alone; she hadn't mourned losing Stan. And along came another epiphany. Fear of being alone had jump-started this fling. Even when her mom was alive, Cali knew she was dying. And Cali hadn't wanted to be alone.

She opened her mouth to apologize for using him because that's what she'd done. She'd used Stan. She didn't want to have sex with him. Had she ever wanted sex with him? No. Oh, this was so bad. She had to give him his bracelet back.

"This isn't working." She meant the relationship and the latch on the bracelet. She looked up to say she was sorry, and to tell him he needed to leave, but the flicker in his eyes stopped her. She dropped her hands to her sides.

"What the hell do you think isn't working?" He slammed his fist on the counter.

She jumped. Her toaster jumped. She considered making a mad dash to a room with a lock. But when you ran, things tended to chase you, and Stan looked ready to give chase. She met his gaze and hoped she appeared braver than she felt. Right then, she knew who her mama meant when she'd asked if Stan reminded her of anyone. She pointed to the door. "Go."

"It's not over." But he grabbed his stuff and stalked out. The door slammed.

"Leave. Leave just like Daddy did," she said, her breath shuddering in her chest.

~

"Cali! You've got to get out of here."

Another dream. Cali tried to push it away. She needed sleep. Deep sleep. Not dream sleep.

"Cali Anne!" Her mom's tone got stern.

"I'm so tired. Can we chat about lesbians later?" She burrowed her face into her pillow.

"He's coming back. He's a bad man. Up to his ying-yang in trouble."

Cali jerked up on the bed. She heard it. Someone tried to open her door. But she'd set the deadbolt. Stan didn't have that key. The doorbell chimed. Half asleep, she hot-footed it into the living room.

"Who is it?" She clutched a fistful of her Mickey Mouse nightshirt in her hand.

"It's me!" Stan sounded panicked . . . or drunk. "Open the door!"

"I don't want to see you now."

"Fuck it, Cali! Open the door!"

"Don't open that door." The voice came from behind her. Her mom's voice.

Was Cali still dreaming?

"Move baby. Move!"

Cali didn't move. She froze. Afraid of what was in front of her. Stan. Afraid of what might be behind her. Her dead mother. But that was silly.

Cali swung around to prove ghosts didn't exist. Of course, ghosts didn't exist. Nothing was there. Nothing.

"Let me in." The door jarred with a splintering thud. A loud blast exploded.

It sounded like . . .

The lamp on her end table lamp banged against the wall and crashed to the floor. She swung around and stared in horror at the hole in her door.

Oh, God. Good shoulders, nice-guy-to-the-elderly Stan had just shot her door.

And if Cali hadn't have stepped back, she'd have traded places with her lamp.

The door knob started turning. Back. Forth. Back. Forth. Another blast sounded. A scream lodged in her throat.

~

"Who's feeding those damn stray cats in the back?" Brit's sergeant's voice boomed down the hall. "Whoever it is, stop! One of them took a shit on my car last night."

Brit's gaze cut to the cans of tuna on top of his file cabinet, but he didn't care enough to hide the evidence. He sat at his desk, two different case files spread out in front of him. Only one mattered. The one they refused to assign him. Keith's photograph stared up at him. He looked away, but saw it in his head. Keith's body lying face up, his empty eyes open, the concrete around his head darkened with blood.

Brit closed his fist, his chest ached. Rina's tip had gotten him nowhere. She'd said she heard the small-time drug dealer, Tony Payne, talking about a gang member who'd shot a cop.

Brit and Quarles had joined the two officers assigned to Keith's case and spent most of the night and all day kicking the dust up in some of Hopeful's more drug-infested streets, looking for Payne. And they got dust for their trouble. Payne couldn't be found.

When they'd returned to the precinct, Sergeant Adams had jumped them for not working the jewelry store murder. Much to Brit's surprise, his partner, who'd never met Keith, had been the one to jump back. "Keith Bolts was one of our own!" Quarles had said.

Brit had walked away before his fist decided to handle what he couldn't.

Now, leaning back in his chair, he tried to calm down.

"Hey." Quarles appeared at the door. "There's shots fired at some nearby apartments. Got one car heading that way, but something's happening across town. They're short of men and need backup."

Brit stood. "Let's go." Maybe some excitement would do him good. Get his mind off the fact that he was no closer to finding Keith's killer today than three weeks ago.

Five minutes later, they arrived. A patrol car, lights flashing, sat in the apartment's parking lot. Guns drawn, Brit and Quarles raced up the steps.

As they hit the landing, Brit saw Officer Logan standing outside apartment 215. Logan's partner's voice echoed from behind the door that was left ajar. The rush of adrenalin lost its edge. Brit slowed down long enough to take a bite of air. Someone was a chain-smoker.

He lowered his Glock. The smell of smoke faded, but the coppery scent of blood assaulted him and had his adrenalin bellying back up to the bar. He gripped his gun. His gaze zeroed in on the white front door, or rather on the red handprints smeared and smudged there. A lot of blood. This wasn't going to be pretty.

Chapter Three

"What we got?" Brit asked Officer Logan, who held his position by the door.

"Domestic disturbance," Logan answered. "One woman inside."

"She hurt?"

"Didn't look like it. Anderson's talking to her. What do you want to bet she won't press charges? These things always end the same."

Brit wouldn't take that bet. He knew those odds—and he hadn't learned them on the job either. "Did you search the apartment?" Brit looked at the blood.

"Why?"

"Because she could be hiding the body in her closet." Brit holstered his gun and wished like hell he hadn't come. Nothing pushed his hot button like domestic situations. He glanced down at the lower half of the door and saw two circular streams of light peering through the wood. Kneeling, he studied the holes. "Shots came from out here." Maybe there really was a body in the closet. Careful not to disturb any evidence, he nudged open the door.

The lingering aroma of smoke evaporated as he moved into the warmth of the feminine-scented apartment—hair spray, perfume, candles. He looked around. The source of all those soft scents sat on the sofa, wearing a Mickey Mouse nightshirt, her arms worry-locked in front of her. He gave her a once-over for injuries. Found none. Then he gave her another up and down for male-related reasons. She shifted. Mickey's ears jiggled with a soft sway of breasts. The woman's gaze, oh-so innocent, found his, and Brit felt his hot button being finger-jabbed to high.

Men who abused women topped Brit's lowlife list, but their victims, who went back to them time and time again, both annoyed and puzzled the hell out of him.

Brit stepped closer to the conversation.

"Are you sure it was your boyfriend?" Officer Anderson shifted his nervous gaze to the notepad as if trying not to look at Mickey's ears.

"I'm sure." She looked sad and a little pathetic, like a lost puppy. They all had that look.

Anderson jotted something down. "I'm going to search the parking lot. See if he's out there, then I'll need to finish getting your statement. You sure you're okay?"

She nodded, her white blond hair whispering around her shoulders. Her blue eyes looked almost doe-like, large and scared. Pretty woman, Brit thought, and he tried to guess her type. Was she the doormat, a fighter, or did she just have a thing for make-up sex after being knocked around? Admittedly, he knew there were a few women who just got caught up in something ugly, but what were the odds of that?

Anderson nodded at Brit, then started for the door.

"You're not leaving?" she asked, as if she hadn't heard anything he'd said.

Practically a rookie, Anderson shot Brit a desperate look. "Uh, Detective Lowell is going to ask you a few questions." Brit's shoulders tightened. He didn't want to get involved. Unless a body appeared, he'd come only as backup. Backup didn't ask questions; backup didn't write reports. Backup didn't care. Brit didn't want to care. He had enough to care about.

He cast her another glance. She fiddled with a bracelet around her wrist. Brit did a rundown of the surroundings, partly so he wouldn't get caught up with Mickey again, and partly to search for signs of a struggle. No signs. Even the books on the shelves appeared to be in perfect alignment.

Maybe too perfect? Suspicion pricked his gut. "Can I take a look around?"

She brushed a lock of hair behind her ear. "He . . . left. I locked the deadbolt. He doesn't have that key."

"Can I look around?" he repeated.

"I don't mind." She yanked at the bracelet as if it were a handcuff. Frowning, she dropped her hands in her lap.

He moved in and inhaled. The scent of shampoo and sleepy woman filled his lungs. But his nose had failed before. "Been drinking?"

Her scared beautiful gaze shifted up. "No."

He felt himself go a little soft. Tension coiled inside his body as he fought the emotion back. "Drugs?"

"No." Her frown tightened.

Before he got caught up in her oh-so innocent eyes or Mickey's ears, he walked down the hall to the bedroom. Nothing seemed out of order. Everything seemed almost too neat. A few clothes hung over a chair, not tossed, but carefully laid out. He opened the closet—no body —mostly women's clothes, but a few hangers with men's shirts and jeans. He looked down at the floor where six pairs of colorful high heels waited like dominos. When he closed the door, the smell of cigarette smoke hit him again.

Moving to the bedside table, he opened a drawer, thinking he might find a gun. Only a pack of condoms and a book of poems. So she read poetry and liked sex. But was she into make-up sex after a knock-down, drag-out? He ran a hand over the pillow when someone touched his shoulder.

He swung around. Nothing. Yet chills ran down his spine. Damn, he needed some sleep.

Giving the room one more glance, he turned to leave, but something caught his eye. A movement. A flutter in the bed skirt. He drew his Glock then slowly he got to his knees. He stared at the white bed skirt, not knowing what he'd find behind it. A body? A boyfriend trying to avoid a trip to the county jail? He pinched the cotton ruffle between his thumb and forefinger, and with his other hand he pointed his gun. Slowly, he lifted up the cotton fabric.

Nothing. Well, nothing except normal below the bed stuff, like a baseball bat and a pair of men's tennis shoes.

Letting out a breath of frustration, he got up and walked out of the bedroom. He ducked his head into the bathroom. It smelled like the woman on the sofa, a clean flowery scent. The smell stayed with him as he ambled back into the living room where he found her as he'd left her—looking like a woman in need of a shoulder. He dug his hands into his jean pockets and tried to decide what he thought was the truth.

"You want to tell me what happened?"

She frowned. "My boyfriend started beating on the door. It was late. I asked him to leave."

"This boyfriend live with you?" The question made her twist her bottom on the sofa. Discomfort usually meant a story loomed right beneath the surface. "He live here?"

She wiggled again. "Only until his apartment becomes available."

"So he came home banging on the door and then what?"

She blinked. "And then he shot . . ."

She hesitated, and Brit waited for her to say who had been shot, to explain the blood on the front door, but she pointed across the room and said, ". . . my lamp."

Brit moved over to the victim, the lamp, and saw the bullet lodged in the brass base. "You two have a fight?" He knelt to get a closer look at the bullet. Looked like a .38.

When she didn't answer, he asked, "What was the fight about?" He stared at her.

She buried her straight, white teeth into the soft, pink flesh of her lip. "A silly argument."

"Humor me," he said, with no amount of humor in his voice. When she didn't reply immediately, he pitched another question in her lap. One she'd feel obliged to answer and prep her to answer the others. "What's your name?"

"Cali McKay."

"Miss or Mrs.?"

"Miss."

"Miss McKay." He walked around, sat in the chair across from her, and purposely didn't look at Mickey. "I'm going to tell you how it is. You called us out here. You got us involved. Now you're going to have to be up front with us."

She glanced away as if to hide the guilt in her eyes. Was she guilty? Most were.

"You hit your boyfriend with something?" he asked, following his guilt theory.

Without looking up, she shook her head. "No. I told the other guy that we didn't fight—not physically. "

And evidence says you did. As a cop, he learned that evidence seldom lied. "Maybe he threatened you. So you hit him, drew blood. He went outside to his car and got his gun." Brit's gaze shuffled around the room again. The thing missing was the blood in the house and the sign of a struggle.

She shook her head again, only this time she raised her eyes. "No. When I got home from work, we argued, no hitting or anything bad. He left but woke me up later, banging on the door."

"What was the fight about?" He watched her. "Well?" He hurried her so she wouldn't have time to think up a lie.

"I wasn't in the mood to be friendly." She blushed.

Brit felt confident he understood the meaning of "be friendly," and guessed the rest of the story. "So he tried to pressure you into having sex. You fought him off. What did you use?"

Her shoulders stiffened. "I told you. I didn't hit him." Anger flashed in her eyes.

And that's what he'd been going for. When angry, a suspect usually gave something away. Let the truth slip out.

"There's blood," he said.

"I didn't hit him!"

"You wouldn't lie to me, would you?"

Chapter Four

She tightened her fist around the image of Mickey's nose. The tug on the fabric brought the hem of the nightshirt up past her knees. His gaze shifted. She had a nice pair of legs to go with those blue eyes and breasts that made Mickey look too damn good.

"I'm not lying," she insisted.

He didn't buy it.

"So he wanted to do the deed and you refused. Some guys don't like to be told no. It's understandable that you'd fight him off." And he did understand. He didn't blame a woman for fighting off a jerk who . . .

"You're not very nice," she blurted out. "I like the other officer better. Can you bring him back?" Lips pursed, she stared at him. "I haven't done anything wrong."

He stood up. Some less aggressive part of his brain told him to back down. But for once, he just wanted to get to the truth. For three freaking weeks, he'd sought the truth about Keith's death. He'd found nothing but dead ends. Zero. Zip.

"How long have you known this boyfriend, and what did you say his name was?"

"Stan Humphrey."

She only answered one part of his two-part question. And he could guess why. "You haven't known this guy very long, have you?"

"He was just staying here until he could move into his own apartment." She clutched another handful of Mickey. Brit's gaze fell to her legs before he could stop himself. Yup, nice legs.

Brit saw Quarles at the door, talking to the rookie Anderson. He swung around and joined them on the threshold. "Find anything out here?"

The man motioned him outside. The moment they cleared the door, his new partner came too damn close again. "You might want to ease up on the chick."

Brit took a step back. "Are you telling me how to do my job?"

"We're all uptight about Keith," Quarles said. "But—"

"You didn't even fucking know him. So back off." Brit spoke low, but his tone hit the dead serious range. He swung back inside and stared at an empty sofa. A noise came from the kitchen. Ease up on the chick. Quarles' words replayed in Brit's head. Damn it, Quarles had a point. He just didn't want him jabbing him with it.

He got to the doorway just as she pulled out a large knife from the kitchen drawer. "Put it down," he told her.

She swung around and knife pointing at him. "I'm not going to use it on you. Even if you were being a jerk." She looked at her wrist and pointed the knife downward.

"I don't want you using it on yourself either," he said his tone curt.

Her gaze shot back up. Her mouth dropped open a bit. "I just want to get this dang bracelet off." She tossed the knife in the sink. It clattered against the white ceramic.

He remembered her fidgeting with the bracelet earlier. Okay, he believed her. He believed a lot of what she'd told him tonight, too. She hadn't hit anyone. Not a fighter, this one. Just a doormat. And he'd pretty much wiped his shoes off on her, too.

Remorse tightened the muscles in his shoulder blades. He noticed the silhouette of body under the thin Mickey Mouse night shirt and looked back at the sink. Silence filled the room.

When he looked back at her, she fidgeted with the bracelet again. He reached for her hand. "Let me help."

~

"He's a bastard!" her mama said.

In Cali's dream, her mom paced around the hotel room where Cali had come for the night. Her mom lectured about Stan while pulling deep drags of cigarette smoke into her lungs as if seeking nicotine solace. "Oh, baby. I picked a lousy time to die, didn't I? With the holidays and now this."

"You know this is a nonsmoking room," Cali said. When her mother didn't answer, Cali remembered this was just a dream. When she'd heard her mom's voice back at her apartment, she'd just been panicked. Grief could do crazy things to a person.

"You're too nice. Too forgiving." Her mom dropped down on the bed and touched Cali's cheek. "I should have raised you to be more of a bitch."

"I'm too forgiving?" Cali thought of Stan, whom she hadn't forgiven, and the jerk, Detective Lowell. She hadn't forgiven him either.

"Stan doesn't deserve forgiving," her mom said. "The cop was testy, but he has reasons."

"You can read my mind, too?"

"I've always been able to read your mind. But yes, there are advantages to being dead." Her mom's eyes teared. "You've got to listen to me. Bad things could happen. I'd die if something happened to you."

"You did die," Cali said, and they both knew Cali hadn't yet forgiven her for that.

"Bad things could happen." Her mom repeated, and her voice seemed to float around the room with the cigarette smoke.

They were already happening Cali thought. Stan was shooting at her apartment door. Her mama was dead. And Cali was crazy because she kept dreaming about her.

Chapter Five

The next morning at school, Cali straightened her desk. Since the funeral, she spent a lot of time straightening, cleaning—her closet, under her bed, her baseboards. Even her catch-all kitchen drawer had been de-cluttered. She'd gotten rid of a lot of junk, a lot of scum, including a louse of a boyfriend. Not that getting rid of him excused her for getting involved. She'd really messed up.

Her classroom door squeaked open. Tanya, wearing a bright red dress and toting an armful of books, walked in. "Hi."

Cali blinked. Suffering from lack of sleep, it almost hurt to look at her friend. The fact that Cali had made it to school should be considered a near miracle. But she had requested the afternoon off. She told the office she needed to do some work on her mom's estate. And while she did have the appointment with her mom's lawyer, she wasn't sure she could muster enough energy to do anything more than drive back to the hotel where she'd stayed last night. Even her toes cried out for sleep. Yet sleeping brought on dreams and those dreams—

The stack of books landed on Cali's desk with a thud.

"Hi." Cali forged a smile.

Tanya, obviously, could spot a forgery. "Dragon slaying went bad, huh?"

"What?"

"You said you had to slay a dragon,"

"Oh. Yeah, it went badly."

Tanya propped her hip on the desk. "You want to talk about it? Or not. I can deal with either."

Cali took a deep breath. The chance to unburden herself seemed too good to pass up. "I'll talk, but . . . it's Jerry Springer, Judge Judy quality."

"Good. I love drama." Tanya wiggled closer. Her earrings, colorful Christmas balls the size of marbles, bounced around her ears. "Spill it."

Cali recounted the night's events. The argument. Stan returning. The shot through the door. The cops arriving. "There was blood all over the door. I don't have a clue from where. I don't know if Stan was hurt or . . ." She'd skipped over the part about the dreams. About hearing her mom's voice. Being crazy was one thing, admitting it another. "That one detective was so rude, and then he thought I was going to use a knife on him. Do I look like a knife-crazed killer?"

"Maybe just a bit around the eyes." Tanya giggled.

Cali laughed. She tapped a pencil on her desk. The drumming sound felt hypnotic. "The first cop wasn't rude. And I could swear I knew him from somewhere."

"Was he cute?" Tanya made a face when Cali rolled her eyes at the question.

"He could have been Brad Pitt. I wasn't thinking clearly enough to consider it." Without warning, a visual of Detective Lowell flashed in her mind, all shoulders and . . .

She grabbed her mental eraser and wiped that image out. Swallowing, she looked back at Tanya. "And then he . . ." Cali ended her tale of woe by telling how the detective insisted she not stay at her apartment for three or four days. "Thanks to Stan, I can't go home."

"That . . ." Tanya lowered her voice, "dickhead."

"Which one?" Cali asked. "The cop or Stan?" The more Cali thought about Detective Lowell, the more she wanted to call someone and complain. She wouldn't though. Partly because her Mom was right, Cali didn't have enough bitch in her, but mostly because the detective had been right. She'd been stupid to allow Stan to stay with her. She'd brought most of this on herself. But it didn't excuse his behavior.

"Both of them are dickheads," Tanya said. "I'd say Stan wins the Big Dickhead award. The cop earns the Little Dickhead award." She rested a palm on the stack of books. "Where did you stay last night?"

"I started to go to my mom's house, but Stan knows where Mom lived, so I went to a hotel." While Stan did know where her mom had lived, in truth, Cali hadn't felt strong enough to face the Cancer House.

"Why didn't you call me?"

Cali wondered if Tanya knew how much her friendship meant right now. "It was so late."

"Doesn't matter." Tanya popped off the desk and collected her stack of books. "Tonight you're bunking with me."

"No." Cali shook my head. "I'm fine." The bell rang.

"No, you're not. Big Dickhead tried to shoot you. Then the hot-looking Little Dickhead Detective accused you of trying to kill him."

Cali frowned. "How did you know he was hot?"

Tanya's smile shot up a degree. "Your eyes went all dreamy when you talked about him. Anyway, you're staying with me. End of discussion." A herd of eleventh-grade students buzzed into the room, and Tanya buzzed out through the maze of teenagers.

Suddenly, the room went silent. No chattering. No morning whining. Their gazes sought hers. Cali's throat tightened at the sight of the sympathy-filled faces. Yesterday, she'd gotten by without most them knowing. Today, she wasn't so lucky. They knew.

They found their seats like mice who knew the maze. Jami, the designated head mouse, wearing her usual tight jeans and sweater, stood beside her desk. "We're so sorry, Miss McKay."

"Thank you." A knot rose in her throat.

"It sucks," said another student. "And we promise not to give you grief today."

"Yeah." Antonio dropped his backpack beside his desk. "If anyone gives Miss McKay lip today, they'll answer to me."

Cali's throat tightened, but she swore she wouldn't cry. "Thanks guys. Everyone work on your art journals." Slipping back into her chair, she started logging grades, anything to keep from crying.

"Miss McKay?" Sara Cane bumped against Cali's desk. Sara, red hair, green eyes, and painfully shy, seldom spoke.

"What can I do for you?" Cali asked.

Sara pulled at a button on her jacket sleeve. "I . . . It's none of my business, but what kind of cancer was it?"

Cali put down the pencil, unsure she could talk about it. But Sara's needy expression loosened the hated word. "Breast cancer. At least, it started there."

Sara's breath caught and her emerald eyes brightened with tears.

"You okay?" Cali's own eyes moistened seeing the emotion.

"My mom found out yesterday she has breast cancer."

"Come on." Cali rose from her desk. Wishing with everything she had that she'd kept her mouth shut, she led Sara to the hall. Sara turned and hugged Cali really hard. They both cried. Then Cali quoted every positive statistic on breast cancer she'd heard for the past two years.

Every positive statistic that hadn't included her mom.

~

Brit walked into his office just after one. He'd grabbed a few hours of sleep, not real sleep, but close enough for his body to remember what it was and to remind him how shitty he felt. Then there had been the dreams. Not just images about Keith, but erotic dreams that involved a blonde in a Mickey Mouse nightshirt. And a blonde out of a Mickey Mouse shirt. He'd reached an all time low—dreaming of victims. He tossed his leather jacket on the chair and ran a palm over his face.

"Back already?" a voice called from outside his door.

Brit looked at Anderson, the officer who'd been at the apartment last night. "You can't talk. What are you doing here?" Brit sat down. His chair groaned, and so did his muscles.

"Came to wrap up some paperwork. I'm off for four days." Anderson leaned his thin frame against the door. "I'm taking my girl to Galveston Beach for some action on the sand if it warms up."

Forcing a smile, Brit looked at his desk where he saw a large brown envelope. Probably images of the jewelry taken from the Goldstein case. He glanced back up. The kid appeared too young and cocky, beaming at the sex he planned to score. Personally, the last time Brit had indulged in beach sex, he'd gotten sand in places where sand shouldn't be.

"Have fun," Brit said, trying to remember when he'd been that excited about anything.

"I will. But I wanted to drop this off." He moved inside and set a plastic bag on Brit's desk. A can of cat food rolled out. "I'm glad I'm not the only sucker."

Brit caught the Fancy Feast. He started to blurt out that he didn't even like cats, that he'd begun feeding the mama cat and her babies because Keith had been doing it. "I'm just—"

"A softy. I know."

"I'm not a softy," Brit said. "Hell, I don't even know what a softy is."

Anderson grinned. "I saw you feeding them the other day. I called a shelter, but they couldn't catch them. Said they'd set traps, but they haven't come back yet."

"They'll kill them if they catch them," Brit said, remembering Keith saying that.

"Nah, I called the no-kill shelter."

Brit nodded and decided he liked the kid. "Good." Anderson started out.

"Hey," Brit asked. "Did you ever get anything on Cali McKay's boyfriend?"

"Yeah." He swung around and leaned on the door frame again. "He has a record. You'll never guess what for?"

"Beating up women." Brit shook his head. Same ol' shit—different day.

"A real charmer this one. He put one girl in the hospital."

"Did he do time?" Brit asked.

"Do they ever? One girl dropped the charges. The one he really bruised up, took out a restraining order and ended up leaving town when he broke it several times."

"Lovely." Brit snatched up the envelope, remembering the pretty blonde.

"It gets worse," Anderson said. "We got a call a couple of hours ago. Someone broke into the chick's place."

Brit's gaze shot back up. "They catch the guy?"

"Nah. I'm guessing it was the boyfriend."

"She wasn't home, was she?" This vision came straight from his dream. All soft, doe-eyed, and naked.

"No. Looks like she did what you told her to do and left. Good thing, too. I tried to call her at work to tell her about her place, and her boyfriend's record, but they said she took half the day off. For some reason, we didn't get her cell phone number."

Leaning back, Brit let air out through his teeth. "You need to get in touch with her. Convince her to get a restraining order."

"Like these women ever do what they should."

"Maybe not, but our job is to try to convince them."

"Yeah, I'll try," Anderson said, his tone implying he wouldn't try too hard.

Brit stared, annoyed at the kid's attitude even while he shared it. Hell, half the cops on the force shared it. Still, someone had to talk to Cali McKay.

"Anderson?" Brit called out as the man started off.

He stepped back into the doorway. "Yeah?"

"Where does she work?"

"She's a school teacher at Wells High." Anderson smiled. "You liked what you saw, didn't you? M-I-C-K-E-Y," the man started to sing, then laughed. "Mickey had some interesting moves last night. Never seen ears look so perky."

Brit frowned. "Did she give you any other number?"

"Yeah, I have her home and work numbers, and she wrote down some number by the closest relative, but then crossed it out. I left a message at the school for her to call me though and even called the number she marked out. Got an answering machine. I think it might be her mom. But no one's called me back." He looked out to the hall. "See ya." He pushed away from the door.

"Hey. Make sure you take a blanket to the beach," Brit offered a bit of wisdom.

"A little sand never killed anyone," Anderson said grinning.

"Yeah, but it doesn't feel so hot between the boys and Mr. Happy."

Anderson laughed. "Make sure you feed the cats," he said as he walked away.

Brit looked down and opened the envelope from the insurance company. "I will," Brit muttered. "But I'm not a softy."

The smell of cigarette smoke seemed to flow from the paper. The first image was of a necklace. And it reminded him how and he and

Keith had gone shopping for a necklace for Laura, Keith's wife, last Christmas.

Closing his eyes, he tossed the stack of photos aside. He didn't want to worry about missing jewelry or soft-looking blondes getting themselves beat up. He needed to be working on Keith's case.

He looked at his cell phone on the desk. He remembered the call he'd gotten earlier. The one he hadn't returned. Laura. Brit figured she wanted to know if he'd caught her husband's killer. Brit couldn't stomach the idea of telling her he hadn't found any solid leads.

Standing up, he yanked his jacket off the chair. The leather fit around his shoulders like a second skin, and he headed out to look for Tony Payne, the man who had info on Keith's killer. He got just past the door and remembered. Darting back into the office, he snagged a can of cat food.

Outside, he popped the can and put it down beside the storm drain in the middle of the parking lot. The cat obviously thought it was perfect place to raise her kittens. He listened and heard the soft meowing. He stepped back and leaned against his car and watched. The mama cat, a gray short- haired stray that didn't appear much more than a kitten herself, came out. She looked around cautiously, her gold eyes wide with worry and fear. He knew the moment she'd spotted him. But she didn't run. They continued to stare at each other. Something was wrong with her ear, part of it was missing. She looked beat up, leery of the world. And he knew exactly how she felt.

A car pulled up on the other side of the parking lot. The feline grabbed the lip of the can and jumped back into the storm drain.

~

Brit got in his car. He had no intention of wasting time on Cali McKay. So why he drove straight to her apartment building was a mystery. Oh, hell, it wasn't a mystery. He'd told her to stay away but, as Anderson said, when did these women do what they were supposed to do?

He parked his car and sat there for a minute before getting out and taking the stairs.

When he got to the second floor landing and found the door ajar, his pulse quickened. He took in the bullet holes again, and reached for his gun just in case the boyfriend had decided to come back. Backing against the wall, he glanced inside the broken window. From here he could see the living room and kitchen. Both empty.

Quietly, he pushed open the front door. Someone had really trashed the place. Knickknacks lay broken, books scattered. He moved toward the bedroom and made the turn down the hall. The door was half closed, limiting his view.

One step, two, and he heard something clatter from behind the door. He raised his gun and put his finger on the trigger.

Chapter Six

He shifted slightly to get a better view.

His breath caught when he saw her. His grip on his gun loosened. She stood with her arms wrapped around her middle, gaping at the mess strewn about the bedroom. Kneeling, she picked up a pair of pink lacy panties.

He holstered his gun and took a few seconds to study her before he made his presence known. She wore loose-fitting black slacks and a matronly looking blouse. Schoolteacher attire, he supposed, but the outfit did nothing to show off the body he thought lay beneath—the body he'd envisioned last night in his dreams.

He cleared his throat and tried to clear his mind. "I told you stay away from here."

~

The unexpected voice took her by surprise. Cali swung around, and dropped her panties. "You scared me."

"You should be scared. I told you to stay away for a damn good reason." He pushed the door the rest of the way open and came inside.

She stared. The man looked like a young Burt Reynolds. Her mom had been a Reynolds fan. Thanks to her, Cali had seen all his movies.

"Who did this?" She stared at his chest covered with a snug-fitting leather jacket. "Did the police do this?"

"Yeah, we get a kick out of going to women's apartments and tossing their underwear around." His gaze moved to the panties on the toe of her shoe. "We didn't do this. We got a call earlier from one of your neighbors. Looks like your boyfriend decided to come calling again. But the million-dollar question is what are you doing here?"

Why did she feel as if she were being chastised? "I needed to grab a few things."

"And what if he'd been here waiting?" His eyebrows rose accusingly.

"What am I supposed to do? All my clothes are here."

37

His blue-green eyes tightened in a frown. Not that the expression looked out of place. There seemed to be a permanent worry line pinching his brow.

He took another step. "I'm sure someone told you if you needed anything from here to call the police and they'd send someone over."

"No. I don't think anyone told me that. But it's the middle of the day. I should be okay."

He shuffled his fingers through his dark brown hair. "People die just as easy in daylight as they do in the dark. You'll need to go to the precinct to fill out a report."

"Can't you just report it?"

His frown tightened. "Did your boyfriend tell you he beat up his last two girlfriends? Real sweetheart, that guy. Do you really want to run into him again?"

Cali opened her mouth to speak, but zip came out. Stan had beat up two women? She didn't want to believe it, but she did.

"Guess he didn't mention it, huh?" He stepped closer and exhaled. "Look, I'm just trying to help. Grab what you need then I'll follow you to the station. We'll fill out the paperwork."

She remembered her appointment with her mom's lawyer. "I can't." Moving to the closet, she pulled out her small black suitcase and a couple of outfits. His dead-on stare followed her. Nervous, she started picking up panties and bras scattered around the room. Instantly, her chest became crowded with too many emotions. Her apartment was a mess. Her life was a mess. And Mr. Looking-Good-in-Leather treated her as if was all her fault. And, yeah, part of it was.

"Can't or won't?"

"Does it matter?" she asked, feeling overwhelmed.

"It should." His authoritative voice hacked away at what little self-confidence she had. Then his gaze shot to a pair of lacy panties next to his shoe and he looked ready to pick them up.

She surged forward and snatched up the panties herself. "I have to be somewhere else."

His frown grew more pinched. Then she remembered Tanya's nickname for him—Mr. Little Dickhead.

Ignoring his ever-present scowl, she snatched up her pink bra, which was also on the floor. She folded the panty and bra and set them on top of the other items in her suitcase.

"Look." He moved to stand beside her and his shoulder accidentally brushed against hers. "You need to get a restraining order. You need to make a report."

Unnerved by his closeness, she shifted to the side and reached to zip the suitcase. It stuck and she jerked at it. He moved in, gently brushed her hands aside, and zipped the case with ease.

"Thanks." The word naturally slipped out of her mouth.

"Don't be stupid," he said.

She stared at him, dumbfounded. Hadn't she said thanks? Where was the normal reply, You're welcome? How did thanks wind up with a comeback of, Don't be stupid? Jeez, he really was a dickhead.

"You need to get a restraining order," he said again.

"I'll go later." More bitchy. She remembered her dream. She crossed her arms over her chest. "And I'll talk to someone else. Not you."

His eyes widened. "You got a problem with me?" He reached down and picked up a pair of black panties.

She raised her chin a notch. "Yeah, you're rude. You treat people with total disrespect. And . . . you've got my panties." She blushed when she realized what she'd said and held out her hand. "I'll take those."

He handed her the underwear. "I'm rude?" he asked. "And here I didn't think you were very discriminating about the men you hung out with."

His remark hit with precision; her throat knotted. She saw regret flash in his eyes, but it was too late. Instinct told her to walk away, but bitches always got the last word. "I am discriminatory. Stan took nine weeks before he got ugly; you've beat his record hands down. I don't like you." She grabbed her case and started out.

"Hey," he called, but she didn't look back.

~

39

"Sorry," Brit muttered to himself. He watched her roll the suitcase out then listened while it thumped down the stairs. Each thud hit against his conscience. Her insult stung like hot sauce that came with a warning on the label. It burned going in, burnt when it hit his gut, and was gonna burn his ass when it exited. If it exited. He had a feeling this was going to hang around his conscience for while, because she was right, he'd been rude. Hell, he'd been more than rude, he'd been an ass.

Regret pumped a little acid to his gut. He'd been trying to help. And did it badly, his conscience countered.

Pressing his palms into his eye sockets, he tried to get a grip on his floundering emotions. Inhaling, he coughed when the air reeked of cigarette smoke. Jeez, was she a chain smoker? Oddly, he hadn't smelled it on her. She'd smelled soft and sweet enough to taste. His gaze went to a pair of panties she neglected to grab from the floor. But holy shit, he needed to get a hold of himself.

Storming out, he shut the door. Realizing she hadn't locked her apartment, he frowned. Then he remembered her broken window. He walked down the steps, headed to his car, but hesitated when he saw the front office. She wasn't his problem.

He took another step toward his car when someone touched his shoulder. He swung around, but no one was there. Brushing his shoulder where he still felt a crazy sensation, his gaze shot to the office door again.

"Shit!" He gave in. Maybe Anderson was right. He was a softy. No, softies weren't rude assholes.

He stepped into the office. A young brunette, dressed in a mini skirt that looked like she meant to hit the bars after work, stood up.

"You need to fix the window in apartment 215," he said.

Miss Hot-To-Trot smacked her gum. "Who are you?"

"Police." He flashed his badge.

She blew a pink bubble with her gum. It popped. She peeled it off her nose and poked it back into her mouth. "I called someone to do it earlier." She flipped out her hand as if she'd done her duty, and all deals were off.

The deals weren't off. If Cali decided to ignore his advice again and came collecting an extra pair of panties, he didn't want her ex waiting on her.

Stepping closer, he scowled. "If something comes up missing from her place, the owners could be held liable. And I'll stand up in court and say I told you. So call them again."

He left, but not before he caught the glare she shot him. Lately, all he got from women were glares. Didn't women used to smile at him? Then he remembered what Cali had said. You're rude. Hell, maybe he needed to work on that.

Crawling inside his SUV, he stared out at nothing. How could he not be in a piss-poor mood?

What kind of a homicide cop was he if he couldn't find his own partner's murderer? The guilt ate at him like vultures picking at a kill. Soon, he would be nothing more than a pile of raw flesh.

His cell phone rang. He pulled it out of his coat pocket. "Yeah?"

"It's Duke."

Brit recognized the voice of the detective who had landed Keith's case. "What's up?"

"I just got a call from one of my informants," Duke said. "Got a location on Payne. Mark and I are headed over there right now. Thought you might like to help us question him."

Brit fired up his engine. "Hell, yeah!"

~

Cali made her two o'clock meeting at the lawyer's office. Attorney Calvin James, a big man stuffed into a black suit, shuffled documents in front of her. A few crumbs from his lunch fell from his red tie onto the desk and he simply brushed them off. In spite of his less than professional appearance, she trusted the man—probably because her mom had trusted him. Feeling emotionally rung out, she signed without doing much reading.

"All together, your mother left you close to a hundred thousand dollars," Mr. James explained. "That's not including her house, which is paid off. It should make things a lot easier."

Easier? A spark of bitterness bubbled up inside her, but the concern in his eyes tempered her anger. "Mama went over all this with me." She fought the desire to stand up and stomp her feet like a two-year-old and demand somebody bring her mother back. She didn't want her mother's money—didn't want to dream about her at night. She wanted her mama. Alive. And without cancer. She didn't want to be alone. Tears watered down her vision.

"It's hard. I know." He pushed a box of tissues her way. "Maybe you could take some time off from work. You can afford to."

She ignored the tissue offer and took a deep breath of resolve. "Work helps." And it did. At school, she managed to forget about her own problems. Maybe because she worried about the students having oral sex, smoking pot, getting into gangs, and quitting school. And their mothers dying of cancer. Her throat grew tighter.

"Are we finished? Because I need to run." It wasn't a lie. She needed to go make a report to the police.

An image of Detective Lowell flashed in her mind, and she hoped she didn't have to see him at the police station.

Rain and cold greeted her when she left the lawyer's office. The drops pelted her face while questions pelted her mind. Where had the blood come from last night? Had Stan hurt himself trying to shoot in her apartment door? Why did her mom have to die?

She stopped by her car, not caring that her new sweater jacket grew rain heavy, or that the Texas-size downpour soaked her hair, or that goose bumps made her skin crawl with the cold.

Nothing mattered. She stopped to dig out her keys, feeling the water wave over the edge of her shoes. She glanced down at the black shoes. Her favorite, most comfortable pair. Maybe she cared a little about them. She moved out of the puddle of water. Remembering her search for her keys, she commenced to digging around in the bag's contents.

"Hate this purse," she mumbled. Her keys always fell to the bottom. Frustrated, she slapped her wallet on the hood, and dug deeper. Tampon, check book, mints. The rain started falling harder.

Finally, she gripped her keys in her hand.

She inhaled, tried to relax, but the air carried the oddest scent of cigarette smoke. Oh, Baby. Her mom's voice echoed in her mind at the same time someone wrapped their hand around Cali's arm. Her breath hitched.

"Hello, Cali." Stan's large frame pressed her against the car.

Chapter Seven

Brit parked his SUV on the side street and ran through the sheets of rain to where he spotted the other two detectives. As he drew closer, he saw Duke had Payne up against a fence in a strip center's alley— the man's arms and legs spread wide as Duke searched his pockets. Duke looked back when Brit's footsteps echoed louder than the rain.

"Look at this," Duke said. "He's got weed on him." Duke dropped the plastic bag on the ground. "Oh, that's not good."

Brit crossed his arms. "Nope, not good." Cold rain beaded on his leather jacket.

"Come on, guys." Payne tried to pivot. Duke slammed him against the fence. Mark, Duke's partner, stood a few feet away as if blocking onlookers from coming down the alley.

"It's not mine," Payne said as a slice of lightning lit up the dark gray sky.

Brit stepped closer. "What do you know about a cop killer? Start talking and we might be inclined to overlook things." Thunder boomed in the distance.

"I don't know shit!" Payne tried to jerk away.

Duke slammed the man against the fence again. "Either you're going to sing, or I'm going to make sure you'll be humming a tune to about five years up in Huntsville. I heard you didn't do so well up there on your last visit."

"I sing, I die," Payne said. "Besides they won't put me away for that little bit." The storm's fury swallowed his words.

Brit leaned his shoulder against the fence, so Payne could see him. "He's right." Brit spoke to Duke, but focused on Payne. "He won't go down for that bit of weed."

"Then you want me to beat it out him?" Duke leaned his shoulder on Payne's back.

Payne's eyes hardened. "You wouldn't do that."

"You'd be amazed what we'll do when a cop killer is involved." Duke snarled the words.

Part of Brit knew Duke wasn't joking. And as much as Brit wanted it, he couldn't allow it. But he wasn't above trying something else. Brit held up his hand. "Beating him is too easy." Brit looked back at Payne. "Besides, some things are worse than a beating. Things like going back into the joint. Right, Payne?"

"That ain't gonna get me no time."

The rain beat down harder. Brit had to speak louder to be heard. "You're right." Another bolt of lightning sizzled through the air. "But I can fix that." Brit wiped the rain from his face. "Assaulting an officer is serious."

"I didn't assault anyone." Payne bumped his head against the fence like an angry child.

"Oh, yes, you did," Brit said. "You see, Duke here has some mean fists. And instead of letting him use them on you, I'm going to let him use them on me. Then I'm going to say you did it. With the weed and assaulting an officer . . . you're going down."

Duke leaned on Payne's back. "I'd rather hit this jerk."

Brit blinked the rain from his eyes and looked at Duke, so he'd know how far Brit would play this game.

"We can't beat him. It wouldn't look good." Brit's words almost got lost in the sound of the rain. "Cuff him so we can get this over with."

Duke cut his questioning gaze to Brit. "You're serious?"

About Duke hitting him, he was damn serious. About going through with the threat if Payne didn't come through. That was yet to be seen. "Cuff him," Brit ordered as the thunder rolled. "We don't want him getting away while you're beating the shit out of me."

Snapping the cuffs from his back belt loop, Duke fit them on Payne's wrists and gave the man a shove. Payne dropped on his ass in the mud and stared up at the two of them.

"This ain't gonna work!" Payne shouted.

Brit wasn't sure it would either, but he was fresh out of ideas.

"I'm not talking," Payne belted out.

Brit ignored Payne and stared at Duke. "Hit me."

~

45

The storm raged in Cali's ears. She felt Stan press closer, and a sick feeling hit the pit of her stomach.

"Why did you call the police?" Stan's unshaven face pressed against her cheek while lightning danced overhead.

"Because you shot at me." She tried to pull away. His grip tightened on her arms and she jerked, slamming her knee against her car. The pain made her flinch—that was so going to bruise. Having taken a few safety courses, she tried to remember what she should do if someone attacked her. Stop, drop, and roll. No, wrong crisis. Scream, kick, scream.

He swung her around. "I didn't shoot at you." His words smelled like beer, but another smell, hideously ugly, clung to his clothes. "It wasn't me." His grasp inched down her arm to her wrist. "Where's the bracelet?" His grip tightened.

"I took it off." The thunder matched the beating of her heart. "Let me go."

He ran his free hand over his face. "Look, baby. I need your help. But you can't call the police. No police."

She wanted to scream she wasn't his baby; that she'd been one woman's baby, but her mom had died. Before she opened her mouth to speak, his head descended, and he kissed her.

The second his lower lip moved between her teeth, she bit down.

The taste of blood flavored her tongue and she gagged. He yanked back. "Fuck it, Cali! Why are you doing this?" He reached for his lip.

She bolted.

His footsteps chased her. Close. Too close. Fear clawed at her. Then his fingers snatched a handful of her hair. The pain sent chills through her skull.

Chapter Eight

It's okay. Cali's mother's voice echoed inside Cali's head. Help's coming.

"Miss McKay? You forgot . . ." The lawyer's secretary came jaunting out into the storm, an umbrella held overhead.

Stan shoved Cali into a parked BMW. Its alarm started blaring when she hit. Stan tore off running through the parking lot toward his truck.

Tears filled Cali's eyes. The taste of blood, his blood, spread to her throat. She leaned over, heaved, and threw up all over her favorite shoes.

~

"I'm serious," Brit said. "Hit me."

Duke shook his head. "I'd rather hit this scum."

"No! Hit me. Come on." He eyed Duke.

Payne shook his head. "You two are idiots."

"Yeah," Brit answered the man sitting on the ground. "We are." Brit gave Duke a jab in the chest. "We're big enough idiots to carry this off. Hit me," he told Duke, and he hoped the cop would play along.

Duke's eyes grew round. "You're really serious?"

Brit nodded. Lightning flashed. "Make it look bad. He's going down for this."

Duke drew his fist back, then pain slapped Brit in the mouth. The punch slammed him against the fence, and he slid down beside Payne. The moment his butt hit the pavement, the cold rain soaked through his jeans.

"Damn." Duke rubbed his knuckles. "You got a hard chin."

"Christ!" Payne said.

Brit wiped the blood across his lip, wanting Payne to get a good look. The storm had lost some of its fury, but droplets rolled down the arm of Brit's leather sleeves. He looked at Duke standing over him. "Is this going to do it? Or should we go for more?"

Duke continued to rub his hand. "I'd better do it again or they may go easy on him."

"Yeah, you're right." Brit got up. He wavered on his feet for show, then spit blood at Payne's feet. The blood was real. Rain washed the red stain away, but not before Payne saw it.

"Maybe do the eye this time. When I see the judge, it'll look really bad. Maybe bruise the throat. I'll say he tried to choke me. Get attempted murder slapped on his ass."

"Fuck!" said Payne. "I'm not going down for this shit."

Brit looked at him. "But you will." He brushed the back of his hand over his throbbing lip. "You want to sing, or am I going to let him hit me again?"

When Payne didn't answer, Brit shuffled forward to stand in front of Duke. "Hit me." He gave the lowlife another glance.

Payne butted his head against the fence. "Okay. I'll talk."

~

"What happened to you?" Adams peered into Brit's office a couple of hours later.

Brit looked up. His lip throbbed like a son of a bitch. "Football."

"In this weather?"

"Boys will be boys." Brit moved some papers on his desk.

"I heard you guys got a lead on Keith's killer."

"Yeah." Brit leaned back in his chair. "It looks gang related. One gang member bragged about what a fellow gang member did. I'm looking through mug shots now to see if I can find someone who fits the description. Our snitch didn't have a name."

The sergeant reared back on his heels. "It's a start."

"I know." Brit just hoped like hell it was enough.

"You know I want this guy as much as you do."

"I doubt that," Brit said.

Adams frowned. "You sleeping at all?" He tucked his hand into his belt. "You look like shit."

Leave it to Adams to point out the obvious. "I'm fine." Brit waved him away. His leather jacket, hanging over the back of his chair, had left a puddle of water on the floor. The coat had dried, while his wet ass still sent a chill through his body.

Adams started to leave, then stopped. He stepped into the office and sniffed the air. "You start smoking?"

"No." Brit snatched a pencil and rolled it in his palms, wishing Adams would go.

"Smells like it." The man stepped closer. "A woman just came in to file a report. Said she'd talk to anyone." He cut a half-ass smile. "Anyone, but you. And here I thought the ladies used to like you."

Cali McKay was here. Brit dropped the pencil. "It's not my job to make them like me." He looked down at his desk, feeling Adams' eyes on him. But relief fluttered through Brit that she'd taken his advice.

"Losing your edge, huh?" Adams still didn't leave and neither did the memory of Miss McKay in that damn Mickey Mouse shirt.

Focusing on the mug shots, he pretended he didn't care that she didn't want to see him. He'd done his job. He flipped a page and tried to ignore the fact that Adams hung over his desk.

"The boyfriend got to her again," Adams said. "Roughed her up a little."

Brit jerked up, his chair banging the wall. "She hurt?" He didn't wait for an answer. He pushed past the sergeant to go see for himself.

Brit didn't slow down until he cut the corner and saw her sitting at Jones' desk. Wet and disheveled, her blonde hair fell out of a clip and hung in a soggy mess against her neck. He studied her face, but didn't see blood or signs of bruising. He walked over to get a closer look.

Jones looked up and stared at Brit's face. "What happened to you?"

Focusing only on Cali, Brit answered, "Football."

"In this weather?" Jones asked.

"Yeah," Brit mumbled and then focused on Cali. "You went back to your place again, didn't you?"

She didn't answer, so he turned to Jones. "Did she go back to her place?"

Jones held up his hands in surrender. "I—"

Brit glared down at her. "What is it? Do you want to get beat up?"

She scowled back, then looked at Jones. Her expression softened. "Are we through?"

Brit answered for Jones. "No. We're not through." Brit picked up the report and read Jones' scribbling. Subject at her lawyer's office. Boyfriend met her outside by her car. Lawyer's secretary stepped out to give her paperwork. Boyfriend ran off.

"What's the lawyer for? Did you get a restraining order?" Brit spouted the first question on his mental list.

She didn't answer. "I have to go." She smiled at Jones.

The smile didn't even reach her eyes. It wasn't a real smile, but it was more than he got from her.

"Thank you," she told Jones and stood up, a little unsteady on her feet.

"Did he hurt you?" Brit asked.

"I'm fine." She slung her purse over her shoulder then started out.

Brit noticed a slight limp as he followed on her heels. After five steps, he accepted the fact that he'd let his temper loose on her again. Which meant he didn't deserve a smile. "I'm just doing my job. I'm not excelling at it right now, but all I'm really trying to do is help you."

Ignoring him, she pushed open the precinct door and walked out into the raging storm without even flinching.

He went after her. Rain pelted him again, and without his leather jacket, the cold made his skin crawl. He matched her steps and went for more questions. "Why are you limping? Does Stan know where you're staying? How did he know where to find you?"

She stopped in front of a silver Honda and began fumbling through her purse. "Blast it!" She tossed a few items from her purse onto the hood of her car. Rain fell on her wallet and a cell phone. She didn't seem to care. Then a tampon rolled off the hood and landed by his shoe.

She looked at it then continued sifting through her purse. Turning the leather bag over, she shook it. Everything rolled out—pens, pencils, and a few coins. Everything, but a set of keys.

"Dang it!" She snatched open her purse and stuffed the waterlogged items back inside. Then she knelt at his feet and picked up the soaked tampon and a pen that had rolled off the hood.

In her squatted position, she reminded him of someone's puppy left out in a storm. Lost. Scared. He'd never wanted to save a puppy as badly as he did right now. A blast of wind whipped her wet hair across her face. He saw her shake as the November-cold cut through his own shirt. But something told him it wasn't just the cold making her shake. How bad had the assault been? His stomach knotted.

Standing, she slung her purse over her shoulder and her blue-eyed gaze locked on him. Her eyes squinted; rain left droplets on her cheeks, or were those tears? "I don't want to talk to you." The distant sound of thunder rolled and he saw her hands trembling.

"Did he hurt you?" he asked again, only this time he let his concern leak into his voice.

Ignoring his question, she started back inside. He followed, matching her brisk pace. When they got to Jones' station, Brit snatched the set of keys off the desk before she did. Jones bit back a grin. Brit wasn't grinning. The woman wasn't in any condition to drive. He remembered when he'd gotten the call about Keith, he'd been shaking so bad he could hardly hold the damn steering wheel. And he'd come within a second of driving right into the path of an eighteen-wheeler.

Wet and disheveled, and somehow still adorable, she held out her palm. "Give them to me." Her voice had an authoritative snip.

Brit remembered her occupation—teacher. Too bad his high school buds had nicknamed him King of Detention and his most common sin had been bucking authority. He wrapped his hand around the keys. "Sit down and have a cup of coffee. Let me make sure you're okay and then I'll give them to you."

"I don't want coffee." Her authoritative edge slipped and her lip quivered.

From the cold or emotion, Brit didn't know. Probably both.

"Look, you're too upset to drive. If I let you go and you had a wreck, I'd feel like shit."

"I'm fine." She held out her hand again, wiggling her five digits, and he saw her trembling.

"You're still shaking." Brit watched her stiffen. He shot her his best smile and spoke in a soft voice. "One cup. Come on. Let me make up for being an ass earlier."

Her left foot started tapping. "I want to go."

Damn, he really had lost his charm. He almost handed them to her, then remembered how close that eighteen wheeler had come to ending his life. If something happened . . . "And I want you to have a cup of coffee."

Her eyes tightened and brightened with unexpected anger. He waited for the explosion, for her to toss out a few four-letter words. So far he'd only heard the words "darn" and "blast" leave those pretty lips.

God knew he'd drawn swear words out of every one of his high school teachers. Not that an outburst was what he wanted; he just wanted to make sure she was safe. He knew it wasn't his problem. It wasn't even his job to take it this far. He didn't want to care. But he did.

Her lips moved as if she counted to ten. Then she looked at the people sitting at the desks spaced around the room. "Would someone please make this jerk give me my keys?"

Lucy, one of the female desk clerks, jumped from her chair and stepped between him and Cali. She shot Brit a look of disgust, then glanced back at Cali.

"Look," the clerk spoke to Cali. "He is being a jerk, which is unusual for him, but unfortunately, he's right. You're not in any condition to drive. So take him up on the coffee, and then, if he doesn't hand over your keys," she cut her eyes back to Brit, "I'll personally hold him down and let you kick him in the balls."

Brit frowned at the clerk, but when he saw Cali's expression soften, he accepted the clerk had accomplished what he hadn't. He couldn't help but wonder if Cali had just finally listened to reason, or if she was hoping to kick him in the balls. Not that he didn't deserve it.

"One cup," he said.

She met his gaze. "Just one."

"This way." He waved a hand. At first she didn't budge, then she started walking, her limp barely noticeable now. He guided her down the hall, two left turns, to his tiny office.

Standing back from the door, he motioned for her to enter. He pointed to the chair across from his desk and kept pointing until she lowered herself into the flimsy piece of furniture. She folded her arms around herself as if to ward off the cold.

"Thank you." He made a dismal attempt to be polite, because for some reason he got the feeling it mattered to her. "How do you take your coffee?"

"I really don't want coffee."

"Cream? Sugar?" He stared at her stubborn expression.

"Cream." She trembled again as she glanced away.

He darted down the hall to collect caffeine. When he came back, she had her arms locked around her middle. Her hair, and the clip, hung in a wet mess around her shoulders. "Here. Hot is all I promise."

She took the steaming coffee, curled her hands around it, and brought it closer as if to absorb the heat.

He touched her shoulder and, as he suspected, the sweater felt saturated. "This thing is soaking wet. Take it off."

"I just want to go home." Steam whispered up from the cup.

"You can't go home." He took the coffee from her hands and set it on his desk beside the cat food. "Take the sweater off before you turn into ice."

"I meant I want to leave here." She glared at him again, but Brit decided that even her glares didn't overshadow her sweet face. The woman didn't use four-letter words. Maybe that explained the face of an angel. A sexy angel.

He continued to stare. A man could get lost in those blue eyes. "Please, take the sweater off," he added, sensing that "please" was her favorite word.

The please worked. Shifting, she began removing the waterlogged material. He decided right then to give politeness a shot from now on when dealing with her.

She pulled her arms from the sleeves. A hard task because of the clingy soaked wool. Underneath she wore the beige blouse she'd worn this morning. The rain hadn't spared it either. Brit envisioned goose bumps rising on her skin beneath the material. Then he saw her breasts, lacy bra, and nipples pebbled against the sheer fabric. Shutting the door on his wayward thoughts, he snatched his leather jacket from his chair and draped it over her shoulders.

His fingers brushing against her neck caused her to jump. "Sorry." He paused. "He really scared you, didn't he?" Brit moved back, giving her space.

She didn't answer. Didn't have to. Fear flashed in her eyes, and it wasn't because of him. He gritted his teeth and wanted to catch the bastard. Pushing back his protective fury, he picked up her coffee and placed it in her hands again. Her appearance—small, vulnerable, and wearing his coat—had his chest tightening.

He moved to his chair and sat. It protested his weight with a shrill screech. One of these days, the damn thing would fall apart. Readjusting his weight, he wondered which one would hold together longer, him or the chair. He'd put his money on the chair. "You want to tell me what happened? It might help to talk about it."

"No." The teacher voice returned, but it didn't deter him. He was too fascinated by the way her rain-soaked hair clung to her cheek.

He had the oddest desire to push the strands away, to pull her against him because she looked as if she could use a good holding. Not his job. He pushed back the desire; he was a cop, not a personal caretaker.

Elbows on his desk, he laced his hands together. "You were limping. Are you sure you're not hurt?"

"I'm fine."

Those two words again. Their eyes met again. "Okay. Then we'll just sit here and stare at each other while you warm up."

She abandoned her coffee on his desk. "May I please have my keys now?"

He couldn't force her to stay here. He knew that. Hell, if the sergeant knew he was holding her keys hostage, he'd get his ass chewed up one way and down the other.

"You won't go back to your apartment, will you?"

"I have to go back there, eventually."

"Not for a few days." He shot her a look that he hoped made the message clear. "This guy isn't someone to mess with."

Her bow-shaped lips tightened. "Fine. I won't go back to my apartment for a few days."

He picked up a pencil and tapped it on a yellow pad. "Where are you staying?"

"With a friend." His coat around her shoulders shifted, exposing her wet blouse.

Her breasts drew his gaze again. The lacy pattern of her bra showed through her shirt. He forced his eyes up. She hadn't willingly entered this wet T-shirt contest, which meant he didn't have the right to enjoy it.

"Does Stan know where this friend lives? What if he—"

"No." Silence thickened the air.

Brit gave the pencil a few more taps, focusing on her face, and trying not to think about her breasts. "Drink your coffee, then I'll return your keys." He ducked his head and pretended to read some paperwork. Instead, he sat there breathing in her scent, for it had taken up residency in his broom closet of an office.

"Oh, that's awful." Her words brought his head up.

The way she looked at the cup made him smile.

"Remember, I didn't promise you it would be good. Only hot." Their gazes converged. Excitement stirred in his gut, and that stirring said he'd like to get to know her. Like to see all her expressions, even a real smile or two. Bad idea. He tugged her keys from his pocket, dropped them on his desk, and slid them to her. "Drive safe. And if you're still limping later, see a doctor."

She set the coffee down and took her keys. She rose. Shoulders stiff, she took a step then glanced back. Those blond strands of hair clung to her cheeks again. "Thanks for the coffee."

He grinned. "I thought you said it was awful."

"It was." She almost smiled. "God awful. But it was nice of you to bring it to me."

Warmth fluttered in his gut. He chuckled, realizing he'd never come across anyone who had manners so intact. She didn't curse and always offered gratitude—even for lousy coffee. He remembered her picking up the useless tampon. Hell, the woman didn't even litter. Obviously, it came from her upbringing. God knew Brit didn't come by manners naturally. Oh, his sister had tried to teach him a few, but they never stuck.

She stood there as if waiting for a reply and, as crazy as it seemed, he wanted to please her. "You're welcome."

He watched her walk out. The seductive sway of her hips, even in those loose black dress pants, reminded him that he hadn't been with a woman in too damn long. It took five minutes before he realized that those hips had just swayed out with his leather jacket. Damn. He loved that jacket. He leaned back in the chair and closed his eyes. When he heard someone clear his throat, he sat up.

Lucy, the desk clerk who'd offered to hold him down so Cali could kick his boys, stood there grinning.

"Thanks for helping out," he said.

She chuckled. "Anderson's right. You're a softy."

"I'm not a damn softy," he muttered after she disappeared.

Chapter Nine

Cali pulled out of the police parking lot before she realized that she'd taken his jacket. She considered turning around. No. She'd drop it off another time.

The rain pelted her windshield and she turned the wipers on high. As she drove, she kept eyeing the rearview mirror, praying she wouldn't spot Stan's white truck. The memory of him coming up behind her, pressing himself against her, made her queasy.

What would have happened if Mr. Jones's secretary hadn't come out? Would he have really hurt her? Tried to rape her? Cali gripped the steering wheel.

"Don't think about it," she mumbled and listened to the squeak of the wipers squeegeeing the rain away. Oh God, she wanted to find herself a soft pillow to cry into. She wished she hadn't agreed to stay with Tanya. All she wanted to do was curl up into a ball and have a good cry. But did she really want to be alone? Just me.

Just me. The words seemed to chase the lump of hurt around her chest. The lump had been there ever since her mother told her about the cancer. Tears blurred her vision as rain coated her windshield. She attempted to hold back the tears; she didn't need more liquid impairing her view.

~

Brit thumbed through another book of mug photos. His vision grew blurry. He needed some sleep or he wouldn't make the night. Eyeing his watch, he decided to go home and try to grab a nap before his shift at eleven. Standing, he stretched his arms over his head. The wet sweater on his file cabinet caught his gaze. Tomorrow he'd drop the sweater off at her work, in exchange for his jacket.

The idea of seeing her again brought a surge of anticipation. His mind created a vision of her breasts against the wet blouse.

57

"Damn!" he mumbled, and mentally tossed the anticipation in the trash along with her cup of cold coffee. The last thing he needed was to get a hard on for some woman mixed up with an abusive boyfriend. He started out, then swung around and grabbed the sweater. He did want his jacket back.

Only a light mist fell when he stepped out the backdoor of the precinct. He stopped to grab his keys from his pocket when something brushed against his leg. Looking down, he saw the pathetic looking mama feline rubbing her face against the hem of his jeans. The animal's gray fur seemed too thin, her chest swollen with milk, and her right ear was missing most of its tip. She'd tangled with someone she shouldn't have. Her gold eyes rose, and she let out a pathetic meow.

"What? I already fed you." He heard her light purr and could almost feel the soft rattle against his leg. "Look, you're better off attaching yourself to that Anderson kid. He's the real softy."

Then Brit wondered if she'd let him grab her so he could take her to a shelter—one like Anderson said, one that didn't euthanize. He'd bet Keith would have known where to take her. Hell, Keith would have taken her home.

Grief fluttered deep in his chest, and he continued to stare at the feline. She looked on the outside like he felt on the inside. Battered, worn down, at the end of an emotional rope. He thought again about rescuing her from the streets. But he couldn't snatch her without her kittens.

"Your crew still in the storm drain, huh?" He bent down, but she instantly backed off and hissed. "Hey, you started this relationship." Studying her, he slowly reached out, but she hissed again and took off, disappearing under the metal fence. He walked over to the storm drain, saw the water had risen pretty high, and he didn't hear the kittens. She'd obviously moved them to higher ground. Smart cat.

~

Thirty minutes later, he walked into his two-bedroom bungalow in one of the older sections of Hopeful, Texas. The place had been one of six homes his Dad had bought during the recession in the eighties.

When the economy took an upswing, old money came in and started turning the neighborhood around and property value shot up tenfold. One of the homes his mom had sold helped put him and his sister through college. Then she gave them each one as a graduation present. His sister sold hers, and his mom rented out the others, living off the profit.

Every few months, someone offered to buy Brit's home. He could make a killing by selling. He refused. Not because of sentimental reasons. Nevertheless, his old man's short career in real estate investment had been the only thing he'd ever done right. Of course, that one good thing had stemmed from his one big win at the track.

Tossing his keys on the kitchen table, Brit walked into his laundry room. He fit the soggy sweater around a plastic hanger. Catching a feminine scent, he pulled the wet wool to his nose. It smelled like her —the light flowery scent he'd noticed that night at her apartment. "Damn you smell good."

"Sniffing sweaters, huh?"

Brit swung around. The sweater fell to the washing machine. "Friggin' hell, Sis, don't do that!"

"Don't do what?" Susan asked.

"Sneak up on me. What the hell are you doing here?"

Her wide mouth thinned to a tight line. "Is it me, or have greetings gone downhill lately?"

He frowned. "You scared the piss out of me."

She eyed him, head cocked to one side. "What happened to your lip?"

"Football," he mumbled as he watched her toss a dark braid over a shoulder.

"God, you suck at lying." She stepped closer and touched his swollen lip. "Ouch."

"I'm fine." He remembered Cali McKay muttering that same lie.

His sister frowned. "You completely forgot, didn't you?" She stared at his lip.

He got a bad feeling. "Forgot what?"

"I called you two weeks ago. Told you I'd be in town for Mom's birthday, and you said I could stay with you."

"Shit! I'm sorry." He closed his eyes and leaned his ass against the dryer. "Was I supposed to pick you up at the airport?"

"Sort of." She arched an eyebrow, then sent him the it's-okay-you're-my-brother look.

"I'm really sorry." He meant it, too. He should have remembered. "Why didn't you call my cell?"

"I tried. You didn't answer. I was worried sick until I called your office and spoke with some guy named Quarles. He said you were working some case."

He yanked his cell phone out of his pocket and realized it was completely out of juice. "Crap. I forgot to charge it."

"You still haven't caught the guy, have you?"

"Not yet. But we've got a few leads." Brit vaguely recalled telling his sister about Keith. Probably the same conversation in which she'd told him about coming down. Susan had met Keith once on one of her trips into town.

She took a step back and did her usual big sister head-to-toe inventory. Up, down. Sometimes he still expected her to check behind his ears and give his fingernails a good inspection. In many ways, Susan had been more of a mother to him than his own mother. And considering how protective he'd been of her, he supposed he'd been a little like a father to her.

She cocked her head and tapped a finger to her lips. "You look like day-old crap with a hangover."

"You're right." He smiled. "Casual greetings have gone to hell in a hand basket."

She grinned, picked up the sweater and hung it up on a hook on the wall. "Whose sweater were you sniffing?"

"Nobody important." He walked into the kitchen and opened the fridge. The only thing inside was some milk.

"I knew that already." Her tennis shoes squeaked on the tile floor as she entered the room.

"Knew what?" He retrieved the milk, opened it, and gave it a sniff test. The sour smell filled his nose. But it was the taste of the sour milk that had him spitting in the sink. He screwed on the top and shoved the container back in the fridge.

His sister rolled her eyes at something. "I knew she wasn't important. Relationships are never important to you. You're a love 'em and leave 'em kind of guy."

"Spare me the talk." He settled for a glass of water. "I swear I haven't broken a woman's heart in about fifteen minutes." Truth was, he hadn't broken any hearts in years. Since the disastrous relationship a few years ago, he'd been careful not to get involved with anyone who wanted to get involved.

His sister twisted her long braid, went to the fridge, and pulled out the milk, checked the date and then rolled her eyes again. "Why would you put it back in the fridge?"

"Because that's where milk goes." He shrugged.

Making a face, she poured the milk down the sink.

When she was done, she tossed the carton into the overflowing trash can then looked back at him. "We're letting them do it to us, you know."

"Letting who do what to us?" He drank his water.

"Mom and Dad. We're letting how they lived their lives affect how we live our lives. We're projecting their mistakes onto ourselves."

"You've been watching too much Oprah." He sat down.

"No. I'm actually seeing my own therapist. Besides, Oprah's off the air, I'm into Dr. Phil now."

He shook his head. "There's nothing wrong with us."

"Then why haven't either of us ever married?"

"Because we're smarter than the average Joe." He toasted her with his empty glass. "How long are you down for?"

"Five days." She sank into a kitchen chair. "Do you want me to stay with Mom?"

"I don't hate you that much." He grinned.

"Thanks." She leaned back in her chair. "You remembered Saturday, right? I'm having Mom's sixtieth birthday party. You said you'd come. You have to come."

"Saturday." He pushed a hand through his hair and let his eyes close for just a second as he recalled agreeing to this, too. "Yeah. Saturday."

"You really look tired." Her eyes softened. "Too tired."

"I'm fine," he lied again. "And I have to be at work at eleven."

"Then go to bed." Standing, she put a hand on his shoulder. "I promised Mom I'd go to dinner with her." Susan kissed his cheek. "Have you talked to her lately?"

Brit nodded. "Yeah, three or four weeks ago." He'd screwed up and forgotten to check caller ID and was forced to talk to her for a minute.

"You should talk to her and see her more often." Susan went to his pantry, opened it, and shook her head. "Are you even eating?"

"See her more? I'm not a masochist. Besides, she has Fred."

"Frank," Susan said. "Fred was her last husband."

"She divorced Fred? Really?" he asked. "Wait. Wasn't he the one she said was her soul mate? Or was that Floyd? What is it with her and men with names that start with an f?"

Susan closed the pantry. "Don't get cute, brother."

"I can't help but be cute." Rising, he shot her a teasing glance. "It's the Lowell charm." He gave his sister's hair a playful tug. "Sorry about not picking you up. Stay as long as you want. You got the key, right?"

"How else would I have gotten in?" she asked.

He shrugged. "You could have taken after dear ol' dad. Breaking and entering was his gift."

She did the eye roll again, only this one appeared serious. "We have to get over the past."

"I have." He started to his room. "If Dad were alive today, I'd arrest his ass." He glanced back. "I'm going to go to bed before I fall asleep standing up."

"I love you, Brit." Susan's words floated down the hall.

He smiled over his shoulder. "Back at you, Sis."

"I'm going to buy you some groceries," she called out.

The bed came into view. "I'll pay you back," he countered, and his whole body felt weak with the idea of sleep. But as soon as his head hit the pillow, his mind pulled up a picture of Keith lying cold in his casket. Why, damn it? There was no rhyme or reason to his death. They hadn't taken his wallet or his car. He'd been leaving the gym after working out. Someone just walked up to him and shot him.

Brit clutched a handful of pillow in his fist. Nope. Nothing was fine. All he could do was keep going. But for how long?

~

Cali leaned back on Tanya's sofa and picked up another piece of pizza. Spicy sauce and melted cheese. Heaven. She couldn't remember the last time she'd eaten.

"This is so good," she said. "I can't thank you enough for letting me come over." And now Cali meant it. As much as she'd craved being alone, being with Tanya chased away her doom and gloom mood.

Tanya smiled. "You want another glass of wine?"

"Yes, but I shouldn't." Cali looked around at her friend's apartment. It suited Tanya. Bright and cheery. Eclectic.

After arriving almost an hour late, Cali crashed on the sofa and Tanya opened a big bottle of Merlot. They ordered pizza and drank while Tanya listened about Cali's suicidal day. Cali managed not to cry, but only because the three glasses of wine had helped. It was still helping.

Tanya refilled Cali's glass and looked at Cali's things in a chair. "New coat?"

Generally, Cali abided by a two-drink minimum. Not tonight. "No. It's his."

"Stan the Dickhead? Let me get my scissors."

Cali grinned. "No, the other jerk."

"Oh, you mean, Mr. Little Dickhead, the detective. How did you get his jacket?"

Cali remembered the detective wrapping his coat around her. For just a second, she'd almost seen some humanity in him. "He put it on me after he stole my keys."

Eyebrows arching, Tanya said, "Sounds sort of sweet."

"Humane maybe, but not sweet. There's nothing sweet about Mr. Little—jeez. I can't even call him an ugly name. I really need to learn to be a bitch." Cali bit into the pizza with gusto and watched Tanya pour the rest of the wine into her glass. They weren't drunk, but they were definitely approaching the silly stage.

Tanya's goofy smile said the stage had already arrived. "Bitch lessons?"

Cali leaned forward. "Yeah. Can you teach me?"

"Shit." Tanya held up a hand, did the attitude head-shake, and smiled. "Are you calling me a bitch?"

"Yeah, but in a good way." Cali chuckled. They'd definitely hit the silly stage. "I'm too nice. Too agreeable. Ask anyone who knows me. If I had dollar for every time I've heard, 'Oh, Cali, you're so sweet.'"

Tanya picked up a piece of pizza. "It's your eyes. Big and blue. You look like a Charmin baby." She pulled a piece of pepperoni off the triangle slice and popped it into her mouth.

"A Charmin baby?" With her pizza poised for another bite, Cali licked a drip of sauce off her lip.

"You know, those baby faces that go on toilet paper."

The bite of thick crust caught in her throat. "I have a face that should be plastered on toilet paper? You see, only a bitch could say something like that."

Tanya dropped back on the sofa. "That's a compliment. Charmin was very particular. I'll bet my mom sent my picture and I was rejected."

"Please, you're exotic looking," Cali said. "I've always wanted to look striking." Picking up her wine, she studied the pizza balanced on her fingertips. "Seriously, I really need to learn to be a bitch. A bitch would have gotten her keys away from that detective."

"You got the keys," Tanya said.

"Only after he got what he wanted."

Tanya chucked. "I'll bet he wanted something else too."

"I don't think so."

"Anyway, you're perfect just the way you are." Tanya tossed the half-eaten pizza slice back into the box and wiped her hand on her jeans. "Did you get that e-mail at school asking if anyone knew of any public officials, as in police officers, who could speak at the At-Risk seminar?"

Cali cut her gaze toward Tanya. "You think I'd ask the detective? Don't think so. Plus, I volunteered at the last seminar. This Charmin face got the cookies and juice donated."

Tanya grinned and picked up the jacket. "Well, Mr. Little Dickhead is a nice dresser. Is he married?"

"Don't know. Don't care." Cali bit into her pizza as the question bounced around her head. Had he worn a ring?

"What does he look like?" Tanya leaned in with interest.

"Burt Reynolds." Cali spoke around the pizza in her mouth.

"Who?"

Cali swallowed. "Burt Reynolds, the movie star. That's who he looks like. But with blue-green eyes. And maybe taller. A little more shoulders."

"Ug, that Burt guy is an old fart."

"Well, the detective is a younger fart, maybe thirty."

Tanya grinned. "Does Mr. Little Dickhead have a nice ass?"

"Haven't checked," Cali told her, but unwillingly she tried to envision it.

"Well, have you checked out his pockets?" She dangled the coat out in front of her, and brown leather danced in the air.

"No." Cali hadn't thought about going through his pockets. But now that Tanya had mentioned it, Cali's curiosity zinged to life, and the wine gave her courage. Not that she needed courage. They weren't going to steal. Just snoop. "Go for it."

Tanya dug her hand into the first pocket and retrieved a half-eaten pack of breath mints. "Well, he cares about his breath." She grinned and went treasure hunting in the second. She pulled out a candy bar wrapper. "He has a sweet tooth." She patted the coat down then turned it inside out. "These coats always have a few hidden pockets." Then she found one. It even had a zipper. She unzipped it and reached in. "What do we have here?" Opening the pocket, she glanced inside. Her mouth dropped. Tanya collapsed on the sofa and giggled.

"What?" Cali downed the last sip of her wine.

Tanya's eyes glittered with humor. "We've given him the wrong nickname." She held up a condom packet. "It's extra large."

They both fell back, snorting with laughter.

~

"He does look like Burt Reynolds, doesn't he?"

Her mama had followed her to Tanya's house, Cali thought. Even in her sleep she worried that it wasn't normal to dream so much about someone who'd died.

"He has great shoulders, too." A smile sounded in Mama's voice.

"I wouldn't know." Cali kept her eyes closed.

"It was sweet of him to give you his coat."

"He's not sweet." Cali pushed her hand into the pillow.

"He's got a lot happening now. He's not normally that gruff. He doesn't even like himself right now."

"Well, I've got a lot happening now, too." Cali nuzzled her pillow with her cheek.

"That's why you should understand. Ease up on the guy."

Cali rolled over and looked up. "Mom, you're dead, and you're still trying to meddle in my life."

"I'm not meddling, I'm just . . . okay, so I'm meddling. That's what mothers do." She dropped down on the edge of Tanya's sofa bed and looked around the room. Her bracelets jingled. "You could teach this girl a thing or two about decorating."

Cali sat up. "You always were a bit of a decorating snob."

"No, I was a real estate professional. I knew what looked good." Her mom lit up a cigarette. "But I like this girl. You two have a good time together. It was good hearing you laugh."

Cali pulled the blanket up around her knees to ward off the chill.

Her mom's expression grew somber as she helped Cali fix the blanket. "You spent way too much of your time with me these last few years. I should have stopped you, but I was selfish."

A hitch of emotion stuck in Cali's throat. "I wanted to spend time with you."

"I know." Her mother smiled, but it faded quickly. "You need to be very careful. The weasel, Stan is still looking for you. Listen to the detective. He's going to help you. And you're going to help him. Sometimes I love the way life works out."

"Help him do what?" Cali dragged a pillow into her lap.

"I can't tell you all my secrets." She glanced at Cali as if she knew things. Her mother was never good at keeping secrets.

"What do you mean?" Cali asked.

"Well, in about ten minutes, he'll be discovering he needs you. Dress nice tomorrow. Wear that pink dress you packed. Let him see that you've got more than a sweet face. Not that there's anything wrong with having a sweet face."

"It belongs on toilet paper." Cali dropped back on the bed.

Her mother reached out and brushed a hand over Cali's brow. "Get some rest, baby."

"I miss you, Mom," Cali whispered.

"I know," her mother said. "I miss you, too."

~

"Okay, let's see what we have." Quarles pushed up the sleeves of his white shirt, rolled closer to Brit's desk and opened the envelope with the jewelry-heist photos.

Brit leaned back. Not as far back as he'd needed to do before. Quarles' presence seemed less intrusive. Not that Brit liked him, but he could almost tolerate him. But why Quarles tolerated Brit's pissy mood was a mystery. Even Brit had to admit, he'd been a pain in the ass.

And speaking of pain, Brit twisted his neck to release the nagging tension. He'd managed to get about three hours of sleep. If you could call it sleep. He woke up about every half hour, his brain actively working on Keith's case.

Still, this evening he felt somehow more together. Maybe it was the lead on Keith's case; maybe it was seeing Susan. Nothing like having his big sis fuss over him. She'd even gone to the store and left him a sandwich waiting in a plastic baggy. Yup, Susan won the Sister-of-the-Year award.

Brit's gaze shifted to the sweater hanging on a hook behind his office door. Maybe his mood had something to do with looking forward to seeing a sexy blonde with big blue eyes. No. He raked a hand through his hair. Tomorrow he would return her sweater and collect his jacket. Maybe remind her to stay away from no-good men. Nothing else.

"Here." Quarles laid out the images on the desk as if they were cards and they were about to play a game. "I thought I'd run by a few pawn shops tomorrow. Show a few pictures around. See if anything has surfaced."

"Yeah." Brit said. "I'll take some too and hit a few on the north side while you go south. I was going to comb the gang hangouts in that area tomorrow anyway."

Rotating his shoulders, his gaze caught on one of the photographs Quarles tossed down. A bracelet—a bracelet with diamonds set in small flower-shaped settings.

"I've seen one like this." Pushing his hand over his face, he searched his mind. With him running on only a few hours of half-ass sleep, the search took longer than it should have.

"Not like this." Quarles placed the other images out on the desk. "Most of these are pretty rare. The old man bought good stuff. Sold a lot to the rich folks."

Brit read the back of the photo. The bracelet wasn't an original, but information printed claimed it to be one of only ten. And it was valued at forty-eight thousand bucks. Then he remembered. "She was wearing it. That's the bracelet Cali McKay was wearing."

Chapter Ten

"Who?" Quarles' green eyes tightened in puzzlement.

"Cali McKay, the woman with the domestic situation we backed up. She had a bracelet just like this."

"Really." Quarles flipped the card and read the back. "It just looked like it. There were only ten of these made."

"No. I remember because I helped her get it off."

Quarles leaned forward. "You think she's in on this?"

Brit crossed his arms over his chest and considered it. He got a visual of her eyes, big blue orbs of innocence. All her pleases and thank yous. "No. But her boyfriend . . ." The word "boyfriend" tasted sour on his lips. "But Stan Humphrey, yeah."

"Did they ever find the guy?"

"No. But I don't think they looked too hard."

"Is she back at her apartment?"

"She better not be. She said she was staying with a friend." A bad feeling bumped around Brit's chest. What if she hadn't listened to him? Damn, this guy could be a murderer.

He fumbled through some scrap papers on his desk until he found her number. He punched it in. Her answering machine caught the call, and he hung up. Leaning back, he drummed his fingers on his desk then stood.

"Where are you going?" Quarles asked.

"To pull the file Jones wrote up on her today. Maybe he got an address where she's staying."

"You thinking about looking her up now? At this hour?"

"If this guy is involved with the jewelry store robbery, he's wanted for murder. So yeah, I'm looking her up." Brit walked out.

A few minutes later, he sat back down at his desk with both Jones' file and Anderson's file in his hand.

"Got anything?" Quarles asked, edging closer.

"Not in this one. But Anderson mentioned he had several numbers." Frustrated, he snatched up Anderson's file and started leafing through it. "Pay dirt. Anderson said he thought it was her mother's number. Maybe she knows where her daughter is staying." Leaning against the edge of his desk, he punched in the number. An answering machine picked up. "Hi, this is Loren McKay. . . ."

"Damn." Brit hung up, collapsing back in the chair. He picked up the file and started reading.

"Ahh, listen to this." Brit looked at Quarles. "Stan plays in a band and travels a lot. Guess where she thought Stan was supposed to be the night he shot at her."

"Where?" Quarles asked.

"Austin. Isn't that where one of the robberies happened?"

Quarles eyes lit up. "Yeah. Interesting."

Brit tapped his knuckles against the desk. "Wonder how many members he has in his band? Want to bet it's four?"

"Wouldn't that be great!" Enthusiasm widened Quarles' grin, and a little of the emotion leaked into Brit.

"I'd love to close this case." Brit grabbed a phone book from his desk drawer and looked up Loren McKay. "Got it," Brit said. "Here's an address on her mother. She might not answer her phone, but she might answer the door."

Standing, Brit reached back for his leather coat. His hand hadn't hit the back of his chair when he remembered the soft swaying hips that had walked out with his jacket. He glanced at the sweater that now hung on the back of his door. He would hold it for ransom until she handed over his jacket. Right then, the anticipation of seeing Cali McKay surged back to life.

~

They went by her apartment first. The window had been fixed. No one answered the door. Then, they drove to the address listed for Cali's mom. The house, a nice white brick, one-story home, sat far back on a manicured acre lawn with an abundance of trees. Brit pulled into the driveway.

"The whole neighborhood seems to be tucked into bed," Quarles said when Brit cut off his engine. The night's silence seeped into the car.

"Yeah." Brit stepped out of his car. There wasn't a light on in the house. Hesitation about waking up an old woman stirred in his gut.

"Look." Quarles nudged Brit's elbow.

Brit turned his head just in time to see a round orb of light dance across one of the front windows. Someone inside the house had a flashlight. Both he and Quarles reached for their guns at the same time.

"The lady could just use a flashlight to get to the bathroom," Brit whispered, using logic.

"Yup," Quarles said, but he didn't put his Glock away.

Neither did Brit. "I'm going around back. Give me about two minutes, then, ring the doorbell."

Quarles nodded, and they both froze as a car rolled by, its headlights casting two sprays of light over the tree-lined lawn. The sound of the car's engine faded, and the dark silence returned. Brit started moving toward the fence.

The gate to the backyard was locked. He found a place to climb over. Falling to the other side, he barely escaped a rose bush. The darkness grew denser. Thick clouds held even the moonlight back. Gun in his hand, he moved toward the back patio.

Brit cut around the corner of the house. A noise brought his gaze up. But too late. Even in the dark, he saw the large object being hurtled at his head. He swung, saved his skull, but took the blow to the shoulder. The impact knocked him to the ground. His gun, jarred from his grasp, hit the concrete. A barbeque grill came slamming down beside him. Charcoal and ashes rained on his face, and he blinked the soot from his eyes. Unsure if he'd be shot in the process, but refusing to go down easily, he lunged for his Glock. He wrapped his hand around the solidness of his weapon and leapt to his feet. Blinking, still half blind, he tried to see his attacker.

No attacker, but he heard footfalls. The bitter taste of charcoal filled his mouth. His eyes, full of grit, stung like hell, but he scanned the shadows of the deep backyard.

Noise clattered behind him. Turning, Brit spotted a dark figure climb over the front fence. He tightened his hold on his gun, but recognized Quarles.

Another noise echoed from deep in the yard. Brit saw someone scrambling over the back fence. "He's running," Brit called and took off. Gritting his teeth, he fled after the grill-slinging bastard.

Heart pumping adrenaline into his chest, he hurdled the fence, and landed in another backyard and obviously in a big pile of dog shit if his nose was working right. He gaze darted around. Nothing. Then, he heard Quarles make the fence behind him.

"What we got?" Quarles' voice stabbed at the dark silence.

"One man. I didn't see a weapon." He pointed. "Go that way." He raced around one side of the house, Quarles the other.

Brit bolted through the open gate just in time to see a white truck, fitting the description of Humphrey's vehicle, hauling ass down the street. "Crap." He spit the bitter taste from his mouth, scrubbed a hand over his eyes, and wiped his shoe on the grass, trying to remove the crap. He smelled like last week's grilled pork chop and dog shit. Lights flickered on in the house of the fence they'd just climbed. "Damn."

"Who's there?" a voice called out from a window.

Quarles walked toward the front porch. "It's okay. We're police."

Brit left Quarles to explain while he ran back the way he'd come. He didn't think Cali was there, but Humphrey could have hurt Cali's mother.

He made the fence, landing with a thud. His shoulder ached, but he kept a firm grip on the Glock. He heard Quarles behind him again.

"Let me call for backup," Quarles said, breathing hard.

"I'm going in." Brit moved to the back door and found it open. Glass from the shattered window crunched beneath his feet.

"Police." He held his gun out. Dead silence permeated the home. "Mrs. McKay? Anyone home?"

No answer. Quarles followed him. Brit motioned for his partner to check the rooms off the living room. Then following his instinct, he darted into the dark hall.

"Mrs. McKay?" he called again. "It's the police. Are you okay?" No one replied. His finger tensed on the trigger. He had a bad feeling. Something about the house felt eerie, off. It even smelled strange.

A few minutes later, Quarles and Brit stood in the middle of the master bedroom. A hospital bed centered the room. Scattered about were all kinds of medical paraphernalia—oxygen tanks, an IV stand. Now he could place the smell he'd noticed earlier—hospital.

Quarles holstered his weapon. "The woman must be sick."

"Yeah." Brit swallowed a bitter taste, then noticed Quarles staring at him. "What?"

His partner grinned and touched his face. "Wish I had a camera."

Brit noticed the soot on his hands and figured he also had it on his face. "He got me with the grill." Brit heard sirens as police cars stopped in front of the house. "Ah, fuck. Did you call for backup?"

"Yeah. You hurt?"

Brit gazed at his soot-covered clothes. "I'm fine." Another lie, but nothing was broken, just bruised, like his damn ego. He used his sleeve to clean his face then rubbed his shoulder again.

"Should you be checked out?" Quarles asked.

"Hell, no." Brit noted a broken lamp on the floor. A few drawers had been yanked out of the dresser and the contents strewn about. "Appears Humphrey was looking for something."

"You think it was him?"

"The guy was driving a white Chevy. It was him." Brit raked a hand over his face. "Damn, I wanted to get him."

"Would have been nice," Quarles said as Brit headed to the front yard to meet the other officers.

He gave them a quick report. Lights flashed on next door, and he mumbled, "I'm going to talk to the neighbors." A woman opened the door and took a step back.

"I . . . thought you . . . were the police." She stared at his soot-covered frame.

"I am." Brit flashed his badge. "Sorry to disturb you. Someone broke into the house next door. No one's home. Do you know how I could reach Mrs. McKay?"

"Mrs. McKay?" the woman asked. "The owner of the house?"

"Yeah. Do you know how I could contact her?"

"Do you have a good psychic? She died last week."

~

73

The next morning, after a shower and her last aspirin, Cali stood in Tanya's living room and went through her suitcase. She saw the pink dress and remembered the dream. They were just dreams. She pulled out the wrinkle-free dress and gave it a shake. The movement sent pain screaming behind her eyes.

"You want coffee?" Tanya, hand pressed to her head, crept past and disappeared into the kitchen.

"Yes, please." Cali bit into her lip, remembering it was Thursday. A week since her mom had died. A week since her entire life had turned upside down. Somehow, some way, Cali had to get her world upright again.

Swallowing, she pressed a hand to her forehead. But first she had to get rid of the doozy of a headache.

"Oh, fudge!" Tanya said from the kitchen. "I'm out of coffee." She appeared in the doorway and collapsed against the wall.

Cali tried not to think about the niggling pain in her heart and head. "Why don't I go by Starbucks and grab us some on the way in?"

"That would be great. Or we could just ride together. You're going to stay the weekend, aren't you?"

Cali shook her head then stopped abruptly when it hurt. "I've intruded enough."

Tanya took a step, moving slowly, as if it caused her pain. "You haven't intruded. Besides I thought they said you shouldn't go back to your place for a while."

"I'll get a hotel." Cali tried to smile, but couldn't.

"You should stay here at least for the weekend."

Cali held up a hand. Her mouth felt like cotton. "I appreciate it. But you've got sex and jewelry scheduled."

Tanya sent her a dismal smile. "I've decided on jewelry. Sex next weekend. You're welcome to stay."

"Thanks, but I need to get some order into my life. I need to go to Mom's and start clearing her house out." Order, Cali thought, and, she almost . . . almost . . . felt capable of pulling herself together. She inhaled and made some quick decisions. Forget about the dreams. Forget about the rude detective. After she delivered his leather coat, she wouldn't have to see him again. And for now, she'd stay away from her apartment so Stan couldn't find her. Making plans gave her a sense of control, even if it was a false sense. What was the saying? Fake it until you can make it. She could do that. Couldn't she?

"Are you going to move into your mom's place?" Tanya stepped beside her.

"No. I'm going to sell it."

"It's a nice house," Tanya said, having attended the memorial service at the house last Saturday.

"Yeah, but . . . The day Mom moved into the house is the day she found out the cancer had come back. I went over there to help her unpack and she was sitting there in the middle of boxes just staring at nothing. Now, every time I think about the house, all I think about is cancer."

"Bummer." Tanya pressed a finger to her temple. "Please tell me I'm not the only one hung over."

Cali grimaced. "Got a whopper of a headache."

"Good," Tanya said. "Misery loves company. I'm gonna shower."

~

Brit paced in front of Cali's classroom. The lady in the office had said Cali usually got here about 7:00. It was already 7:15. Had something happened to her? For about the hundredth time, he wished he'd made her tell him where she was staying.

He'd searched her mother's home up and down for telephone numbers that would lead him to Cali. But nothing. Today, he wasn't leaving without knowing how to reach her.

Of course, finding out how to contact her wasn't why he was here. He needed to find that bracelet; he needed to find Stan Humphrey. And he needed to apologize for being an ass. Her mom had just died and then he'd come along and took his bad mood out on her.

Still, he was here strictly for work-related reasons.

"Right," an internal voice echoed from deep in his gut. He was attracted to her, had already spent too much time envisioning her naked.

Leaning against the wall, he rubbed his shoulder and chose to ignore all the voices. With as little sleep as he'd had, it was amazing the voices made any sense at all. Maybe if he hadn't been so exhausted, he'd not have let Humphrey get the upper hand.

He should have been more alert than that. He glanced at his hands. Ten minutes scrubbing in the shower and he still had soot under his nails.

Closing his eyes for a second, he thought about how Keith would have laughed his ass off at the sight of him, covered in charcoal and smelling like grilled meat and dog shit. Brit remembered the few jokes Quarles had tossed out last night. Brit smiled, then an unexplainable stab of guilt hit his gut. Somehow it felt like a betrayal to Keith.

The tap of high heels echoing down the hall brought him to attention. He waited to see if it was Cali who made the corner. A frown tightened his lips when a brunette wearing an orange sweater over a jean skirt came into view.

She clicked past him, a stack of books balanced on her hip. Brit's gaze, moving on its own accord, zeroed in on her backside. She swung around.

He raised his eyes, nodded, and offered her half a smile. It was, after all, the polite thing to do after being caught checking out a woman's ass. Not that he was even interested.

She frowned.

Brit's smile faded. Yup, the Lowell charm had vanished.

"You're looking for Cali, aren't you?" She shifted her armload of books.

"As a matter of fact, I am. I'm—"

"I know who you are. Little . . . er, Detective Lowell, right?" Her cutting tone could have etched glass. Deep etching.

He nodded and gave her a quick once over. "Have we met?"

"No." Her frown pulled at her brows. "Cali is my friend."

"She mentioned me, huh?" Maybe a little of the ol' charm still lived.

"Yeah, and if you're rude to her again, I'm gonna make sure she files charges against you." The books on her hip slipped and scattered on the floor. She leaned over, stopped, and pressed a hand to her head. "Damn."

Brit knelt and collected the books. When he stood, he said, "I . . . didn't know her mother had died. I was doing my job, but if I'd known about her loss, I probably would have been easier on her." He handed her the books.

She took them, and her gaze cut over his shoulder. "You were still an ass."

He gritted his teeth. "I plan on apologizing."

"You do that." She pivoted on her three-inch orange heels and entered a nearby room.

Her door slammed, then, he heard someone behind him. "What are you doing here?"

Chapter Eleven

He turned and faced Cali. She had two coffees in her hands. But his gaze didn't linger on the coffees. He couldn't take his eyes off the dress. Actually, it wasn't the dress. The neckline wasn't low, the hem wasn't short, it wasn't tight, but it did fit, and it didn't leave a curve to the imagination. Steam billowed from the cups she held in her hands. But the coffees weren't the only things hot. Damn, she looked good.

"Hi," he said, hoping to rescue some of the Lowell charm.

"What do you want?" she asked.

Four hours with you in bed. He chased that little thought away. But when she moved and the pink fabric shifted across her breasts, the thought zipped right back, only this time it insisted on five hours.

She shifted ever so slightly drawing his attention back to her hourglass figure. Maybe six hours.

"I need to talk to you about the case." He tucked his dirty nails into his pockets.

"Did you find Stan?" She lowered her voice as someone walked by.

"Can we go in your room?" he asked.

She took a step, then stopped. "Yes. But . . . I'll be right back."

Stacking her coffees, as she walked, she pushed open the door where the brunette had disappeared. Brit watched her go and the sway of her hips made his mouth go dry.

Seven hours.

Work-related reasons, he reminded himself.

"Yeah, right," echoed that damn internal voice again.

~

Cali heard a thud as she hit Tanya in the head. Her friend had obviously been listening at the crack. "Sorry," Cali said and handed her a cup.

Tanya rubbed her forehead. "I was just making sure he wasn't being a jerk again."

Cali smiled. "Did I hear you call him an ass?"

"Yeah." Tanya made a face. "Do you think he's going to arrest me for it?"

"I don't think so." Cali pulled the tab back on her cup and sipped the hot coffee. "You've got to teach me to be a bitch."

"He leave?" Tanya frowned back at the door.

Cali shook her head and remembered her headache thanks to the painful messages the movement brought on. "No." She pressed a hand to her forehead. "I'm practicing being a bitch and making him wait."

"You go, girl." Tanya grinned and sipped her coffee. Cali sipped hers. They both sighed as the caffeine seeped into their hung-over bodies.

That's when Cali remembered her mom telling her to wear the pink dress because she was going to see Brit. That she was going to help Brit. Her headache pounded a bit stronger.

"Why do you suppose he's here?" she wondered aloud.

Tanya did the hung-over shuffle to her desk where she dropped into her chair. "He said he was going to apologize."

"Really? Well, I better go collect my apology." Cali took one step. "Or should I let him wait a while longer?"

"Go. I'm cheering for you." Tanya winced at the sound of her own voice. "Quietly, of course."

Cali bit into the edge of her cup, making teeth prints. "He's messing up my plans."

"What plans?" Tanya asked.

"I was going to forget about him."

Tanya grinned. "He's too hot to forget. You got a plan B?"

"No plan B."

"Then come up with one. Fast." Tanya's eyes twinkled with mischief, even in their hung-over glaze. "He's really hot."

Cali sighed and went to face the detective. She found Mr. Hottie pacing in the hall. Meeting his gaze, she almost flinched and her stomach sent the hot coffee gurgling. She hadn't realized she went for the Burt Reynolds type. But the flip in her stomach said otherwise—definitely the "you're attracted to this man" flip.

"This way." She walked into her classroom.

Cali looked at her watch as she placed her coffee on her desk. She tried not to notice how wide his shoulders were, or how long his legs looked encased in those form-fitting jeans. Glancing away, she reached up to loosen the clip in her hair, hoping to relieve some of the tight pounding behind her eyes.

"I have exactly seven minutes before the bell rings." When she looked at him, she could swear the man was staring at her breasts.

She cleared her throat, forgetting that the throat clearing muscles were connected to the headache muscles. She winced.

He jerked his gaze up, looked a bit guilty, then, he frowned. "I'm definitely going to need more than seven minutes."

"Why more time?" Cali shifted and knocked over her cup of pencils. Seeing him in her classroom, in this part of her world, felt odd —as if the craziness in her outside life had followed her to school. Her headache throbbed as she collected the lead #2s. Right now even her false sense of control was slipping.

He tucked his fingers into his jeans' pockets, winced, pulled his hands out, and rubbed his shoulder.

"I tried to find you last night. It's about the bracelet you had on." He looked at her wrist.

"Why do you care about that?" She remembered him helping her unlatch the bracelet. Then, she remembered the couple of smiles he'd offered her yesterday at the police station. The man was a mixed bag of emotions. And he wasn't smiling now. She noticed his shoulders again. Not that she was actually taking Tanya's advice and coming up with Plan B.

She simply had a shoulder fetish and his looked good in his navy windbreaker. The thought of his leather jacket popped into her head. She'd left it in her car.

"Your jacket. I . . . it's in my car." She suddenly remembered the condom in his pocket and felt her face heat up.

"Where's the bracelet?" he insisted. "Do you have it on you?" He edged closer and those shoulders shifted making him look even more masculine.

She hesitated, completely at a loss as to why he cared about . . . She pushed a finger against her temple and tried to remember his question. Oh yeah, the bracelet. "I threw it away."

"What?" A cop edge sharpened his words. "You did what?"

His tone vibrated in her aching ears. She held her spine straight, reminding herself that this was her turf. At least in this room, she ruled the roost. "I threw it in the garbage."

His dominating gaze cut into her, and she didn't feel so in charge of her roost anymore.

"You threw a diamond bracelet away?"

She set her coffee down. "It was Zirconium. Not real."

He studied her for a second, then pulled something from his pocket and held it out. "Is this the bracelet?"

She stared at the photograph. "It looks like it. But why would you —"

"Where did you get it?"

"Stan gave it to me." She took the picture, flipped it over, and saw a price. "No. He couldn't have afforded to buy—"

"He didn't buy it. He stole it."

Her nervous chuckle loosened the jackhammers in her head again. "No. Stan wouldn't . . ." She closed her mouth before she choked on her size-seven pink pumps. She didn't know Stan. Good shoulders, nice-guy Stan had beaten up his other girlfriends, and he'd shot at her. Cali vaguely remembered Stan saying he wasn't the one who had shot . . .

"Oh my." She fell into her chair.

"Look, I need your help here."

Well, in about ten minutes, he'll be discovering he needs you. In the dream her mother had said he—

"Has your garbage been taken out since that night?" He stepped closer to the desk, crowding her space and thoughts.

She stared at her coffee as if she could visually soak up some of the caffeine and clear the muddle from her brain.

"No. It should still be there." The dream meant nothing. Just a coincidence. The fact that she had a stolen forty-eight thousand dollar bracelet in her garbage, well, that piece of info meant something.

"Good. Can you come with me to your place to find it?"

She looked at the clock on her wall. "I can't leave." Okay, having stolen merchandise was like illegal. "I mean, I need to get someone in here to watch the class."

"Okay. Get someone."

She didn't move. She just stared at him, thinking she'd love to just go home and paint her toenails right now.

"Sometime today, maybe?" He waved a hand to the door.

She stood up. "Do you always have to be rude?"

A shade of guilt colored his eyes. "You're right. I'm sorry." The bell rang, and he ran a hand over his face. "Really sorry." His apology sounded sincere and made him sound less like a big bad cop.

Oddly, she wanted the cop back. Big bad cop's shoulders were less noticeable. "Wait here. When the kids come in, tell them to start on their art journals."

"Do what?" His eyes filled with panic, but she left as her students crowded into the room.

When she returned a few minutes later, she found Anthony and Chris arguing over a girl, paper airplanes zipping across the room, and someone's CD player blaring Dido music.

Beside her desk stood Detective Lowell, feet slightly apart and arms hanging limply. He wore a wide-eyed perplexed expression.

"Class!" Cali snapped. The detective jumped. She might have smiled if the rise of her voice hadn't brought the headache dancing in the forefront again.

The music clicked off. Anthony and Chris grew quiet. The last paper airplane nose-dived against the detective's chest. Silence filled the room.

"Start on your art journals, please," she said.

Papers ruffled, seats were taken, order replaced chaos. She walked over to Lowell. "You can handle criminals, but you can't handle a few teenagers?"

He leaned close. "Criminals I can shoot."

She smiled this time. A small one.

"Can we go?" he asked.

She glanced over at her desk. "I have to wait until a substitute comes."

"How long?"

"Thirty, forty minutes."

He stared at her as if she'd condemned him to years.

"You can wait in the office if you'd like," she offered.

He edged closer, his shoulder brushing against hers. Close enough she could smell him. And it was a nice scent, too. "And abandon you to the wolves?" His grin came on slow, sexy.

She almost smiled again, then remembered that she didn't like this man. "Have a seat."

"With them?" He leaned close to her, too close again.

She took a step back. "They don't bite."

"Promise?" he asked and moved to an empty desk at the back of the class.

"Hey, everyone." She rubbed her hands together to stop the tingling in her palms. "I've got a substitute coming—"

"I thought he was the substitute." Tony pointed to Lowell.

"No. This is . . . a friend." The last thing she wanted was to start a rumor mill about her being involved with a crime.

"Boyfriend?" Anthony asked. "You're breaking my heart, Miss McKay. I told you I was going to grow up and marry you."

Laughter erupted.

"He's not my boyfriend." She met the detective's smiling eyes. The man seemed more relaxed in the back of the class than up front. She had a quick vision of how he might have been as a high school student—tough, bad boy, with a string of girls holding their breaths to be noticed. And she would have been part of that string, not that he'd have given her a second look; he wouldn't have been interested in the sweet, good girl of the class. Hadn't she been named "the girl most likely to graduate a virgin" in her junior year? And they were right, too.

"Come on, Miss McKay. Don't lie to us," Jamie said. "I mean, look at him. He's kind of hot if you like old dudes."

Cali couldn't help but chuckle when Lowell looked appalled.

"And you're hot," Jamie said. "You two match."

"I don't think so," Cali said.

"Are you her boyfriend?" Tony swiveled around in his chair to speak to the man in question.

The detective's expression now twinkled with humor as if he might say something to embarrass her. Or even worse, tell them he was cop.

"We're just friends," he said.

The knot in her stomach lessened when he hadn't told the truth. "Get to work." She wrote the assignment on the board. After five minutes, she decided to let Tanya know she'd be leaving. She started out, but Lowell caught her hand as she passed. And if the giggling she heard was any indication, at least a dozen of her students noticed.

His touch caused her pulse to sing again and she pulled her fingers from his warm palm.

He leaned closer. "You're not leaving me alone with them, are you?"

"I'm just going to tell Tanya where I'll be."

"What if they go crazy again?" he asked.

"Then control them," she whispered. She remembered the question Tanya had asked last night. Her gaze cut to his hand. No ring. "You . . . you're a cop, for goodness sakes."

"So I'm allowed to fire a few warning shots, huh?" He grinned.

"You don't really have a gun. Do you?" she asked.

His brow wrinkled. "Of course, I do."

She frowned. Maybe she was a little sensitive where guns were concerned, but after seeing her lamp mortally wounded, her feelings were justified. Plus, if anyone spotted his weapon, then they might guess he was here on police business.

"I think you should wait outside," she said.

He frowned. "I was teasing."

"I don't care. I'll meet you in front of the school when the substitute gets here."

~

Thirty minutes later, she stepped out of the school and into the crisp fall air. The sun caused her to squint, and the slight muscle reflex did nothing to help her hangover headache. She saw him standing beside the flagpole and started toward him. Something like anticipation bubbled in her chest.

He spotted her and she felt his gaze on her as he headed her way. She watched the way his body moved, even but quick steps that exuded power and confidence. Male confidence—the kind that had her body responding in a purely impure want-that-man kind of manner.

She remembered the condom again and without warning, her gaze lowered to his zipper.

Oh, gracious! Was she really thinking about the size of his penis? It's the hangover. Had to be the hangover. Her life was a wreck, she so shouldn't be thinking about sex right now.

"That wasn't necessary," he said, probably referring to her asking him to leave the classroom.

"I don't like guns." The wind picked up, the flag popped in the air. "I especially don't like them in my class."

"I'm a cop, Cali. Nothing was going to happen." He pressed a hand to her waist. "Come on. I'm parked over here."

She walked faster to escape his touch. When had he started calling her by her first name? Probably about the same time you started thinking about his penis.

"I'll follow you in my car." She took a sharp left.

He caught her arm, gently, his touch soft. "Ride with me."

"But . . ." His touch caused her heart to do another somersault.

"I need to talk to you." His gaze softened and he started moving his thumb in tender little circles on her forearm. "Please." His tone held so much tenderness and right then so did his eyes.

She relented because she was a sucker for politeness and not because his touch felt good. But just in case, she pulled away from his hand. They continued walking. He stopped at an SUV, opened the passenger door, and waited for her to get in.

A second later, he pulled himself up in the driver's seat, put the key in the ignition, but didn't start the engine. He shifted his wide shoulders and looked at her. "I know I've been an ass lately. I've had . . . a lot on my plate." He passed a hand over his face. "But that's not your problem. I'm sorry."

A bitch probably wouldn't accept his apology. She stared at him and saw sincerity. She also saw something else, something familiar. Worry and stress.

"I understand." So okay, she didn't have the bitch thing down yet.

"Thank you." He continued to stare. "I didn't know about your mom's death."

The ever-present grief hiccupped in her chest. She glanced out the window. "Did Tanya tell you?" She watched the flag flip in the wind.

"No. Last night after I saw the picture of the bracelet, I was trying to find you. You'd given Officer Anderson your mother's address."

She looked at him. "I did?"

"Yeah, you listed it under closest relative."

"Habit," she said. "I must not have been thinking."

"You were upset. It's understandable," he offered.

She nodded.

"Anyway, my partner and I went to your mom's looking for you."

Cali nodded, assuming her mom's neighbors had filled him in. She continued to stare out the window, not wanting to succumb to tears. It had been almost a week now since she buried her. Shouldn't she be over the crying stuff? Stan thought she should be. But oh yeah, Stan was a first class jerk, and probably, a jewelry thief.

"Stan Humphrey was there. He broke in."

Cali swung around to face him. "At my mom's place?"

"Yeah." He ran his hand over the steering wheel.

"Did you catch him?"

He shook his head. "He got away."

She closed her eyes briefly. "Please tell me he didn't ransack her place like he did my apartment."

"It's not as bad, but he did toss a few things around."

"Did he steal anything?" She felt her bottom lip tremble, and that hiccup of grief grew to a large lump of throbbing pain.

He shrugged. "Not knowing what your mother had, I can't say. I'm sorry. But I thought after we find the bracelet, we could go to your mother's place and check."

She slumped back into the seat, feeling her backbone lose its starch. The lump of pain moved up from her heart to her throat. Her head still throbbed and tears formed in her eyes.

His gaze, filled with sympathy, met hers. "You okay?"

"Am I okay?" All the emotion she'd felt this last week bubbled to the surface. "My mother dies, my boyfriend turns into a gun-toting jewelry thief, and my apartment gets ransacked. I'm kicked out of my own apartment, Sara's mother gets cancer." She was ranting, but she couldn't stop. "And my mom's lawyer tells me how lucky I am because my mother died and left me some money. Lucky. Who knew?"

She let out a deep breath and told herself to calm down, but she wasn't listening, venting felt too good, so she started again. "I get assaulted again by the gun-toting jewelry thief, and learn he broke into my mom's house. I'm stuck dealing with a sometimes rude, sometimes nice gun-toting cop. Oh, let's not forget that I'm having crazy dreams where my mother talks about lesbians. Does it sound like I'm okay?"

The moment her last words came out of her mouth, she realized what she'd said. "Sorry." Emotion rose in her throat. "You didn't really need to hear all that."

"Lesbians?" he asked.

"Sorry," she muttered. Suddenly, she needed to get away—to be alone. To gather her wits, if she had any left. Frankly, nothing made sense. Not the dreams. Not her thinking about his penis. Not her having dated a criminal or having stolen evidence in her trash can at home. She fumbled with the door handle and nearly fell out of the SUV.

She marched toward her car. She got within a foot of her Honda, when she realized she'd left her purse and keys in his SUV. Suddenly, the sound of glass being crunched beneath her pink pumps filled her ear. She looked up at her car, which was now minus a window. Tears filled her eyes. Somebody had broken into her car. How much more could she take? She pressed her hand to her lips, to hold in her sobs, but she couldn't stop the tears.

"Hey." His hand brushed over her back, then he pulled her against him, a wall of warm muscle. He felt solid, an anchor, a lifeboat. Someone to hold her. And he smelled so good.

A bitch would have been able to pull away. A bitch wouldn't have needed to be held. She wasn't a bitch. She was a Charmin-faced girl. She buried her baby face on his shoulder, a very nice shoulder, and continued to cry.

Chapter Twelve

She didn't know exactly when it happened. Perhaps, after he convinced her that she didn't have to feel bad about her mental breakdown. Maybe after he called a glass company to come fix her broken window. Or it could have been when he stopped off at the gas station and bought her a diet soda and a bottle of aspirin. But at some point in the last thirty minutes, she'd decided that Detective Lowell might not be a dickhead. Not even a little dickhead.

He pulled into her apartment's parking lot and sent her a comforting smile. "You ready?"

She remembered how it felt when he'd held her. The way his hands pressed against her lower back. The way her head had rested on that soft, yet firm, spot between his shoulder and chest. But remembering was causing all kinds of havoc—emotionally, physically. Oh yeah. She needed to forget.

She grabbed her purse and got out of his SUV. He got out, too, and fell in step beside her without talking. When she fitted the key into the door, he touched her arm and she started remembering again.

"I just thought of something," he said. "When you saw Stan, did he appear to be hurt?"

Cali recalled the blood on her door. "Not really," she said. "At least, I didn't see any signs of it."

He nodded, and Cali turned the key. The familiar smell of her home greeted her, but nothing about the disaster before her looked familiar. She'd seen it once, but in her weakened emotional state, it hit her harder. Her brass lamp, the one Stan had shot through the door, lay on the floor, only now her ceramic lamp lay in pieces beside his brother lamp, the last victim of Stan's malice. Did the man not like her lamps?

Oh, hell, it wasn't just her lamps. Sofa cushions were scattered about, and books littered the room. Even the snow globe her mother had given her last Christmas lay upside down beside the coffee table. Thank God, he's spared her this. She moved inside and picked it up, holding it tight.

"I'll help you pick up, but let's find the bracelet first." He stepped over the mess and ducked into the kitchen.

Giving the snow globe one final squeeze, as if it somehow would offer her some moral support, she set it down and followed him. He stood by the stove, his gaze shifting around.

"Garbage is here." She opened the cabinet where she kept the trash can. As she reached to start sorting, he caught her hand.

"I'll do it. Do you have another trash bag?"

She supplied the bag and held it open as he sifted through her garbage. Not a dickhead, she thought again. He dropped items into the second bag—a black banana peel, accompanied by fruit flies, coffee grounds and junk mail. He was almost at the bottom. Her heart thudded at the thought that Stan had found the bracelet in the garbage.

Lowell reached into the very bottom and when he looked up, he smiled. "Pay dirt."

He stood, bracelet in hand, and grimaced as if stretching down into the bin had hurt, then he pulled the photo from his pocket. "Looks like I have to confiscate this. Sorry."

"I didn't want it," she said. The tender way he looked at her made her want to cry. And something told her if she cried again, she'd end up in his arms again. As tempting as that sounded, she couldn't go there. She wouldn't go there. Stiffening, she walked out of the kitchen and headed down the hall, stopping at her bedroom door. The topsy-turvy sight brought a moan to her lips.

Lowell stopped behind her. He touched her shoulder. Obviously, after she'd cried all over him, he thought touching her was acceptable.

"When he met you at the lawyer's office, did he say anything about the bracelet?"

She turned around, thinking. "Yeah, he did, but then I ran."

"I think that's what he was looking for. That would also explain why he went to your mother's house, and why he broke into your car."

He glanced around and his eyes widened. "Shit!" He darted past her and dropped on his hands and knees beside the bed.

"What?" she asked.

"He took it." He stood up, a frown creasing his forehead.

"Took what?"

"There was a baseball bat under here before." He met her eyes.

"Yeah, it was his."

"I figured that." He rubbed his shoulder again. "A bat was used in the robbery."

"Oh." Shame for allowing herself to get mixed up with a criminal bit down like a big, hungry dog on her conscience. "I swear, I never knew. We met when my mama was going through chemo. I guess I wasn't thinking straight."

He nodded.

Unsure what else she could say, she looked around at the mess and picked up a lamp.

"You start picking up in here," he said. "I'll start in there." He stepped for the door.

"You don't have to help."

"I don't mind." He cast a quick smile over his shoulder.

She watched him walk away, and remembered Tanya asking if he had a nice ass. She checked. It was nice. Really nice.

Great. Now she was thinking about his ass and his penis. Not to mention his shoulders.

Her stomach did that wiggly thing it did when she was attracted to someone. Not good.

Taking a deep breath, she started putting her things back in their proper places. And mentally she did the same thing, which meant the whole attraction thing had to go right out the window. It was too soon. She was too vulnerable. Look where her last relationship led her.

She inhaled a breath meant to induce calm, but the air smelled like cigarette smoke. She recalled the dreams. The madness of it all had her heart racing. The busy work gave her a few minutes to convince herself that she wasn't crazy. She was just grieving.

Ten minutes later, she walked into her living room. Lowell had a broom in one hand and his foot was wedged against the dustpan. He stopped to rub his shoulder.

She knelt to hold the dustpan. He swept up the shards of broken ceramic lamp into the dust pan, and she emptied it in the trash.

"We make a good team." He smiled and she noticed the bruise under his lip again. "Did you finish in the bedroom?"

"Good enough." She studied him. "What happened?" She touched her lip.

"What?"

"Your lip. And you keep rubbing your shoulder. And don't tell me football."

He grinned. "It's nothing." His gaze lingered on her face. "Do you need anything from here before we go?"

"My life back." Then she smiled to make light of it. "Do you really think it's dangerous for me to come home?"

"Don't even think about it." The authoritative tone returned with an even rougher edge. "You're not coming back here until we get this creep behind bars. I'm serious."

She let out a deep breath. "But it could take days to—"

"It could take weeks." He leaned in. "I don't care. It would be stupid to come back here. He's wanted for murder, for Christ's sake."

Her mind wouldn't wrap around the word. "Murder? He . . . killed somebody?" She'd slept with a murderer? The non-bitch, the Charmin-faced girl, had slept with a murderer? Her stomach cramped.

"The jewelry store your bracelet came from, they beat up the old man who owned it. He died of brain injuries later."

She dropped on the sofa, remembering Mrs. Gomez's praise of Stan. "But Stan was so nice to old people. I can't believe—"

"Then you'd better try harder to believe it." His tone sounded sharp, angry.

She looked up. The pinch between his eyebrows had returned.

Her mind kept trying to make sense of everything. "I just can't believe he would do something like that. He helped my neighbor bring her groceries in. He was nice to the old man who runs the donut store. And—"

"If you're about to tell me how much you still love him, you can stop now." Gone was the detective who'd smiled and held her so nicely. In his place was Mr. Little Dickhead.

She raised her chin. "I don't love him."

"But you still think he's a good guy?"

She stood. "Not good. I just don't see him hurting an old person."

He stared at her with so much frustration, she didn't understand. "Are you ready?"

"Ready for what?"

"To go to your mother's house," he said curtly.

"Yeah," she lied. The last thing she wanted to do was go to the Cancer House. The place where she'd watched cancer slowly take her mom's life.

~

They hadn't exchanged a word when he parked at a fast-food restaurant. "I'm hungry."

And obviously hunger put him in a foul mood, Cali thought.

Once inside, he ordered a hamburger and fries. She ordered a salad. Pulling a ten from her wallet, she laid it on the counter. He glared at the money.

"I got it." He pulled out his wallet and tossed down a twenty.

"Let me pay," she said. "You're already helping me enough."

"No!" He stuffed the ten back in her purse.

Cali grabbed her salad and soda and planted herself at a table. He sat down in front of her. Refusing to look at him, she forked a piece of wilted lettuce, her appetite nonexistent.

"I just don't get it." With the corner of her vision, she saw him rip the paper from his burger. He leaned toward her to get her attention. "What makes women do this?"

"Do what?" She looked back down, cut her tomato and forked part of the tomato wedge.

"Allow a man to treat you like crap, and then stand there and defend him."

She set her fork down. "I'm not defending him. I just—"

"Don't want to believe he's guilty." He scowled at her.

She felt her stomach tighten. "I didn't say that." When she met his eyes, bright with frustration, she stopped herself from trying to explain. "Look, I'd really appreciate it if you just ate and took me back to my car."

"Fine." He stood up and walked out of the restaurant.

She stared at his untouched food and, just because it felt good, she gave her salad another jab. Taking a deep breath, she got up, tossed her salad in the trash, then went to the counter and asked for a to-go bag. She rewrapped his burger, packed his fries, and picked up a couple of ketchup packets on the way out.

It wasn't until she saw him sitting in his SUV that she realized he could have left her there. But no, he waited and even had the passenger door open. She climbed in and dropped the bag between them. "You forgot this along with your manners."

He frowned. "Do you always have to be so nice?"

She considered his words. "You're right." She snatched up the food, got out of the car, hot-footed it to a garbage can in front of the restaurant and dumped the bag in with the rest of the garbage.

Head held high, she climbed back into his SUV, and slammed the door. "I'm working on being a bitch. You know, you really do earn the nickname Tanya and I gave you."

"What is it?" he asked. "Asshole? Jerk?"

From his voice she could tell he'd lost his attitude. Not that it mattered. He still deserved hers. "No." She met his gaze head on. "Little Dickhead."

Shock widened his eyes. "Little?" He fell back against the seat and laughed. The deep rumble sounded rusty, as if he hadn't laughed in a long time. When his laughter stopped, he rested his head back and stared up at his ceiling. He let out a deep breath. "Damn, I'm tired." He closed his eyes for a second, then he tilted his head to the side to stare at her. "I got out of line again."

"You think?" she asked.

"It comes with the job. Sort of. We see so much—"

"So only dickheads need to apply to be a cop?"

He sighed. "I deserve that." He closed his eyes a second as if to collect his thoughts. "In my line of work, I've seen way too many men do terrible things to women. And nothing grates on my nerves more than when I see those women turn around and go right back to the men."

"And you think that's what I'm doing?"

"When you defend Stan, yeah, that's what I think."

She sat up a little straighter. "I'm not defending him. I'm voicing my opinion. I broke up with him."

"I hope you meant it." His gaze met hers and held and when the silence grew awkward he said, "Now, can I please take you to your mom's house and see if anything was taken so I can finish making out that paperwork?"

She nodded, even though the idea of walking into her mom's house right now was almost more than she could bear.

Five minutes later, he pulled into the driveway. She sat staring at the white-brick home, mentally seeing the word "cancer" written in red across the front.

"You okay?" he asked.

"Yeah," she lied. She wasn't okay. Nothing was okay.

~

Brit watched her as she walked up the sidewalk. Each step looked measured, forced. He remembered the hospital bed, the medical supplies, the smell. How hard was it to watch a person die slowly, piece-by-piece, day-by-day? And when that person was your mother . . .

Not that he had any overwhelming love for his mother, or his old man who'd died instantly of a heart attack, but he couldn't imagine losing his sister, Susan. Then he thought about losing Keith. That pain had been quick, deep, and while it still hurt like he'd been gut-shot, he hadn't had to watch his friend die slowly.

"We could do this later," he said, regretting being a dickhead.

She looked up, pain in her eyes. "No." Fitting the key inside the front doorknob, she opened it and walked inside.

The first thing Brit saw were the black footprints trailing across the beige carpet. His black footprints. Guilt made him want to remove his shoes now.

Moving like a robot, she picked up a lamp from the floor and set it on a table. She went to the back window, covered with a piece of wood that he'd found in the garage last night.

"I could call someone to fix it." He pulled out his phone. "And to clean the carpet. I think that might have been us that left—"

"No. I'll call someone later."

He looked at his cell phone. "Do you have a cell phone?"

"Yeah."

"I'm going to need that number." He turned on his phone. "What is it?"

"I don't know it. I just got a new one." She took off down the hall.

He snapped the phone shut. Did she not want to give him her number, or did she really not know it? He heard her opening the door to the master bedroom. He thought about the hospital bed, the oxygen tank, and the cold feeling of a terminal illness he'd gotten from the room last night.

Slipping the phone in his pocket, he went to join her. She sat on the edge of the hospital bed. He expected to see tears, to hear the sniffles that she'd let out this morning when he'd held her. Her eyes were dry, but he saw pain in her expression. He felt it. Grief. It dominated the room like a living, breathing animal. He stood there, sensing her pain seep into his skin and curl up into his chest. Odd how there was even any room in him to feel her pain when he had so much of his own.

It hit him then. They shared the same monster. This was probably why he felt so connected to her, why he couldn't stop himself from caring or from being so damn pissed off by the thought of her allowing some man to abuse her.

And because she's so damn sexy. But deep down he'd known it was more than the attraction he felt. Hell, he'd dealt with dozen of cases involving beautiful women before and managed to treat it like a job and not a personal agenda.

"Do you see anything that's missing?" he asked, wanting to get her out of here.

She looked around and then met his eyes. "My mom." She bit down on her lip, slipped off the bed, and followed the black footprints he'd left on her mom's carpet last night.

He stood in the room, listening to the soft thud of her footsteps moving away from him. The hospital smells seemed to evaporate, replaced by the smell of cigarettes. He looked around. Had Cali's mom smoked while using oxygen? Shaking his head, he went to find Cali. She waited on the sofa, eyes still dry, sitting with her hands clutched in her lap. One look at her and he knew she was lost in her private world of grief. Damn if he didn't know how she felt.

He had the urge to pull her up and into his arms. To hold her like he did earlier. She'd felt good against him, soft in all the right places. But it hadn't just been her being female or soft that made it feel good. It had felt . . . right somehow.

But it wasn't. As tempting as it was to give in, to make this more than just a case, he couldn't. He couldn't for a dozen or more reasons. And whether he wanted to admit it or not, he wasn't a hundred percent sure he believed Cali wasn't just a tad like his dear ol' mom. Too nice. Too willing to be some man's doormat.

"Ready?" he asked.

She shot up, walked out, locked the door after he exited and then climbed in his SUV without saying a word.

He didn't know if she was back to being mad at him, or just mad at the world. Either way he could understand. Grief did that to you.

He drove back to the school where he'd left her car but he needed to ask her more questions about Stan. He wasn't looking forward to it, but it was his job.

His stomach grumbled and felt as if it was gnawing on his backbone for nourishment. He pulled into a coffee shop. "I need to ask you some questions about Stan. And I'm starving."

"Haven't we already tried to do this once?" she asked.

"Yeah." He shrugged and felt the guilt sitting on his shoulders. "Just a few questions. And I'll stop being a dickhead. Scouts' honor."

She looked suspicious. "You never were a boy scout, were you?"

He grinned. "Touché. But you have my word."

She inhaled and then nodded. A wave of relief washed over him and he again found himself wanting to stop fighting the attraction, to see where it took them. But damn, where was his willpower? Probably off in some corner of his empty gut dying from hunger and lack of sleep. After some food and rest, surely he'd be back on top of his game.

He went to remove his keys from the ignition when his cell phone rang. Pulling it out of his pocket, he saw it was Quarles. He looked at her. "Sorry. I have to take this." He answered it. "What you need?"

"Hey," Quarles said. "Where are you?"

"Right outside the beltway. Why?"

"You need to come in." Bad news shadowed Quarles' tone.

The feeling rumbling in Brit's empty gut reminded him of how he'd felt when Adams had called him about Keith. He prayed he was wrong. "Why?" He gripped the phone harder.

Chapter Thirteen

"There's been another shooting," Quarles said. "Another officer. The same MO as Keith's."

Brit's hold on the phone clenched. His lungs held on to the oxygen of his last breath as he put out the one—word question. "Who?"

Quarles cleared his throat before speaking. "Mike Anderson. The kid who worked that domestic violence case with us. He's dead."

"No, it can't be him. He's in Galveston with his girlfriend." Brit got a vision of Mike standing at his office door, holding a bag of cat food, and beaming about his plan to have sex on the beach. Brit's mind refused to believe the kid with such a zest for life and a soft spot for strays could be gone. Gone like Keith. "He's with his girlfriend," Brit repeated.

"He never picked her up," Quarles said. "When he didn't show up, she assumed he was mad. But when he didn't call, she finally went over to his place. She found him in his garage. Two shots to the head."

The truth kicked Brit in the gut. He didn't want to believe. But refusing to believe something wasn't going to change a God damn thing. He'd proved that the hour he stared at Keith's body in the morgue, swearing it wasn't him.

"Christ." Brit slammed his hand on the dashboard. "I'll be right there." He dropped the phone in his lap.

Cali stared at him with questions in her eyes. "Something wrong?" Her voice radiated concern, tenderness.

"Yeah."

"With my case?"

"No." He didn't say anything else. He couldn't. He put the car in drive and started back to the school.

~

Cali watched Lowell's SUV pull away. His silence as they'd driven back to the school had left her with the impression that something terrible had happened. When he'd turned to say goodbye, her breath had hung in her throat. The pain darkening his eyes was too familiar—like looking into a mirror. Currents of empathy flowed through her heart. It was as if whatever was affecting him was the same thing that was hurting her right now. Grief. Of course, in her emotional state, her ability to read emotions could be impaired.

She recalled how it had felt to be in her mom's home. To be able to smell the perfume she once wore, to sit on the bed where she'd taken her last breath. "Miss you, Mama," she whispered.

Turning back to her car, she remembered that only a few hours ago, the window had been smashed. Whoever Lowell had called had come out and done a fine job. The next time she saw him, she should remember to tell him thank you. Then it hit her. There might not be a next time.

He'd come for the bracelet, and he had it. He'd said he had more questions, but maybe not.

When that thought sent a vibration of disappointment rattling around her chest, she chased it away. Any emotional involvement right now would be a big mistake. Wrong time. And, oh yeah, wrong man. In spite of being attracted to him, in spite of him having moments when he came across like a hero, he was still a bit of a dickhead. A little one. A smile somehow broke through her emotions as she recalled how he'd laughed when she told him his nickname.

She got into her car. For just a second, she had a crazy feeling of someone watching her. Twisting around, she checked the parking lot. Nobody. Taking a deep breath of resolve, she spotted his jacket in the backseat. She'd forgotten to give it to him. Reaching back, she snagged it. She brought the worn leather to her nose. It smelled like rain, and like him. She recalled with clarity how good it had felt to be in his arms.

Realizing what she was doing, pining over something that she couldn't, or at least shouldn't want, she dropped the jacket in the front seat and started the engine.

Now, if she only knew where she was going.

~

An hour later, Brit joined the crowd in the meeting room at the precinct. Sergeant Adams, his thick brows puckered into one line of worry, paced in front of the room. He and Anderson's lieutenant had called a meeting. "Here's what we know. It's the same MO as Keith Bolts. Possibly the same gun . . . we're checking ballistics."

Adams' gaze cut to Brit. "We've got a good lead. Sounds like we might be after a gang. Last year there was talk about a pop-a-cop initiation. This could be that." The man curled his hands into fists. "The informant said a young gang member, we think belonging to the Blue Bloods, was bragging about one of his buddies taking out a cop. We've got to find these guys." He stopped pacing. "I know we'd like to push everything else aside. But we can't shelve our other cases. I got upstairs to agree to pay overtime. So let's do this. Go find these punks. But don't forget your other cases."

A few more words were tossed out by Anderson's lieutenant. Brit could hardly focus. Finally everyone stood up. No one spoke. What could they say? Another one of their own had gone down. Grief and a need for vengeance hung like fog in the air; fear made the fog denser. Who would be next? No one in the room would admit to being scared, but Brit saw it in their eyes. He remembered Keith saying that only the stupid weren't afraid.

Sometimes Brit admitted to being stupid—especially since Keith's death.

Brit spotted Logan, Anderson's partner. With a hitch in his throat, he put a hand on the man's back. "We'll get them." He didn't wait for Logan to reply. Brit knew how Logan felt. Less than a month ago, he'd been Logan—a cop without a partner. A cop with the need to kill whoever killed his friend. Hell, he still was that man. Nothing had changed.

Suddenly needing his own space, Brit lit out of the room. He stormed into his office, and the first thing he saw was the cat food. Grabbing two cans, and his thin coat, he took off to the parking lot.

Outside, he pulled the metal tabs and set them down on concrete. Thoughts of Keith and then of young Mike Anderson, both animal lovers, ripped at Brit's heart. Closing his eyes, he leaned against the building. Emotion gripped his chest so tight, he longed to scream.

Instead, he let himself slide down the brick wall, and sit on the cold pavement. Elbows perched on his knees, he buried his face in his hands. He dragged one deep breath after another into his lungs, hoping to loosen the godawful pain.

The touch against his ankle brought his head up. Mama cat, with her missing ear and gold eyes, stared at him with caution. Brit swallowed the lump down his throat. "You're stuck with me. Seems only the good die young."

She let out a meow and tapped his leg again with the side of her face. Brit wanted to reach down to stroke her, but instinct told him she'd run. "I gotta get you off the streets."

Footsteps sounded on the concrete. The cat jerked back and darted off.

Quarles walked over, eyeing the cat food cans. "You okay?"

"Yeah." Brit got up and masked his emotion behind a frown.

"Good," Quarles said. "Because I just got a call from a buddy of mine, a homicide cop with Clear Lake. I think we've got a break on the jewelry store case."

~

Nothing smelled quite like days-old death. The smell permeated the hotel room. Brit looked around, but hung close to the door. He'd seen worse, but not by much. A huge red stain had dried into the motel's worn beige carpet. Ditto for the specks of gray brain matter mixed with blood spattered on the pale yellow wall behind the bed. Two bodies. The one missing the top of his head from a gunshot got the credit for the wall decor. The other with his throat slit had added the coloring to the carpet. And as hard as it was to look at it, it was even harder to smell.

On the bed were plastic bags with the jewelry store logo and a bank deposit bag. Against the wall leaned a guitar.

"Our guys." Quarles' eyes were only a shade darker than his green-tinted skin. When Brit had pulled up a few minutes after his partner, he'd found Quarles standing beside his car, hurling his lunch on the pavement. Obviously, his new partner had a weak stomach. Not that he could blame him. Thankfully, Brit didn't have any lunch to lose, or he'd be out there now doing the same.

"What do you have?" Brit asked, after one of the Clear Lake officers walked up and Quarles introduced them.

"Looks like the murders took place late Tuesday. We spoke to the hotel manager, and he said some guy came in and out of here this afternoon. Big guy, black hair."

Stan Humphrey. Then Brit remembered the blood. He looked at Quarles. "Did CSI get some of the blood off McKay's door?"

"Yeah." Quarles wiped a hand over his mouth and seemed to think. "You think the blood at her house is from this crime scene?"

Another detective walked up. "I hear you might have something on these guys," he said as he pinched his nose.

"Yeah." Quarles turned back to the open door as if to get a breath of clean air.

Brit tried not to breathe through his nose, but air filtered through. Oddly, the first scent he got was cigarette smoke.

The other detective continued, "We found a cell phone in the bathroom. The last call made was about one o'clock today. Possibly from that Humphrey guy. I don't think either of these guys made that call. What kind of sick fucker stays here in this?" The officer shook his head.

The same kind of sick fucker who would beat up women, Brit thought.

"Maybe he came back here looking for something," Quarles said.

Brit tried not to look at the dead man's face. God knew he already had enough images to keep him awake at night. "Where was the last call to?"

"Here's a weird one. It was to Wells High School."

A cold chill drummed through Brit's body. Cali. He stared at his watch. Four. He'd dropped her off at the school around two. What if that bastard had been waiting for her?

He looked at Quarles. "I just remembered somewhere I need to be." As he lit out to his car, he saw an image of Cali McKay's sweet face and prayed he wasn't too late.

He never stopped for a light. He wasn't sure he ever hit the brakes the whole drive. He kept remembering how she felt up against him. Warm. Soft. Alive. Her car wasn't in the school parking lot. Only a couple of cars were left in the lot. "Damn."

He parked in front of the school and ran to the front. He jerked on the door, but it didn't budge. Locked. He banged on the glass then caught movement in one of the open office doors. He pounded the door harder, louder. A dark-skinned woman, wearing a business suit, finally peeked outside the main office.

He snatched his badge from his pocket and pressed it against the glass. Surprise widened her almond-shaped eyes, then she hurried to the door.

"I'm trying to find Cali McKay," he said. "I need her cell number."

"I'm Mrs. Jasmine, the principal. Is she in trouble? She's such a sweet girl. I can't—"

"No. She's not in trouble. I just have to find her."

He followed the woman back into the office, and she told him again how sweet Cali was, how Cali loved her job, how good she was with her students. At last the woman pulled open a file cabinet and thumbed through the folders as if she had all the time in the world. "A . . . B . . ." He wanted to nudge her aside and find it himself.

"Here." She pulled out the file. "Her home number is—"

"I have her home number, I need her cell number."

Her brightly painted fingernails trailed down the paper. Then she glanced up. "Her cell number is scratched out. I remember now. I tried to call her last week about her mom and it was disconnected."

"Fuck!"

The woman flinched.

Brit held up his hand. "I'm sorry." Then he remembered the other teacher from this morning. She might know where Cali was. "What about the other teacher, the young brunette who teaches in the classroom beside her?"

"You mean Tanya Craft? Bright, colorful dresser?"

"I guess." He didn't remember what she'd been wearing. Didn't care. "Give me her contact information and address."

The principal turned back to the file cabinet and opened the drawer. "A . . . B . . ."

~

Tanya Craft wasn't answering her phone. He tossed the phone in the passenger seat and squealed off the school grounds. Ten minutes later, he pulled into the parking lot of her apartment building, praying he'd see Cali's silver Honda. Nothing. He parked and took off in search of apartment 105. Music blared behind the door. He knocked. Hard.

"Ease up!" a voice said as the door jerked open. Tanya's brown eyes went wide. "Wow, it's the cop with an attitude. What do you want?"

He frowned. "Is Cali McKay here?"

She tilted her head back. From the twinkle in her eyes, he knew she was going to give him some lip. Before she could speak, he leaned forward. "I need to know where she is. Now!"

She drew back. "Cali's right. You really are a dickhead."

"She could be in danger," he said, trying to take it down a notch, but he remembered the scene at the hotel that Humphrey left behind, and knowing he might have Cali chewed on his last nerve.

The chick's eyes rounded. "She's . . . staying at a hotel off Highway 6. I tried to get her to stay here, but she wouldn't."

"What hotel?"

~

Brit saw Cali's silver Honda in the hotel parking lot. Pulling in beside it, he cut off the engine and dropped his head on the steering wheel. A few deep breaths later, he headed to the front office, his badge drawn.

"What room is Cali McKay in?" He showed his badge.

The clerk's round face tensed. "Is she a hooker? I swear, I didn't know."

"No." Brit shoved his badge back in his pocket. Who could look at Cali and think hooker? "Just give me a room number."

The man turned to the computer and pecked on a few keys. "Room ten. Five rooms down on the left."

After rushing to the door, Brit hesitated. What was he going to say to her? "I thought I'd lost you." Hell, she wasn't his to lose. Then he remembered he had a reason to be here, besides just needing to see her alive. He needed information on Stan. And to inform her about their suspicions concerning her ex. She needed to know how dangerous the freak really was.

He knocked. No answer.

He knocked again.

"Cali? It's me, Brit." It suddenly occurred to him that she hadn't ever called him by his first name. Had he even given her his first name? Jeez. He'd made love to the woman in his mind, and he hadn't even given her his first name.

"Cali, it's me, Detective Lowell. Brit Lowell." He knocked again. "Cali?" All the panic he'd felt earlier and just released suddenly U-turned with a rushing force. "If you're in there, open the door. Please."

Nothing. Visions of her lying on the bed with her throat slashed filled his head. Then he considered that maybe she just didn't want to see him.

"I'm sorry again for being a dickhead. Open the door, please."

Still nothing. He stormed back to the front office. "Give me the key to her room."

The desk clerk shot him a cocky look.

Fear of what he'd find behind that locked door churned in Brit's stomach. He reached across the counter, grabbed the man's shirt, and jerked the clerk so close that Brit knew the man had onions with his lunch. "Give me the damn key."

Seconds later, key in hand, he ran back to her room. "Cali?" He pushed open the door, his gut knotted, ready to be sick.

Chapter Fourteen

An hour later, Cali sat across from Betty, her mom's hospice nurse. She knew the conversation would be hard—talking about her mom always was—but she also knew she had to do it. Just as she had to do other unpleasant things, like find a new place to stay. Luckily, she'd found a hotel only a block from the hospice center.

"I always try to keep my distance, emotionally," Betty said. "You have to in this line of work." Betty's hazel eyes clouded with tears. "I couldn't do it with your mom. She was so easy to talk to. So genuine."

Cali's chest tightened. "She appreciated you so much."

Betty smiled. "Your mother had a way with people. I told her things about myself that I haven't told my therapist."

Betty, my hospice nurse, she's a lesbian. Her mom's words still rang in Cali's mind.

"She loved people. Loved to know everyone's business." Cali grinned even as a wave of grief swelled inside her. She looked out of the office window. The afternoon traffic whizzed by. "I went to her place today. But I couldn't stay."

Betty rested her hand on Cali's. "Have you talked to someone? A counselor, a therapist?"

"No. I had to work." And I'm running from a murderer.

"Our psychologist is here now and she just had a cancellation. I'm sure she'd see you. You really look as if you could benefit from talking to her." Betty's gaze pleaded. "Let me call her."

Was she ready to know if she was crazy? That was the $50,000 question. Cali took a deep breath and nodded. "Okay."

~

"Thanks for seeing me." Cali sat down on the sofa a few minutes later.

Doctor Roberts, a mid-fiftyish, petite woman, smiled and settled in the chair across from her. "No problem."

Soft classical music played in the background. Cali looked around the room nervously, noticing the pale, soothing colors, and then confessed, "I've never talked to a therapist."

"You've never lost your mother before, either."

Cali looked into the woman's kind green eyes, eyes that whispered, "trust me." "It's hard," Cali admitted.

"How long has it been?"

"A week." Cali gazed out the window. The sky had darkened to a deep purple, but streaks of pink painted the horizon. "Every time someone offers me their condolences I almost cry."

The doc shifted in her seat. "Have you let yourself cry?"

Cali thought about Lowell holding her. "Oh, yes."

"I mean really cry."

"You should have seen Lowell's shirt this morning." She tried to laugh, but it sounded more like a sob.

"Lowell? Is he your boyfriend?"

She suddenly realized she didn't know if Lowell was his first name or last. But someone had called him Lowell. She'd cried all over a man and didn't even know his name. Emotion swelled in her throat. "No. It's not like that."

"Not like what?" Dr. Roberts handed her a box of tissues.

Cali set them beside her and drew one out, wrapping it around her fingers like a rope. "I'm not attracted to him." The lie hung like a dense cloud around her. "Okay, I am attracted to him. Every time he smiles, my stomach does that flip thing." She pressed her hand to her middle. "I've got a lump of grief in my chest and my stomach's flipping. I shouldn't be feeling this when I should be thinking about Mom."

Dr. Roberts tilted her head to one side. "It's okay to be attracted to someone even when—"

"Okay, so maybe it isn't wrong." She snatched another tissue when her vision blurred with tears. "But he's a dickhead!"

Dr. Roberts smiled and jotted something down on her pad. Cali wondered if the doc wrote down that she'd said "dickhead."

"I'm sorry. I'm practicing being a bitch. Mom said . . ."

"Your mom said what?"

The question set Cali's confession loose. "I've been dreaming about my mom. She tells me things."

"What kind of things?" Dr. Roberts asked in a calm voice.

"Like to leave the apartment because Stan's trying to break in."

Confusion puckered the doc's brow. "Someone broke into your apartment?"

"My boyfriend. My ex-boyfriend." Cali tightened her hand around the wad of tissue, then added another to her collection.

"And his name is Lowell?" the doctor asked.

"No. Lowell's trying to catch Stan. He's a detective."

"Did Stan do something wrong?" she asked, leaning forward.

Cali nodded. Soft music echoed in the background. Everything she'd been scared to think about suddenly bubbled to the surface.

"He robbed a place and killed someone." Cali twisted the tissues together and more words spilled from her lips. "Mom told me to wear the pink dress because I was going to help Lowell. And he showed up and asked for help."

Dr. Roberts tilted her head to the side as if to contemplate. "Who did your boyfriend kill? Or was that just a dream?"

"No. Not a dream." Cali snatched another tissue, and her tears flowed. "He robbed a store, and gave me a bracelet. Now he wants it back."

"And he tried to break into your apartment to find the bracelet?"

Cali nodded. "And he tried to shoot me."

Shock widened Dr. Robert's eyes. "My God, are you okay?"

Cali nodded and her tears rolled down her face. "But my lamp didn't survive. And then he took out the other one." She tried to smile, but couldn't.

Dr. Roberts held up her hand. "Let me see if I understand. Your boyfriend broke into your apartment and tried to kill you."

"He didn't get in. He shot through the door. But yeah, he broke in later." Cali's voice shook. "I wasn't there. But he ransacked my apartment. The detective helped me clean it up." A few more tears rolled down her cheeks. "After I cried all over him." The lump of emotion kept growing and she kept talking. She dropped the tissues and grabbed a clean one. "Then the dickhead broke into my mother's place."

"Wait." She held up a hand. "The detective broke into your mother's place?"

Emotion caught in her throat; she pushed it away and kept talking. "No, Stan, the bigger dickhead. And he broke my car's window after he found me at the lawyer's office." Cali clutched her hands. "He kissed me. I hated it. I don't think I ever liked kissing him. And I keep having these dreams about my mother. Oh, and the detective wouldn't give me my keys." Cali gave up trying to make sense; she just let it all out. "And Sara's mom has cancer." Cali's tears flowed.

"Who's Sara?" The doc's voice sounded a little less calm.

"My student. She asked what happened to my mom." Her voice shuttered. "I told her. But I didn't know her mom had cancer. And now she thinks her mom is going to die, too. I feel terrible."

Dr. Roberts stood behind her desk and moved to sit beside Cali. "Good Lord, you've had a bad week, haven't you?"

"You think?" Cali wiped some more tears from her face.

For the next fifteen minutes, Cali calmed down enough to explain things better. And she told the therapist everything. About all the dreams and how they made her feel nuts. When she finished, Cali looked into the counselor's eyes and asked the all-important question. "Am I crazy?"

A smile washed over the doctor's face. "Your life's been crazy, but I don't think you're crazy."

"But what about the dreams?"

"What do you think about the dreams?" Dr. Roberts asked.

"I asked you first," Cali said, and looked at the empty Kleenex box. In her lap, she had a baseball-size wad of tissues. Cali spotted a small trash can beside the sofa. Leaning over, she tossed them away, keeping one for emergency use. "Are you sure I'm not crazy?"

The woman folded her hands neatly in her lap. "At hospice, I deal a lot with people who have lost loved ones. You're not the first person I've counseled who said she's felt the presence of someone who passed away."

"But I don't feel it," Cali insisted. "They're dreams. Sort of."

"I know, and that's my point. Feeling close to our loved ones who have died generally brings us comfort. I've never seen a ghost, but I can't say they don't exist. However, you're not even seeing ghosts. Most of the time when we dream, the people appearing in our dreams are usually a projected image of ourselves."

The doctor got up and poured them each a glass of water. "If you dream of a child, you're really dreaming of your inner child. If you dream of your mother—"

"So my mom is really my maternal psyche trying to help me." Cali accepted the water and leaned back.

The doctor smiled. "You catch on quick."

"But what about the things she tells me?"

The woman sat down beside her again. "Everything you've told me she said could be easily explained. You heard Stan opening the door. During the funeral, you probably noticed Stan flirting, but were too upset to really think about it. Even with Lowell showing up. You're an intuitive person. He's a cop trying to find your ex-boyfriend. It makes sense he would need your help."

Cali let out a deep breath. "So I'm not losing my mind. I'm okay?"

"Besides the fact that you're grieving, have a murderer after you, and are having to deal with a detective who could use a few manners." She grinned. "Yes, I'd say you're okay." She paused. "Do you want to talk about why you got involved with someone like Stan?"

Cali bit down on her lip. "I know that one. I didn't want to be alone. And he was there." She recalled what Lowell had said about her being the kind of woman who allowed men to abuse them.

"What about past relationships?"

"What about them?" Cali asked, now afraid Lowell might be on to something.

"Have there been many?"

"Some." Cali set her water down. "But not for a long time. The last few years I've spent most of my time with Mom."

"Were they good relationships?"

"If they were good, wouldn't they have lasted?" She thought about Marty, the man she thought she'd marry—the only one she'd really loved.

"Not all relationships can last. But there's still a difference between good and bad."

Cali considered it. "Some of them were okay, but most of the guys ended up being jerks." And one chose a career over me. Or did I choose my mother over him? Cali stiffened. She had enough to cry over, she didn't need to dredge up Marty memories.

"What was your father like?"

The question hung in the air. "I don't know. He left when I was young. Mom said . . . he wasn't a keeper."

Dr. Roberts raised an eyebrow. "You don't remember him?"

"Vaguely." Cali started shredding the tissue and tried to listen to the music. It was a Christmas tune now. A time for family gatherings. Something she no longer had.

"Was he a dickhead, too?" the doctor asked with a touch of humor.

Cali raised her gaze. "The detective?"

"No. Your dad." She paused. "It's very common for girls who witnessed their mother being mistreated to fall for men who mistreat them. Did your father mistreat your mother?"

Cali looked at her hands. Was Lowell right? "He yelled a lot and would throw things. He left us."

"Your mother told you this?" Dr. Roberts asked.

Cali inhaled a shaky breath. "I guess I remember more than I want to."

The doctor's voice softened. "Sounds as if this is a new issue you need to explore."

"Don't I have enough already?"

"If only we could schedule our problems." The counselor gently smiled.

Cali tried to grasp it all. "So you're saying I choose bad men. That if I'm attracted to a guy, it's because he's a jerk like my daddy was."

"Well, it's not as if you can't be attracted to a good man. I'm saying the tendency would—"

"So I'm more apt to fall for dickheads." She thought about the detective. Oh, yeah, the proof was in. She had a serious thing for dickheads.

The doc laughed, then got serious again. "I think you should be careful about who you allow in your life. If you know your weaknesses, then you'll be wiser for it."

Cali looked up at the window. "It's late."

Dr. Roberts looked at her watch. "Goodness. It's almost six-thirty."

"I'm sorry," Cali said. "You should be at home. Not listening to some crazy talk."

"It's not crazy talk. And if you would like to see me again, all you have to do is call." Her gaze softened and she patted Cali's hand. "You should listen to the detective and not go home for a while. He sounds a little crusty but he probably knows what he's talking about."

Cali nodded. "I got a hotel room just down the street." She stood up. "Thank you." Cali looked at the trash can, overflowing with mascara-smeared tissues. "I'll replace the tissues."

"You are too sweet."

Cali frowned. "I really am working on being a bitch."

The doctor chuckled.

After saying her goodbyes, Cali walked out of the office into the dark night. The November cold seeped through her cardigan sweater. She remembered that she'd left her heavier sweater at the police station. Remembering the police station made her remember Lowell and the warm jacket that he'd placed on her shoulders. Her stomach did another cute-guy flip as she remembered how it had felt leaning against him. Remembering Lowell made her think of Stan. Could he really have taken part in killing an elderly man?

She recalled him snatching her by the hair in the lawyer's parking lot. She remembered how repulsive she'd found his kiss. Had her stomach ever flipped for Stan? She didn't think so. So I'm more apt to fall for dickheads. Did that mean Lowell was a bigger dickhead than Stan?

Streetlights and passing cars cast sprays of light across her dark path. She wasn't the only pedestrian braving the cold night, but fear still shimmied down her spine. She thought she heard someone behind her. She jerked around, expecting to see Stan. But no Stan. Just shadows. Only her mind playing tricks on her.

Biting into her lip, she walked faster. Her warm breath easing from her lips floated up like cigarette smoke. That made her think of her mom. Thinking of her mom made her feel just a little safer. Or it did until she heard footsteps behind her.

Probably nothing, she told her. Probably just someone else like her trying to get out of the night. Probably.

Chapter Fifteen

After forty-five minutes of combing the area, visiting all the restaurants where Cali McKay might have walked to, Brit returned to her hotel room and finally cratered and called for backup. If Stan Humphrey had Cali, it might take more than him to find her.

Brit wore the hotel's carpet down to another layer of thread as he paced. Pausing, he stared at the two officers who'd just arrived—Wolowitz and Edwards. "I called her friend again. She hasn't heard from her,"

"Does she have other friends?" Edwards, the force's newest female officer, asked.

Brit stared at the bed. "I don't know." Cali could have all sorts of men friends waiting to take Stan's place. His shoulders blade tensed at the thought.

"What time did they say she checked in?" Wolowitz asked.

"Around four. She called a friend and told her she was here. She didn't say anything about going anywhere." Brit rubbed his shoulder.

The vision of Cali lying somewhere bleeding kept flashing in his head. Then the vision flashed worse. He saw her lying somewhere with a cold stare of death on her sweet face; the same look he'd see on one of the bodies just a few hours ago in another hotel room. The same cold look that Brit saw on Keith's face in his dreams.

If anything happened, it was his fault. He'd dropped her off at the school. He hadn't stayed around to see if that creep had been waiting for her.

"Okay," Wolowitz said. "We'll comb the area again. Either she's on foot or a friend picked her up."

Or Humphrey had her.

The door pushed open. They all swung around. Cali, still dressed in the pink dress but now topped with a white sweater, stood in the doorway.

Her eyes widened. "What's going on?"

Brit's breath lodged in his throat. He gave her a quick onceover to make sure she wasn't bruised or bleeding. She wasn't. And that had him feeling like an idiot for overreacting.

"Where have you been?" The question came out harsher than he'd like.

Her red-rimmed eyes focused on him. "Why?"

The possibilities suddenly crossed his mind. "Have you been with Stan? If you're hiding something, you could go down with him."

She frowned, her shoulders tightened and every inch of her went on the defensive. "I haven't seen him."

"Then where were you?" Even as he asked it, he believed her about not being with Stan. Did she already have Stan's replacement lined up? It shouldn't bother him.

But it did.

~

Cali looked at the female officer as if needing an ally. "He's a total jerk and I don't like it. Does he have the right to treat me this way? Do I even have to answer him? I didn't call anyone this time. He's like a bad penny. He just keeps showing up."

Edwards hesitated. "I think Detective Lowell was worried."

"And I think he's being obnoxiously rude. Oh sure, he's been nice a few times, but then he goes back to being rude." She turned around and stared at him. "Are you bipolar or something?"

Brit frowned and raked a hand through his hair. "How did I go from being a dickhead to bipolar?"

"Please, if you're going to quote me, get it right." Her chin angled upward in a haughty tilt. "The name I dubbed you is, Mr. Little Dickhead. Now, if you'll excuse me, I need to run to the bathroom." She skirted into the bathroom in a wave of pink fury and slammed the door.

The loud whack served as his wake up call. She was right. He was back to being a dickhead. Again. Brit saw the smile on Edward's face. "You two can go."

Edwards shot a questioning glance at her partner.

Brit released a deep gulp of frustration. "It's fine. She's just upset with me, but she'll get over it."

"So you two are . . . ?"

"No," Brit said, but it felt like a lie.

After they left, he sank down on the edge of the bed and dropped his face into his palms. He couldn't chase the image of a bleeding Cali from his mind. He was so tired. So damn hungry. And confused. Why did he keep screwing up where she was concerned?

The answer came hurtling back at him. Because you're scared she's like dear ol' Mom. Because you like her. Like her a lot. And the last thing he wanted was to find himself being attracted to someone like his mom; because then, by damn, that might mean he was like his dear ol' dad.

The bathroom door opened. She'd washed her face, combed her hair, and if the fire in her eyes was any indication, she'd somehow gotten angrier in the process.

"Why are you even here?" she asked. "This is my hotel room and I haven't broken any laws."

He ran a hand over his face, and decided to run with the truth, or the partial truth. "Two bodies were found this afternoon. Murdered."

He saw her trying to compute the information. "Stan?" Her color faded ever so slightly.

Did she care about the asshole? He got another shot of ire to his gut, remembering how his mom had cared about the numerous jerks she'd allowed in her life. He pushed it back.

"Not Stan. It was two of his band members. Ted Pratt and John Soles."

Her eyes widened. "I met them once. What happened?"

The image of the two dead men flashed in Brit's mind. The truth didn't require details. "Their bodies were found in a cheap motel."

"You think Stan did it?"

Brit didn't hesitate. "Yeah. His phone was found at the scene. The men were killed sometime on Tuesday. We think the blood on your door could be theirs. We're having it tested now. Plus, Stan was there earlier today. "

Her color went paler. "He was there with the bodies today?"

Brit nodded. "We don't know if he was searching for something or what. But the last call he made was to your high school. This afternoon."

She dropped beside him on the bed as if her knees had given out.

"When I heard about the call to the school, I thought . . ." He took a deep breath. "I was worried Stan might have been waiting for you this afternoon. I thought I'd dropped you off right in his lap. And when your car was here and you weren't, I thought the worst."

She looked overwhelmed, as if only half listening. "How did you find me?"

Brit noticed her puffy eyes again and his gut clutched. "I went to the school. Your principal gave me Tanya's number." Brit remembered his last phone conversation with Cali's friend. He pulled his phone out and hit redial and handed it to her. "Your friend's worried. She made me promise I'd have you call her when I found you."

He listened as she assured Tanya that she was okay. She kept it short, no explanation of where she'd been. When she dropped his phone back in his palm, he felt her hand shaking.

"When you weren't here, I overreacted." He fought the urge to brush his finger over her cheek.

Her baby blues looked away, and he hoped she'd tell him where she'd been. He believed she hadn't been with Stan, didn't he? Yeah, he did. Just like he'd believed her about the bracelet being in the garbage. And so far she hadn't lied to him.

"Now what?" she asked.

You tell me where you were. "You like Chinese? There's a restaurant next door. You hungry?"

The slight grumble of her stomach filled the quiet hotel room. He smiled. "I think that's a yes."

She placed a hand over her abdomen. "I guess so. I keep forgetting to eat lately."

"Me, too." He realized this must be a symptom of grief. And then not wanting to think about grief, he added, "And then someone threw my lunch away."

She frowned. He smiled. "I'm joking." He paused. "I need to talk to the hotel clerk. Assure him everything is okay with the cops being here. Give me five minutes and then we'll do dinner."

She nodded and he started out. "Lock the door," he called and he waited until he heard the lock click. Just because Stan hadn't been here yet, didn't mean he hadn't followed her.

He walked to the front office. The same clerk from earlier sat behind the desk. Now, Brit wished he'd been less abrupt. His people skills could use work. Or they could these last few weeks. Losing Keith had turned him into an asshole.

"Hi," Brit said to the clerk. "Remember me?"

"Like I'd forget." The man sneered.

"Sorry about that. We had a situation. And still do. I want Cali McKay's name pulled off any and every record you keep here. Put the room under my name." He tossed down a credit card. "If someone calls, there is no Cali McKay here. But you get in touch with me ASAP." He put a twenty on the counter next to his card. "Understood?"

The clerk's blond brows pinched together. "There's not going to be any trouble, is there?"

"Not if I can help it."

~

As they walked next door to the restaurant, the tangy smell of Asian food reminded Cali of how the wind always carried with scent of the Oriental restaurant by her apartment. What she wouldn't give to just be able to go home. Maybe paint her toenails and veg.

There was a wait on a table, so Brit suggested they order take out and go back to the hotel. Thoughts of being in a hotel room and eating takeout food with him seemed too intimate. But she hadn't argued.

As soon as they'd eaten, she was sending him on his way. When they got back to the room, she sat on the bed, thinking he would be more comfortable in the chair. Instead, he followed her lead, and the mattress swayed. Cali's spine tightened. Hotel room. Bed. Man. Good-looking man. Yup, way too intimate.

How had she arrived here? Why had she agreed to this? Taking a deep breath, she pressed a hand to her quivering stomach.

He opened one of the white boxes, and looked up at her. "I'll share my chow mein, if you'll share your cashew chicken."

"Sure." She watched steam rise from the box and for some reason, she thought of her mom.

They split the dishes and ate mostly in silence.

"You going to eat that?" he asked.

"I'm done." She watched him pop her half-eaten egg roll into his mouth. First they shared a bed, then food, now he was eating her leftovers. What was next? Was he planning on staying the night?

He looked up; their gazes met. She turned away. Another silence swam around the thick awkwardness in the room. She heard him swallow, felt his stare.

Time to tell him to leave.

"Look," she said.

"My name's Brit," he interrupted her. "What's yours?"

"You know my name."

He shrugged. "I know. I'm thinking maybe we could try it over again. A fresh start."

She looked at him, unsure if she wanted to restart or end it with a clipped goodbye. But one glance into the hope shadowing his eyes and her heart softened. Caught by his gaze, she realized it wasn't just hope, but some other emotion, something familiar. Grief?

"Cali. My name's Cali McKay."

"It's a pleasure to meet you, Cali." He grinned in that devilish way men do. Or the way some men do. Actually, very few she'd met had such a kiss-me grin.

"Thanks for having dinner with me."

Her stomach did the flip thing again. He handed her a fortune cookie. She looked down at the plastic-wrapped cookie in her palm. "I'm scared to open it. I haven't had what anyone would call good luck lately."

"Maybe it's about to change." He opened his own cookie.

She watched him silently read it. "What does it say?"

He looked up, then down at the slip of white paper again. "It says . . . 'Stop being a dickhead, Dickhead.'"

She laughed. His blue-green gaze locked on her and she suddenly felt too warm, too crowded. Scooting over a few mattress inches, she opened her own cookie. The crackle of plastic echoed in the silent room.

"And?" Humor still danced in his eyes.

She tried to think of something funny to say, but it didn't come, so she just read it. "Listen to your dreams." The message vibrated through her head. Just what she needed, a little doubt. No, not doubt. She believed Dr. Roberts. Her dreams were just—

"Nothing about me being a dickhead, huh?"

"Nothing." She grinned and stacked the empty containers.

"I'm really not a dickhead. Not normally."

She remembered what the doctor said about her being attracted to the wrong type of men. The silence grew loud again.

"What did your fortune cookie really say?" she asked.

"What? You don't think they'd say dickhead in a fortune cookie?" He picked up the slip of paper and read. "Don't pass up the next opportunity." His gaze moved to her mouth.

Cali got up and carried the empty containers to the small waste basket. "Thanks for dinner," she said, remembering he'd refused to let her pay again. Wringing her hands, she tried to figure out how to suggest he leave.

"You're welcome." He studied her. "I need to ask you some questions about Stan," he said, as if he'd read her mind.

She continued to stand in the middle of the room. "You can ask, but when I filled out the report, I told the other officer all I know."

"I'd still like to hear it." He crossed his legs at his ankles, perfectly comfortable in her bed.

"Okay." She remembered the bracelet. "Did you find out if the bracelet was really from the jewelry store?"

"It's being checked by the distributor. But we're pretty sure it is." He rubbed his shoulder. "Where did you meet Stan?"

She didn't see how this was important to the case. "At the coffee shop near my apartment. I'd seen him there before. One day I was digging in my purse for some change to pay for my coffee, and he came up and paid it for me. He asked if he could join me. The shop was crowded and no more seats were available. It seemed rude to say no, so I said yes. He was there most days when I showed up, so we sat together. He seemed nice, or at least he did at first. I was . . . my mom was dying." She felt the grief tighten her chest. "I guess I needed someone to talk to. About a month later, he asked me out."

Brit sat there just listening.

She remembered that he thought she was the type of woman who got off being a victim. And while he might be partially right—she might run from conflict and try too hard to be nice—she refused to believe she'd really allow a man to abuse her.

"I needed to forget about my problems, so I went out with him. A few days later, I had car trouble and he drove me to my mom's, and even fixed my car for me. Before I knew it, he told me he was having problems with his roommate, and his new apartment was supposed to be ready in a week or so. Mom's health started going downhill really quickly, and I wasn't even at my apartment most of the time, so I told him he could just stay there. Then she died and I realized he'd been there for almost a month."

Brit continued to study her but didn't say anything, and nervous at what he might think of her, she kept talking. "He never came across like someone who would rob a store," she added. "He was even nice most of the time."

"Unlike me," he said and frowned.

Chapter Sixteen

"I'm not going to disagree with you, if that's what you think." She grinned.

He chuckled, then settled back against the wall. "Besides the band members, do you know any other of his friends or family?"

"No. He said he hadn't been in town long. Said his family was from Oklahoma. That his parents had passed. He said the band was about to get a record deal with some small recording studio in town."

"Did he ever mention any other girlfriends?"

"No. He was alone and I think I was scared of being completely alone." She moved and sat in the chair beside the bed and stared at the pictures on the wall. Contemporary art—splashed with reds and blues. She didn't want to think about Stan anymore.

"Where were you this afternoon?" This question came out in a different tone. Almost as if she didn't have to answer it if she didn't want to, but she did.

"The Hospice Center. It's down the street. I had to sign papers about my mom. I was coming to sign some papers and saw the hotel and decided to stay here." Another shadow of guilt touched his expression. Had he really believed she'd been with Stan today? The thought hurt.

At least the dickhead had a conscience. As well as great shoulders, she noticed again.

"I'm really sorry." He folded his hands over his flat stomach. "Why didn't you stay with Tanya?"

"I stayed there last night. She's a jewelry artist and I know she has work to do." And possible sex scheduled, even if she did say she was postponing it.

"You have any other family?" He yawned.

"No. It's just Mom and me." Her chest clutched again. "Just me." Needing a new focus, she asked, "You got family?" She looked at the empty spot next to him on the bed, but didn't move from the chair.

"A sister and a mom. A few cousins here and there. We're not really close." He leaned against the pillows.

"With who?" she asked.

"Who what?" He uncrossed his ankles and stretched out, letting his body sink deeper into the mattress.

"Who are you not close to?"

"My cousins . . . My sister is a great gal." He shifted his shoulders as if to get a kink out and closed his eyes

"And your mom?" Cali asked. Having just lost her mother, she couldn't believe anyone wouldn't value having a parent.

He opened his eyes. She noticed for the first time how tired he looked. His blue-greens were rimmed in red, bloodshot, and he had that crease between his brows. She remembered her mom saying he was going through something. And the shadow of pain in his eyes was familiar.

Had he lost someone he loved? The question lay heavy on her tongue.

"My mom is . . . complicated." His eyes drooped shut and he scooted down just a bit, getting more comfortable.

Was he really going to go to sleep in her bed? "Complicated how?"

He didn't answer. His head dropped an inch to the side. She remembered him telling her that he'd been working the night before when he found the picture of the bracelet. Then she recalled him being there the night Stan had shot at her. Did he work third shift? If he did and he showed up at the school this morning, that meant he hadn't slept in over thirty-six hours. Okay, she'd let him nap for a few moments.

She checked the time. Almost nine. She frowned. He wasn't the only one tired. She had to get up at six. She stood, turned on the television, and cut the volume on low.

Flipping channels, she found the nightly news. She saw a picture of a police officer on the screen. He looked familiar. Sitting on the foot of the bed, she listened.

"Officer Mike Anderson was found shot at his home earlier this afternoon. Police are . . ."

She stared at the face again and it hit her. "Oh, God!" He was the officer who had come to the house that first night. She remembered thinking he'd looked familiar then, too. As if she'd met the man somewhere else.

Looking back at Detective Lowell—okay, Brit—she wondered if he knew about this man's death. Then she recalled him getting that phone call while they'd been in his car. He'd been upset. For just a second she wondered how one dealt with a job that could involve so much ugliness—crime, death.

She gave Brit another glance and considered waking him. But he looked so peaceful. His brows were no longer pinched and even, slow breaths moved his chest up and down. Rolling her eyes, she cratered. She'd let him sleep a few more minutes.

Kicking off her shoes, she decided she had a right to be comfortable, too. She stretched out, her head on the end of the bed, far enough she didn't touch him. Then with her chin on her folded arms, she watched the news.

~

Brit felt the vibration in his jeans pocket. It took him a second to realize it was his phone. Opening one eye, he stared at the pair of feet resting on his chest. He blinked and opened both eyes. Where the hell was he? Everything came back at once: Chinese food, Cali, the motel. Cali's feet?

He raised his head off the pillow an inch. Yup, Cali's feet. Pretty feet with red toenails. Nice legs. Nice . . . pink panties. Her dress had ridden up to her waist—showing off a beautiful rounded ass covered with a thin piece of pink silk. He inhaled and felt his blood ride south. Really nice view.

He reached for his phone, regretfully gave up the nice view, slipped out from beneath her soft legs, and got out of the bed. The television was on, flickering light, and very little sound in the room. Taking a few steps, he couldn't help looking back one more time to savor what he left on the mattress. Holy hell, what he wouldn't give to crawl back in that bed and pull that dress the rest of the way off and explore all of Cali McKay with both his hands and mouth.

He went into the bathroom. When he turned to close the door, he saw the time on his phone. Twelve-thirty. Damn, he was late for work. "Lowell," he whispered.

"Are you going to show up for work?" Quarles asked.

Brit ran a palm over his face. For the first time in weeks, he'd actually slept. The kind of sleep that made a body feel human.

"You okay?" Quarles asked.

"I overslept. Be right there." He hung up, washed out his mouth, then walked back into the room. He found the remote and clicked it off. Cali lay curled up on her side, her hands tucked under her cheek in the place of a pillow. His gaze whispered down her hot body. Damn she had a beautiful ass and legs. He swallowed, letting his gaze linger on her soft backside while his mind conjured up an image of putting his finger on the back of her knee and moving up her leg. All the way up—to the pink panties. He envisioned running his finger under the elastic band and . . .

His body responded to the images in his head. He frowned. Just what he needed to carry to work with him, a hard-on. Exhaling, he tried to chase the thoughts from his mind and draped the blanket across her legs.

Before he walked out, he looked back and got another kick in the gut. He didn't want to leave. What if that idiot had followed her here? You're overreacting, he told himself. Tomorrow, when she went to school was when he should really worry. And he could be there then.

Would be there.

He walked to the door, his protect-and-serve instinct hitting hard. Then thinking about Keith and Anderson, he left.

Fifteen minutes later, Brit found Quarles sitting at his desk, going through mug shots. Quarles looked up. "Everything okay?" Concern flickered in his partner's eyes.

"Fine, why?"

"I've spoken with your sister three times. She's been trying to reach you."

"Oh, shit. I forgot her again. I'm an ass." He remembered seeing her number flash on his phone while looking for Cali and not answering it. He walked to his office, snatched his phone out. Sure enough, she'd also called while he'd been sleeping and he hadn't woken up. He jabbed in his home number.

"Hello," Susan answered, fully alert and probably pissed. He didn't blame her.

"I'm sorry," Brit said. "It's been a hell of a day."

"I heard about the other cop, and I've been worried about you."

"I know and I'm really sorry, Susan. I've been a dickhead lately. I can't think straight, I'm losing my temper at the least little thing. I'll make it up to you, I promise. I'll be home in the—" He remembered he had to make sure Cali got to school okay. "I'll be home by ten in the morning. I swear, I will."

"Did you sleep at all today?" she asked.

"Yeah. As a matter of fact I overslept."

"Where were you?"

"I—"

"If you were out with some girl, the least you could have done was to have called me."

"It's not like that. Really. I'll explain it tomorrow. I promise."

She sighed. "I'm just relieved you're okay."

"Thanks. I'll see you in the morning." He hung up and raked a hand over his face.

"You sure you're okay?" Quarles stood in the doorway.

"I'm fine." He thought about Cali alone in the hotel room. Then he glanced at the mug books in Quarles' hands.

He remembered the all-night diner across from Cali's hotel. "How about us setting up office somewhere else tonight?"

"Like where?"

"I'll show you. Grab our files and bring the mug books." Brit reached back again for his leather jacket. It wasn't there, and he remembered Cali's sweater tucked in the back of his SUV. Tomorrow he'd give it to her. The idea of seeing her tomorrow sent a shot of anticipation through his blood.

He vaguely recalled thinking that once he got some food and rest, he'd be able to fight the attraction.

He'd been wrong.

"I don't mean to upset you, dear." Cali's mom sat in the straight back chair beside the bed, smoking again.

A dream—her maternal psyche trying to take care of her. Then Cali remembered the detective, and she jerked her gaze to the empty bed.

"He left," her mom said. "He had to go to work."

Cali stared at her mom. This is a dream, isn't it? "You're not real."

"I just want to make sure you're okay, and then I'll go."

Cali suddenly felt guilty as if her mom thought she didn't want to see her. "The dreams just freak me out a little."

"I should have made him leave a lot sooner." Her mom took another drag on the cigarette.

Cali thought about the detective. "Asked who to leave?"

"Your father. I let him stay, and I shouldn't have."

Cali saw regret in her mom's eyes. "It wasn't your fault."

"Yes, it was. I let that man treat us something terrible. But I thought I loved him. And I was scared to raise you alone."

"You did fine," Cali said.

"You're the best thing I did. I'm proud of you, baby. Did I tell you that?"

"Every day for the last three years," Cali whispered, remembering their time together at the end. "You tried so hard to prepare me for your dying. I should have been ready, but I just wanted you to try one more time. The chemo might have worked."

"It wouldn't have worked, baby. It would have just made me sicker." Her mom smiled with so much love that the ache in Cali's heart lessened. "You can't prepare yourself for this," she said. "Plus, that Stan guy messed everything up."

"I know." Cali watched her mom inhale and release. "I thought he was nice, but he wasn't."

"No, he wasn't nice. He took advantage of you. But he didn't kill those two men."

Cali heard her mom, but almost didn't believe it. "What?"

"Stan didn't kill them. It was the other guy, the other band member. And he's after Stan now. Stan needs money to get out of town. That's why he's looking for the bracelet. But he's still not a nice guy. He loses his temper just like your dad did. And he's feeling desperate and desperate people do bad things sometimes."

"How do you know?" Cali asked.

"I told you. There are some benefits to being dead." Her mom looked around the room and took another drag of her cigarette. "He covered you up before he left, you know."

"Who?" Cali asked.

"Brit. Your Mr. Reynolds look-alike. He's a nice guy. He cares about you. You need to listen to him."

"He's not mine."

"He could be yours. You two match. Your auras kept flowing together when you two were sleeping. It was as if they couldn't keep apart. And when they blended, the colors were amazing. You two go together really well."

"Our auras? Mom, you don't even believe in auras."

"Sweetheart, there's nothing like dying to make you more open-minded." She took another drag on the cigarette and her bracelets jingled in the smoky silence.

"He's a dickhead," Cali said.

Her mom smiled. "Yeah, but remember, he's just Little Dickhead." She chuckled and then sobered. "He's got a good heart, Cali. You should see him feeding the stray cats. He's just going through something right now. You'll help though."

"I don't want to help him," she said, but it was a lie and she felt it in her stomach. She had to learn to be a bitch.

"Yes, you do. You always want to fix people. You wanted to fix my cancer and couldn't. You want to fix your students. Even Stan. The counselor is only partly right; you might have a little weakness toward men like your father, but more than that, you just want to fix people. You saw Stan as lonely, like yourself, and that's why you let him in your life. Bad decision, but for a good reason."

Cali recalled believing that Stan had seemed lonely. She looked away, not wanting to think about Stan. "So I just have to stop caring."

"No, dear, you don't stop caring. You just accept that you can't win them all. But you can't give up."

"You gave up," Cali said. "If you'd done one more treatment, it could have worked. We could have at least had Christmas, New Years, and maybe Easter."

"It wouldn't have changed things," her mother whispered in a voice so low that her words seemed to float away. "I was so tired of fighting cancer."

Cali turned her head, hoping her mom wouldn't see the anger that still lingered in her heart. She had wanted one more time.

"You wanted to fix me, dear. We couldn't win this one. But I have one that you can win. Actually, I have several that you can win. And I'm going to help you. Help you help others. But you're going to have to listen to me."

"Listen to what?" Cali asked, her breath shaky.

"Don't go to lunch. Stay at the school." Her mother's voice seemed to float away again.

"What?" Cali asked as a noise tried to shatter the dream.

"Do you hear me, Cali? Don't go to lunch. And think about that officer–the one who was killed. It's important, Cali. You need to remember."

The noise. Cali heard it again. She jack-knifed up and opened her eyes. It took one second to remember where she was. Then she heard something and looked at the door. Her breath caught when she saw the knob turning. Had Stan found her again?

Chapter Seventeen

When the door pushed open, Cali's scream lodged in her throat.

Then Brit stepped into the room.

Perched up on her knees, staring at him from behind a curtain of blond hair, she managed to close her mouth. She remembered the dream, then she remembered watching the news. "You fell asleep," she said.

His bad-boy grin teased her sleepy mind. "I don't normally fall asleep when I have a beautiful woman in bed with me."

She frowned. "What are you doing here?"

"I wanted to make sure you got to school." He shoulder-shut the door while focusing on her. "You all right?"

She realized the brightness sneaking around the window treatments. "What time is it?" She knee-walked off the bed, his teasing smile, too much, too early. She should have woken him right when he fell asleep. Once again, being sweet had gotten her into a pickle. A bitch would have kicked him out.

"It's almost six." He looked wide awake and wonderful. "I got us breakfast." He set a bag on the dresser.

She pushed a hand through her blond mess, trying to untangle her thoughts more than her hair. Had she slept all night with him? She remembered her mom saying something about him leaving. "Did you work last night?"

"Actually, I overslept." His smile gave his words more meaning than she understood. "But yeah, I went to work." He pulled two coffees from a bag and held one out to her. "Coffee now, or after you shower?"

She blinked, her brain on overload. "How did this happen?"

"What happen?" He set the bag and one coffee on the dresser. He wore the navy windbreaker. It didn't look as if he'd changed clothes.

"This." She waved a hand between them. "You here and talking about showers and bringing me coffee."

"I was just trying to be nice." He pulled the top of the coffee off and sipped from the rim. The smell of chicory and caffeine made everything seem more real.

She eyed the clock again, figuring how much time she had to get to work, then she looked back at him. "Why are you here now?"

The steam from the cup rose around his face. "Because I want to make sure Stan isn't waiting for you at the school."

She remembered her dream again. Her mom had said for her not to go out for lunch. She pressed her palms against her eyes.

"You sure you don't need a coffee?" He took two steps closer. She took two back.

"No." She grabbed her suitcase and stepped into the bathroom. Before she closed the door, she looked over her shoulder. "Is this normal?"

"Now that you mention it. No." His grin came on slow. "Normally, when I bring a woman breakfast in bed, she's a lot nicer."

She frowned. "I mean, do you do personal wake-up calls and bring coffee to all the people you meet on your job? Aren't you taking the protect-and-serve motto a tad to the extreme?"

His smiled faded. "I'm just trying to make sure you stay alive. The guy after you is suspected of three murders now."

She nodded, recalling her dream where her mom said that Stan hadn't been the one doing the killing. "So that's all that's going on?"

He raised his coffee and sipped from the cup. His blue-green eyes stared at her through the steam. "What else could there be?"

~

"So that's all that's going on?" He spent the entire time waiting on her to shower and telling himself that enough was enough. She was right. He was taking this too damn far. And it could backfire on him big time.

But the moment she stepped out of the bathroom, his resolve took a hike. It was her eyes. Big and blue. It was her body. Soft and sexy. But it was the mere possibility that the same asshole who'd killed the two guys back at the other hotel could do the same to her that sealed the deal. He wasn't backing down.

He let his gaze move over her. The khaki pants and a pink sweater hugged her body in all the right places. His hands itched to reach around her waist and pull her against him. To feel her against him. Breathing in air that smelled like freshly showered woman, he envisioned removing each article of clothing she wore and pulling her into the bed and getting acquainted with every naked inch of her.

"Coffee now?" He held out her cup.

She accepted it and pulled off the lid. A bit of steam rose from the cup as she put her lips to the edge. Taking a small sip, she glanced up at him. "Thank you."

He smiled. "You're welcome." He reached for the bag of donuts. "I just got plain glazed."

"That's what I like."

He offered her the bag and she reached in and pulled one out.

They sat on the bed and drank coffee and ate donuts that were still warm. He remembered last night, the comfortable place they'd slipped into, right before he'd fallen into the first real sleep he'd had in almost a month.

"Sorry if I scared you this morning," he said.

She nodded. "I'm sorry I was grumpy."

The donut melted on Brit's tongue. But he thought about something else he'd rather taste. Her. She licked her finger, then popped the little digit into her mouth, seemingly unaware of how sexy she looked. A flake of sugar clung to her bottom lip and he longed to lean down and taste it with his lips. His lower body tightened and the evidence of his arousal pressed against his zipper. He inhaled and tried to stop the blood from flowing south.

She finished her donut, and he offered her another.

"No. Thank you."

That flake of sugar still clung to the side of her mouth. He reached over and brushed it aside. Their gazes met and held.

"Sugar," he said, unable to look away.

She blinked and turned away, but then she looked back. "I saw the news last night about the officer who was killed. The second one to be killed in the last month."

Brit's donut lost its flavor, and the erotic images in his mind faded. He inhaled. "Yeah."

Concern filled her eyes. "Wasn't he the same officer who came to my house?"

He nodded. "Mike Anderson. Just a kid. I . . . hate it." He dropped the rest of his donut in the bag and tossed it in the trash with last night's dinner containers.

When he looked up, she blinked those big blues at him. "I'm sorry. I imagine it must be hard to lose a fellow officer. I know it's hard when people ask questions about someone you lost."

"Yeah," his voice gave the word more meaning than he wanted. From the look on her face, she'd heard and understood it.

She sipped her coffee and looked into her cup as if lost in thought.

"Coffee okay?" he asked, longing to fight the wave of grief trying to nudge its way into her mood again.

"Yeah, it's fine. You remembered how I take my coffee. Thanks."

"You're welcome." He shrugged. "Told you I wasn't a total dickhead."

She smiled. He had to stop himself from leaning in and kissing her. But damn he wanted to taste her. To taste the sheen of oil from her lips. To taste the sweetness of sugar on her tongue.

"Do you know where he lived?" she asked.

"Who lived?" he asked.

"The other officer. Mike Anderson. That first night, I remember thinking he looked familiar, and again last night when I saw his picture on the news. I thought maybe I knew him from somewhere. Maybe the grocery store or something."

He hesitated, but remembered from Mike's file. "In Springville, just north of here."

"Were you two close?"

He shook his head. "Not really. But from what I knew of him, he was a decent guy."

She pressed her lips to the cup and stared at him over the rim. He could almost feel her trying to read him. "Did you know the other officer who was killed?"

Damn, he didn't want to talk about this. "You ready to go?" He stood, hoping to leave the question behind.

"You knew him better, didn't you?"

He pitched his coffee in the garbage. "Yeah." He exhaled. "He was my partner. And my best friend."

~

His SUV stayed behind her as she drove. Cali thought about the pain she'd seen in his eyes when he talked about his partner. She'd sensed earlier that they were both going through something. She'd been right. They were both grieving. Her heart ached for him. Was that why she felt drawn to him?

He's going through something, she remembered her mom saying. How had her mom known? When Cali pulled into the school parking lot on automatic, her mind chewed on the dreams and the crazy possibility they presented.

No, her mom didn't know. Her mom was gone. The dreams were exactly what the counselor said they were—her maternal psyche verbalizing her own intuitiveness.

Stopping her car, she stared at the nearly empty parking lot. "Where is everyone?" The realization hit. Oh yeah, today was an in-service day. The kids wouldn't be here, which meant she'd be in meetings all day.

Normally, she enjoyed a break from the daily grind, but this morning in the shower she'd worried about Sara and hoped to check in on her. As Cali parked, she decided she'd give the girl a call. It never hurt to let someone know they weren't alone.

Brit's SUV pulled in beside her. She waved at him, thinking he might just take off. But nope, he got out and met her as she closed her car door. She remembered how he'd looked at her while they'd been eating donuts. For a second there, she thought he'd been going to kiss her—which probably wouldn't have been a good thing. But it hadn't prevented her from wishing he'd tried.

Not that she would have allowed it. Or at least she told herself she wouldn't have.

He stopped in front of her. A cold wind gusted, and she was tempted to move closer just because he looked so warm. She recalled again how she'd cried on his shoulder almost in this very spot. Recalled how good it had felt to have his arms around her, too.

"What time are you off?" he asked.

"Three, but I don't expect you to come back."

"Why not?" He shifted closer. Tall, dark, strong. And warm. She met his eyes and saw the shadows of grief there, the same thing she felt. It took everything she had not to lean against him. She wanted to console him and be consoled.

"Because . . ." She couldn't think with him this close.

"Don't leave the school until I get here. I'm serious."

Don't go to lunch tomorrow. Her mom's warning whispered in her head.

"But—" She closed her mouth as he pressed a finger against her lips. The touch felt intimate, soft, and caring. He cares about you. Her mother's words filled her head again.

"Please, don't argue." He brushed his finger down to the edge of her jaw and under her chin. With the slightest pressure, he tilted her face back. She watched his tongue brush a layer of moisture onto his bottom lip, and his blue-greens stared at her mouth.

Tanya's gold Toyota darted past, and the moment shattered like dropped crystal. Tanya had lousy timing. Or great timing. Did she want him to kiss her?

"It's an in-service day." She threw words at the awkwardness.

"A what?"

"Kids are off. We'll have meetings all day."

He looked at her mouth again, then glanced away. "You have security here, don't you?"

"Yes. Roberto Garcia; he patrols the lot." Right then, Roberto's security car pulled around the side of the school.

"I'm going to talk to him." He started off.

She grabbed his hand. The warmth of his palm against hers gave her a jolt. She released him. "I wish you wouldn't tell him about all this."

"He needs to know. Humphrey broke into your car yesterday, and he could come back."

Cali knew Brit was right, but something he'd said yesterday teased her mind. "Did you tell Mrs. Jasmine about everything?"

"Mrs. Jasmine?"

"The principal? You said she gave you Tanya's number."

He nodded. "I only said I was worried you could be in danger. I didn't stay to explain things."

Cali sighed. "Guess I'll be called into the office today."

He frowned. "I didn't mean to cause trouble." Concern darkened his eyes.

She offered him half a smile. "I'll survive." Silence fell again. More awkwardness.

"I'll be here at three. You wait inside. Promise me?"

She nodded. He gave her mouth one more glance, then walked away. But he looked back and then smiled and winked. The quick flutter from his eyelid spread to her stomach.

"I'm in so much trouble," she muttered.

"Why?" Tanya appeared beside her. "Because he has a nice ass?"

"Yeah. And awesome shoulders, too. And a good heart." Cali frowned.

Leaning in, her friend asked, "So is he still a dickhead?"

Cali considered it. "Let's just say, he's a smaller dickhead than I thought."

Tanya grabbed Cali's arm. "I'm scared to ask if you mean that literally."

They giggled like teens all the way inside.

~

Brit heard laughter, but didn't look back. If he did, he was afraid he would go snatch her up and kiss her like he wanted to, like he felt damn sure she wanted to be kissed. But he had to leave. He had

Keith's and now Anderson's killer to look for. And Susan to see. But not until he spoke to the security guard.

"Hi." Brit approached the older man as he stepped from the car. "I'm Detective Lowell, HPD." He purposely didn't mention the homicide division. It usually made people nervous.

"Roberto Garcia. Retired HPD. What can I do for you?"

Brit liked knowing the guard had carried a real badge and offered the man his hand. "It's about one of your teachers."

"Someone in trouble with the law?"

"Nothing like that. You know Cali McKay?"

The quick smile made the old man look younger. "She baked me a cake for my birthday last year. Don't know how the woman knew it was my birthday, but I tell you, she's one angel."

An odd sense of pride swelled in Brit's chest, as if Cali was his to be proud of. "Yeah. Well, there's trouble with one of her old boyfriends."

"Stalking her?"

Brit glanced back to where Cali had parked. "Her car was vandalized yesterday."

Garcia frowned. "It could just be a kid. You have no idea what—"

"I don't think so. This guy's trouble. I have a mug shot in my car. I want you to take a look at it. Keep an eye out. We believe he's driving a white Ford pickup. An older model."

They walked back to Brit's SUV. He reached into his file and took out the mug shot.

The man studied it intently. "What's he wanted for?"

"We're looking at him for a murder," Brit answered.

"That serious, huh?" Garcia frowned. "How did someone like Cali get mixed up with someone like that?"

The question hit hard. "Just watch out for him." Brit reached into his front pocket. "My card. If you even think you see him, call me, then call 9-1-1. Don't try to apprehend him yourself. But keep him away from Cali."

"Don't worry. I owe Miss McKay." Garcia widened his shoulders. "I may look like an old codger, but I still got it."

"I don't doubt it." Brit shook the man's hand again. Garcia's grip held firm, solid. Getting in his car, Brit felt better about leaving Cali. A little better.

Chapter Eighteen

Before heading home, Brit stopped by his office to feed Mama Cat. Good thing he had, too. He ran into Duke and his partner and they told him they had interviews set with a few gang members about to go down for some other small charges. They hoped when pressed, they might offer up some info on Keith's murder for leniency on their charge. Brit almost told them he would go with them, but remembered his date with his sister.

Before he left the precinct, he got wind of a rumor that a task force was being formed to track down the cop killers. Brit marched into Sergeant Adams' office and demanded he be added to the team.

Adams perched his elbows on the desk. "Keith was your partner. Being too close to a case can get in the way."

"I'm the one who found the only lead we've got right now." Brit clenched his fists. "Every one of you pushed this case off as a random killing. I knew better. Being close to this case isn't going to get in my way. Put me on it, or I'll just work it on my own." Brit met Adams' stare.

"You look like shit. When was the last time you slept?"

"I'm fine. Let me work eight to two, then I'll come back and work half a shift on third. I swear I won't let you down. I'm putting in more hours than that now. I need this, damn it!"

The man clenched his jaws. "You'll stay grounded?"

"Yeah." Hope stirred in Brit's gut.

Adams' brow puckered. "We'll start tomorrow. But– "

"I'll be here tomorrow." Brit didn't want to hear any buts.

"Fine. Go home and sleep. And, oh yeah, stop feeding those damn cats."

"It's not me," Brit lied and only felt slightly guilty. Keith wouldn't have stopped feeding them no matter what Adams thought. Neither would Mike Anderson.

"Bullshit," Adams said.

~

Brit went home—after he fed the cats—not to sleep, but to eat crow from his sister. If he was lucky, he could eat crow, then crash a couple of hours before taking her out to a make—up lunch.

He walked in his house and found Susan in the kitchen pouring coffee. "You talking to me?"

"Let's see." She smirked. "You forget I'm coming down, you forget to pick me up at the airport, you spend thirty minutes with me then go to bed, leave, and don't come home for twenty—four hours." Her finger wagged at him. "Tell me you weren't out breaking some woman's heart last night, and I might forgive you."

"I wasn't breaking any hearts." Brit opened the fridge and found it stocked. "Food. I love you." He pulled out the milk and filled a glass to the rim.

"I'll believe you love me when you show up at Mom's party tomorrow night."

Brit guzzled the milk, then frowned. "What time?"

"I've only told you three times. I've sent you an email invite and snail mail." Her mouth thinned. "It's at six in the afternoon at Fancies' Restaurant and Bar. It's two blocks down from that gym you used to belong to."

"Okay." Brit gaped at the bluish milk in his glass.

"Okay, you'll be there?" she asked.

"I will do everything in my power to be there."

Susan's chin snapped up. "I don't like how that sounds."

He finished his milk, even though it had no taste. "Look, sis, I promise if I can, I'll be there. I'm drowning in work. There's Keith and Anderson's case, Cali's case, and—"

"Who's Cali?"

"She's just a girl in trouble and I'm trying to help."

"Was that who you were with last night? Why you didn't come this morning?"

He leaned against the fridge. "Yes, but it's not like you think. We're not together."

"She married?"

"No."

"Is she engaged, old or ugly?"

He got an image of Cali coming out of the bathroom this morning —wearing a pair of loose khaki slacks and her pink sweater.

"Well?"

"No. She's prim and proper."

"Which means you haven't had sex with her?"

"And we probably won't have sex." The probably in the sentence gave him a jolt. Hadn't he already gone over this in his mind, convinced himself this shouldn't happen? Yeah, but that changed when he'd seen her eat a donut. Or was it when he saw her in her pink panties? Maybe it was when he saw the pain in her eyes and she cried on his shoulder.

"Why not?" Susan's eyebrow arched up.

He ran a hand over his chest. "Because she's not my type."

"So she's prim and proper and ugly, huh?"

"No. She's . . ." Too much like our mom. But damn, he didn't really believe that, did he? He remembered the guard asking how Cali could have gotten mixed up with someone wanted for murder. Did getting messed up with a lowlife make a woman a doormat?

"Was that her sweater you were sniffing? Hmm?"

"Don't hmm me." He yanked her ponytail. "Can I catch a few Z's before I take you out for a fantastic lunch?"

"I insist on it." She kissed his cheek. "Oh, I went by your office this morning on my way to meet Mom for breakfast." She brushed a lock of hair from his brow. "Your partner said you'd taken off early."

"I did." Brit set the glass in the sink.

"He seems nice." A sly smile teased the corners of her mouth. "Is he married?"

"Quarles? John Quarles?"

"Yeah."

Brit frowned. "Why do you care?"

"Because he asked me to have breakfast with him."

"I thought you were meeting Mom."

"I was, and I did. But he asked for a rain check." Her smile faded. "What's wrong? Is he married? Gay? A womanizer?"

"No. He's not married, not gay, but all men are womanizers." He pointed at her. "I don't want you seeing him."

"Why not?" She snapped her chin up.

"Because if you have sex with him, I might hear about it. And then I'll have to kill him. That's a brother's job. To kill any asshole who has sex with his sister."

Susan laughed. "I tell you what, if I have sex with him, I'll tell him not to brag about how good I was. How's that?"

"Friggin' fantastic," Brit snapped. "No. Seriously, no. Don't go there."

Her eyes went tight. "I think I've grown past the age where little brother tells big sis what she can and can't do. So give up trying." She nudged him in the ribs. "Now, go get some sleep."

That didn't mean she was going to date Quarles, did it? Too tired to think straight, too tired to argue, he shuffled down the hall.

"Hey?" Susan voice made him pause at his bedroom door. "Are you going to bring Cali to Mom's party? There's going to be dancing."

"No," he called back over his shoulder and crawled into the bed, fluffed the pillow, and waited for sheer exhaustion to take him under. By God, he needed to sleep. Sleep like he had last night for those few hours at Cali's hotel room. Deep sleep.

Real sleep.

Instead, he tossed and turned, and his mind flipped images in his head—images of Keith, of the two corpses, and images of Cali in pink lacy underwear. He didn't know how his mind could change channels from the horror of death to a soft woman in sexy pink underwear, but his mind did what it wanted. He finally dozed off, but he never fell into a deep sleep.

At eleven he got up and showered. Walking into his bedroom, he tugged on the towel hanging around his waist, visions of pink underwear still dangled in his mind. He tried to call Cali at the school. Her main line rang, but a machine picked up. He smiled when he heard Cali's voice on the recording. Dropping the phone, he didn't leave a message. But he called back again just to put a voice to the fantasy that had teased him awake. The one where he'd finally removed those panties.

~

The message machine on Cali's desk blinked. Two hang ups that listed as an unknown number. She turned a pencil in her hand and wondered why she expected to hear from Brit. She was a case to him. That's all she wanted it to be.

She started drawing hearts on a notepad. Liar, she thought and scratched out a heart. She wanted more. But deep down, she knew this was one lie she needed to overlook. Plain and simple, she was in no emotional shape to let what she felt for Brit go anywhere.

She remembered what the counselor said. She had a tendency to fall for men like her dear old dad. Men who yelled and threw things. Men who left.

Then she remembered what her mom said. She was a fixer. And Brit Lowell needed fixing. Just like she did. Was it wrong to want to fix someone who was in the same boat you were in?

Releasing her hair from the banana clip, she stared at the phone. Then she remembered the call she'd told herself she'd make.

She found Sara's number and dialed. "Hi, is this Sara?"

"Yes," the voice answered.

"It's Miss McKay."

"Miss McKay? At school?"

"The same one." Cali tried to keep her tone light. "I was just calling to see how things are. I missed seeing you yesterday, and I just wondered if everything was okay."

"It's fine, I guess." Sara's voice came out low. "Mom saw the doctor. They said they'll probably do surgery next week. They're hoping they can just remove the lump."

"I'm sure it will be fine," Cali told her, hoping she sounded positive.

"I hope so." There was hesitation in Sara's voice. "But shouldn't she get a second opinion?"

"She hasn't gotten a second opinion?" Cali asked.

"No. She seems to like the doctor, but when I went to the office with her, he called her by the wrong name. I just got this strange feeling that if he didn't care enough to even get her name right, then how could we put her life in his hands?"

Empathy for Sara stirred up sharp, painful memories. How many times had Cali watched a physician treat her mother as if she was simply a means to a paycheck?

"She needs a second opinion," Cali said. "I could give you my mother's oncologist. He was really good."

"I'd appreciate that," Sara said.

Cali repeated Dr. Tien's name and number. How sad was it that she knew the number by heart? "Let me know if you need anything— anything at all. And tell him I sent you."

"Thank you." Sara's voice sounded a little tight.

Cali hung up and sank back in her chair. Her heart ached for Sara. You can't win them all. Cali remembered her dream.

She bit down on her lip. "Please let me win this one."

The door squeaked open, and Tanya popped in. "Let's go."

Pulling at her banana clip, Cali looked up. "Go where?"

"To lunch. Mrs. Jasmine is buying. I'm ordering steak."

Cali squeezed the hair clip and let it pop closed. She inhaled, and a whiff of cigarette smoke filled her nose. A chill ran down her back. "I might just hang here."

"Don't go there. No arguing, girlfriend." Tanya sashayed up to the desk and snatched Cali's purse. "Now come on. We're going to lunch and we're going to have a good time."

~

Brit took a bite of his burger and watched his sister. Then, frowning, he watched the man two tables away watch his sister. The jerk had been watching her since they walked in.

"Mom asked about you," Susan said. "She said she left ten messages after she heard about Keith. You never called back."

"I'll see her tomorrow night." While he added a fry to his mouth, Susan forked her salad. Normally Susan ate burgers and fries. Normally, he didn't worry about his sister dating his partner. And normally, men didn't stare at his sister. Brit looked at the man who had been ogling Susan since they walked in.

Susan flipped her long hair back. "Do you want me to pick her out a gift from you?"

Something was different about Susan. Brit edged back in the chair. What had he missed? "Yeah. I'll pay you back."

"You got any ideas what you'd like to get her?" Susan asked.

"You're a woman. You pick." Then he figured it out. And it was about her figure, too. She was less of a woman than before. He looked at the man again, who still gawked at his sister as if he were undressing her in his mind.

"How much do you want to spend?"

Frowning, he popped a fry into his mouth. "I don't care."

Susan dropped her fork. "Don't care? Look, I know she wouldn't win Mother-of-the—Year award, but—"

"Mother-of-the-Year? Right." His laugh rolled out with sarcasm. They had both blamed their dad all those years. Then by the grace of God, the old man died. It wasn't six months until Brit's mom had a replacement. Just as mean. Maybe meaner.

Susan leaned in close. "She wasn't perfect, but—"

"No buts. What is it, husband four now? Was it number three who put her in the hospital? Do you know I almost got fired for breaking that fucker's nose?"

"It's a sickness. And she's seeing a therapist right now. And I actually like her new husband."

"Maybe it's a sickness. And by God, I hope she gets help. I pray this man treats her well, because I don't enjoy beating up old men." He clutched his fist. "I know she's my mom, that's why I'll still beat the crap out of anyone who lays a hand on her. And barring disasters, I'll be there tomorrow night. But don't ask me to pretend like we're this big happy family. Because you know who my family is? You. You're my family."

"I just wish—"

"Wishing doesn't fix things. I gave up trying to fix Mom."

Susan leaned in. "What about fixing yourself, Brit?"

"Don't start." Brit pushed his plate back.

"It's just. . ." Her fork hit the plate, and she sent him one of those, I-love-you looks.

That look always got to him. "Eat." He pushed his plate over to her. "And finish my burger. You're too skinny."

"I'm down forty pounds. I didn't think you noticed."

"I didn't. Not until that man over there noticed, and kept noticing your ass when we walked in. Men aren't supposed to notice my sister's ass. And my partner isn't supposed to be hitting on you either."

His sister's eyes lit up and she leaned in. "That man really looked at my ass?"

Brit laughed. The waitress brought over the check and he dropped a twenty on the table.

Susan crossed her arms over her chest. "I'm not the only one who has changed. Our waitress has been eyeing you like a piece of candy she wants to unwrap."

"Which one?" Brit pretended to scan the room.

"Brunette, big tits, tiny waist. Normally, you'd have had her phone number and bra size by now."

Now, he glanced around in earnest. "Big tits?"

"And you didn't even notice. Which makes me wonder if this too nice, too sweet Cali hasn't worked some spell on you."

"There's no spell," he said.

"You like her. And don't deny it. You don't go around sniffing some woman's sweater you're not attracted to."

He chuckled and then nodded. "Okay, I'll admit it. I like her. But more than I like her, I want to protect her. And even considering how much I like her, I'm not sure letting it go anywhere is a good idea."

"Why not?"

"Because she's part of a case. And because with all this other crap going on, I'm not sure I'm thinking straight," Brit said. Since Keith had died, he hadn't given women or sex much more than a passing thought. Until Cali. He remembered getting hard just staring at her in bed this morning.

His cell phone rang. He answered it. "Lowell."

"De . . . tective?" The winded voice didn't sound familiar. "It's . . . Garcia at the school. We got . . . trouble."

Chapter Nineteen

Brit clutched the phone in his hand. "Is Cali okay?"

"I think I spotted him," Garcia said, his words jarring as if he were running as he talked. "I was making my rounds. When I got around front, I saw a white pickup leaving. I'm . . . not sure, but I think it was following a van full of teachers. I ran to my car, but by the time I got there, both vehicles had gotten away. I'm running . . . inside now to see if Miss McKay went with them."

"I'm on my way. Call me as soon as you know if she's there. If she's not, find someone who knows where the hell they went, and you get me that information."

The line went dead.

"God damn it," Brit seethed. He looked at his sister. "Let's go. It's Cali."

He drove like hell was on fire and chasing him. He called the station and got an APB put out on a white pickup around the school. He kept his phone clutched in his palm, waiting for Garcia to tell him if Cali was at the school or out to lunch. Why the hell hadn't he told her not to leave the school?

Susan tried to ask him questions. "Not now," he snapped and concentrated on running red lights.

Ten minutes later, he came to a rubber-burning halt in front of the school, still clutching his phone. Why hadn't Garcia called back? Brit jumped out of his car and sprinted to the front door. It was locked. He banged his hand on the glass. Behind him, he heard Susan get out of his SUV.

His phone rang and he snapped it open. "Where is she?"

"She's fine," Garcia answered. "I found her in the teacher's lounge."

Brit let out a breath he felt as if he'd held for ten minutes. "Get someone to let me in. I'm standing out front."

"I'm right there," Garcia said.

When he looked up, Garcia and Cali made the corner. Brit stared at Cali's face. She looked shaken, pale, reminding him of the first night he'd seen her at her apartment. He dropped his phone into his shirt pocket, itching to hold her instead.

Garcia opened the door. Brit pushed past him to Cali. "You okay?" He brushed his hands up and down her arms. She nodded, but didn't look okay. "What happened?"

"Nothing. I didn't go to lunch. I stayed here." He felt her trembling.

He squeezed both her hands. "Stan called you, didn't he?"

Her frightened eyes met his. "No."

He stared at her and as clearly as he could see her face, he could see she was hiding something. What the hell was she hiding?

"What happened, Cali?"

She blinked and shook her head. "Nothing."

Garcia walked past him, and Brit heard the door whisk open . "Can I help you?" the security guard asked someone. Brit remembered Susan. When he looked back, sure enough she stood at the door.

A cold wind entered when his sister stepped inside. "I'm with him," his sister said.

Brit nodded at his sister and went back to staring at Cali. "You're shaking," he said. "Tell me what happened. You have a problem with the principal?"

"No. It's fine."

Brit's phone rang. He put the phone to his ear, but didn't answer quite yet and continued to study Cali's washed-out expression. "Did you see Stan Humphrey?"

"No," she said.

Frowning, he hit the talk button. "Lowell."

"Hey, detective. We've pulled over a white pickup. It's not the right license plate, but the man fits the description. What do you want me to do?"

"Hold him until I get there. And be careful. We're looking at him for murder. Where are you?"

The cop gave an address and Brit memorized it. "I'll be right there." He hung up the phone and looked at Cali again. Was he imagining she was hiding something from him? Hell, with such little sleep as he'd had, maybe he was seeing things that weren't there.

He gave Cali's arms another squeeze, then looked at Garcia now standing beside him. "They've pulled over a white pickup. I'll call you when I know something." He looked back at Cali. "Remember, don't leave until I get here." He wanted so bad to lean down and kiss her, but he didn't.

When he turned around, he met Susan's gaze. "Let's go." He placed his hand on her lower back and guided her out. Crawling into his car, he prayed the man driving the pickup was Stan Humphrey. Damn, but he wanted to catch this bastard.

~

Cali watched Brit and the brunette walk out. It didn't matter. It didn't matter that he had a beautiful woman with him. He was just a cop and she was just a case. And the fact that Stan had been spotted in the parking lot, that her mother had warned her not to go out to lunch, that she'd smelled smoke when Tanya had come in, insisting she go out to lunch, it didn't matter either. Because the dreams were only her subconscious.

It was totally logical. She could almost hear Dr. Roberts' calm voice explaining it. "You always go out to lunch on an in-service day. Stan probably knew that. You knew Stan would know. Therefore, it was logical that you turned Tanya down. It wasn't your mom telling you this—it was your subconscious warning you. And you listened to your subconscious because it was logical. Not because you believed your mom was communicating with you."

But logic could go fly a kite in a hail storm because Cali didn't feel better. Not about the dream, because she hadn't remembered today was an in-service day. Not about the beautiful woman with Brit because she hadn't realized he had a girlfriend.

Cali had seen the woman checking her out, too. And though Cali hated to admit it, she'd done her own checking—the old compare and contrast and she-has/I-have inventory. The brunette, with long hair that hung past her shoulders, had looked older than Cali. Some men liked older women and longer hair. The brunette had larger breasts. Men liked larger breasts. The brunette was taller and seductive, wearing a snug pair of black jeans and a snugger red sweater that hugged her slightly bigger breasts. Cali was a sweet girl with a Charmin face. The brunette was exotic looking.

If it had been a competition, hands down the brunette won.

But it wasn't a competition. Brit Lowell was just a cop trying to protect her. He'd even said as much this morning when she'd asked him. And he hadn't tried to kiss her because he hadn't wanted to kiss her. And as soon as she got that through her thick skull, and quit doodling hearts on paper, the better off she'd be.

~

"Stay in the car," Brit told Susan as he pulled up behind the squad car and a white pickup.

As he got out, he spotted a dark-haired man talking to Officer Wolowitz. Brit eyed the pickup; it was the right make, the driver had the right hair color and height. Hope stirred in his chest. But then the man turned around and Brit saw his face and his hope shattered. Not the right man. Not Stan.

After leaving a message on Cali's machine that it hadn't been Stan, Brit drove Susan back to his place. She asked a few questions, and he answered her with as little information as he could.

He parked in the driveway, and bet himself he wouldn't make it out of here without his sister interrogating him about his concern over Cali. Not that he had anything to hide. He remembered his gut telling him that Cali was keeping something from him. And now his gut shouted out another bit of wisdom. He couldn't let this attraction go anywhere. Not when there was the least bit of doubt about her relationship with a suspected murderer.

But damn it, nor was he going to let Humphrey get to her.

Susan slid out of the seat, then turned and faced him.

"I might not be home until in the morning," he told her.

Her frown deepened. "You're not sleeping enough, brother."

"I'm going to get some sleep," he said, hoping this afternoon would go just like it had yesterday. That he could hang with Cali at the hotel and get some rest.

"You're going to kill yourself going like this."

"I'm fine." He waved her off with his gotta-go tone because he wanted to stop at the station to visit with Duke and Mark and see how the interview went with the gang member.

He also planned to talk to Adams about putting a man on Cali. Stan seemed adamant to get to her. He knew Adams would balk, but someone had to take care of her. And maybe he wasn't the right person to do it.

"She's really pretty." Susan stood outside the SUV's open door.

"Yeah." His mind went back to the panicked look on Cali's face. What had upset her? What was she not telling him? He jammed the car into drive and took off.

~

"I can't do that," Adams said. "We'll work the case, but I can't afford to put a man on the girl. Especially when the school already has security."

Brit leaned forward. "He's broken into her apartment, her car, and her mother's house. Now, we're almost certain he was at the school again today. He's wanted for three murders."

"Yeah, and chances are she's meeting him for quickies every afternoon. You know how these women work."

Brit's gut flinched as if someone had punched him. "She filed charges against him. She gave us all she knows."

"Says who?"

"Says me." Brit jammed his hands into his pockets to keep them off Adams' neck.

"What you want to bet when we catch the guy, she'll be in court crying her eyes out because she knows he really didn't mean to do it? The answer is no. Do the job. Find the guy and bring him in, but I'm not putting men out there to protect some girlfriend when I've got cop killers running the street."

Brit stormed out of Adams' office ready to hit somebody. He slammed the door of his broom closet of an office and dared anyone to try to talk to him. He'd expected Adams to deny his request, that wasn't what had blistered his balls. It was the fact that everything Adams said was exactly how Brit had felt a few days ago. And while most of those feelings had been pushed aside, the smallest thread of doubt hung loose. And that thread seemed to be the one thing that could unravel Brit's sanity.

~

Cali sat in the last meeting for the day, wishing the moments away. Mrs. Jasmine had the floor again and it took everything Cali had to pay attention.

"The At Risk Kids Foundation is still looking for volunteers to help them coordinate their biannual meeting. And they've sent out e-mails asking if anyone knows any civil servants that would volunteer as speakers. I've already offered up my husband, who is a fire fighter." She shuffled through her notes. "If anyone has a few hours to donate, I'd appreciate it."

Cali felt Mrs. Jasmine's eyes zoning in on her, but she glanced away. It wasn't the program. A.R.K. helped teenagers who were thought to be at risk of quitting school. Cali seriously felt the program had merit, but right now, she should be asking for volunteers to help her piece her own life back together. Cali got a vision of her standing up and announcing, "Excuse me, would someone please volunteer to convince me that my dead mother isn't visiting me in my dreams, and if anyone else could do something about my ex-boyfriend, the murderer whom I slept with. Well, I'd appreciate it."

"Didn't you volunteer last time, Cali?"

Cali glanced up, caught in the woman's target. "Yes, it's a great program." Then she clamped her mouth. You can't fix everything, Cali. Her mother's voice echoed in her head. Let somebody else help the A.R.K. program this time.

"Well, everyone think about it," Mrs. Jasmine said.

"I'll do it," Tanya said, sitting next to Cali.

"Thank you, Tanya." The meeting continued and Tanya leaned over. "Do you think Mr. Little Dickhead would come speak at the meeting?"

"I don't know. You did call him an asshole."

Tanya grinned. "That's why I was thinking you could ask him for me. I think he likes you."

Not as much as he does the brunette, Cali thought.

~

After simmering a while in his office, Brit left to find Duke or Mark. To see if their chat with the other gang members had given them anything.

"Nothing," Duke mumbled and shoved back from his desk. "The bad thing is I believe they're telling the truth. Either Payne is shooting us a line of bull or he got something wrong."

Brit felt his blood pressure rise a notch. "Maybe it's not the Blue Bloods. Maybe it's a different gang."

The toothpick between Duke's lips rolled to the other side his mouth. "Maybe. But he said Blue Bloods, didn't he?"

Gritting his teeth, Brit nodded. "Did they get anything from the crime scene at Anderson's?"

"No, it was clean. Just like Keith's."

Brit picked up the file. Two bullets to the head. The same as Keith's. Same gun, a .45. Keith was killed in a parking lot. Anderson died at his house.

"You know," Brit said, "I always found it odd that Keith didn't have any defensive wounds. Keith was a fighter and if he'd seen anything coming, he'd have fought. And I've never seen anyone sneak up on him, either." Brit thumped the file. "It says here that Anderson's place wasn't broken in to. So we have to assume that he might have known the killer."

Interest piqued, Duke sat up. "Then it would have to be someone they both knew? So is Payne's story a crock? Neither Keith nor Anderson worked on the gang force. I checked. Even you said that Keith and Anderson hardly knew each other."

Brit popped his knuckles. "They didn't. Sure, we ran into Anderson while working a case or two, but that's it."

"Maybe we should look back at those cases," Duke said.

"Maybe. But hell, I'm just thinking out loud. None of those cases ever felt like trouble." Brit gritted his teeth. He was so tired of not finding answers.

"Keep thinking," Duke said. "Because I sure as hell have hit a brick wall." The toothpick shifted to the left side of Duke's mouth.

"I'm on the task force now, too." Brit looked at the clock. "I'll see you tomorrow at ten."

As Brit walked out, he decided to give Payne a call—see about meeting him again. Maybe Payne had gotten the gang wrong. Back in his office, he got Payne on his cell phone. As usual, the man only wanted to gripe about how he was putting his life on the line.

"We offered you police protection," Brit insisted when Payne balked about meeting him.

"Then they'd find out for sure," Payne snapped.

Brit got the feeling that Payne refused protection because he was doing his own shady business, not because of being fingered as a snitch. "They wouldn't," Brit said.

"I don't want to have a cop up my ass."

"Then if you get hurt, it's on you." After a few more minutes of dialogue, Brit jotted down the address where Payne finally agreed to meet him. "You be there at midnight or I'll come looking for you. And if I have to look for you, I swear to God, I'll find some reason for you to do time."

When he hung up, he remembered that last night, he and Quarles had spent most of the night combing through the files and going through mug shots at the diner across the street from the hotel. He'd kept an eye on Cali's hotel door all night.

He wouldn't be able to do that tonight. And that thought didn't sit well with him. The fact that he cared didn't sit well either. The fact that he wanted to be in that hotel room with her, both of them naked, annoyed the hell out of him.

Fighting back a jumble of emotions he blamed on lack of sleep, he headed out. He was almost in his car, when he saw the cat darting across the parking lot toward him.

She stopped a few feet away, stared, and then slowly inched closer. Her gold eyes studied him, and she let out a soft purr.

"I left food earlier. It's over there."

She did a figure eight around his leg, gazing up at him with a needy expression.

"Don't do this." He scowled. "We're not buddies. I'm not the attaching kind."

He squatted down and held out his hand. She moved in and rubbed the side of her face on the tip of his fingers. When he turned his hand over, she darted back a foot. "Still don't trust me, huh?"

She moved a bit closer. "Okay, since we're talking, the white Buick isn't a litter box. Crap on Adams' car again, and the shit will hit the fan." He glanced at his watch. "Now go. I got another woman to see about."

~

Brit called her when he parked in front of the school. Then, hungry to see her, he got out and waited by the glass doors. When she came strolling down the hall, he watched her body move toward him, and his blood thickened with sexual awareness. He smiled. The smile she returned appeared forced, and he remembered how she'd looked today. Terrified. But of what? Was he right that she was hiding something?

She pushed the doors open and as she got closer, his gaze moved to her lips, and he was hit with the longing to kiss her. He didn't do it, but he did put his hand on her lower back.

He felt her flinch and she stepped away from his touch. For some reason, her reaction reminded him of the cat. Scared. Jumpy. She didn't trust him. The thought hurt. Then he recalled how he'd been an ass to her in the beginning. Trust needed to be earned.

"Bad day?" he asked when he caught up with her. Hoping he would find the answer to what she might be hiding.

"Bad day, bad week, bad month. Bad few years."

"How can I make it better?" he asked and meant it. Because damn it, he understood how she felt. Grief wasn't easy to deal with.

"Tell me I can go home to my apartment. I just want to get back home and start my life over."

"You will soon enough." They walked, only their footsteps filling the silence. When they got to their cars, he glanced around again. While there wasn't a white pickup in sight, Brit had decided to drive around a while to make sure no one followed them. Leaving her tonight would be difficult, but it would be impossible if he didn't do everything in his power to make sure that Stan couldn't find her.

Still aching to touch her, he cratered. He reached up and brushed his hand down her cheek to her neck. This time she didn't pull away. A few strands of blonde hair on her neck caught in his fingers. He remembered how it had looked that first night at her apartment—all loose and soft, shimmering around her shoulders. What he wouldn't give to yank that clip from her hair; what he wouldn't give to feel her hair on his naked chest.

"You follow me, okay? I'm not going straight to the motel. I want to make sure no one is trailing us." He brushed his hand to the back of her neck, mesmerized at how his palm fit perfectly into the curve of her neck. He wanted to touch her like this everywhere, without clothes. To know every dip and sway of her body.

"We're going to catch this guy," he said.

She caught his hand, pulled it away, and released it, but she continued to stare up at him. "Do you ever sleep?"

He was so caught up in her blue eyes, he barely heard her. "Huh?"

"Your eyes are bloodshot. You work all night and now you're working today."

"I'm not on duty now."

"Then what are you doing here?"

"I'm making sure you're not being followed."

"But you're not getting paid."

"I'll let you buy dinner tonight." And maybe you'll wear your hair down for me.

"You don't have to do that."

"Okay, I'll pay for dinner." He grinned and took her keys from her hands and hit the button to open her doors. As he leaned forward, he caught her scent, that soft flowery perfume. He remembered her sweater in his car. "I have your sweater."

157

"I have your jacket," she said. "It's in the backseat." She glanced to her back seat and started to reach for it. He stopped her.

"I'll get it later. Let's get out of here before we get company."

He rode around for almost ten minutes, keeping his eyes on Cali's Honda behind him and any cars behind her. Finally, satisfied that no one tailed them, he headed toward the hotel. Toward temptation, and he was feeling damn weak right now. He reminded himself that she might be keeping secrets, but even that didn't sate his need to have her. To have her close.

~

Cali pulled into the hotel parking lot and practiced her send-off speech one more time. "I'm really tired, and all I want to do is go to bed and sleep, so if you don't mind, I'm just going to skip dinner. Besides, I'm sure you've got better things to do. Like that hot little babe you brought to my school today. Remember, the one who has bigger tits and longer legs than I do?"

She startled when he opened her car door.

"You talk to yourself very often?"

"Only on Fridays," she quipped to hide her nervousness and got out. A cool breeze brushed past them. She pulled her thin cardigan closed, recalled her speech, and decided to leave out the bigger tits and legs part. "I . . ." She stuttered to a halt when he reached out and released her banana clip, letting her hair fall. "What are you doing?"

His sexy grin came on strong. "If you can talk to yourself on Fridays, you should be able to let your hair down." He tossed her banana clip in her front seat, pulled her to the side, and shut the car door. "Where do you want to take me for dinner?"

She ran a hand through her hair. Then she remembered her talk to send him packing. "You don't have to stay." Her breath caught when he pressed a finger over her lips.

"I want to." He stared at her mouth. "I want . . ."

Chapter Twenty

"You probably have plans," she said against his finger, and when she looked up at him she got the idea that he was considering kissing her. She stepped back, but butted against her car.

He pressed closer. "I do have plans. I'm having dinner with you." His gaze went to her mouth again. "Do you have any idea how badly I want to kiss you right now?"

Her breath caught. "No, but . . ." She remembered the woman he'd had with him today. "I don't think you should do that."

"Why not?" He moved in. His lips were so close she could feel the moisture from his breath.

"Because . . ." She forgot why it wasn't a good idea.

He moved closer, his head lowered just a bit. His lips brushed ever so lightly against hers.

"Because . . ." There had been a reason why he shouldn't kiss her. She'd known it, but it was gone.

"Too late now." His lips melted against hers.

She forgot about telling him to stop—forgot everything. The only thing she knew was that he tasted so good—felt so good. The ache she felt in her heart for the last week, even the ache she'd felt since she'd heard her mom had cancer, lifted like fog. An odd thought ran though her mind. This was what it felt to be alive. A part of her had died with her mother, and had been dying since she learned her of mother's cancer.

When his tongue slipped between her lips, she opened her mouth, invited him inside. His hand moved through her hair to cup the back of her head. He tilted her head slightly to the side to deepen the kiss. She leaned into him, let her tongue move into his mouth. Her breasts slid across his chest. His other hand moved between her and the car. His palm glided under her cardigan, under her pink sweater, and his palm moved over the bare skin of her lower back.

"Get a room," someone yelled from a passing car.

They jerked apart. She covered her mouth with her hand. "You shouldn't have done that," she said behind her fingers.

She darted off toward her room—part of her hoping he would leave, another part hoping he wouldn't. His footsteps echoed along with hers. When she opened her door, she turned to give him the speech.

"I'm tired." She couldn't remember what came next in the speech. Oh, yeah, he should leave. She opened her mouth but—

"Me, too." He nudged her inside and shut the door.

They stood there, staring at each other. She noticed his breathing sounded as labored at hers. Hands clenched, she glanced at the bed. His taste still lingered on her tongue, the feel of his body against hers echoed in her memory like a sweet dream, or a poem too good to be forgotten. She glanced up and caught him studying the bed.

Her breath caught; the memory of his kiss vibrated through her. She turned and stared at the wall and then she swung around. "I'm not having sex with you,"

He exhaled so hard she saw the hair resting against his brow flutter with his breath.

He nodded. "I can deal with that." He looked around for a second and then back at her. "I didn't mean for that to get out of hand." He looked at the clock. "We'll have an early dinner and—"

The send-off speech, she needed to do the speech. "I think you should leave."

He stared at her, frowned, and then ran a hand through his hair. "And I don't think that's a good idea."

"Well, I'm not so sure that your opinion—"

"Three!" He blurted out. "Count them. Three." He held out three fingers. "Three people connected with Stan Humphrey have ended up dead. And now he's after you. And . . . because of a kiss, because of a moment that got out of hand you want to put your life at risk. The kiss was a mistake. It won't happen again."

Angry, confused, and still so weak, she tossed her purse on the chair, grabbed her suitcase, and went into the bathroom to take a shower. A cold shower.

She'd never needed a cold shower before. However, she'd never felt that achy emptiness between her legs like she had now. Never felt her entire body tingle with need, want and desire. Sex had always been something she thought was overrated. Most of the times she didn't cross the finish line and she just faked it. She'd even considered the fact that something might be wrong with her. She'd gone for two years without getting naked with someone before Stan, and her experiences with him showed her she hadn't really been missing anything.

So what was happening? Why now? Why Brit? Why did she feel as if she would die if he didn't make love to her? Oh yeah, her mother had explained that their auras had the hots for each other.

Maybe Dr. Roberts was wrong. Maybe she was crazy!

Ten minutes later, she came out of the bathroom, showered, cooled off, and feeling a bit more in control. Her gaze lit on him, stretched out on her bed, shoes off, both pillows stacked behind his head. His eyes shut. He'd turned the television on and the remote rested on his flat stomach.

But she'd bet beneath the shirt he wasn't flat. She'd bet he had those ripples caused by tight muscles. She'd imagined him without his shirt. Imagined her in bed beside him without his shirt. Her breath caught when she realized what she was doing. She was literally undressing the guy in her mind. Men did that. Not women. She jerked her gaze up to the ceiling.

Dang those auras!

Not that she believed, but she needed something to blame it on. And blaming auras was as good as anything.

Her gaze shifted back to him again. Asleep. Had it been so easy for him to forget the kiss? Her ego took a direct hit.

Suddenly his eye lids fluttered open, and they stared at each other. She felt his gaze whisper down her body. Saw the male appreciation warm his blue-green eyes. Okay, so her ego felt a little better, but her willpower took another nosedive.

She'd purposely gone through her suitcase and found the most unappealing thing she'd brought with her. Gray sweats and an extra large white T-shirt. She had also put her hair back up, because she hadn't missed the way he'd watched it tumble down around her shoulders after he'd unclasped it.

"You like Italian?" he asked.

He looked part Italian. Yeah, she liked. But he meant food, and she should be thinking food. She'd never eaten lunch and the donut he brought her for breakfast had worn off hours ago.

He sat up, shifted his weight and pressed against the headboard. "There's an Italian place right around the corner. I think they deliver." He pointed to the phonebook he had open beside him. "Someone told me they have wonderful chicken marsala and veal parmesan. We could get one of each and share."

She laced her fingers together. Just like that she remembered another reason this whole thing felt wrong. And by "whole thing" she meant the kiss, his being in a hotel room with her, her lusting after his body. "Seriously, don't you have somewhere else that you should be?"

"Nope." He reached for the phone. "I'll order."

"What about your girlfriend?" The question slipped out. A question she felt compelled to ask, but shouldn't.

"She dumped me about eight weeks ago." He pulled the phone book closer and punched in the number.

"She didn't look too upset today." Oh, crap, why didn't she just shut up? He was going to' think she was jealous. And she wasn't jealous. Or was she?

He glanced up, his eyes widened at her question. "Is that why you were upset today?"

She flushed. "I wasn't upset."

He held up a finger. "I'd like to place an order to go. Chicken Marsala and Veal Parmesan."

When he stopped talking, she jumped in. "I wasn't upset. It's none of my business. But she should be upset."

He placed his hand over the phone. "I don't think she would care. That was my sister."

Sister? Suddenly hit by the resemblance between the two of them, she felt like an idiot. She should have known. Even more, she should have never mentioned it.

"Do you want salad and bread sticks?" He arched his eyebrows at her.

She nodded, then dropped into the chair and only halfway listened as he finished ordering and gave the hotel address. Then he hung up.

She stared at the television. She felt him watching her, not the TV.

"Her name is Susan," he said. "She lives in Austin. I guess it was rude of me not to introduce her, but I got the call about the pickup and I didn't think."

"Maybe you should go spend some time with her."

"I did while you were in school."

"Bet she'd like to see you again. Living out of town and all." Cali's focus stayed glued to the television. Not that she listened.

He said something to her, and she glanced at him briefly. "Can we just watch some television?"

His gaze shifted back to the television and then back to her. "It's a commercial."

"I like commercials," she said.

"So erectile dysfunction is of a real interest to you?" He chuckled.

She refocused on the television, saw the man and woman lounging in bathtubs and blushed. "This whole thing is too awkward."

"What's awkward?"

"This." She eyed him. He still looked good, too good. "You, laying on my hotel bed and ordering takeout food. You being nice one minute and a jerk the next."

The sudden crease between his eyebrows hinted at his frustration. "I admit I wasn't on my best behavior in the beginning, but I've been working on that."

"And that's confusing me. So go back to being a jerk."

He frowned. "Look. All I want to do is make sure you're okay. Make sure you come out of all this without being hurt."

"Really? That's all you want? And that kiss out there was what?"

"The kiss was probably a mistake."

Probably? He stared at her as if waiting for her to throw the next verbal blow, but she didn't have one. She really did need to learn to argue better.

The news broadcaster announced a news flash on the television. Their argument went on pause, and they focused on the screen. "A woman's body was found. We're told Galveston police suspect the boyfriend to be the killer."

"You see!" he said. "That's why I'm here. You could be next." He jumped off the bed, tossed the remote down, and stormed into the bathroom. The door thudded closed. And Cali's heart thudded with it.

The sound of shower spraying water onto the plastic curtain became apparent. The news continued. She focused on that, anything not to think about him being naked in the shower. The reporter shifted subjects to a report about the Houston cops who were recently killed. They splashed Mike Anderson's photo across the screen. She remembered him from her apartment, but she also remembered him from somewhere else, too. But from where?

It's important, Cali. You need to remember. Her mom's voice echoed inside her head.

Chapter Twenty-One

Still frowning, Brit stepped out of the cold shower and grabbed the towel that hung over the curtain rod. The moment he buried his face into the nubby white cotton, he regretted it.

The musky aroma of woman mixed with a flowery fragrance clung to the damp cloth. Her scent. The vision of her rubbing the towel over her naked curves filled his head. The memory of the kiss whispered through his mind. The recollection of how soft her skin had felt when he'd slipped his hand under her sweater to caress her bare back had him aching to touch more. He breathed in, letting the aroma of the towel drive him crazy, because sniffing towels and sweaters was as close as he could afford to get to her.

He hadn't been kidding about the kiss being a mistake. Since when did he lose his head and start making out in public? He wasn't a sixteen-year-old hormone-crazed kid anymore. What the hell had he been thinking?

He moved the towel down his chest and lower, only to discover the cold shower hadn't helped. Friggin' hell. He couldn't face her with his dick as hard as wood. And taking care of the problem with her in the next room didn't feel right.

Leaning against the sink, he tried to think about something that would make him go limp. The thought that tomorrow he would have to attend his mom's birthday party did the trick. The fact that his mind took him to his mom, reminded him how he'd compared Cali to his mother in the beginning. He remembered thinking she was hiding something earlier when he'd shown up at the school after Garcia had called. Had it only been seeing him with Susan that had her upset? Or was it more?

He pulled his underwear and jeans off the towel rack where he'd hung them. His jeans weren't zipped when he heard the knock on the hotel's door.

"Don't you dare open that," he yelled and stepped out of the bathroom as he finished zipping.

She stood next to the door, her purse in her hands. Her eyes rounded. "It's . . . our dinner."

He stepped to the window and carefully slid the curtain back. At the sight of the young teenage boy, he relaxed, and called out. "Just a sec." He reached in his back pocket for his wallet.

"Here." She shook three twenties at him. "Take it."

He took the money, opened the door, and exchanged the twenties for plastic bags full of food. Backing up, he set dinner on the dresser, and started pulling out the white boxes. When he looked up, he met her frown.

It suddenly occurred to him that he didn't have a shirt on. Frowning, he dropped the food and headed for the bathroom to finish getting dressed.

When he came back out, she sat on the bed, one of the boxes balanced on her lap. Her knife and fork were unwrapped and she had a napkin spread out on part of her lap. She glanced up and picked up her plastic silverware as if she'd been waiting for him before she began to eat. Another sign of her impeccable manners. He walked to the dresser, collected his own box, and sat on the other side of the bed.

When his weight shifted the mattress, a frown pulled at her mouth. He considered getting up and sitting in the chair, but that felt silly. He wasn't going to attack her. Besides, he couldn't sleep sitting up in a chair, and that's exactly what he hoped to do after dinner.

Tense silence filled the room, and he could feel her trying to build a wall around herself.

He didn't want a damn wall between them.

"How's your dinner?" he asked.

"Good," she said.

One word. And she didn't even look at him. Yup, she was building a wall.

"How was your day?" he asked, determined to tear it down.

"Fine."

One word.

"Did your principal talk to you about me showing up?"

"No."

One word.

"Did you want to share entrees?" he asked.

She wrapped some pasta around the plastic fork, cut the few strings of pasta hanging off with her knife. "I'm fine."

Two words.

But he needed more. "Why not?"

He saw her shoulders tightened, and while making her mad wasn't his objective, sometimes that's what it took to bring down someone's wall.

She dropped her fork and knife and raised her eyes. "I'm not sure I know you well enough to eat after you," she said in an oh-so-polite manner. While anger flashed in her blue eyes, obviously it wasn't enough, because the wall she built between them still stood. Mentally, he could see her add another few bricks.

"That's funny," he said.

"What's funny?" Her tone was tight enough to strangle someone.

"You worried about germs. It didn't stop you from putting your tongue in my mouth in the parking lot."

Her gorgeous mouth dropped open. "I didn't do that."

"Yes, you did."

She opened her mouth to deny it and then closed it. "But you started it."

"You didn't tell me to stop."

Her frown deepened. "I already told you that I'm not—"

"Having sex with me. Yeah, I know, I heard you the first time. But I'm not talking sex. I'm talking about sharing your Chicken Marsala. And maybe sharing a conversation. I hate the silent treatment. I don't see any reason why we can't be civil to each other."

She looked down at her food and stared at her chicken. "I wasn't giving you the silent treatment." She paused. "Okay, maybe I was, but this is crazy."

"What part of this is crazy?" he asked, wishing she'd look at him again.

"All of it." She finally raised her eyes. He somehow sensed the wall she'd built was gone.

"It does feel crazy," he said, meaning what was happening between them. He took a bite of his veal and the tomato sauce and cheese flavored his tongue.

She exhaled. "Here." She handed him the box of food. "Let's swap."

"You sure?" He smiled.

"Yes."

He couldn't help but wonder if he could change her mind about the sex that easily.

He waited until she took a bite from his box before he started eating. They ate in silence, but it was no longer the tense, angry kind of silence.

"Save room for dessert." He forked another piece of sauce-laden chicken and a mushroom into his mouth.

"What did you get for dessert?" She started to close her box lid.

He reached over and pierced the last piece of veal from her box and brought it to his lips.

"Italian cream cake," he said around the flavors in his mouth. As he ate the last bite of chicken, he suddenly realized something. For the last few weeks, he'd eaten when his gut hurt from hunger, but he hadn't tasted or savored food. Hell, he hadn't tasted or savored life.

And while he didn't quite understand it, he sensed the change had something, or rather everything, to do with her.

~

After eating two small bites of dessert, Cali, still sitting on her side of the bed, set the cake down beside her and started gathering up the to-go boxes. When she looked over at him, he was watching her.

"You not going to finish that?" He pointed his fork at her and gazed at her cake.

"No. I'm full." She passed him the Styrofoam box with her half of cake in it and she watched him devour it in three bites.

When he looked up, he flinched to see her watching him.

"What?" he said around the cake and covered his mouth. He swallowed. "Did I break some manner thing?"

She grinned. "No." She'd actually been thinking she liked how he ate with enthusiasm.

"Then why are you looking at me like the manner police?"

"I'm not looking at you like the manner police," she said.

"Bull crap. I've seen the way you eat, all proper-like. You used your knife and did that roll thing with your fork and pasta." He pointed at her with the fork. "And you put your napkin in your lap."

Her mouth dropped open a bit. "Wait. Are you accusing me of making fun of how you eat, or are you making fun of the way I eat?"

"I'm not making fun of you. I'm just saying you eat like you're at some richified dinner party."

"I do not," she said, not really insulted, because of the humor she saw in his eyes. He didn't smile nearly enough. "I just eat the way my mother taught me to eat."

"Which is richified," he said and chuckled. "And then there's all the pleases and thank yous you hand out."

She rolled her eyes. "Since when did being polite become a bad thing?"

"I didn't say it was bad. It just makes you different." He continued to grin at her, then scraped the bottom of his Styrofoam make-shift plate and slid the fork into his mouth to savor the last of the icing. He pulled the fork out of his mouth slowly. "I'll bet you wouldn't have done that," he said.

"I do that all the time."

"You don't cuss." He pointed at her again with the fork. "When you were mad the day you couldn't find your keys, you said 'darn it.'" He laughed again. "Do you know what I say when I lose my keys?"

She frowned. "I can imagine. Anyway, I don't use bad language because I'm a teacher."

"Teachers don't cuss?" He repositioned himself lower on the bed, and looked at her through his thick lashes.

"If I cuss outside the classroom, then I'm likely to cuss inside the classroom. And the last thing a teacher needs is a student going home and telling their parents that Miss McKay used bad language."

He rested his hand on his flat stomach and continued to look up at her with his smirky grin on his face. "I bet you couldn't say shit if you had a mouthful of it."

"I can say dickhead."

He tilted his head back and laughed. "You know I'm just teasing you."

"Right," she said and still was only half-annoyed. What was it about him that made her feel lighter?

"Seriously, you're perfect." His smile faded to something softer, something that reminded her of how he looked before he'd kissed her.

He kissed just like he ate, as if he really enjoyed it.

"Don't change a thing," he said.

He picked up the remote and flicked channels until he found a movie.

Sneaking a peek, she found him watching her and not the television. She stood up. "I'm going to brush my teeth. Are you going to make fun of me for doing that, too?"

He smiled. "No."

She started for the bathroom.

"But can I borrow your toothbrush when you're done?"

She swung around. "No!"

She heard him laughing as she shut the bathroom door. When she looked up at her reflection, she was smiling. She almost didn't recognize herself. Maybe he wasn't the only one who needed to laugh more.

~

When she walked out a few minutes later, she grabbed a pillow and stretched out with her head at the foot of the bed. Pillow tucked beneath her, she latched her arms around it and pretended to watch television.

"You have to work?" she asked without looking back.

"Yeah," he said. "I'll have some cops ride by."

"I'm sure I'm fine," she said. Burying her chin deeper into the pillow, she thought about Stan catching her at the lawyer's office. Fear did a number on her full stomach. Then for some reason, she recalled Stan saying he hadn't been the one to shoot at her. She almost told Brit that, but thought better of it. He'd just think she was defending Stan again.

Then she remembered the dream last night, when Mom had said . . . No. Her maternal psyche had said that Stan hadn't killed anybody—that Nolan was after him, and that Stan was looking for the bracelet because he needed money to get away. Could Nolan have been the one who shot at her door? Had he been aiming at Stan?

There had been blood on the door. Was it blood from his two friends? Or had Stan been shot? She closed her eyes and tried to remember if he'd seemed hurt when he came at her at the parking lot.

No, he had seemed fine. Then all of a sudden, she recalled that he'd smelled really bad. Had it been because he'd been in the hotel room with the dead bodies? Oh, God, what kind of person would do that?

She chewed on those thoughts and questions while chewing on her lip. Footsteps sounded outside the door. She stiffened, then relaxed when she heard them pass. Taking a deep breath, she glanced over her shoulder. Brit was asleep. Something told her all she had to do was scream, and he'd be up. But what if Stan showed up while Brit was at work? Suddenly, she wasn't so eager for him to leave.

~

Cali heard the beeping noise, but pushed it away. The warm mattress beneath her shifted slightly. Or was it a mattress? It felt too warm, too much like . . . someone. A male someone. Oh, crap!

Everything came back. Brit in bed with her. She felt the warmth of bare skin under her cheek. When had he removed his shirt? When had she decided to trade out her pillow for his chest? Bare chest. She started to jerk up when she heard and felt him take a sharp breath.

Mortified, she feigned sleep. That's when she realized her head wasn't the only thing on top of him. Her right arm and hand rested across the man's bare stomach. Yup, mortified pretty much defined her mood right now.

Chapter Twenty-Two

He inhaled again, sharply. He shifted and through the tiniest slit in her eyes, she saw him look at his watch.

Slowly, as if not wanting to wake her, he picked up her hand and removed it from his stomach. Then she felt him slide out from under her. Cali's head dropped to the warm spot on the mattress. She kept her eyes shut, praying he wouldn't guess she was awake. She felt the mattress shift as he left the bed. She heard him heading to the bathroom.

In a few minutes, he came back and sat on the edge of the bed. She felt him staring. He leaned down and pulled the blanket across her. The mattress shifted ever so slightly and she felt his breath on her ear. Lightly, he pressed his lips against her cheek. The minty scent of mouthwash filled her nose.

"Damn, you're pretty," he whispered and stood up.

Her heart stopped beating, and she wished he'd crawl back in bed, pull her into his arms and make love to her.

Instead, she heard him gathering his things from the bedside table, and he moved to the door. He didn't leave quickly, but stood there for several seconds before finally walking out.

As soon as the door clicked shut, she rolled over and pulled the pillow he'd been using closer to her face. It smelled like him.

Closing her eyes, she shut everything out, and let herself drift off.

~

Brit stood at the motel door. He had to think about Keith and Anderson, he had to go to work. How long had she been in his arms tonight? He wished he'd been awake the entire time. Sweet heavens, she'd felt good. For that, he'd give up sleep.

He pushed a hand through his hair, realizing it had happened again. He'd slept. Really slept. It was her. Something about being with her allowed him to let go of the grief that had bunkered down in his soul. And not just the sleep, but he could taste food again. Being with her felt too damn good. He felt alive again.

Breathing in the cold November air, he looked around the parking lot. Perhaps, being with her felt good, but leaving her felt wrong. But he had to, didn't he? Thoughts of Keith made his feet move away from the door.

He got into his SUV and fit the keys in the ignition just as a car pulled into the lot. It parked two doors down from where Cali slept. Brit's hands curled around the steering wheel. He waited. A man got out. Dark hair, large build. Brit couldn't see his face. The stranger walked past the first door and stopped in front of Cali's room. Brit reached for his gun.

~

Cali had just drifted off, when she smelled the cigarette smoke. The dream pulled her in.

"You need to call her," Mama said.

The mattress shifted, and Cali rolled over. Her mom sat at the foot of the bed. Just a dream. "Call who?"

"Sara. Your student, the one whose mother has cancer. Call and remind her that her mom needs a second opinion."

Cali recalled the fear she'd seen in Sara's eyes. "What do you know?" Cali's chest constricted.

"Just that you need to call, dear. Convince her."

In the dream, Cali sat up and watched her mom blow smoke rings.

A smile tilted her mom's lips. "Do you remember when you sat in my lap and asked me to make smoke Os?"

Cali nodded. "Yeah, I remember."

Her mom studied the cigarette. "I would have never smoked around you if I'd known how bad it was." Silence fell like a soft rain, and her mom toyed with her bracelets. "You know, your father wasn't all bad in the beginning."

Cali considered telling her that she didn't want to talk about him. Her mother had brought him up once or twice those last weeks of her life, but Cali had always managed to steer the topic away. It hurt to talk about him. Hurt to remember the few vague memories she had of the man who'd walked out of her life.

Her mother pulled the cigarette to her lips. "I should have made him leave. But I wanted to fix him. Like you, I was a fixer. I thought if I loved him enough he would change." Her mom stared at Cali as if trying to read her mind. "Oh, God," her mom said as tears filled her eyes. "You heard us that night, didn't you?"

"What night?" Cali felt a familiar ache stir in her chest.

A tear rolled down her mom's face. "Why didn't I figure this out?"

The memory surfaced in Cali's mind. She was four. She hugged her worn teddy bear in her arms and stood outside her parent's bedroom door. The loud voices had woken her up. Sometimes he screamed really loudly at her mother, and Cali wanted to make sure her mama was okay.

"I'm so sorry," her mother said. "I should have realized. That's why you hated kindergarten and summer camps. You were afraid I'd leave you."

Cali closed her eyes as the memory replayed her father's voice. "Just leave her. She's always in the way. Someone else will care for her. The state has homes for kids. Come with me." Her father had wanted her mom to give her away.

"Oh, baby." Her mother's voice shook with emotion. "You've been afraid all this time. And now I have left you."

Cali swallowed the lump of pain. "You were a great mom." And she meant it. Her mother had put her first—over her career, over the occasional men she'd dated. Cali had never questioned her place in her mother's life. She'd been first. Now Cali wondered if that had been right for her mom to do that.

"We did okay, didn't we?" Her mother brushed a hand over Cali's shoulder. Warmth seeped from her touch, and the age-old hurt began to disappear.

Her mom swung around and looked at the door. For a second, she appeared panicked, then she relaxed. "The detective really isn't a dickhead, Cali."

"I know," she said.

"And there's nothing wrong with how you eat."

Cali sighed. "I know that, too." She leaned back into the pillow and felt the next realm of sleep calling her. "I'm so tired, Mom."

"You shouldn't stay here again. Tomorrow, find a different place." She stood and went to stand by the door, staring at it as if she could see out. "Find another motel room, or—"

"I'm fine." Cali felt her mind slipping away.

"You're not fine. Don't tune me out, girl. You have to listen. Cali . . ."

~

Brit quietly opened his car door, gun aimed, finger on the trigger. He made it to the hood of his SUV when the man walked to the next hotel door, pulled out a card key from his pocket and let himself in.

Relaxing his grip on the gun, Brit took a deep breath. He couldn't do it. He couldn't leave her when a man who'd already committed three murders was looking for her. Grabbing his cell phone from his pocket, he hit the memory button until he found Quarles' number.

Brit spoke as soon as his partner answered. "Remember the diner from yesterday? Meet me at the hotel parking lot across the street."

"That chick's there, isn't she?" Quarles asked.

Brit hadn't explained last night, but he knew Quarles had been suspicious. Brit hadn't wanted to admit it then, but now he didn't care what Quarles knew. "Yeah. Just meet me there. And tell Adams we're going to be out all night." Brit looked at his watch, thinking about his appointment with Payne at midnight. "And hurry."

~

Twenty minutes later, his partner pulled up beside him. Brit gave him the short explanation about his meeting with Payne.

"No," Quarles said. "Let me go talk to Payne. You stay here and babysit. You're the one who has the hots for her."

"Look, you don't know Payne. You don't know how he works. I do. He won't talk to you. I just need you to watch out for her. Look, you're my partner. And I'm asking this as a favor."

Brit didn't know how Quarles would react to him throwing down the partner card. Considering they'd only been partners for two weeks, and the fact that Brit had mostly treated Quarles like a stomach virus, he honestly figured Quarles would tell him to blow smoke up someone else's ass.

"One hour," Quarles said. The man held up a finger. "After that, I'll come looking for you."

Brit thumped Quarles' shoulder. "Thanks."

"Thank me by getting your ass back in one piece with something that we can use to take down these guys."

"You got it." Brit started to walk away, but he heard Quarles speak.

"By the way, I took your sister to dinner tonight."

Brit turned, his brotherly instincts on alert. "Why?"

"Because I was hungry." He paused. "Because I like her. Because she's beautiful." His voice didn't waver. "Is this going to be a problem?"

Brit looked at his partner. "She doesn't even live here."

"She visits regularly. And Austin isn't that far away."

Brit popped his knuckles. "What do you want to come of this?"

"Come of it?" Quarles chucked. "It's a little soon to be asking me my intentions, isn't it?"

Brit frowned. "I swear, if you hurt her, I'll shoot you. And I'm not joking."

Quarles didn't flinch. "I'm not planning on hurting her. We had dinner and we actually had a nice time."

Frowning, Brit got into his SUV and drove to meet Payne.

As his tires hummed against the pavement, he mentally collected everything he knew about Quarles. He'd talked about a few women he'd known in the past—relationships that had fizzled out. He was probably Brit's age, maybe even older. His family lived somewhere in east Texas. The man had a dog and took the damn thing to the vet constantly. Truth was, Quarles seemed decent enough. And Brit respected that he'd been upfront with him. But Brit simply didn't want to know the man who was trying to get into his sister's pants.

However, Big Sis probably wasn't waiting for baby brother's approval either. Susan had always done things her way. A freelance photographer, she'd made a name for herself and didn't live her life by anyone else's rules. He actually respected that about her, too.

After a minute, Brit decided he didn't have the right to tell Susan what to do. But he hadn't lied to Quarles. If the man hurt his sister, he'd answer to Brit.

Turning the corner to the house where Payne had said he'd be, Brit noticed the knots in his shoulders had lessened. The sleep he'd had in Cali's presence had worked magic again. Hope vibrated in his chest, and for the first time he felt like he might be able to do this. Find Keith's and Anderson's killer, live through the grief, and Cali . . . What with Cali? That was the million-dollar question.

"I'm not having sex with you."

Something told him that might change. Or maybe it was just him hoping.

After checking the address twice, he parked his SUV in the driveway. He got out and looked up and down the street at the overgrown lawns, the wrecked cars parked in the front yards. Not what you'd call suburban paradise. Rent must be cheap.

His gaze moved again to the shack of a house. Not a light on in the place. The tension crawled back into his shoulders. He pulled his gun out of his holster and eased toward the porch.

He took the first cracked step up to the house. The wood slats on the porch moaned. The door stood ajar. Something felt wrong. Deadly wrong. Then he smelled the blood.

Chapter Twenty-Three

"I'm going to be longer than an hour," Brit said into his cell phone thirty minutes later when Quarles answered his line.

"What? Payne's not talking?" Quarles chuckled. "Can I be the guy who hits you this time?"

Brit pressed a thumb against his temple. "Duke told you about that?" Not that he cared.

"Oh, yeah. He's quite proud of it." Quarles paused as if waiting for Brit's comeback. When Brit didn't offer one, Quarles cleared his throat. "What's up?"

"Someone got to Payne."

"Dead?" Quarles asked.

"Yeah."

"Crap. You think it's about his talking to us?"

"What else can I think?" Brit stepped away from the door as the paramedics wheeled Payne's body out.

"I know for a fact that you offered that lowlife protection. This isn't your fault."

"I know," Brit said. "But he's still dead, isn't he?" Guilt pinched at his gut.

"Where are you? I'll be right there."

"No. Don't leave her."

"Brit. The chick's fine. If that bastard Humphrey knew she was here he'd already have shown up."

"Please." Damn, did he really say that? Cali's manners were rubbing off on him. "I'm wrapping things up here, and I'll be back there. I don't know if Adams told you, but I'm only working half shifts. I'm on the task force."

"Me, too," Quarles said. "I talked Adams into it when I heard you were on it."

Brit leaned against the wall, trying not to look at the blood smeared on the floor. But damn, he'd seen too much death this month. "You didn't even know Keith."

"He was a fellow officer. That's all I need to know."

"Yeah." Brit stepped outside on the porch and took a deep breath, hoping to cleanse himself of the images. "Keep an eye on her. I'll be there soon."

~

Soon turned into three hours. It had taken him an hour to fill out the dreaded report and another two to find Rina Newman and get her under police protection and set up in a hotel. She'd insisted on it being a five star. Brit hadn't argued. If Adams refused to pay for it, not having her death on his conscience was worth the price of a fancy hotel for a few days.

The way he figured it, Rina had tipped someone off about Payne's slip of the tongue or Payne had done it himself. Either way, whoever had gotten Payne could get to Rina. Brit didn't think his conscience could take another hit.

Quarles wasn't happy when he finally returned to Cali's motel, and neither was Brit. He looked at his partner. "I told Adams you were chasing leads on the jewelry heist murder," he informed him.

"You mean you lied." Quarles' tone rang with frustration.

"Humphrey is a lead on the jewelry heist."

"Yeah, then why didn't you just tell them I was here babysitting?"

Brit didn't answer. "I'll see you tomorrow." He started toward the motel room door, wanting nothing more than to crawl into the bed with Cali and lose himself to sleep. Okay, maybe he'd like to lose himself in her. But that wasn't an option.

"Hey." Quarles' voice brought Brit around. Concern darkened the man's eyes. "Are you going to be okay?"

Brit squared off, not wanting to appear weak. "Yeah, but I've met my quota on seeing dead people for the month."

"Hell of a way to make a living, isn't it?"

"Yeah." Brit waved and let himself in, quietly. Cali, asleep on her stomach, lay on his side of the bed. Well, the side he'd slept on for the last two evenings. She didn't stir, and he hoped she wouldn't because she might push him away. He took his gun out and quietly set it on the nightstand as he toed off his shoes. Then he stripped off his shirt and dropped it on the floor. Out of habit, he undid his jeans and started to push them down when he caught himself. Would she balk that he'd stripped down to his boxers? Oh, hell, he was too tired to care. He shucked off his jeans and socks. Careful not to let his weight shift the mattress, he crawled in beside her and pulled the cover up over his waist.

Staring at the ceiling, he questioned if even her magic would bring him sleep tonight. The snapshots began to play inside his head—Keith, the dead men in the hotel, and now Payne.

A soft sigh escaped the sleeping woman beside him. Brit held his breath and hoped like hell that she didn't wake up and ask him to go. Instead, she rolled over, found his shoulder and rubbed her soft cheek against his bare chest. Her hand dropped to rest low on his abdomen and he rode the wave of pleasure that followed her feather-light touch. The softness of her breasts melted against his side and his loose boxers suddenly felt tight.

He swallowed and tried to just enjoy having her close, because he knew he couldn't have more. But why couldn't he? Obviously, all the blood he needed to work his brain had gone to other parts of his body, and he struggled to remember why he couldn't dip his head down and taste her mouth again, to let his hands roam up and under that T-shirt, to—

"I'm not having sex with you."

Yup, there was the reason he couldn't make a move. Now. When he made a move, and yes, he figured he eventually would, it would be when she was wide awake.

She turned her head and the wispy feel of her hair flowing across his chest actually brought a smile to his lips. Drawing in a careful breath, he let her scent fill his lungs.

Hearing the even sound of her breathing, he braved his next move. He rested his hand on her back. So damn soft. Then, even as his body cried out for sexual release, he found himself closing his eyes, letting go of the images haunting him, letting go of the pain. And he could let go as long as he held her.

~

A door slammed in the room next door and startled Cali awake. She opened her eyes and raised her head. When she did, she found herself staring into a hooded pair of blue-green eyes. Brit's eyes.

"Oh goodness." She lay stretched out on top of him like a blanket. Her panic came on quickly. The panic increased when she recognized the impressive bulge pressing against her abdomen.

With lightning speed, she rolled off him. Which might have been a good move had they not been on the edge of the bed. She landed with a thump on the floor, face down. She turned her head and rubbed the end of her nose. Moving her hand, she found herself staring at a men's pair of jeans and a shirt on the floor. One thought did a fast track around the corners of her sleep-dazed mind. If his clothes were down here, then what was he wearing up there?

Suddenly a pair of large feet landed a few inches from her face. He knelt. His position offered the answer to her question. His position also offered a better vista. A three-dimensional vista. Knees, round and dusted with hair, behind them extended thighs with firm muscles, and, holy moly, the man filled out his pair of navy boxers quite nicely. She stared, blinked, and stared some more.

Reality hit. Ogling a man's crotch was not polite. She turned her head, resting on her other cheek, and eyed the fabric fuzz on the top of the tan vacuum-damaged carpet.

"You okay?" His hands reached down as if to help her up.

"Fine." She let him help her stand and then she stepped away. She'd seen him shirtless last night and had been impressed, but now she had the whole package, well except for the boxers, and, oh boy.

"Bathroom." She lunged forward, but her foot wedged in his jeans. She tripped. He caught her around her waist, pulling her into his hot, almost naked body. Her hands and cheek pressed against his chest, and she pushed back.

He studied her, his hands still on her waist. "You sure you're okay?"

"Yeah." Her pulse sang while her heart tried to hum along.

He moved his hand from her waist and touched her cheek. His smile appeared sleepy and sexy. "Your nose is red." His voice came out husky with an early-morning drawl that oozed over her like warm honey.

"That happens when I fall on it."

He chuckled. "You're cute in the morning."

Rolling her eyes, she went to the bathroom and tried to find some of her dignity. And she knew exactly where to look for it—in the toilet.

~

It took two cups of the diner's strong coffee before Cali was able to put the embarrassment aside of waking up on top of him. She still wasn't sure how he'd talked her into coming here, but she suspected it had something to do with his saying please.

With caffeine pumping in her veins, she found a question that needed to be answered. "Did someone appoint you as my bodyguard?"

He dropped the menu and held his coffee cup between two palms. "I thought we covered this last night."

"Yeah, but I just don't get it." She took a deep breath and the smell of something cinnamon, like French toast, wafted as a waitress skirted by. Cali's stomach grumbled and she realized she was actually hungry. "Have you been assigned to me?"

He pulled his cup to his lips. "Not officially."

"Then unofficially, have you been told to protect me?"

"No. Why?"

"Because . . ." She reached for her own cup and hot liquid spilled from her heavy mug. "I'm just trying to figure out how we got here." Unwrapping her silverware, she let it clank against the dark veneered table.

"I think we walked across from the hotel," he answered with humor.

She frowned. "You know what I mean. I've know you less than a week and now I'm waking up in bed with you." She soaked up the coffee with a napkin and raised her gaze. "Is this what you do, go around saving damsels in distress?"

His eyes crinkled into a sexy smile. This morning, he wore a black T-shirt. Over the snug fitting cotton fabric, he'd donned a light blue buttoned-down shirt, which he left open. "You're a damsel?"

"I'm a serious damsel." She arranged her silverware. "How did we go from me not liking you to this?"

He pressed his forearms to the table and leaned so close she could smell the coffee and toothpaste on his breath. And since he didn't have any toothpaste, he'd probably borrowed hers. Had he used her toothbrush, too? Why not? They shared meals, a bed. What was a toothbrush thrown in?

"I don't know how we got here," he said. "But I'm not complaining. Are you?"

"It's scary," she confessed.

He frowned and leaned back. "What can I do to make it less scary?"

She considered it. "Give me a break from you."

He frowned. "What about Stan? I'd think he might scare you more."

She considered that, too. "He does."

"Then I say we just move slowly. No pressure."

She inhaled. "I guess."

Time ticked by while they each stared at the menu. "The omelets are good," he said, but Cali continued to hide behind the menu.

"What are you having?" He reached across and lowered her menu so he could see her. "No silent treatments, okay?"

She frowned. "Eggs and toast. And I'm not sharing my breakfast with you." It was a silly thing to say, but she felt the need for some barriers.

He nodded.

After they ordered, Brit asked, "What are your plans today?"

She poured cream into her coffee. "I'm visiting Tanya."

He lifted his freshly-filled cup to his mouth and steam rose around his lips. "Does Stan know where she lives?"

"He's never been over there."

"Does he know her last name? Is she in the phone book?"

Cali stirred her coffee, watching the dark chocolate color wash to a light brown. "I don't think he'd expect I would go to her house. We've just become friends."

"Okay." He stared into her eyes. "I get off at two."

What did he expect her to say? 'Good, I'll meet you back at the hotel for nap time and let you use my toothbrush again.'

"I could swing by Tanya's when I get off. It might be around five," he said. "We could eat dinner out for a change."

"You know where Tanya lives?" she asked.

"Yeah, I went by there the day I was looking for you, remember?"

"Yeah." She studied her silverware, to keep her eyes off him.

"Does that sound okay?" he asked.

So he expected to spend the afternoon with her again. And probably the night. She wasn't sure if she was happy about that or not. Or maybe she did know. The fact that she looked forward to it scared her.

"You work really odd hours," she said, wanting to change the direction of her thoughts.

He sipped from his cup again. "It's not always like this. We just have a lot of cases."

"You mean the cases about the two officers?" Her question brought the sadness back into his eyes, and suddenly she didn't feel so awkward anymore. She could relate to him in a big way. Two people, nose deep in grief. "I'm sorry about your partner."

His expression tightened, and Cali understood. She hated hearing those words, too. Yet now she understood everyone on the other side, wanting to let her know that they cared, that she wasn't alone. And she wanted to do that for him. "Death sucks."

The look in his eyes softened. "Yeah. How are you coping?"

"I miss her." The moment leant itself to the truth. "A lot."

"Are you still dreaming about her?"

She dropped the spoon. "How did you know—?"

"You told me," he said. "The day your car got broken into. Remember? The whole dreams and lesbians talk." He grinned slightly.

She bit down on her lip. "Oh, yeah. During my meltdown."

A smile made his eyes crinkle. "You seemed to bounce back."

She sipped her coffee, and bits and pieces of last night's dream started swimming through her mind. What had Mom told her?

"So you're still dreaming about her?" he asked again.

"Some. But I'm not crazy," she added and immediately wished she hadn't.

"I never thought you were." Honesty gave his voice a deeper quality, and Cali decided she liked his voice, along with everything else about him.

"You dream about your partner?" she asked.

He unrolled his napkin-clad silverware. "Not dream. I keep seeing him in my head at the morgue. Then I see an image of his wife." He inhaled. "It's not pretty."

"So he was married?"

"Yeah." He looked down at his phone on the table. "She's called a couple of times. I know she wants to know who killed her husband and I can't tell her."

Her chest hurt for Brit. "I'm sure she understands," she said.

"How could she when I don't?" He looked away.

"What was he like? Your partner?" She knew the question was unwanted, but she felt compelled to get him to talk about something besides the grief.

"We were as different as night and day. He was a Republican. I'm a Democrat. He believed in silver linings. I'm a realist. He was analytical. I'm a fly by the seat of my pants type. He was married, had a kid, went to church on Sunday for God's sake. I'm different."

She pondered his words. "So you're a spontaneous atheist and a diehard playboy who believes in taking care of the little guy, but doesn't want to add to the world's population because you really think the world is going to pot."

He laughed and curled his hands around his cup. "Yup, something like that." His grin lingered in his eyes, and Cali noticed he looked less tired this morning. He didn't resemble a dickhead at all, just someone who needed compassion. And she wanted to reach deep into her soul and offer him a big handful.

He twisted his cup in his palms and stared at her. "That sounds like something Keith would have said." He hesitated. "So you got me pegged. Tell me about you."

"What about me?" She tried not to look at his hands. He had nice hands. She remembered the kiss yesterday and how his palms had felt as they found their way under her sweater. The touch had lasted seconds, but the memory hung on.

"Did you always want to be a teacher? You're good at it."

Cali basked in his praise. "Thanks. I enjoy it, but I really only got into it because I loved art. I knew I needed some sort of income while I tried to make it as an artist. It wasn't until I was student teaching that I got the teaching bug."

"What kind of art?" he asked.

"Painting," she said. "Watercolors mostly."

He leaned back and draped one arm over the top of the booth. His shirt draped open and his T-shirt spread over his chest. Tight. "Are you good?"

"Of course. The first painting that I ever exhibited sold for a thousand dollars."

His eyes widened. "I'm impressed."

Cali grinned. "Don't be. My mother bought it."

He laughed. "Well, maybe she had good taste."

"She did," Cali admitted. "But I think she might have been a wee bit prejudiced."

"I didn't see any of your work in your apartment."

She glanced down and realigned her silverware. "I haven't painted since Mom got sick."

The waitress appeared with two plates weighing down her arms. She dropped the plates with a thud and refilled their coffees. They ate and talked about casual stuff, his job, her job.

She finished and pushed her plate to the side.

She watched him butter his toast, then he forked a bite of her eggs from her plate and put it in his mouth.

"Oh." He grimaced. "I forgot. We weren't sharing."

She rolled her eyes. "It's fine."

He sat there staring at her with a smile on his face. A sexy smile. Were they going to sleep together tonight?

"Tonight you're sleeping in your jeans," she said, then couldn't believe she'd said it out loud.

He dusted some crumbs from her chin as his smile widened. "Deal."

Chapter Twenty-Four

Brit followed Cali to Tanya's apartment. He didn't get out of the car, afraid if he did, he'd be too damn tempted to kiss her. So he simply watched her go inside. Then he went to check on Rina. He'd told Rina last night that she wasn't to leave the hotel and was to order meals from room service. But since when did women listen? He rode the elevator up to the tenth floor.

"Who is it?" Rina asked hesitantly when he knocked.

Good, Brit thought. Her fear would keep her in line and hopefully alive. "It's Detective Lowell."

The door swung open and Rina stood there wearing nothing but a white towel. And it wasn't a big towel either. "Come in." She arched one shoulder and smiled seductively.

Brit's gaze swept over her once before he took the step. Inside, he focused on the sun streaming through the window. When he glanced back, her towel had dropped a little lower.

"Why don't you get dressed," he said, his voice controlled.

"Why?" she whispered. "You see something you like?"

Brit spotted her clothes on the bed. "Get dressed."

She snatched up her clothes, and turned to go into the bathroom. But a step away from the door, she let the towel fall to the floor. Brit got a nice view of her naked ass. Then she turned around and gave him the full Monte.

She wiggled her fingers at him. "You want to take a shower with me?"

He couldn't say he didn't appreciate the view, because he did. But there wasn't an ounce of him that wanted to do more than appreciate it. "I said, get dressed."

"Your loss, because I'm good." She walked out.

Brit stood there, waiting to feel something more. Like regret. But nope. He hadn't even felt the normal male twitch. Considering it had been eight weeks since he'd buried himself inside a woman, it seemed odd.

He heard the shower spray, but instead of thinking about the woman who'd just appeared naked before him, he thought about Cali. Of how damn good her towel had smelled when he buried his face in it. If she'd made him the shower offer, he'd be rock hard and getting wet right now.

This morning, when he'd woken up with her on top of him, he'd entertained several ideas of how to proceed. All of them involved getting her naked. Thankfully, she'd taken the edge off his desire by taking a nosedive to the floor.

Letting out a breath, he settled into the hotel chair.

In a few minutes, Rina stepped out, looking wet and annoyed. "So if you're not here for a freebie, whatcha want?"

His impatience brought him to his feet. "I want to make sure you understand how serious this is."

"I told you last night. I didn't tell anyone."

"And what if Payne did?"

She frowned. "I can't stay here forever. I've got to work."

"No, you don't. I could get you some help until you got back on your feet." He recalled making that offer once before. Of course, she hadn't taken it.

"Why? I like my job." she said sarcastically. "I'm good at it."

"You want to die like Payne? Because let me tell you, it wasn't a pretty sight."

Her dark eyes widened. "But . . ."

"No buts. You don't leave this room. Order anything you want from room service. I'm going to talk to my captain today, and we'll probably move you to a safe house."

"But I barely saw the guys."

Her words hit like sharp ice chips. "Saw them? You said Payne told you. You didn't say you saw anyone. Them? There was more than one?"

She crossed her arms over her chest. "Two. One kid was waiting in the car. But—"

"What did he look like?" Hope swelled in Brit's chest.

She blinked. "I don't want to get in this any deeper."

Brit glared at her. "You're in this about as deep as you can get. You know Payne wouldn't have thought twice about giving you up to those guys. Besides if you saw them, then they saw you. The only way you're going to save your ass is to help us catch them. So just tell me. What did the other guy look like?"

She frowned. "They were both kids. One white and one black, the one who talked to Payne was black. He didn't say he'd killed anyone. He said one of his gang buddies had done it."

"What about the other one? Did you get a look at him?"

She wrung her hands together. "He had long hair. Red."

"Did you know what gang they were from?"

"I don't know gangs. They don't like to pay for sex."

Brit let out a deep breath. "Come on. I'm taking you in."

"But I thought I was going to stay here. Order room service, watch cable. Judge Judy comes on in an hour."

"I'll get you something to eat at the station," he said.

~

Cali sat at Tanya's kitchen table, drinking coffee. Tanya, who wore jeans and a neon purple sweater, stood at the sink washing a few dishes. "Oh, I want to show you my last three pairs of earrings." She dried her hands. "I want your honest opinion."

Cali followed her into a room where a big table was filled with a small welder, and gold wire, and where tiny beads were scattered on top.

Eager to show off her wares, Tanya held up a pair of earrings that looked like tiny acorns.

"They're beautiful," Cali said and meant it. Truth was, most of Tanya's pieces were beautiful, but they weren't Cali's style. These were different.

"You really like them? Because they're different from anything I've done. But when I was designing them, I thought about you."

Cali smiled. "They're really pretty. Honestly."

"Good. I made them for you." She handed Cali the pair.

"No." Cali set them down. "You need to give these to the gallery. They're waiting for you to replace the others."

"I already made those."

"You're serious?" Cali asked. "You made these for me?"

"Yes, now don't get mushy on me. Just say 'thank you.'"

"Thank you." Grinning, Cali went to the mirror and put them on. "How do they look?" She turned, tilting her head to one side, then the other.

"Classy," Tanya said. "The artist who designed them must be absolutely fabulous."

"She is." Cali looked around the room that served as Tanya's studio. "You must have been very busy."

"I was. Stayed up past midnight last night."

"What about Eric?" Cali asked.

Tanya frowned. "I'm going to meet him for dinner tonight, but I'm putting sex off until next weekend."

"Why?"

"You were right. Date three is too soon."

Cali flinched. "I was joking, I didn't mean—"

"I know you were joking. But you were right. I don't want to rush things. I'm always dirtying up the bed sheets with a guy, and then I'm sorry I didn't wait to find out if he was worth the price of laundering the sheets."

"Do you think Eric's a dickhead?"

"No. I just think I need to slow down. But speaking of dickheads, how's Brit?"

"He's fine." Cali looked back in the mirror at the earring.

"Just fine?"

Cali dropped down in a chair beside Tanya's work table. "Oh, heck. He's so fine."

Tanya rubbed her hands together like an excited child. "Details, I want details."

Cali spent ten minutes telling Tanya about Brit kissing her, then sleeping in the same bed with her.

"So nothing happened?"

"No. Nothing."

"And you're fine with that?" Tanya asked.

"Of course."

"You don't lie worth a shit," Tanya said.

Cali shook her head. "I don't know what I want. One minute I'm telling him we're not sharing food let alone bodily fluids, and the next, I wish he'd try something."

Tanya grinned. "What time is he picking you up?"

"He said around five."

"Great, that's just enough time."

"Time for what?"

"Shopping. I think you need to buy something new. Something sexier than your teacher attire."

~

Brit had delivered Rina to Adams and had just gotten settled into his chair when he felt someone staring at him from his office door. He hadn't looked up when he heard the sultry voice.

"Hey, Sexy."

Brit looked up and met the assistant DA, Shane Paxton's brown eyes, head on. His gaze traveled down her body. Her fitted black suit didn't hide all the curves that she loved to show off. It had been that body, coupled with her long red hair that had attracted him to her in the beginning. And it had been her willingness to accept a casual relationship with no expectations that kept him with her for two months.

He nodded. "How are you doing?"

"Lonely." She smiled.

"I don't buy that," he said. The woman had a list of men waiting in the wings. Shane didn't hide the fact that she liked to fuck, so much so that when Brit wasn't available, she'd make do with someone else. Oddly, he hadn't even been upset when he'd stopped by her place and found her ex walking out of the bedroom. Or at least, he hadn't ended things with her until a week later when she'd been rude to Keith's wife at a barbeque he'd taken her to.

"I have a case I'm looking into and then I'm going to leave work early and go home—all alone."

"Sometimes being alone is good," he said, trying to be diplomatic.

She frowned. "I came by to pay my condolences several times for Keith, but you were always out. I know how that had to hurt you."

"I appreciate it," he said and he did.

She moved in a bit. He didn't appreciate that.

She gave him a pouty frown. "You could look happier to see me, you know."

No, he couldn't. He wasn't even sure he had the energy to fake it. As much as he prided himself on having relationships that were purely physical, he'd learned a valuable lesson. In order to enjoy being with someone for longer than a time or two, at the very least he needed to like the person. He didn't like Shane.

His mind went to the blonde he'd had breakfast with. He liked Cali McKay.

A lot.

"What do you need, Shane?"

She grinned. "I could tell you, but I think it's still illegal in Texas."

He shook his head. "Sorry. I'm going to have to pass."

She frowned. "Is there someone else?"

"Maybe."

"She'd never have to know," Shane said.

"I would."

She laughed. "Please tell me you haven't gone and really fallen for someone. Not you."

"Maybe," he said again, thinking it was a lie, but deep down he knew it wasn't. And that pretty much scared the shit out of him.

~

At almost eleven, after pretty much having to out and out tell Shane that he wasn't going meet her later and screw her, Brit sat at a table with the six other officers on the task force. They were combing through everything they had, sifting through old files on gangs, new files on gangs, reading both Keith's and Anderson's old cases, trying to find a link between the two.

Adams walked in and looked at Brit. "Good call bringing Rina Newman in," he said.

Hope stirred. "She identify anyone?"

Adams shook his head. "Not yet. But just the information she did give us is going to help. I feel it in my gut."

"Are you going to put her in a safe house?" Quarles asked.

"Yeah. But she's bitching that it won't be the Marriott."

Brit grinned. "Hey, she's not a cheap date."

"I hear she runs about two hundred," Duke said. "But according to one john, she charges more for small deposits and early withdrawals."

They all laughed, even Adams, but he was the first to flip back to serious. "Well, all I can say is you better get this guy fast. I'm not sure we can keep her curtailed long. I heard she has a small habit."

Quarles leaned forward. "Then have her watched like a hawk. We might need her to testify when we catch those bastards."

"I will." Adams looked at the files strewn across the table. "You find anything we can use?"

"Not yet," Brit answered.

Adams looked at Quarles. "Did you come up with anything last night on the Goldstein homicide?"

A moment of silence hit before Quarles answered, "Nothing new."

"Nothing?" Adams asked. "Seems like with all we've got, this case should be easy to break."

Brit spoke up. "We've visited most of the connections to Humphrey and the Nolan guy. So far, no one knows anything."

"Have you talked to club owners where they played?"

"That's next on my list, sir," Quarles said.

"What about the girlfriend? Is she giving us anything?"

"She's told us everything she knows," Brit said.

"You sure?" Adams asked. "You know how her type is."

Brit sat up straighter. "Yeah, I'm sure."

"Have you talked to her, Quarles?" Adams asked.

"Mostly Brit's taken care of that."

Adams' uni-brow puckered. "I thought she didn't like you. Isn't she the one who came in here?"

"Yeah," Brit said. "But we've come to an understanding."

"What kind of an understanding?" Adam crossed his arms, and suspicion deepened the grooves in his forehead.

Brit leaned back in the straight chair until he had it balanced on the back two legs. "She's told me everything she knows. I believe her. She's a victim in this, not a suspect."

"Maybe Quarles should question her. To make sure." Adams kept his gaze on Brit as if reading between the lines.

But damn, was he that readable? "He wouldn't get anything that I haven't already gotten."

"Make sure what you're getting doesn't get us in trouble."

Brit snapped his chair forward. "What are you saying?"

"You know what I'm saying. We might need her to testify. Don't do anything to jeopardize this case, Lowell." He turned back to Quarles. "From now on, all contact between that girl and this force happens through you. Lowell stays away from her."

"That's bullshit." Brit gritted his teeth. No way would he stay away from Cali. He wasn't sleeping with her. Well, he was, but that's all he was doing. The fact that he wanted to do more was none of Adams' damn business.

"It's not bullshit. I call the shots." Adams tossed down an envelope in front of Quarles. "Ballistics came back on the bullet they got out of the chick's apartment. It's the same one they pulled out of the Clear Lake motel . We haven't gotten the blood results back, but it looks like the boyfriend is the guy. Make sure that she isn't trying to protect him."

~

The owner of the first honky-tonk where Stan and the band had played wasn't in when Brit and Quarles stopped by. The manager at the second bar could talk someone under the table, but he offered nothing new.

When Brit and Quarles got back into his SUV, Quarles moved the files to the back seat. His partner, normally too chatty, had been quiet since they left the precinct. Brit had an idea what kept Quarles from being his chipper self, too.

"I'm not having sex with her." Yet. Brit started the engine.

"I didn't ask," Quarles said, knowing exactly who "her" was. "But I do need to know how you want to work it."

"I'm not going to change a damn thing just because Adams believes I'm getting it on with her."

"That's fine. But Adams might be right. If I questioned her, maybe I'd be able to get something more."

"She's told me everything she knows."

"Are you sure?"

"I'm sure." And he was. Wasn't he?

"Fine." Quarles held up his hands. "But you'd better be right, because if she's lying, it's my ass on the line, too."

~

Brit snatched his windbreaker and headed out of the building. He'd had a frustrating day and the only thing he craved right now was Cali. Pushing open the door, he stormed across the parking lot.

A terrible soulful sound of a cat's cry brought him to a quick halt. He swung around and saw a white van parked with the back doors opened. Then he noticed the painted paw prints on the vehicle's door. The shelter? A heavyset man walked to the van with a cat carrier in his arms. The box dangled from side to side as if heavy.

The cat's cry echoed again. Brit's stomach clutched. This was the right thing, he told himself, and took another step to his SUV. Anderson had called the shelter. The one who wouldn't kill her or her kittens. Right thing.

He got into his SUV, put his key in the ignition. The cat's cries echoed again. Right thing. He closed his eyes.

He got out and hotfooted it to the van just as the man climbed into the front seat. "Hey." Brit knocked on the van's window.

The man rolled down the glass. "Yeah?"

"Mike Anderson called you, right?" At the sound of Brit's voice, the mama cat howled. The pitiful sound made his chest clutch.

"Anderson?" the man asked.

"You're the shelter that doesn't put them down, right?"

He shrugged. "We try to adopt them out, but we've got so many."

Brit gritted his teeth. "You're not from the no-kill shelter?"

He shrugged again. "Look, I'm just doing my job."

The cat howled again. "Shit!" Brit said.

~

An hour and a hundred dollars later, Brit stood in his laundry room filled with cat supplies. He had the cat box set up and food and water doled out. The three or four-week-old kittens, one black and two grays, and their mama hid behind the drier. Mama Cat, not happy about being relocated, stuck her head out and hissed at him.

"It's just temporary," Brit told her. "As soon as I find a no-kill shelter, you'll get a real home."

Hurrying to get a shower, he wondered where Susan was, but since her car wasn't out front he figured she was either at his mom's or with Quarles. But damn that whole thing didn't sit well with him.

He grabbed his work files from the table. Passing the door to the extra bedroom, he spied the wrapped gift on the unmade bed. "Damn!" He'd fucking forgotten about the birthday party from hell. As tempting as it was to bail out, Susan would have his head and then would probably go after his boys.

The idea of taking Cali to the party popped into his mind, but he slammed the lid on that one really quick. With his mom and whatever husband-of-the-week showed up with her, God only knew how the evening would go. The last thing he wanted to do was to try to explain his mom to Cali or explain Cali to his mom.

He raked a hand over his face and decided he'd get Quarles to watch Cali. Brit would only make an appearance at the party. Susan would balk, but if he explained, she'd understand. Yeah, he needed to talk to Susan.

Maybe he needed to talk to Cali, too, about Humphrey. Just to reconfirm she hadn't neglected to tell him something.

Brit walked into his bedroom and tossed his files on the dresser. Snatching up his phone, he dialed his sister.

She answered the first ring. "Don't you dare tell me you can't come."

"I'm not going to tell you that," he said. "I'm just not going to be able to stay long."

"Why?"

He hesitated to tell her the truth, but then did it. "It's Cali. She has some nut after her, and I don't want to leave her alone."

"Then bring her."

He dropped down on his bed and raked a hand over his face. "Don't you remember what happened a couple of years ago?"

"No. I try not to focus on the bad shit. Unlike you."

"Fred or Frank or whatever the fucker's name was she was married to at the time, he got drunk and shoved Mom into the Christmas tree and I had to break his nose."

"You didn't have to," Susan said and chuckled, but he didn't see the humor in it.

"He hurt Mom. I had to stand up for her because she wouldn't stand up for herself. Oh, but did she appreciate it? Hell no, she got mad at me. Did you know the jerkwad reported me to my captain? I got my ass in a sling at work and Mom takes his side."

"She was wrong," Susan said, the humor gone from her voice. "She knows that now. She's trying to change, Brit."

"Women like her never change," he seethed and an image of Cali flashed in his head. Cali wasn't like that, he told himself. "Look, I need to run. I'll see you tonight, but I can't stay long."

He hung up and dialed Quarles' number. When no one answered he left a message. "Call me. It's Brit." Then he went to take a shower.

~

Cali and Tanya both stood in front of the bathroom mirror putting on makeup. It had been a perfect girl's day out, and Cali almost forgot that her life was in chaos.

Until now. Tanya sent her a worried glance. "I saw the story last night on the news about the jewelry store robbery and the two dead men. Stan hasn't tried anything else, has he?"

Cali brushed some color on her cheeks. "No."

"Do you think he killed those two guys?"

Nibbling on her lower lip, Cali answered, "No. I don't. I mean, if a week ago you'd told me that he robbed a jewelry store, I'd have told you I didn't think he could have done that either. And maybe I'm wrong, but I just don't see him killing anyone. I know they found Stan's phone at the hotel and everything points to him, but I don't believe it." She shook her head. "The guy helps old people bring in their groceries. He even unstopped my elderly neighbor's toilet. He's not evil. Not all evil."

"He shot at you." Tanya sent her a cutting glance.

Cali dropped her blush applicator. "What if someone was shooting at him? That's what he told me that day at the lawyer's office. I mean, if Stan did the murders then he should have the money and the other jewelry, so why is he trying to find the bracelet he gave me? Why would he hang around for one piece of jewelry?"

Tanya cocked her head as if thinking. "That's a good point. Have you mentioned that to Brit?"

"A little, but . . ."

"But what?"

"He thinks I'm trying to defend Stan. He got all angry and turned into a dickhead about it."

Tanya frowned. "Well, you kind of are defending him."

"No. Okay, maybe a bit. I mean, I believe he beat up his girlfriends. I saw his temper. I just don't see him killing anyone."

Cali added another stroke of blush, and not wanting to think about Stan, she attempted a conversational U-turn. "Where is Eric taking you to dinner?"

"Some Italian place. It's supposed to be romantic. I know he's going to try to change my mind about tonight."

"But you're not going to give in?"

"Probably not." A smile spread across Tanya's lips.

Cali laughed and reached for her purse to get her lip gloss.

Tanya grabbed her hand. "No. Use the red one you bought. It's sexy and besides, it goes with your sweater."

Cali scrutinized her image in the mirror. The red sweater fit like a coat of paint. Its neckline dipped down in the front, not too low, but definitely hinting at cleavage. And it came just above the navel. And the hip-hugging jeans fit just below. When Cali walked, the barest hint of belly skin peeked through. According to Tanya, belly skin drove men bonkers.

Did Cali want Brit bonkers?

~

"I'm just saying don't go looking for trouble." Adams' voice roared over the phone. For some reason, the sergeant felt the need to personally call Brit with another warning about Cali.

"I'm not looking for trouble." Brit looked up at Tanya's apartment building where Cali waited.

"Don't mess up this case," Adams said. "We might need her to testify."

I'm not having sex with you. Brit recalled Cali's words. Maybe he really should abide by her wishes until Humphrey was caught.

"Yeah." Brit hung up and got out of his car to collect Cali. He frowned as he made his way across the parking lot, dreading having to tell her that he needed to postpone dinner until later.

The moment Cali opened Tanya's front door, looking like sex in high heels, he knew he was in deep-shit trouble.

"Hi." She smiled. Her red painted lips slid moistly across her white teeth. Her hair, long and wispy, hung loose around her shoulders. Her sweater wasn't loose. Oh, hell it fit. Fit really nicely. And it was red. Like her shoes. Of course, he didn't appreciate the shoes until after he noted how good the jeans hugged her hips and then his gaze followed them to her thighs . . . then down to her calves. The visual trip to heaven and back ended with a pair of red high heels. Shoes that he'd once heard described as, "fuck me heels."

Not that there was even one thing indecent with Cali's clothes—well, except the instant desire they induced in him to remove them.

"Uhh." He let his gaze whisper over her. Up and then down. There wasn't a safe spot, not one un-hot place to focus.

A gulp of desire squeezed out his breathing room. How the hell was he going to keep his hands off her?

Oh, hell, chances were he was going piss Adams off royally.

Chapter Twenty-Five

"Just ride with me," Brit insisted. "We'll come and pick up your car later."

Cali agreed and followed him to his car. As she slid into his SUV, her new shoes pinched a bit and so did her disappointment.

Okay, it sounded lame, but she'd bought a new outfit and took extra time with her makeup, and she'd sort of hoped for at least a little compliment. Instead, he didn't even seem happy to see her.

Oh, he'd given her a head-to-toe glance, but he'd been frowning the whole time.

"Bad day?" Cali asked, when a few minutes later, he pulled into a service station for gas.

"Yeah." He looked at her, frowned again and got out of his car to pump the gas. She watched him pull out his phone and try to call someone. It appeared they didn't answer, because his expression soured again.

When he got back in, he looked at his watch.

"Is everything okay?" she asked.

He released a deep gasp. "No. I'm supposed to be somewhere right now. I have something I have to do."

Hadn't he invited her to dinner? She had to work to not let her feelings show on her face. The she recalled the obligations of his job. Was he on call?

"Just drop me back off at Tanya's to get my car," she said.

"I don't want you to be alone." Concern tightened his eyes.

"I'm fine." The rejection she felt in her chest pinched tighter than her new shoes.

"You've got a murderer after you. That's not fine."

"He doesn't know where I am," she said. "Besides, I've been staying by myself at night." In some distant place in her mind she remembered last night's dream. What was it her mother had said?

He palmed the steering wheel. "Not really. I set up office at the diner across from the motel. When I wasn't there, I had my partner watching out for you."

Her mouth fell open a little. "Why?"

He turned and looked at her, the frustration in his expression reading loud and clear. "Because I don't want to see you hurt." He reached out and ran the back of his hand down her face. "You look amazing. I didn't even tell you that, did I?"

"No." She cut him a grin. "But thank you."

He looked at his watch again. "You know what? You're just going to have to go with me." He pulled into traffic then thumped his palm on the wheel.

She looked at him. "I don't want to intrude."

"You won't." He met her gaze. "Please come with me."

Between her fear of being alone and the soft pleading in his eyes, she relented. Silence followed. "Where are we going?" She thought about the type of police business he did. Homicide work.

He shifted his shoulders. "My mother's birthday party."

She chuckled. "And I'm thinking it's a crime scene."

He clenched his jaw. "I wish. This could turn out to be a lot uglier than that."

~

Brit led Cali into the restaurant. Hands down, this wasn't a good idea. He paused. Hell, it could be a disaster on acid.

"Am I dressed okay?" Cali sounded insecure. "This looks more like a cocktail-type place."

"You're fine." His gaze moved over her body. "No, you're hot." He kissed her cheek. He knew kissing her was wrong, but he was past caring. He paused, letting himself appreciate what he'd just complimented, hoping to chase away the ill feeling being near his mom brought on.

At Cali's soft smile, the thoughts of his mom melted like ice cream on a hot sidewalk. If it wasn't for his sister, he'd be hightailing it back to the hotel, Cali in tow. But tonight he'd better sleep in his car.

A hostess pointed them to a backroom. Brit heard his mother's voice and hesitated. Cali squeezed his hand, her palm molding smoothly to his. The perfect fit brought a sense of comfort.

"Sorry I'm late," he said, stopping at the door. People, at least two dozen or more, were crowded in the room. Some sat around the table, others stood nearby visiting. Brit recognized some—friends of his mom from way back, a few neighbors, a cousin or two. Most of them he didn't know. Probably some of the friends and family of her latest husband. Was he number five or six? Brit lost count.

Susan's glare chastised him for being late. But then, her focus shifted to Cali, and forgiveness softened her eyes.

"Better late than never." Susan approached them. "Hi." She focused on Cali. "We sort of met the other day at your school. Of course, my rude brother didn't introduce us."

Cali smiled and leaned against his shoulder. Her weight felt good there, too.

"In your brother's defense," Cali said, "he did tell me who you were later."

Brit wasn't used to people coming to his defense, but with some work he thought he could get used to it. He could get used to Cali. With that thought came the slightest bit of warning.

"Well, I'll give him a break then." Susan, a twinkle in her eye, looked back at him. "You want to explain the vicious lioness guarding your laundry room?"

"Sorry. I should have told you about Mama Cat. You didn't let her out, did you?"

"No, but I put my life at risk rescuing my undies from the dryer. And the black kitten took a liking to my bra. So mama kitty decided what little kitty wanted, she got. In short, if they destroyed it, you owe me a Victoria's Secret bra. And it wasn't the cheap kind."

"Sorry for that, too." Brit glanced at Cali, who was grinning and looking surprised.

"You have a cat and kittens?" she asked.

"No. It's a temporary thing. I don't even like cats. She's a stray and—"

"Brit?" A familiar female voice called out in the crowd.

He emotionally flinched when he saw his mother stepping forward.

She held onto the back of the chair as if it hurt to move. His gut squeezed, and he scowled at the man standing beside her. Had she let her latest man use her as a punching bag? Things never changed.

"Excuse me for hobbling," his mother said. "Susan and I worked in my yard this morning, and I'm afraid my gardening muscles are raising cane."

Brit looked to Susan to see if she flinched at his mother's version of the truth. She didn't, and he tried to relax.

"Mom, this is Cali. Cali, my mom Linda." Crap. Brit didn't know her last name. He hadn't made the wedding four months ago and had only met the groom once at the engagement party his sister put together and insisted he attend a few months before that.

"Linda Swain." His mom gave Cali's hand a squeeze. "It's a delight to meet a friend of my son's."

"It's a pleasure to meet you, too," Cali said.

While Cali, his mom and sister chatted, Brit looked around the room at the other attendants. A familiar face in the crowd had him refocusing. What was he doing here? He walked over. "So this is why you didn't return my calls?"

"Calls?" Quarles pulled out his phone and snapped it open. "Whatcha' know? Out of juice. Hope it wasn't important."

Brit knew a lie when he heard one, but he bit back the resentment. Quarles didn't owe him anything. They weren't friends and were barely partners.

Quarles' eyes moved to the front of the room. "Wow. Is that the McKay chick?"

"Yeah."

"She looks hot." Quarles grinned.

Brit frowned. "Aren't you supposed to be here with my sister?"

"I am." Quarles smiled, and his gaze shifted to Susan. "I was just about to say that she's almost as hot as your sister."

~

It took Cali only a few minutes to relax after she decided she liked Brit's family. She got the feeling, however, he wasn't anywhere nearly at ease as she was. When dinner was served, steaks with red potatoes and salad, Cali ate, but Brit, who usually ate with gusto, spent more time scattering his food on the plate than eating it.

Eventually, most of the party attendees meandered out to listen to the band in the main room. The soft cadence of music shimmered through the door and attempted to set a cozy mood, but Brit's rigid posture chased it away.

"You okay?" She leaned into his tense shoulder.

"Fine." Rolling his neck again, he eyed his mother and her husband sitting at the other side of the large table. Cali found it odd that they hadn't scooted over to converse with them. From what she could see, his family appeared perfect. She supposed appearances could be deceiving. Nevertheless, considering she'd just lost her mother, it took everything she had not to pull his face close to hers and say, "Love them, Brit. You won't have them forever."

"Come on," Susan called from the door. "We're dancing. Brit, Cali. You too, Frank and Mom. It'll do the muscles good, Mom."

Brit stood. "We should leave." He led her to the door.

"No," Susan said when Brit whispered his goodbye. "We haven't opened presents or cut the cake. And we're not going to until you dance with Cali. Now go cut a rug, brother." She shot him a firm glance and Cali got the feeling that whatever reservations Brit had about his family, it wasn't with his sister.

Brit's frown deepened, and he turned back to her. "Would you dance with me so we can get this show on the road?"

She put her hand in his and smiled. "I'd be honored."

He walked her to the dance floor just as a slow song started. He exhaled. "This could be dangerous."

"It's just a dance." She placed her hands on his shoulders.

He put his hand on her waist. "You're lethal tonight." His breath smelled of wine.

"Thank you." She sighed when his fingers found that spot between her jeans and sweater and he touched her bare skin.

Just a dance. She told herself.

The music flowed. So did they. The band changed songs, but kept the pace body-brushing slow. Brit's fingers kept slipping under her sweater and onto her waist. He never explored too high, or too low, but the feel of his warm hands against her body made her dizzy. She leaned her head against his shoulder.

"Thanks for coming with me," he whispered in her ear.

"Thanks for asking." Why did this have to feel so good?

"I would have asked you earlier. It's just . . . my family can be hard to take sometimes."

She looked up at him. "Susan is a joy and your mom seems sweet."

"Oh, she's sweet all right." His voiced dripped with sarcasm.

She continued to move with him. "Is it her husband? You don't like him?"

He brushed his face against her cheek. "You smell so good." His fingers slid under the sweater again. "You feel so soft."

She laughed nervously and pulled back. "Behave."

He gave her an inch, but her breasts still brushed his chest as they swayed, and an inch wasn't enough. She felt her body tightening and longing to move back in. "Is it her husband?" she asked again.

He frowned. "Could be, but I keep forgetting which husband this is. Can we not talk right now?"

"She loves 'em and leaves 'em, huh?" She rested her head back on his chest.

"Something like that."

His hips brushed against hers. "Where's your father?"

His body grew tense. "He died when I was fourteen."

Empathy filled her instantly. "I'm sorry." She looked up.

"Don't be. He deserved it."

She flinched at the bitter words.

"I'm sorry," he said. "That was cold, considering you just lost your mom."

"What did he do?"

He moved around the dance floor with practiced ease. "Women, booze and crime."

"And you blame your mom?" She met his steps, even as those steps brought them closer. His hard body felt right.

"I blame them both." He stared down at her. "What about you? Where's your father?"

"Gone," she said.

"Dead?"

"Don't know." She rested her face back on his shoulder, and part of last night's dream vibrated through her thoughts. She remembered what her mom had said about her dad. Then she remembered something else. Don't stay at the same hotel.

He leaned his head down and asked, "Did you get along with your mother?"

"Yeah. I mean, we had our share of disagreements, but we loved each other." She pushed the thoughts of the dream from her mind. They were just dreams.

"What kind of disagreements?"

"Small stuff," Cali lied, remembering the very last disagreement they'd had.

He stepped back just a bit and stopped dancing. "Your mother didn't like Humphrey?" His tone held the slightest edge, reminding her that he was a cop, and she was still his case.

"She never met Stan," she said honestly. She couldn't tell him that since her mother died she'd nicknamed the guy a weasel. But she hadn't really nicknamed him. Those were just dreams.

"Why not?" He moved her back into the easy rhythm of the dance.

"Because she was so sick and maybe because I knew she wouldn't approve."

"Smart lady."

"Yeah." Cali looked away.

"What else?" he asked. "What else did you fight about?"

The knot tightened her throat and the truth just slipped out. "About her treatments."

He almost stopped dancing. "You mean for cancer?"

She nodded. "She refused to have any more. She gave up."

He caressed her cheek, his gaze as tender as his touch. "That must have been hard."

"Not as hard as knowing that I spent the last weeks of her life mad at her." Cali closed her eyes as the ache flared.

With a gentle sweep of his fingers through her hair, he pulled her into his warmth. "I'm sorry."

"Maybe we should talk about something different." She raised her head when he started moving again.

"I have a better idea. Let's not talk." He kissed her. A slow, deep kiss that tasted like red wine—sweet, tangy. She became lost in want. Nothing existed but him, the kiss, and their bodies, together. She closed her eyes and just let him lead her.

Finally, Brit pulled away. Cali opened her eyes and realized the music had stopped. They were almost alone on the dance floor. His hooded gaze met hers. He offered her one of his slow, sexy smiles, the kind with a lot of heat. "I told you this was dangerous."

Aware of how dangerous she felt, of how far she'd let herself go, she stepped away. Embarrassment rained down. Had they really made out on the dance floor in front of everyone and God? Yup.

She started back to the room where his mother's party was happening.

He caught her. "Not so fast."

"We should go back to the party. Everyone else has."

He arched a brow. "Let's stand at the bar and give me a minute."

The slow tune of passion still hummed through her, but the embarrassment and the fact that she'd let things go too far chased her back to this side of sanity. "Why?"

He cut his gaze toward the front of his khaki slacks.

She saw the bulge behind his zipper. She jerked up her gaze. "Oh." She blushed.

Smiling, he touched her cheek. "Damn, you're precious."

~

Fifteen minutes passed before they rejoined the others. For some reason, either the second glass of wine, or dancing with Cali, he'd managed to forget about his issues with his mom and just started enjoying himself. He even managed to eat the birthday cake.

He was eyeing the uneaten piece of Cali's cake when his cell phone rang. He pulled it out of his pocket, forked one big bite of her cake in his mouth, and moved to the quieter side of the room.

"Hello." Brit felt Quarles watching him. The man had watched him all evening. And part of Brit knew the man was worried about his relationship with Cali. Down deep, Brit shared the concern, but not enough to do a damn thing about it. With Humphrey's phone at the crime scene and blood evidence on Cali's door, chances were they had enough evidence on the man and wouldn't need Cali's testimony.

"Lowell?" the husky female voice didn't jar his memory.

"Yes?"

"This is Lucy Edwards, Officer Edwards. I met you the other day at the hotel. We answered the call about the missing woman."

"Yes, I remember you. What I can I do for you?" And how did she get his cell number?

"Actually, it's what I can do for you."

Chapter Twenty-Six

Brit hesitated. "What's that?" he asked, uncertain he was reading this right.

"I'm back at the hotel. Some idiot took a few punches at the guy working the front desk to get the key for room 112. He tore through the room pretty good. The clerk had your card with your number on it."

"Tell me you got the guy."

"Sorry. He was gone when we got here." She took a deep breath. "Aren't you at all concerned about the woman?"

Brit looked at Cali, sitting and talking to one of his mom's friends, and he remembered how close he'd come to leaving her alone tonight. Acid let loose on his stomach. "I know where she is."

"Good, because I was going to tell you that she's not here."

"Did you get a description of the guy?"

"Yeah. White male, dark hair, big fellow."

Brit palmed the phone tighter. "Can you call out an APB and comb the area for a ninety-eight F-150 pickup?"

"Is there something we should know about this case?" Edwards asked.

"Yeah. I'll be there in ten minutes to fill you in."

He snapped the phone closed.

Quarles appeared beside him. "Trouble?"

Brit nodded. "Humphrey just beat up the hotel clerk for Cali's room key. He trashed Cali's hotel room."

"How did he find her?" Quarles asked.

Brit glanced back at Cali. "She originally put the room in her name. I told the clerk to change it. I bet the jerk didn't do it."

"Or she told him where she was staying," Quarles said.

"She hasn't talked to him," Brit said. And he believed that. He did.

"Should we head out?" Quarles moved closer.

"I am," he said. "You can stay. But I'm going to ask Susan to take Cali to my place."

"I'm with you," Quarles said.

"Something wrong?" Cali appeared beside them.

Brit saw again the doubt in Quarles' eyes as he stepped back to talk to Susan. Brit focused on Cali. "Stan just roughed up the clerk back at your hotel."

Her eyes grew round. "Is anyone . . . badly hurt?"

Brit raked a hand through his hair. "It didn't sound like it. I'm heading there to check things out. I'm going to get Susan to take you back to my place. I'll get your things."

Worry etched her brow. "I should go with you."

"No." He continued to study her. "Do you know how Stan could have found you?"

"He must have followed me."

Brit frowned. "Not when I was with you, he didn't."

"Then I don't know." She looked around the room, panic showing in her eyes.

"What is it?" he asked.

"Nothing," she said, but it didn't look like nothing. "Could you just take me to another hotel? I would prefer that to going to your place."

He frowned, getting the feeling again that she wasn't being completely honest with him. "Just go with Susan. We'll talk when I get back."

~

Cali left the restaurant with Susan. She could have called a taxi, and she even gave a quick thought to phoning Tanya, then she remembered Tanya's date. Deep down, however, she chose to stay because of Brit.

"I'm sorry to impose like this," Cali told Susan.

"You're not imposing. I'm just glad that whatever pulled him away didn't keep him from showing up at Mom's party. And I'm thrilled he brought you."

"Well, thank you." Cali looked out the window and thought about her dream last night. Don't stay at the same hotel. How had her maternal psyche figured that one out? Chills marched up her spine and she wondered if maybe she should go see Dr. Roberts again. Have her convince Cali that the dreams weren't really her mother seeing the future.

"Have you and Brit been dating long?" Susan asked.

Cali inhaled. "We're not . . ." She wasn't sure what they were or weren't doing.

"Dating?" Serious doubts played across Susan's expression.

Cali had a hunch that Susan had seen them on the dance floor. "I mean, we're not really dating. I'm a case."

"That's what he said, too." Susan stopped at a red light and faced Cali. "I didn't believe him, either." She smiled. "You two look good together."

Cali nodded. "It's just the wrong time." She hoped that would stop Susan from asking more questions.

"It's never the right time." Susan sent her another smile. "But I know it's probably more about Brit's job and him getting his ass in sling for dating someone involved with a case."

"Yeah." Cali gave that some thought. She didn't want him getting his ass in a sling.

"But Brit's always bucking authority." Susan chuckled.

Cali nodded. A change of subject was needed and she pulled one out of thin air. "Brit said you lived in Austin. Do you visit much?"

"Every month or two," Susan answered. "I'm a photographer, freelance, so I travel quite a bit anyway."

"I took photography in college," Cali said. "Loved it."

"You teach art, right?" Susan turned the wheel.

They talked for the next ten minutes about painting and photography. Comfortable conversation. Then Susan pulled into a driveway. The quaint, red brick bungalow was located in one of the refurbished areas of town.

"Nice," Cali said.

"You haven't been here before?" Susan asked.

"No." Suddenly, her decision to stay with Brit didn't seem right. He wasn't sure about what was happening between them. He could get in trouble with his job. Staying at his home meant crossing a line.

Cops didn't bring home their witnesses. Neither did they make out with them on a dance floor.

She looked at Susan. "I'm thinking that staying here might not be a good idea."

"Why?" Susan, eyes the same blue-green color of Brit's, studied her.

"Because your brother has already done too much. Because . . . it's the wrong time." Because I'm scared. Because I've got a bad habit of dating dickheads. Because my dead mother talks to me in my dreams.

"Brit doesn't do what he doesn't want to do. Besides, he's not even here." Susan got out of the car. Giving in, Cali followed her to the porch.

Susan unlocked the front door and reached in and hit the lights. "If you don't mind me asking, what kind of case are you involved in?"

"It's a long story." Cali stepped inside, crossing the line into Brit's personal world. She took in the decor—masculine, but nice. Dark leather furniture and bookcases. With the exception of some black and white photography, very little wall art. She glanced back at Susan. "A real long story. Is this your work?" she asked, hoping for a change of subject.

"Yeah." She took a few more steps inside. "I like stories. Come on. I'll get us something to drink."

A soulful meow cried out. "Is that Brit's cat?"

"Yeah, but I wouldn't recommend getting close." Susan raised her sleeve and showed off some scratches.

"She attacked you?"

Susan smiled. "No, I was just certain if she'd let me hold her, she'd fall in love with me. I'm a sucker for the underdog."

"Me, too."

They ended up at the kitchen table, drinking wine. After a few minutes, Cali gave Susan the short version of how she'd met Brit.

Susan studied her hands. "I should have guessed."

"Guessed what?"

"Well . . ." She hesitated as if to choose her words carefully. "It's Brit's nature to protect women."

"The cop in him, I guess." Cali sipped the wine.

"Yeah, but our mom sort of fell into bad relationships. You know how the story goes, a victim always in search of a man to victimize her. A real loser chooser."

"That sounds kind of grim." Cali thought about Frank, Brit's mom's husband. He hadn't seemed like a loser.

"Not as grim as Brit would put it. He spent most of his childhood trying to protect her from our father. After Dad died, he protected her from the next guy, and the next. He grew bitter. Not that I blame him, but Mom's trying to change and Frank's different. Brit, of course, can't see it."

Cali chewed on that piece of information. "And you think his protecting me is somehow related to all that?"

Susan took a sip of wine. "What do I know?"

Cali could tell from Susan's voice that it was exactly what she believed. And the shoe fit. Not a pretty shoe either. At least now Cali understood why he'd been so hard on her in the beginning. The idea that he lumped her into a category with a woman who'd gone from one bad relationship to another didn't feel too good, but if what Dr. Roberts had said was true, maybe Brit hadn't been that far off the mark. Great. *Am I really a loser chooser?*

"You and Brit seem close," Cali said, wanting to change the subject.

"We are. With a lot of drama always happening when we were kids, we kind of looked out for each other. Can you believe he had a fit because I went out to breakfast with his new partner? He said he didn't want to know the guy who was trying to get into my pants."

Cali grinned.

"So I told him I wouldn't let his partner brag about how good I was in bed."

"So you are dating him?"

"Maybe, I mean, I had breakfast with him and then he came to Mom's party tonight. But I like him. I haven't dated anyone in two years. I gave up men and took up ice cream about two years ago."

"Bad breakup?"

"I'd say. I came home early from an out of town job and found my fiancé in bed doing the deed with an anatomically correct doll."

"Seriously?" Cali had to work to keep from giggling.

"Seriously. He'd even named the doll." She made an odd face. "George."

A giggle leaked out. "Sorry."

"Please. I know it's funny. Now. Not so much then. Anyway, I finally kicked the ice cream habit and lost the forty pounds it cost me."

They talked for at least another twenty minutes, before Cali yawned.

"Are you tired?" Susan asked.

"Yeah, a little."

"Why don't I set you up in Brit's room?"

"I would prefer to just sleep on the sofa." Cali saw Susan's surprise. "We're really not dating."

"Looked like you were dating." Susan held up a hand. "I'm sorry. It's not my business."

"It's okay." Cali felt obliged to tell the truth. "I'm not going to say we're not attracted to each other, but we haven't . . . We aren't . . ."

"Getting naked, yet?" Susan grinned.

"Yeah." Cali looked around the house, Brit's home. She'd crossed a line by being here, but if she kept her head, she could step right back over it.

"Well, unlike my brother, I don't have a problem with it. So you have my blessings to get naked with him." She stopped talking and frowned. "Okay that sounded awkward."

They both laughed.

"He's a great guy. Honest. Loyal. Doesn't have a thing about blow-up Ken dolls." She sighed. "Grumpy as a bear with an African bee up its butt sometimes, but he's good as gold when it counts."

Cali sighed. "I know."

Susan stood up. "Okay, I'll stop playing matchmaker. However, Brit's sofa sleeps like a bed of rocks. And I've trashed the extra bedroom pretty badly. So, sleep in his bed. Besides, Brit works third shift. He won't be home until morning."

Cali followed her into Brit's bedroom. When Susan turned the light on, Cali's gaze went to the unmade king-size bed.

"Don't worry. Brit actually has a housecleaner. She came a few days ago. And he's only napped a couple of hours since then. So the sheets are pretty clean." Then Susan smiled. "I think he keeps an extra toothbrush in his medicine cabinet."

~

Brit and Quarles met Officers Wolowitz and Edwards in front of the hotel. Within a few minutes, Brit had updated them on the case. While Quarles talked to Wolowitz, Brit walked to the hotel room with Edwards.

"Why hasn't Adams assigned someone to her?" Edwards asked following him as she pushed a lock of dark hair back behind her ear.

Brit tensed. "I asked, but with the cop killings going down, he couldn't see doing it."

"Well, let this guy get to Miss McKay and Adams will wish he'd seen it differently."

"He won't get to her." Brit poked his head into the hotel room where he and Cali had stayed for the last couple of days.

"We don't know if anything was taken," Edwards said.

Brit stepped inside. A few of the dresser drawers had been yanked out. Cali's suitcase had been emptied and her clothes lay strewn around. Was the jerk still looking for the bracelet or was it Cali he wanted? For just a second, Brit considered letting it leak out that the police had the bracelet. The acid in his stomach started to churn when he recalled again how close he'd come to leaving her here.

"Do you think the guy stole something?" Edwards followed him inside.

Brit picked up the suitcase and set it on the bed. "I'll have Miss McKay go through her things. If anything's missing, I'll call you."

"So you know for sure that she's safe?" Edwards asked.

"Yeah." He picked up a pair of Cali's panties the asshole had obviously handled. Frowning, Brit tossed them in the trash.

Edwards looked at the discarded undies, then back at him. "No luck finding the pickup."

"The guy's slippery. We get anything more from the clerk?"

"No, but he was pretty upset then. We might want to have another go at him."

"I'll do it." Brit turned to leave.

"You two an item?" Edwards' question sounded more female-related than cop.

Brit looked back. "No, but I don't want anything to happen to her."

"Because you care?" She laughed. "I saw it the other day. You were too worried."

The denial lay on the tip of his tongue, but he couldn't say it. "Yeah, I care."

A grin softened the lines of her face. "You know, my partner was right. He said you were an okay guy."

"Don't believe it. I can be a jerk." As Brit headed to the office, he considered how he had left Cali at the restaurant. He wondered if she was going to be pissed.

Two men sat behind the counter. The man holding a bag of frozen butter beans to his eye was the same one Brit had confronted earlier. Both men's heads bobbed up when Brit cleared his throat. "I need to talk to you." He pointed to the victim.

The clerk removed the frozen veggies. "Not sure I feel much like talking." He was going to have one fine shiner. However, the man had faired a lot better than any of Stan's other victims. Why?

"This guy kills most of his victims," Brit said. "He could come back to finish the job because you may be an important witness to this case. Of course, if you don't want to help us find him . . ."

The man's shoulders snapped back. "Whatcha want to know?"

They walked to the office in the back and sat down at a table. Brit asked the basic questions. The answers reconfirmed what Brit already knew. Humphrey had come looking for Cali. "Did you see a vehicle?"

"No. But I really got a good view of the front of his knuckles," the clerk said sarcastically.

Brit leaned against a table. "Who did you tell that Cali McKay was staying here?"

"Tell? I didn't tell anyone."

"Did you change the paperwork like I told you?"

"I deleted her name from the records, and canceled her charge, just like you asked and put the charges on your card. Hell, you stood there and watched me do it. Remember?"

"What did this guy say when he first came in? Did he act as if he knew she was here or was he just asking?"

"He knew she was here. He demanded I give him her room number. I said she wasn't staying here. He called me a liar. No, he called me a 'fucking liar.'"

"He didn't say how he knew she was here?"

"We didn't sit down for tea and conversation."

Brit frowned. "Then what happened?"

"When I denied the chick was here the second time, he got ugly."

"How ugly? Did he threaten you with a gun or knife?"

"No, his fists were pretty convincing."

"But you gave him the room number and the key so he could beat up on a woman?"

To the clerk's credit, his eyes widened with concern. "I thought the female officer said she wasn't there."

"She wasn't. But you didn't know that then, did you?"

Brit turned to leave and practically ran over Quarles standing at the door. Brit kept moving until he made the parking lot. The cold surrounded him, and he zipped up his flimsy jacket, and thought about getting his leather coat.

He gave a verbal report to Wolowitz and Edwards. After a few minutes, they left. Brit went back to the room to finish gathering Cali's things. Quarles followed on his heels. Too close.

"You're in too deep." His partner leaned against the door.

Brit dropped the suitcase on the bed and didn't reply.

"You need to step back," Quarles said. "Let me find her a new motel. I'll keep an eye on her. Give yourself time to think before something happens you'll regret."

"I'm handling this." Brit zipped up the case.

"I saw you handling it on the dance floor. Adams will have your ass if you mess up this case."

Brit gritted his teeth. "I'm not going to mess it up."

"It looks bad." Quarles reared back on his leather shoes.

"Ask me if I give a damn how things look. Besides, you're trying to get it on with my sister. I think that's a hell of lot worse than me being interested in someone who may or maybe not even be considered a witness in a case."

"I'm not trying to—"

"I saw the way you were looking at her tonight. Like she was a candy bar that you were dying to unwrap."

Quarles rolled his eyes, but he didn't deny it. "At least let me question Cali, just to make sure she's not still talking to this guy."

"She's not talking to him." He scanned the room once more and the smell of cigarette smoke filled the air. Was Humphrey a smoker?

"If you believed that, then why were you drilling the clerk about how Stan knew she was here?"

"I was doing my job." Brit snatched up the suitcase and left.

~

Cali moaned into the mattress. Everything smelled like him. Burying her face in the pillow, she recalled their little make-out session on the dance floor. Her body warmed with the memory. She threw the top sheet off and tugged on the flannel pajamas Susan had lent her.

Staring at the ceiling, she let her thoughts skitter from one issue to the next; the dreams, Stan, Brit thinking she was a weak-hearted woman who loved to be abused.

She thought back to the three real relationships she'd had. Her first, at nineteen, had cheated on her with his brother's wife, but the moment Cali discovered his indiscretions, she'd told him to take a long walk down a busy railroad track.

Her second boyfriend had been a control freak, and while he'd wanted to control Cali, she'd freed the shackles of that three-month fling pretty quickly. Then Marty. As Dr. Roberts had said, not all relationships were bad. She had loved Marty.

He'd gotten a dream job offer in New York, and he hadn't wanted to go alone. The night she'd gone to break the news to her mom, her mom had broken her own news first. She'd found a lump. Cali couldn't leave her mother, and Marty couldn't turn down the job of a lifetime. Both had made choices.

He had visited the first few months, twice, but as Marty had put it, "Long distance relationships are hard nuts to crack." But Cali's heart had cracked. She had lost the man she loved and, at the same time, she'd been fighting not to lose her mom.

After that, Cali had gone through her mom's up and down dance with cancer. Not until Stan had paid for her coffee that September morning had she even considered indulging in a relationship. Sad as it sounded, she hadn't missed sex or men. Being with Stan convinced Cali that she hadn't missed out on much. But meeting Brit sure had.

With her relationship evidence laid out in her mind, she didn't feel so bad. Yeah, she'd known a few jerks, and she'd admit that she needed to learn to be a better bitch. But she hadn't been anyone's doormat.

Unable to sleep, she flipped on the lamp and followed her bladder to the master bathroom. Once relieved, she went to the sink and rinsed her hands. Running her tongue over her gummy-feeling teeth, she tried to open the medicine cabinet, in hopes of finding a new toothbrush.

The mirrored door didn't pull open easily, so she gave it a yank. The mirror swung open and half the cabinet's contents came raining down on the sink. Pills, a pack of toothbrushes. Then a thirty-six pack of extra large condoms hit the counter, bounced off and landed in the toilet.

"Oh shit!" She slapped her hand over her mouth at having let the four-letter word out.

Forcing herself into action, she grabbed the first things she saw, a toothbrush in a holder on the sink and tried to fish out the box of rubbers floating in the toilet.

Finally, by sticking the end of the toothbrush into the carton's side she got the pack out, and dropped the soggy box of rubbers and toothbrush into the sink. Closing her eyes, she tried to figure out what to do. The condoms were not exposed to the toilet water, but yuck on the idea of using one that had made the trip to the potty. And then there was the toothbrush. A big yuck.

Suddenly, a giggle left her lips as she tried to imagine explaining this to Brit. Oh, hell, what was she going to do?

Maybe what she needed to do was just toss them and then tomorrow when she got her car, go buy him another pack. She envisioned doing that, and her face heated up and she started laughing again.

~

Five minutes later, toothbrush hidden in a drawer and condoms pushed all the way under the bottom cabinet, she went back to the bedroom. Every few minutes, a nervous giggle would erupt. She still wasn't sure how or if she was going to tell Brit.

On the way back to bed, she passed the dresser and bumped into some files resting on top. They fell to the floor and papers scattered. Kneeling, she gathered the items. A photograph caught her attention—a dead man, sprawled out on concrete, blood marking his forehead. His eyes were open—empty.

The nervous giggles vanished and she stared at the image as she may have an accident on the side of the road—horrified, yet drawn to the horror.

Another photo from the second file floated to the floor. Her breath caught. Stan. Trembling, she slipped the mug shot back inside, rose, and set the files back on the dresser.

She took one step, then stopped and glanced back at the files. Maybe if she read everything Brit knew about Stan, then she'd believe him about him killing someone.

Making up her mind, she picked up the file that contained Stan's photo, and sat down on the edge of the bed.

Chapter Twenty-Seven

It was after midnight when Brit pulled into his driveway. He'd stopped off at the precinct and lost himself going over Keith's and Anderson's old cases, hoping to find something that tied them together. If he could just find that piece of the puzzle, he was sure the rest would fall into place.

When it hadn't surfaced, he'd gone to Quarles' desk and spent the next hour combing through the new information that had come in on Humphrey and the other band members. He'd digested it and then re-digested it because it was his job and he'd needed to know.

He'd told himself that working on his night off had nothing to do with avoiding Cali, or the fact that she was at his house, maybe in his bed. It was then he'd given up and headed home.

Getting out of his SUV, he noticed the home's dark windows staring back at him. Only the porch light waited up for him. Letting himself inside, his gaze went to the sofa, and he felt relief that Cali hadn't insisted on sleeping there. The pricey piece of furniture sat well, but slept like a torture chamber.

The cat's meow called out to him. He opened the laundry door. Mama Cat sat on the dryer. She looked ready to hiss then she stopped, jumped down, and bumped his leg with her gray face.

"You over being mad at me?"

Two of her kittens staggered from behind the washer. Brit knelt down. Mama hissed. Frowning, he stepped out and shut the door.

The dark hall greeted him. Stopping, he peeked into the extra bedroom where Susan slept when in town. The sight of her sprawled across the bed, garbed in Disney flannel PJs, brought on a smile. Leaning against the doorframe, he stared at his sister. He'd been a lousy host to her this time, and he should try to turn that around.

Taking the next few steps down the hall, he felt his blood begin to thicken. Memories of Cali dancing against him sang through his mind and hummed a sexy tune on his body.

He eased open his door and slipped inside. Cali hadn't shut the blinds and the street light washed over her in a silver glow. She lay uncovered, on her side, and curled up. She looked so small in his bed. A smile brushed his lips when he noted she wore a pair of Susan's flannel pajamas. Mickey Mouse PJs. He grinned and recalled she'd been wearing a Mickey Mouse nightshirt when he first met her.

Brit stepped closer. Flannel had never looked so good. The sweet curve of her bottom and the swell of her full breasts covered in soft, faded cotton gave his heart a good workout.

Swinging around, he went to sleep on the torture chamber. On the way, he stopped at the bathroom to grab his toothbrush.

~

"That picture drew you to it, didn't it?" her mother asked.

Cigarette smoke filled Cali's senses as the dream began. She slipped into the realm willingly. "Which picture?" The gruesome images in Stan's file flashed through Cali's mind—a picture of an elderly man, eyes closed, a cold blue tint to his skin, then the other images of Stan's two band members. Cali had never seen anything so awful. Had Brit seen it in person?

"Not those," her mom said, reading Cali's mind again. "The one of Brit's partner."

"I wasn't drawn to it." Cali sat up as her mom took her place at the foot of Brit's bed.

"Then look at it again. It's important." Her mom's bracelets jingled.

"I can't go through his other files," Cali said. "I only went through Stan's because it involved me." And what she'd read disturbed her. Yet, try as she may, she still didn't think he'd killed anyone. From the written report, it seemed obvious Brit and the police felt differently.

"Brit won't mind if you look at it." Her mom's gaze moved around the room. "Nice house. Do you know how much homes are going for in the area?" Even dead, her mom talked real estate. "Four hundred thousand at least." She pulled a cigarette to her lips and stared at Cali. "I'm not just your maternal psyche."

"Are you a ghost?" Cali asked, not that she would believe even if Mom said yes.

"No. You have to really want to hang around to go to that level. I'm just a not-ready."

"What's that?" Cali pulled her knees to her chest.

"It means I'm not ready to pass on. I've got unfinished business. There are a lot of us here."

A tingle spread down Cali's spine and she looked about the room. "Where?"

"Around."

"What unfinished business?" Cali asked.

Her mother smiled and her bracelets played a soft jingle. "You. I need to help you."

"Help me do what?" Cali drew a pillow closer.

"Well, at first I thought I was just going to help you move away from the grief, but then everything went to shit—Stan and the other murders." Her mother frowned. "But I'm not any good to you if you don't listen. I told you not to stay at that hotel again. If you hadn't gone with Brit, Stan would have found you. And it wouldn't have been good."

"Great, nothing like knowing your dead mom has to haunt some guy to get you a date."

"Please. I didn't haunt him. He did that because he cares." She chuckled. "He actually is really good at ignoring me." She hesitated. "Seriously, you should see your auras. You two can't be in the same room together without them practically attacking each other. And I mean in a good way."

Cali blushed. "Well, I can't control what my aura does."

"I'm not saying control it. I think you should go for it." She paused and looked back at the door. "I also said for you to call Sara again and remind her to tell her mom to get a second opinion."

Cali stared at her painted toenails. "I'll call tomorrow." And not because her dead mom told her to. But because, well just because.

"Don't be hard on yourself." Her mother pulled a drag of smoke into her lungs. "We also talked about your father."

"I don't want to talk about him," Cali said, surprised that she had spoken so bluntly.

"We don't have to talk. You just need to know that it wasn't your fault. He left because he didn't have the balls to stand up to his responsibility. We both wanted to fix him, but we couldn't."

"I hardly remember him."

"You remember." The night's silence followed. Her mom sighed. "You're not a doormat. You have a weakness for the dominant male, but most women do. And most men have the tendency to be dominant. It doesn't mean they are all abusers, like Stan. Or your dad. But like I told you, you're more of a fixer than a victim."

Her mother went to the window and stared out. "Think about those relationships again. They all had something you wanted to fix, didn't they?" The lull of the night seemed to move her mother farther away. The dream almost faded when her mother said, "You can't fix people Cali. Not even Brit. You can help him, but he has to fix himself."

~

"Damn it." Brit sat up and quit pretending he could sleep. He needed Cali to sleep. It was a king-size bed, and she wore his sister's pajamas for God's sake. He wouldn't touch her.

Remembering his promise to keep his clothes on, he slipped on his jeans and shirt and crept down the hall to his room, ignoring his better judgment with each step.

Trying not to look at her, he pulled the covers back and slipped between the sheets. One deep breath of her sweet scent and the tension in his shoulders melted. The mattress shifted, he felt her roll over. Unable to resist, he turned to see her.

Her lashes, blond but long, rested against the tender skin beneath her eyes. Her nose, perky and small, tilted up ever so slightly. Her mouth—she had lips that could wet a man's dreams. So lost in looking at her lips, he didn't realize that she'd opened her eyes. But when he saw those beautiful orbs of blue, his breath caught.

She lifted up on her elbow. The flannel around her breasts tightened and so did he. He realized his mistake then; it didn't matter who the pajamas belonged to, it was the woman in them that interested him. He fluffed his pillow, just to keep his hands from drawing her against him. "Didn't mean to wake you."

"I thought you'd be at work."

"I'm off tonight." He looked at her and his chest swelled with fear that she'd send him away.

"Oh." She looked toward the door. "I'll sleep on the sofa."

He frowned. "We've done this before."

"Yes, but . . ." She sat up a little higher. "There wasn't a sofa in the other room."

"I'll go." He reached for the blanket. She caught him. The warmth of her touch sent a wave of emotion to his chest.

She studied his face then glanced at the bedside clock. "You look beat again. You don't sleep but a couple of hours a night."

"Thanks to you," he said.

"How do I stop you from sleeping?" She moved her hand from his arm.

"You don't stop me. You help me." He wished he hadn't said that, because he could tell from her look that he would have to explain. "Since Keith's death I haven't slept worth a damn. I'd doze, but never really sleep until that night in your hotel."

"I put you to sleep." Humor laced her voice. "Just what every woman wants to hear."

He grinned. "You do a hell of a lot more than put me to sleep." Damn, even draped in Mickey Mouse flannel, she brought erotic images to his mind. More than that, she looked . . . right in his bed.

She must have noticed him eyeing the pajamas. "Your sister loaned them to me."

He grinned. "You wore Mickey Mouse the first time I saw you."

"And I didn't think men noticed a woman's wardrobe," she said.

He grinned guiltily. "It was the ears."

"The ears?"

"They jiggled." He chuckled.

"The ears?" Her eyes got wide. "Oh, you are terrible." She gave his chest a thump and he caught her hand and held it against him.

They just stared at each other. She finally spoke. "I accidently knocked over the files on your dresser. I noticed Stan's name on it, and

I leafed through it. I saw the photos of the band members." She slipped her soft palm from under his.

There were no secrets in the file, so he didn't mind her seeing it. "Not exactly bedtime reading."

"It was awful. Did you actually see the bodies?"

"Yeah," he admitted, but wanted the subject closed.

She let go of a deep breath. "I'm sorry."

"For what?"

"That you would have to look at that. No one should have to see that."

He stared into her beautiful eyes and realized for all the evil existing in this world, in her eyes was just the opposite. "Somebody has to deal with it."

"I guess." Her words whispered over him, followed by the sweet brush of her fingers as she pushed his hair from his forehead. He closed his eyes and thought about those gentle fingers moving over other places. His body grew hard, then her hand pulled away, and he wanted to beg her to touch him again.

"Anyone ever told you that you look like Burt Reynolds?"

He looked at her. "Yeah. I've heard that once or twice."

She grinned and her smile was the most precious thing he'd ever seen. Innocent like a child's, yet sexy like a woman's. And tonight it was the woman he needed.

"My mom had a serious crush on Burt Reynolds." Her voice came out wispy.

"What about you? Does he do it for you?"

Her smile quivered, her eyelids lowered. When they fluttered back up, he saw the answer in the warmth of her gaze. Brit knew he was a goner. And he'd never been happier.

"He's okay," she teased.

"Just okay?" He reached across and tucked a lock of blond hair behind her ear. Then he traced his finger down her neck. "You don't find him just a little irresistible?"

She moistened her lips. "I should let you sleep."

"I don't want to sleep." He slid closer until his jeans-covered knee brushed up against flannel. If she'd flinched, given him one sign that she didn't want this, he'd have backed off. "What do you want?" Her voice rang soft and willing.

He moistened his lips. "This."

He tasted her mouth, ran his tongue across her bottom lip, telling himself he would stop after a kiss. It was the biggest bold-faced lie he'd ever told himself. But damn it, he wanted her. No, it went deeper than want. He needed her. Her touches, her smiles, her pleases, and thank yous.

She suddenly jerked back and slapped her hand over her mouth. "Toothpaste!"

"What?" he asked, confused.

"You taste like toothpaste." She spit out the words from behind her hand, when she really wanted to spit. Then the humor of it hit.

"You don't like the taste of toothpaste?"

She giggled and looked sexy as hell doing it.

She moved her hand. "Please tell me you didn't brush your teeth. I thought I hid it."

"Why?"

"You don't have a garbage can in your bathroom, so I hid it in the back of a drawer."

"Why would you hide my toothbrush?"

She bit down on her lip. "Because you shouldn't use that toothbrush. Ever. Never again."

He studied her. "Why?"

"It . . . had a little accident and it went into the toilet."

"In the toilet?" He chuckled. "Well, lucky for you, I couldn't find my toothbrush, but I had an extra one under the cabinet." He paused and saw the devilish grin brightening her eyes. "How did my toothbrush end up in the toilet?"

She made a funny face. "It was an accident and. . ." She made another funny face and bit down on her lip.

"And what?" He leaned in again.

"Nothing," she said quickly. Rather too quickly and his suspicion rose.

He started to question her, but his gaze fell back on her lips. And more than answers, he wanted to kiss her. He wrapped an arm around her waist and pulled her close. With both of them on their sides, the distance between them melted into a lover's joining. Every part of her came against him. The kiss started light but deepened. Her tongue danced with his, slow, easy, just as their bodies had danced a few hours ago.

Shifting his hand to the front, he released the second button on her pajama top. The back of his hand brushed over flannel-covered breasts. He slipped his hand up under her shirt and touched sweet orbs of flesh. His erection, almost painfully pressed against the crotch of his jeans.

The feel of her budding nipple against his palm took him to the next level of hard. His hands started to shake with a sudden need to be there, to be on top of her, to have her nipple in his mouth, his hardness inside her.

He pressed his leg between her thighs. Rolling her on her back, he rested on top of her. He shifted his hips against hers, and she met him in the age-old rhythm. They moved together, rocking against each other, but the clothes got in their way.

Shifting slightly to the side, he reached down, found the elastic bottoms of her pants, and slipped his hand inside. Down past the flat abdomen, pass the soft patch of hair. No panties. His fingers found the wet lips of her sex and he heard her in inhale.

Somewhere in his mind, he remembered her telling him she wouldn't have sex. "Tell me to stop and I will." He lowered his mouth to the curve of her neck, certain she wouldn't call an end to this trip to heaven. He found the flutter of her pulse on her neck with his tongue. "One word and I'll stop. Or not."

"I don't want you to stop, but . . . we probably should." She reached inside her pajama bottoms and wrapped her hand around his wrist. "I'm sorry."

Ice water would have been more welcome. He pulled his fingers out from between her thighs and rolled completely off of her and stared at the ceiling—the tightening in his crotch bordered on pain. He hadn't been this close and told no since he was a teen in the back seat of his mom's old Chevy. And he hadn't particularly liked those days either.

He dropped his hand on his chest and tried to find the right thing to say. But his next breath came scented with the sweet, musky scent of her sex and another wave of desire shot though him.

"I'm sorry," she repeated.

"No problem," he managed to say, if you didn't count the worse case of blue balls he'd ever had as a problem. His dick—hard as wood —slid across his zipper as he sat up and he almost moaned.

Chapter Twenty-Eight

"You could get in trouble at work by crossing a line with me." Her heart raced while her body was one big ball of want.

She saw the desire bright in his eyes and she knew the look mirrored her own. Her body shook. She could still feel his touch between her legs, the ache, the desire to beg him to continue working his magic was so strong that she grabbed a couple of handfuls of blanket into her fist.

"That's the reason you stopped this? Because I don't see how what I do on my off time is anyone's business. The chances of you having to testify aren't even that great. That asshole pretty much sealed his fate when he left his cell phone at the crime scene."

She bit down on her lip. His complete confidence in Stan's guilt and her lack of it suddenly seemed like a bigger issue than his getting in trouble at work—especially when she remembered the conversation with Brit's sister.

Without completely meaning to, the question just came out. "Do I remind you of your mom? Is that why you were so hard on me in the beginning?"

Even in the semi-darkness she could see his frown. See the emotion playing across his expression. "Why would . . . What does that have to do with this?"

"Just answer me."

His frown deepened. "Big sis has been talking, hasn't she?'

"Can you just answer me?"

When he hesitated, she recalled everything her mom had said in the dream, about her not being a doormat, but being more of a fixer. Taking a deep breath, she continued, "Maybe I have a little issue with choosing the wrong men, and Stan was wrong. But I'm not the type to let men abuse me."

He inhaled and raked his hands over his face. She remembered where his hand had just been and she tightened her legs to fight the ache there.

"How did Stan find you?" he blurted out.

"We met at the coffee shop. I told you that."

"No. How did Stan know you were staying at the hotel? Someone had to have told him."

She felt the accusation all the way to her painted toenails. "You really think I told him?"

"All I know is he found you. And the desk clerk swears he changed all the paperwork and never told a soul."

What he said got hung up somewhere between her head and her heart. Brit believed the desk clerk, but he didn't believe her. Her need for his touch vanished. "Then he had to have followed me." The hurt echoed in her tone, but she didn't care.

"Not when I was there. And if he'd followed you the first night why did he wait a few days later to come after you?"

"I don't know. But I didn't talk to Stan. And I think I've already told you that. And yet you don't believe me, although you were going to make love to me. How could you do that?"

Guilt and then honesty flashed in his eyes. "I want to believe you. I want to believe you so bad it's eating me up inside."

"But you don't trust me." His distrust hurt, hurt more than she wanted to admit. She stared at the ceiling, because looking at him stung too much. Silence thickened the darkness. She tried to decide what she needed to do. Would Brit take her to another hotel? She needed to get away. She needed to think.

"I'm a cop, Cali. I get paid to be suspicious. I see the worst in people. It's not you. It's me."

A distant and familiar chirping filled the air.

He sat up and pushed a hand through his hair again. "Damn, that's my cell phone." He'd barely got to his feet when his home phone started to ring.

"Friggin' hell," he muttered.

Both phones stopped making noise. She saw him bury his face into his hands.

Then, she heard the footsteps from the hall. She'd forgotten about Susan being here. A knock echoed.

"Uh, Brit. Are you in there?"

Cali wanted to bury herself under the covers, feeling like a teen being caught in bed with a guy.

"Yeah." His tone sounded so tight it might break.

"It's John. He says he really needs to talk to you."

"John who?"

"Quarles. Your partner," she answered with sarcasm.

He frowned.

"I'll pick up in here." He walked around the bed and reached for the phone. His gaze met hers and before he reached for the phone, he whispered, "I'm so damn sorry."

She cut her gaze away. Sorry for what? For not believing her. For doubting her and still planning on having sex with her? For his sister catching them?

He snatched up the phone. She snatched up what little dignity she had left. Which wasn't much.

"What is it?" he asked.

She listened, but pretended not to.

"Fuck," he muttered. "I'll meet you at the hospital," he said and hung up. He glanced back at her. "I've got to go. There's been another cop shooting."

~

Brit found Quarles pacing in the surgery waiting room at the hospital. "What do we know?" Brit demanded.

Quarles motioned for him to follow him outside the room. As he turned to leave, Brit noted a pregnant woman sitting in a corner. Silent tears fell onto her pale cheeks while her hands splayed across her round stomach as if to protect the life within her. Several uniformed troopers surrounded her. The wife. Pain filled Brit's chest. He hurt first for her, then for Keith's wife, Laura. He still hadn't returned her call.

He clenched his fists, the need for revenge singeing his heart.

Each of Brit's footfalls fell harder than the last, and his chest clenched tighter. "They can't hear us now," he snapped. "What do we have?"

Quarles turned around. "One shot to the chest."

"One. Chest," Brit repeated.

"I know. It's not the same MO. I'm not sure it's connected. He was making a routine stop. Something went bad."

"Did he call in a license number?"

"There wasn't a tag, which is why he pulled the car over."

"Do we have anything?" Brit closed his hand so tightly his nails cut into his palms.

"Yeah." Quarles pulled out a small tablet from his front pocket. "His call in stated it was a 2003 Honda Civic, silver."

The information stirred up another piece of data from Brit's brain. "Civic, silver," he repeated, trying to connect the dots of what he heard to what he knew. Then the dots merged. "Damn."

"What?" Quarles asked.

"One of Stan Humphrey's band buddies, the drummer with his throat sliced, he had a silver Civic. His car never turned up."

"You think Humphrey is behind this shooting?"

"Do we know the type of gun that was used yet?"

"No."

"Where did the shooting take place?"

"Around Main and I-45."

Brit's brain juggled that information until something else hit. "Didn't someone in the band rent a house around there?"

"Yeah," Quarles said. "But I checked and the landlord said they moved out three weeks ago. Left the place in shambles."

Brit combed a hand through his hair. "Which would mean the landlord hasn't rented it. And maybe Stan is hanging out there."

Quarles squared his shoulders. "Let's go."

~

They stopped by the precinct to grab the address, then hightailed it over to the house. Only one out of ten street lights cast a small globe of brightness. Both he and Quarles looked out at the darkness. Brit's gaze shifted to the house on the corner. No white pickup. No silver Civic. Not even a light on in the house. Yet, his sixth sense told him that someone waited.

Quarles must have felt it, too, because they both reached for their guns at the same time.

"Should we call for backup?" Quarles asked.

Brit considered it. "We don't know if anyone is there."

"You're right." Quarles opened his door, but didn't get out. "You want the back or front?"

Raking a hand over his face, Brit wished like hell he'd caught a few hours sleep. Being dead on your feet in a time of crisis could land you dead on your back.

Brit's grip tightened on his gun.

As if reading Brit's mind, Quarles asked, "You okay?"

"Yeah," Brit said, and collected his wits as he squared his shoulders. He could do this.

"Ready?" Quarles asked.

"Yeah. Why don't I take the front this time?" Brit's gut told him if Humphrey hid within those shabby walls, he'd shoot before trying to escape. The longer a man ran, the tenser the situation got and the quicker he drew his weapon. If bullets were going to be fired, Brit would rather they were aimed at him. He couldn't live through losing another partner.

Their eyes met. Quarles shifted. "You die on me and I'll get fucking pissed. I'm not breaking in another partner."

Brit smiled. "Back at you." Right then, Brit knew for certain that somehow Quarles had jumped over Brit's emotional hurdle. He hadn't wanted a partner. He'd been determined to keep a distance between them, but that distance had been bridged.

"Let's do it." Brit opened his door.

They got out of Brit's SUV and moved in the shadows leading to the house. With every step Brit took, the more his gut told him to get ready. Something was about to go down.

Chapter Twenty-Nine

Brit zipped up his thin coat to shield himself from the bite of cold. As he watched Quarles slink to the back of the house, every noise seemed amplified—the distant roar of traffic traveling with the cold rush of November air, the scratchy vibrations of maple leaves finding a place among those that had fallen before, and the sound of Quarles' footsteps moving around the house.

Brit counted to fifty before taking action. The wood porch creaked with his steps. He blocked out all the other sounds and trained his ears to listen for a noise from inside the house. A sign that someone lingered there, that someone knew they were here. He heard a scuffle, maybe a footstep. His heart stopped. Suddenly, the smell of cigarette smoke filled his nostrils. Someone was inside smoking.

Instinct screamed for Brit to move. He darted to the side of the door, his gun raised. He drew cold smoke-scented air into his lungs.

"Police!" Loud pops of gunfire filled the night. Brit pressed his back against the wall. Splinters from the wood door fell like snow to the porch. "Give it up!"

Footsteps pounded, the sound shrinking as those steps moved deeper inside the house. "He's going out the back!" Brit shouted, praying Quarles could hear him.

Brit lurched off the porch and ran to the back. He heard the backdoor open then slam.

"Police! Stop or—"

Quarles voice rang in unison with the cracking pop of gunfire. His unfinished sentence hung in the darkness.

Cold air lodged in Brit's throat. No! "Quarles!" Brit bolted around the corner, following the darkest shadows against the house. His gaze darted left, right.

Then Brit saw him—saw Quarles hunkered down behind an old Chevy truck. Dead vines clung to the bumper.

Quarles waved. Alive. Hopefully, unharmed.

Brit let out the gasp of air that lodged in his throat.

Quarles pointed to the patch of pine trees clustered to one side of the yard, then started shouting orders. "Throw down the weapon! Come out with your hands up."

Brit spotted the caved-in fence behind the perp that led to the alley in the back. If he was the perp, that's where he'd run.

Brit started moving in. Quarles shook his head, but Brit had made up his mind. Humphrey wasn't getting away, not this time.

The cold bit into Brit's skin, even as sweat pooled on his brow. He inched closer, his steps muffled by the layered pine needles blanketing the ground. Finally, he made out a figure crouched behind a tree. Quarles continued talking and the perp's gaze appeared trained toward the rusted Chevy, giving Brit just the opportunity he needed.

An old wheelbarrow lay upside down on the ground and Brit moved toward it. His foot came down on a twig. The snap rang in his ears. The perp swung around, gun aimed, and Brit dove for his cover. The smell of wet earth filled his nose as gunfire erupted.

"Don't do this!" Brit yelled, rolling to his side, using the wheelbarrow for cover. "It's not a good day to die."

"We got you covered." Quarles' voice rang in the frigid air as if to remind the lowlife that he was out numbered.

But Brit would have been a hell of a lot happier if the ass was outnumbered by one more. They needed a guy behind the fence. Then again, this idiot didn't know how many there were. "Watch out, Tompkins. He might come your way and try for the fence," Brit yelled.

All was fair in shootouts—even lying. Brit sighed and spoke to the man again. "My partner has been aching to kill somebody today. You're going to make his day if you try to make that alley."

Quarles must have figured out what Brit was up to, because he saw his partner pick up a rock and toss it at the fence.

Brit saw the lowlife jerk his gaze toward the fence. "Be ready," Brit called to the non-existent officer.

Silence fell on the backyard.

"You don't want to die tonight," Brit spoke to the perp again. "Do the right thing."

"Okay, I give up," came the voice. The gun hit the ground with a hollow thud.

"Come out with your hands up," Brit said. "Lay face down on the ground and cross your legs and arms."

"Do it now!" Quarles ordered.

Brit saw the man step out from behind the tree.

"Down!" Brit yelled, frowning when the man moved into the spilled moonlight. Unless Humphrey had just lost about four inches of height and dyed his hair blond, the man falling to his knees wasn't him. So who the hell had they snagged?

~

For two hours, Cali had roamed Brit's house with silent steps, determined not to wake Susan. Yet Cali's emotions were not so silent. Her emotions flipped from anger to desire then to fear. Anger that Brit didn't believe her. Fear that he might be the next cop killed. And then desire. Want it or not, still angry at the man or not, the memory of their kiss, of his gentle touch, had her body tingling in places that hadn't tingled in a very long time.

Oh heck, who was she kidding? Her body and those places had never tingled like this before.

For the first time in her life, she felt she understood what the big fuss was about sex. Those few moments of feeling on fire with passion, feeling submersed in the world of want, had been unlike anything she'd ever experienced. Sure she'd enjoyed sex before, but never had it felt so intense. She'd never been so lost in it, or maybe it was that she'd never been so present in the moment. Whatever it was, it was different.

Cali moved back into the kitchen and looked at the open laundry room door. Mama Cat's gold eyes stared up at her. She didn't look too approachable.

"I'm not going to hurt you. I'm a friend. Actually, I could use a friend."

The cat hissed and disappeared. She didn't want to be friends. Cali just stood there, eyes trained on the door, in hopes of getting a peek at the kittens. No luck. It seemed mama had warned them not to meow to strangers.

Feeling closed in, Cali stood by the window in the living room, waiting for the day to arrive as if her confusion about last night's events would clear with the sun.

As the sky turned bright orange, Cali didn't feel clearer, except she knew she needed some time to think. And she couldn't do that here. The phone book lay open where she'd left it earlier. She punched in the number. Brit wouldn't be happy, but she needed to think about what was right for her.

She waited by a window until the cab arrived. Afraid Susan might wake up, and not wanting to face her, Cali hurried out. Walking out the door, her purse slipped off her shoulder and landed at her feet. When a light inside came on in the extra bedroom, Cali snatched up her purse and took off.

~

The sun had risen an hour ago, but even in the daylight, Brit and Quarles were in the dark about the man they'd arrested. The bastard had lawyered up and refused to talk.

Adams wasn't happy. "So you're telling me that you don't know if this lowlife is involved with either of these cases?"

Brit slumped in a chair, too tired to fight. "We know who he isn't. He isn't Humphrey or Nolan Bright, the other band member. And until Trooper Garland is able to talk—which according to his doctors won't be until tomorrow—we won't have an ID on the man who shot him. I think the guy's connected to the jewelry case, not Keith's murder. The gun our guy used is at the lab. If it's a match to the one used on Garland, we'll know."

"So basically you have shit," Adams growled.

"That pretty much sums it up," Quarles stated, his tone colder than a witch's tit, his shoulders held ramrod straight.

Glaring at the two of them, Adams pounded his fist against on the table. Brit could see that stress had Adams in a piss-poor mood. The man wanted answers, he wanted the assholes who'd killed Keith and Anderson and had attempted to kill Trooper Garland.

No one wanted that more than Brit, but people in hell wanted ice cream, the kind with marshmallows and nuts. And they friggin' weren't going to get it just because they wanted it. Neither would he or Adams. And no amount of brow beating on the sergeant's part was going to change it.

"So why the hell did you bring him in?" Adams snapped. Obviously, he hadn't heard the whole story.

Quarles, his green eyes bright with anger, looked at Brit as if to see if he wanted to take a stab at the question. Brit shrugged, and his partner took the lead. "Well, let's see. Maybe at this precinct you let assholes shoot at your men, but where I came from, we are accustomed to dragging their asses in and locking them up until we find out why they chose to fucking try to kill us."

Adams' nostrils flared, giving him a cartoonish appearance. "I didn't know shots were fired."

"You could have asked or read the report before jumping up our asses," Quarles snapped back.

Even running on weak fumes, Brit could see this wasn't going to end well if someone didn't intervene. So he intervened. Or, he did the next best thing. He took the focus off his partner and brought it down on himself. He and Adams had a history; they knew how to fight fair.

Brit got to his feet. Sometimes the best way to show a smart man he was being an idiot was to become a bigger idiot yourself. "I tell you what, sir. I'm going to go in there and beat the crap out of that guy, and I'll bet he'll tell us what we want to know."

Adams shoved a chair closer to the table, its legs scraping on the tile floor like chalk on a blackboard. "Go home. Both of you look like the walking dead, but when Garland wakes up, I want someone over there to find out what he knows."

Brit opened the door and motioned for Quarles. His partner snatched up the file and stormed out of the room. Obviously driven by anger, Quarles didn't stop until he stood in the parking lot. He cut Brit a sharp glare. "Adams is a fucking ass."

"He can be," Brit said, feeling that persistent tightness pulling at his shoulders. "But there are worse assholes." Brit pressed a hand on Quarles' back. "Come on, I'll take you back to your ride."

A few minutes later, they pulled up at the hospital beside Quarles' truck. Quarles turned. "Are you headed home?"

Nodding, Brit thought about Cali. "Yeah."

"Tell Susan I'll call her later," Quarles said. "What time does her plane take off this afternoon?"

Brit blew out a deep breath. "I don't remember the exact time." In truth, he hadn't remembered period. But hell, he'd pretty much been an ass to his sister this trip. He was going to have to do some major sucking up later on.

Quarles put one foot out the door, then looked back. "We worked good together today. Don't you think?"

"Yeah," Brit said and meant it. He didn't want to mean it, hadn't wanted to start replacing Keith, but it was happening.

Quarles shifted, but didn't leave. "I know how you feel."

"Feel about what?" Brit blinked the grit from his eyes.

"About Keith. I lost my partner last year. He was working security part time for a grocery store. The bank inside got held up. It's part of the reason I transferred down here."

Brit stared at Quarles. Now he understood why the man had taken so much shit from him these last three weeks. "Sorry."

"Yeah," Quarles said. "So am I. Sorry about Keith."

Brit leaned back. "Did you catch the bastard who shot him?"

Quarles' smile sounded in his voice. "His trial is next month. They're asking for the death penalty."

"Good," Brit said.

"We'll get Keith's killer, too." Quarles sent him a nod.

"Yeah."

Brit watched the man get in his car. Leaning back, Brit closed his eyes as his mind juggled the issues weighing on his chest.

Keith—finding the sorry son of a bitch that took him out. Laura—Keith's wife—whom Brit hadn't spoken to since the funeral.

Thoughts of Cali sifted through the worry funnel and landed with a thud on his chest. What kind of reception would he get when he got home? Hell, would she even talk to him?

He drew in a pound of oxygen and let it out slowly. When he reached for his keys, his cell phone rang. Too tired to think straight, he snagged it from his pocket and answered it before checking the number.

"Yeah."

"Detective?" the male voice asked.

"Yeah?" he repeated while his frazzled mind, almost too tired to work, attempted to put a name to the voice.

"It's Bradley Faith, from the hotel. I got beat up last night."

Brit ran a hand over his face. "What's up?"

"Well, I found something that the jerk left here. It concerns the girl, so I thought you might want to know about it."

~

Cali stepped up to the apartment door and knocked. She knew she was going to wake Tanya. If Eric was with her and Cali interrupted their "morning after", she was going to cry.

Actually, she was pretty sure she was going to cry anyway.

She heard footsteps then saw the peephole go dark. The door opened. Tanya wore a pair of green panda-bear pajamas. "Cali?"

Her friend's non-sexy attire gave Cali hope that Tanya was alone. "Please tell me you don't have Eric in the bed with you."

"No. We just had dinner. No hanky panky. Come in." She threw open the door.

"I was just going to get my car and find a hotel, but I think my keys fell out of my purse at Brit's." Cali's heart ached.

A cold wind tousled Tanya's hair, and she wrapped her arms around herself. "Something bad happened, didn't it?"

Cali hesitated. "Sort of."

"What happened?" Tanya stepped back into her apartment.

"I don't know where to start." Cali bit down on her lip as her sinuses started to sting.

Tanya's eyes tightened in sympathy. "Come on, I'll fix us some hazelnut coffee. There's nothing flavored coffee can't cure. It's right up there with chocolate."

"Make it a big pot." When Cali got to the kitchen, she spotted the phone. "Before I weep, or OD on caffeine, can I make a call?"

"Yeah." Tanya went to the cabinet and got the coffee.

Opening her purse, Cali found Brit's card and saw he'd written his home and cell phone. Susan answered on the second ring. "Hi. This is Cali. Is Brit home?"

"Hey," Susan said. "I saw the taxi and tried to catch you."

"I'm sorry. I just had to . . . to get out for a while." Cali didn't know what else to say. After insisting she wasn't dating Brit and then having Susan discover them in bed, Cali knew Susan probably considered her a real loony-toon. "I didn't want Brit to worry. I'm at a friend's. I'm safe, and I'm going to stay here for a while. Can you tell Brit I'll call him later?"

"Sure," Susan said. "But why don't you try his cell number?"

Cali considered it. "I don't want to disturb him at work. Can you just leave him a message?"

"Sure." Susan hesitated. "Is everything okay?"

"Fine. Except, I think my keys may have spilled out of my purse on Brit's front lawn. Can you check? I'll come by later."

"Okay." Susan paused. "He's really a good guy."

"I know." When Cali hung up, she leaned against the wall and tears filled her eyes. She swallowed and looked at her feet. Painted toenails make you happy. She recalled her mother saying. She kicked off her shoes. "Do you have some nail polish?"

Chapter Thirty

The smell of freshly brewed coffee filled Brit's nose as he unlocked his front door. He dropped his keys on the table as he walked inside. He heard someone in his kitchen and prepared himself to eat crow, beak and all.

As he stepped inside the room, he saw his sister. Susan turned around, holding a box of cereal. His gaze cut around the room. Cali must still be asleep. Good. He'd only have to eat one bird at a time when he apologized to them separately—his sister for ignoring her and Cali for doubting her about talking to Stan.

He touched his pocket where he'd tucked the computer printout of Cali's MasterCard bill. Somehow, Humphrey had gotten her computer password and printed out the paperwork that showed Cali had charged a room. When Stan had been tossing the clerk around to get the key, the paper must have slipped from the idiot's pocket. The desk clerk had found it after they'd left.

"Hey." Brit removed his windbreaker and pulled out a chair.

Susan looked him up and down, her sisterly gaze checking him over with protectiveness. "You're going to kill yourself. You can't keep going like this without sleep."

He pushed a hand through his hair. "I'm too mean to die." Brit noticed the laundry room door standing open. "Are the cats okay?"

"Fine. The mama still won't come out. But the kittens peeked out a couple of times.

You want some cereal?"

"Sure." He glanced back down the hall toward his bedroom. He watched Susan place a ceramic bowl in front of him, then turn to get a spoon. "What time does your plane leave?" He leaned his chair back on two legs.

She turned around, spoon in hand, surprise widening her blue-green eyes. "You remembered?"

He shrugged, not wanting to admit he hadn't, but willing to admit his bigger mistake. "I've been a piss-poor host."

"Yeah, you have." She dropped the spoon in his bowl and rested her hand on his shoulder. "But I understand." She ruffled his hair the way she used to do when he was a kid. "I need to be at the airport at five. However, I have to drop off the car at the rental place. It's right by the airport and they offer a shuttle service."

Brit watched his sister sit down across from him, peel a banana, and slice it into her bowl. "I'll follow you and drop you off. It's the least I can do."

She looked up and offered him a smile and half of her banana.

"No, thanks." He stood, even though every muscle in his body begged him not to, grabbed a cup and helped himself to coffee. "I'm sorry I had to skip out on Mom's party."

"At least you showed up. I didn't think you would." She poured him a bowl of dry sounding flakes. "It meant the world to Mom that you came."

Do I remind you of your mom? He recalled Cali asking him.

He didn't want to discuss his mother. He settled back into his chair. A meow called from the door. Brit turned and Mama Cat was sitting on the threshold. Slowly, she edged out, until she stood beside his leg. Dipping her head down, she rubbed her face on his ankle.

"Look at that," Susan said. "I've tried food, sweet talk. But no, I'm not good enough. You just like men, huh? Slut," Susan said, pointing at the cat with her spoon.

"It's just because I've been feeding her," he said as his sister turned back to her cereal bowl. "What happened to donuts for breakfast?"

"Got to keep my girly figure." She smiled at the cat. "Guess I like men, too." She poured blue-looking skim milk into his bowl of flakes. "Five more pounds and I'm at goal weight."

"You were fine the way you were." The cat gave his leg another tap before disappearing back into the laundry room.

"I was fat the way I was," she said. "But, thank you."

"I'm really sorry for not being here this time. Between Keith's case and Cali's, I've been running in tight circles."

"I like her." Susan spooned a bite of banana and cereal into her mouth. The crunch filled the silence.

"Me, too." For the life of him, he didn't know where the relationship was going. Until Cali, the idea of a real relationship would have sent him running for cover. But now, he was still scared, but not so ready to run.

"Has Cali gotten up yet?" He deposited a bite of cardboard flakes floating in watered-down milk into his mouth.

Susan's eyes widened. "She didn't call you?"

"Call me?" He swallowed the bad feeling along with this sorry excuse for a breakfast.

"Yeah. She left first thing this morning."

"Shit!" He sprang to his feet so fast he hit the table. The milk in his bowl sloshed over the edge. "You let her go?"

Susan dropped her spoon. "Let her? Oh, I didn't know you were keeping her against her will. If you'd told me, I'd have handcuffed her to a doorknob."

"I didn't . . ." Tension curled up in his body.

"She called." Susan took her spoon for a lap around her bowl. "She said she was with a friend. Said she planned to stay there."

"Did she say it was Tanya?"

"She didn't give a name." Susan stood and grabbed a dish towel.

Brit grabbed his phone and started hitting buttons to find Tanya's number.

"I don't think she wants to talk to you." She wiped his mess from the table.

He looked up. "She said that?"

"Not in so many words, but she apologized for skipping out and said she just needed to get away. Then she said she would call you later. And the way she said it sort of implied for you not to call her."

He popped his phone closed. "Did she mention that her ex-boyfriend is a murderer and now he's after her?"

"She told me some of it." Susan dropped the towel in the sink. "But she also said she was safe. Do you think the boyfriend could find her at this friend's place?"

He hadn't thought it the other day, but right now, thinking took energy he didn't have. He wanted Cali here. He needed her here. Pocketing his phone, he turned to leave.

"Brit?" Susan's tone gave him pause, and he faced her.

"What?" he asked, annoyed and not hiding it.

"If she isn't in any danger, maybe you should give her some space. She sounded, I don't know, upset or something."

"Well, then I'd best go and resolve things."

"When a woman wants time to think, it's best to leave her be. Let her call you when she's ready."

"I know you just want to help, but don't. Butt out!" He started for the door.

Of course, Susan followed him. His sister never backed down from a fight. "Take a nap first. If you go there now you might make things worse."

He couldn't take a friggin' nap. He needed Cali to sleep.

Susan stepped in front of him. "Get some rest. You're grumpy, you're tired, and you're bound to mess something up when you talk to her."

"Mess things up like Dad always messed up?" he asked, suddenly remembering Cali asking him some hard questions.

"I didn't say that," she snapped. "Good God, Brit! You're nothing like him."

"Then why did you talk to Cali about Mom?"

"I didn't. I just said that you grew up wanting to protect women."

He shook his head. "Look, Sis. I don't like knowing that my partner is the guy trying to get in your pants. But I'm not butting into your love life, so get out of mine."

Her chin snapped up. "Really? And what do you call threatening to shoot John?"

So Quarles had told his sister that, huh? "That wasn't butting in, that was just me telling a guy what will happen if he starts dicking with my sister."

She almost smiled. "But maybe I want some—"

"Just stop right there. I don't want to hear it."

Susan's eyebrows suddenly arched. "This thing between you and Cali, it's serious, isn't it?"

He snatched his keys from the end table. "I don't know. But I won't find out if I don't bring her back here."

Chapter Thirty-One

Cali sat in Tanya's kitchen. "And then I don't know why, but I grabbed his toothbrush to fish out the condoms."

Tanya held her stomach because she was laughing so hard and, for some reason, so was Cali. It felt good to laugh, almost as releasing as a good cry.

"So did you ever tell him about the condoms?"

"No. I just hid them in the bottom of his cabinet."

Tanya's doorbell rang and was followed by a loud whacking knock. "Ten to one, that's Mr. Little Dickhead," Tanya said. "Probably wanting to know what you did with his condoms."

"Oh, shit!" Cali said.

"Did I hear you right?" Tanya snickered. "Did you actually say a naughty word?"

Cali frowned. "Yeah, I guess this Charmin-faced girl has been hanging around the wrong people lately."

"Is he so wrong?"

"I was talking about you." The doorbell rang again.

Tanya laughed again. "What do you want me to do?"

Cali pulled her knees up to her chest. Her toenails, freshly painted with two coats since she'd arrived at Tanya's, stood out like beacons in red. She moaned. She didn't know what she wanted.

Talking to Tanya had taken the edge off Cali's panic, or maybe it was the toenail painting. Either way, she'd even told Tanya about the dreams. Her friend had basically agreed with Dr. Roberts—the dreams were just Cali's mind dealing with the stress and grief. But what did Cali believe?

Great. She didn't know what she wanted, or what she believed. She was just one indecisive chick, with some really bright red toenails.

The doorbell rang again. Cali hugged her knees.

"It's your call," Tanya said. "I can tell him to go float his boat down a different stream, and we can paint your toenails again, or I can ask him in, and give you two some space."

The knock came harder. "I don't think I should stay with him anymore."

"Then I'll tell him." Tanya started to get up.

"No," Cali said. "I'd better tell him myself." Barefoot, toenail polish still gluey, she duck-walked out of the kitchen.

"Okay," Tanya said. "But stick to your guns, be strong."

Guns ready, and trying to keep her toes apart, Cali moved to the door. She pressed her eye to the peephole, just to make sure it was Brit. The last thing she wanted was to confront Stan. And if he'd found her at the hotel, maybe he could find her here.

She saw blue-green grieving eyes, and her heart melted. She opened the door, swallowing a lump of raw emotion. He looked like the walking dead. The man needed to go to bed. She got a flashback of them in his bed last night. To sleep, she added to the thought.

He didn't speak. Just stared. She cleared her throat.

The muscle in his cheek twitched. "We need to talk. Will you please come home with me?"

She inhaled, remembering she had guns to stick to. But where were her guns and what exactly was she supposed to stick to? Then she remembered. "I think I should stay here, Brit."

"Why?" Hurt echoed in his voice. Her heart responded, and her grip on her guns weakened.

"You know why." She stood a little straighter.

He pushed a hand over his face. "You said no and I stopped."

She stared down at her toenails and decided they could use a dozen or so more coats. Then squaring her shoulders again, she faced him. "It's not that. Or only part of that."

"Then what else is it?" He fell against the doorframe.

His scent surrounded her, and she closed her eyes for a second.

"You think I'm lying to you about Stan," she said. "You think I'm like your mother. And you don't even like her very much. And while I don't think I'm anything like her, I sure as heck don't like you thinking I'm some kind of perverted woman who likes to be abused."

He reached up and pinched the tip of his nose and closed his eyes as if trying to gather his thoughts. "You're right. I was wrong to accuse you of talking to Stan."

"Oh, and you just suddenly believe me, huh?"

"I wish I was that smart. But no. The hotel clerk found a print-out of your online credit card bill. Stan somehow got your password and printed out the charge to the hotel. And I know that makes me an even bigger ass, but I'm trying to be honest."

She tried to figure out why her resolve was fading. Perhaps his honesty. Perhaps that he looked so tired. Perhaps because even tired, he looked so damn sexy.

He suddenly continued, "And I'll even admit that in the beginning I did associate you with all the things I didn't like about my mom."

He inhaled deeply. "And if you're standing here waiting for me to give you a reason for my behavior, well, we're going to be standing here a long time. I could tell you it's because I'm exhausted, and I am. I could tell you it's because I'm torn up inside with grief, and I am. But that doesn't make it okay. So basically, the only excuse I can think to offer up right now is that I'm an idiot. But I'm an honest idiot who's apologizing."

Another wave of empathy ran through her. She wanted to wrap her arms around him. She needed to help him, to erase the grief from his eyes—because somehow helping him, helped her own grief.

And yet, deep down, she remembered something her mother had said. You can't fix, Brit. He's going to have to fix himself.

Did that mean she needed to be working on fixing herself too?

He pushed a hand over his face. "Come home with me. I need to know you're okay. I need you to sleep."

She looked at him and felt herself wavering again. "What's happening here?" She waved a hand between them.

"I just want to protect you." His words stirred her anger again and she managed to find her guns.

"So that's what this is all about? You, protecting me. There's nothing happening between us?" Maybe she wouldn't just stick to her guns, maybe she should load, cock, and fire them on him. "Do you seduce all the women you come across in your job? Take them home and crawl in bed with them and stick your hand down—"

"Cali." He took a deep breath. "Look, I'm sorry. You're right. This isn't just about me protecting you." He closed his eyes for a second, and when he opened them, he stared right at her, his red-rimmed blue-greens pleading. "I don't understand everything that's happening. I'm not going to pretend I do. But all I know is that I don't want to walk away from here without you. I think if we're going to figure this out, then we need to do it together. Please. Please, come home with me."

She studied her toenails again because if she looked hard enough, she'd find her guns down there hanging out at her feet. The guns she was supposed to stick to, but had dropped. He reached out and touched her face, and she no longer wanted to find the guns. She wanted to fall into him, to let him comfort her, and offer him comfort in return.

He pulled his hand from her face. "I won't even . . . Nothing will happen that you don't want to happen."

"And in that lies the problem." She raised her gaze.

He smiled as if understanding exactly what she meant. He reached back up and ran a finger over her cheek. "Then why is any of that an issue? We're both consenting adults."

"The case," Cali said. "The fact that you and I barely know each other. The fact that both of us are going through something awful right now, and it isn't wise to start a relationship."

"Whoa," he said. "First, you know more about me right now than most of the guys I've worked with for eight years. You even met my mother. No one has ever met my mother. Hell, Keith hadn't even met my mom." He hesitated. "And I'd like to think I know you. As for the case, even without your testimony we've got solid evidence. The worst that could happen is that I get my ass chewed out by my boss. I'm willing to take that risk. And hell yeah, we're both going through something, and that's part of the reason we should be together. To help each other. I need you. Please."

She bit the inside of her cheek and noted the lines of stress around his eyes. Any fight she'd had in her went the way of the guns. "Let me say good bye to Tanya."

Relief filled his eyes as he leaned in and kissed her. Not a let's-have-sex kiss, but a thank-you kiss. "I'll wait here."

When she went back in the kitchen, Tanya held out Cali's purse. "I don't know how you held out so long."

Cali took the purse. "I lost my guns."

"The hell with guns. I just want to hear all the juicy details later."
Tanya hugged her.

Cali hugged back. "Thanks for being here. I owe you."

"Yeah." Tanya walked her to the door. "And pay backs are hell."

~

While Brit waited, his phone rang. He looked at the number and
frowned. Keith's wife. He cut it off and dropped it back in his pocket.
When he did, he felt the folded piece of paper. Forgetting what it was,
he pulled it out. It was the printed copy of Cali's credit card bill. He
was about to drop it back in his pocket when an idea hit.

If he hadn't been so tired, he'd have realized sooner. This was the
key to catching Stan. He'd charge another room on Cali's card, and
wait for Stan to show up. Hope fluttered inside him. His smile widened
when Cali walked out.

She looked at the paper in his hands.

"It's what the hotel clerk found," he said as they got into his SUV.
"Your online credit card bill."

She buckled up and then glanced again at the paper and frowned.
"I was trying to fix it so I could pay my bills online. He offered to
help."

Which you should have refused, he thought, but he didn't say it.
He started the car and headed to his house. "Actually, I think this is
going to help us end this case."

"How?" Her big blues, tired blues, met his.

"I'll rent another hotel room with your card. This time when Stan
comes to call, my partner and I will be waiting."

"Okay," she said.

She didn't say anything else, and Brit wondered why she didn't
seem as happy about this as he was. But even as doubt pulled at his
mind, he pushed it away. But the closer they got to his house, the
quieter she got. When he pulled into the garage, she looked almost
afraid.

"Something wrong?" he asked.

She glanced at him. "I'm sure your sister thinks my hair color is an indication of my mental capabilities."

"Don't be silly. Susan told me she likes you."

"Right," Cali said, and they walked inside. A note on the table said Susan had gone to have lunch with John and wouldn't be back until around three.

"Why is she doing this?" he muttered.

"Doing what?"

"Dating my partner. It's going to end badly."

"You don't know that," Cali said.

Brit frowned. "If he hurts her, I'll have to kill him and I think my sergeant will frown upon that."

She rolled her eyes. "Why do you think he'll hurt her?"

"Because he's a man," he snapped.

"Hmm," she said. "So maybe I should stay away from men, too."

He exhaled. "I guess it's a brother thing."

"I guess so." She offered a shy smile. "Good thing I don't have any brothers."

He remembered that she'd practically told him that she wanted to have sex with him. Not that he'd actually forgotten it. The thought had caused a tightening sensation low in his belly since she'd said it.

He opened the fridge, not knowing what he needed most, food, sleep, or to make love to Cali. "You hungry?"

"I ate, but thanks." She ran her hand over the table as if nervous, and he decided sex would have to wait until later. Besides, he wanted to be at his best their first time, and with only a couple of hours of sleep in the past thirty-six hours, he didn't think he'd be at his best. Food first, sleep, and then sex. Funny how sometimes the most important things got put last.

He pulled out the milk and frowned when he saw the nonfat label. Shoving the milk back in, he grabbed the carton of orange juice. After pouring a glass of OJ, he spread some mayonnaise on a slice of bread, added a piece of cheese, topped it with another slab of bread, and ate standing up.

Cali studied him. "Are you afraid to sit down because you might not be able to get up?"

He swallowed. "Yup. Did you sleep okay last night?"

She shook her head. "I never did go back to sleep. I'm pretty tired myself."

He looked at her without trying to hide the want in his eyes. "Then you won't blame me when my head hits the pillow and I'm out cold. And we catch up on other stuff when we're both feeling recharged?"

"That's fine." Her cheeks grew redder and he knew she knew what he meant by catch up.

He leaned against the counter and grinned. "You're blushing. You're so damn refreshing."

"I am not," she said.

"Yes, you are. Can you even say sex without turning red?"

Her eyes widened. "Yes. I can say sex."

He pointed a finger at her. "You're turning redder." He chuckled and polished off his sandwich. "Come on." He wrapped his arm around her waist and led her to his bedroom. The bed had been made and his sister's pajamas lay folded neatly on top. Cali's doings, no doubt. His sister had never won any prize on neatness.

He pressed a kiss to Cali's temple and moved her to the bed. She sat down on the edge. He kicked off his shoes, removed his shirt, and unsnapped his jeans, never taking his eyes off her.

"You gonna sleep in your clothes?" he asked.

"I'm plenty comfortable." She sounded so prim and proper.

"Right," he teased.

"Really, I'm fine." She stood up.

Grinning, he removed his jeans, but left on his boxers for fear of shocking her that he was already hard for her. Then he pulled back the covers and motioned for her to climb in.

She pushed off her tennis shoes, nudged them beneath the bed with her foot, then dipped under his arm and crawled between the sheets. She kept crawling all the way to the other side. He went in after her. Sliding them back to the middle of the bed, he draped his arm across her stomach and buried his nose in her hair. Her blond strands caught on the stubble on his face, reminding him he needed to shave, and he breathed in her scent. Damn, she smelled good—felt good, too.

"Are you going to be able to sleep?" he asked, wondering if he could. He was getting harder and his mind teased him with thoughts of taking off that red sweater, of tasting every place he'd touched last night.

Obviously, some muscles in his body didn't need sleep. He rose up on one elbow to see her face. And what a face.

She cut her gaze toward him. "I think so."

He kissed her cheek and noticed the tension in his shoulders had already loosened. "Thank you for coming home with me."

"You're welcome." She shifted and looked at the clock. "Should we set it so we'll be up when Susan gets here?"

"Why?"

"Because I told her that we weren't getting naked together. And this will be the second time that she's caught me in bed with you."

He chuckled. "When she gets here, I'll tell her we're now getting naked and having sex." He winked. "She'll be happy."

Cali set her mouth in a firm line. "I don't think so."

Brit gave in and set the clock. When Cali rolled over on her side, he followed her. He wrapped his arm around her waist and pulled her soft backside against him. Even too tired to think, he wasn't too tired to feel. And he felt every sweet inch of her against him.

He had almost closed his eyes when he heard her mutter, "Shit."

He pressed his face into her hair and grinned. "You're a teacher, you're not supposed to cuss."

She rolled over and frowned. "I just remembered."

"Remembered what?" From the look in her eyes, it appeared serious. His gut tightened, thinking it was about Humphrey. "What did you remember?"

"A reason why we can't have sex." And she blushed when she said the three-letter word. But he was more concerned with what she had to say than the blush this time.

"Why's that?" He propped up on his elbow.

She frowned. "I'm afraid that your condoms went the way of your toothbrush."

"Say what?"

"They went in the toilet." Humor danced in her eyes, yet she bit her lip as if trying not to laugh.

"You threw my condoms in the toilet?" Laughing, he pulled her against his chest. Somewhere between the spurts of laughter, he assured her he had another stash of condoms. Right in the bedside table, waiting for when they woke up. Then, in spite of wanting her so badly he ached, the laughter and having her warm sweetness so close chased away the grief, he slept. His last thought was of how heavenly she felt against him and how he could get used to this.

Used to having her in his life.

Chapter Thirty-Two

When the alarm went off, he came out of a dead sleep—the kind of sleep that refueled the body. He blinked away the mental cobwebs and looked around. The other side of the bed was empty.

"Cali?" He slapped off the buzzing alarm, pushing a hand over his face. His palm met with the bristle of his two-day-old beard. He needed to shave. He needed a shower.

He needed to make love to Cali.

Desire tightened his boys and a smile brushed over his lips.

Tossing back the covers, he got up and heard laughter. He moved down the hall. Cali and Susan sat at his kitchen table, chuckling like old friends and digging through a box of photos on the table.

Mama Cat sat on the threshold to the laundry room watching them. Something about seeing the three of them—three women that all had gotten under his skin—all together in one room made the air in his lungs feel fresher. Another smile started inside his chest and fluttered up to his lips.

He leaned against the doorframe and enjoyed the strange emotions doing laps around his chest. "What's so funny?"

They both swung around. Susan spoke, "I'm showing Cali all your naked baby pictures."

"Hey, in my defense, it was cold when they were taken."

Susan laughed. The cat meowed. Cali grinned and he saw her cheeks warm to a soft pink color. He also saw her gaze brush over him, slowly, as if gathering details to save to her memory. He liked the look in her eyes. He liked where that look could take them.

Hell, if Susan wasn't here, he'd strip off his boxers and tell her to take a long and hard look. And he was going to get long and hard if he didn't corral his thoughts.

Susan must have noted Cali's red face because she clucked her tongue. "Men have no decency. Go get your clothes on and quit trying to impress Cali."

Chuckling, he turned away before his sister saw just how much Cali impressed him. "I'm going to shower and shave." A cold shower.

Looked as if he wouldn't get everything he needed until he put his sister on that plane. As his body tightened, he wondered if he could book her on an earlier flight.

~

Cali watched Brit give Susan a hug. The airport noise bounced around the light gray walls like ping pong balls. Families whispering goodbye, voices raised with excitement as they spotted loved ones, and an occasional beep of security catching someone's keys in their pocket. Glancing around, she saw what appeared to be a mother and daughter embracing and Cali's chest tightened. For just a second, she felt so completely alone. Alone in a world where everybody had someone.

Not wanting to go melodramatic, she focused again on Brit and Susan.

"I love you," Susan said to her brother.

"Back at you," Brit said, hugging her. Glancing over his sister's shoulder, his gaze met Cali's and he winked.

Cali smiled.

Susan pulled away from Brit. "Promise me you'll call Mom occasionally."

"Have a good flight." He raised an eyebrow at her.

Susan frowned and turned to Cali. "It was a pleasure to meet you." Her hug took Cali by surprise, but she didn't mind.

"Make my brother behave," Susan said. "If he keeps running around in his boxers, threaten to post one of those naked baby pictures on the Internet. The one taken on that cold day."

"I will." Cali laughed. Having never had a sibling, she found their teasing something to be cherished.

As Susan walked away, Brit pulled Cali close. "Told you she liked you," Brit said.

"You're lucky. I wish I had a sister," Cali said. As soon as Susan passed security, Brit led Cali out of the airport.

They stepped out of the elevator and into the parking garage. "I thought we'd order in tonight," he said as he hit the clicker of his SUV. "What do you want? Chinese? Italian? Me?"

His tone grew soft. His gaze met hers. Then he pulled her into his arms and, leaning her against the passenger door, he kissed her.

His hands traveled up her ribs, dangerously close to her breasts. When the kiss ended, he leaned his forehead against her and took several long breaths. "Alone at last."

"You don't work tonight?" Cali asked, a little out of breath herself. Every place he'd touched her, and some places he hadn't, pulsed with pleasure. The memory of his touch on her bare skin in intimate places had the pulse of pleasure increasing.

"Not until tomorrow." The heat in his eyes made promises.

She wanted those promises. She didn't know what would happen after Stan had been brought in, after she learned to deal with her mother's death, or after Brit learned to deal with the loss of his partner. How much of this magical feeling was situational? When the situation changed, would things change between them? Either way, right now she wanted to let herself feel this.

"Good." She smiled. "You need a full night's sleep."

He arched an eyebrow. "Sleep is so overrated."

She kissed him, leaning close—all of her against all of him. She slipped her tongue inside his mouth. He gently pressed his hips against hers and she met him in the sensual motion. Footsteps and the sound of rolling luggage broke them apart.

He grinned, his eyes dark with want and his lips wet. "I'd better get you home before you have your way with me right here."

She felt her cheeks grow red and heard his chuckle.

"I think I'm figuring you out. You can have sex, but you can't talk sex." He leaned in and whispered in her ear. "Before it's over with, you're going to be talking dirty to me."

Before it's over with . . . ? Brit's words rang in her head. Was he too wondering how long this could last?

~

"Shit," Brit mumbled as he spotted Quarles' truck parked in his drive way. Then he spotted the man on the porch, his cell phone in his hand. Brit's cell phone started ringing.

Quarles looked over his shoulder at the SUV and closed his phone. Brit glanced at Cali as he pulled to a stop. "Have you ever seen a grown man cry?"

She bit down on her lip and offered him a shy smile.

Frowning, he got out of his SUV. "What's up?"

Quarles looked toward the driveway as Cali stepped out of the SUV, then he met Brit's eyes with sympathy. "Sorry."

Brit didn't attempt to hide his frustration. "You should be."

"It's Rina," Quarles said. "She disappeared from the safe house. I stopped by the precinct, and the officer watching her called in while I was there. He thinks she took off in search of a hit. Said she looked like she was having a meltdown."

Brit raked a hand through his hair and glanced back at Cali. He wanted to tell Quarles he didn't give a rat's ass about Rina and insist he call someone else to track her down. But he couldn't.

~

Lady Luck liked him today. He found Rina the first place he and Quarles looked—a rundown bar where a lot of hookers hung out on their down time. In the back of the smoky room, she half sat, half lay sprawled out over some guy's lap. As Brit and Quarles approached the booth, Brit noted Rina's unfocused stare. She'd found what she came looking for. And the man with his hand up her dress thought he'd found what he was looking for, too.

Clearing his throat, he flashed his badge. The man jumped to attention. He pushed Rina off his lap. She landed with a thump against the side of the booth.

She pulled herself up and dropped both her elbows on the table. Her half-gone gaze met Brit's, and she smiled. "Hey. You shouldn't be jealous. I offered you a freebie earlier."

Brit motioned for the chump to leave. When he scurried away, Brit pulled Rina up by the elbow. "Come on."

"I don't want to go back there." She tried to wiggle away.

"You don't want to end up dead, either." Brit had to put his arm around her to guide her out of the bar.

"Don't you want to fuck me, Lowell?" She put a hand on his chest, attempting to pole-dance herself down his leg, but in her drugged state, she nearly fell over. He caught her.

"No, Rina, I don't." He held her further away. Right then, Brit realized more than ever how deep his feelings ran for Cali. Because he didn't want to fuck Cali either. He couldn't remember when he'd felt something this genuine for a woman.

He'd always liked women, and never stopped short of respecting them. But it had been about sex. He hadn't been a selfish lover. He offered pleasure when he took his, but with Cali it wasn't just about pleasure. He remembered how right it felt laughing with her in his bed, talking to her the other morning at breakfast, how seeing her with his sister and that damn cat had melted his heart. And if that wasn't enough of a difference, he recalled how comforting it had been when she'd squeezed his hand when he'd been about to face his mother. Everything he felt for Cali was different. Genuine.

Rina looked over at Quarles. "You want to fuck me?"

Quarles' eyes lit up. "I'm going to have to pass, as well. But thanks for offering. My ego would have been hurt if you hadn't."

They took Rina back to the precinct and another officer drove her to the safe house.

"Do you think Rina is going to ask him to fuck her, too?" Brit asked.

Quarles shook his head. "Nah, he's not nearly as good looking as we are." They both laughed as Quarles followed Brit back to his office where they filled out some paperwork.

"Heard anything on Garland?" Brit sat down in his chair.

"He's out of surgery, but they're keeping him sedated for a while. The doctor said we couldn't see him until tomorrow."

Brit nodded. "Good." He could now go spend the evening with Cali. His body tightened with anticipation.

"Did you get Susan to the airport?" Quarles asked.

"Yeah." Brit cast a look at his partner, still not too happy about the man's interest in his sister.

"She said she'll be down for Thanksgiving," Quarles added.

"She usually comes down for the holidays." He looked at his desk. "You still pissed about me seeing her?"

"You got a sister?" When Quarles nodded, Brit added, "How old?" He purposely put some sleaze into his voice.

"She'll be eighteen next month. The baby in the family."

"What if I told you I wanted to get to know her?"

Quarles' eyebrows shot up. "I'd say you're too damn old."

"But I like 'em young. And I'll bet she's hot."

Quarles frowned. "Okay, I see what you're getting at. It makes a brother uncomfortable, but that's just tough. I like your sister. I don't know where it will lead. But we're both adults. And if say so myself, I'm not a bad catch. And I'd never, ever screw a blow-up doll, male or female."

Brit sighed. "She told you about Edward, huh?"

"Yeah. Bastard."

Brit's negative feelings about Quarles and his sister lightened. "Just make sure it doesn't lead to her being hurt."

"Hey." Adams appeared at the door. "Good work snagging Rina." He stepped inside the office and shut the door. Both Brit and Quarles looked at each other with concern. Adams leaned against the closed door because there wasn't room for him anywhere else. "About the guy you brought in yesterday—I was out of line."

Brit noted that Adams mostly looked at his partner. The sergeant obviously depended on their history to make things right and didn't feel Brit expected an apology. Brit didn't.

"You two did good bringing him in." Adams ran a hand over his unshaven face. The whole damn police force looked sleep-deprived because of the cop shootings.

Brit actually felt good knowing he wasn't alone.

"Did he give us anything?" Quarles asked the question sitting on the end of Brit's tongue.

Adam looked at Brit. "Not much. But you were right. He's not our cop killer. The gun he had and the one used on Keith and Anderson weren't the same."

"Did you compare that gun to the slug that was pulled out of Cali McKay's apartment?" Brit asked.

Adams butted against the door. "We did. It isn't a match. But the guy is connected to the Humphrey case. We got a hit on his prints. His name is Trent Bright. Cousin to Nolan Bright. He swears he doesn't know anything. That his cousin called him and asked him to meet him at that address. Claimed he thought you guys were trying to rob the place when you approached."

"Was that before or after we informed him we were the police?" Quarles muttered.

Brit grabbed a pencil and rolled it between his palms. "Do me a favor. Have Ballistics compare the bullet pulled out of McKay's apartment to the one that shot Garland."

Adams scratched his raspy cheek. "You think Humphrey shot Garland?"

"I'm thinking it could be a possibility," Brit said. "Maybe Humphrey, Nolan and his cousin are in this together."

Adams tugged at his belt. "I'll have it checked out. Now all we got to do is find a way to catch Humphrey."

Brit pulled out the computer printout of Cali's credit card bill. "I think I've got that figured out, too."

He'd planned to wait until tomorrow, but the sooner he had Humphrey behind bars, the sooner he could see clear to what was really happening between him and Cali. The thought brought just a bit of panic marching through his chest, but Brit no longer felt so eager to deny the emotions. Instead, a part of him whispered, "March on."

An hour later, they had everything planned. They'd managed to get four rooms at an out-of-the-way hotel. They wanted the adjoining rooms empty in case trouble broke out. And the next day they'd have the hotel posted on Cali's bill. The thought of having to spend the next few nights watching the hotel room made Brit even more eager to get home to Cali now.

It was almost eight when he walked onto his front porch, juggling bags that contained strawberries, champagne, and take-out Chinese food from his favorite restaurant.

When he rearranged the bags to slip the key into the lock, he realized his palms were sweaty. He hadn't been nervous about being with a girl in years, but he felt it now. It wasn't just the thought of sex giving him pause. It was how she made him feel. And then there was the talk they needed to have. After considering everything, he decided Cali should take some time off from school. Humphrey had already tried to get to her at her school twice. Brit didn't want there to be a third time.

He opened the door, and the saucy smell of the food floated from the paper bags.

"Cali?" She didn't answer.

Emotions fluttered inside him like a trapped bird. What if he'd been wrong about her being safe here? What if he'd been wrong about her wanting to be here? The second thought sent him hurrying into the kitchen. He'd hunted her down once today. If she ran again, he wasn't sure his pride would allow him to go after her twice.

Then the thought of losing her wormed its way into his gut, and he knew his pride could be damned. He'd go after her again and probably again, if he had to.

"Cali?" he called louder.

No answer.

He checked the extra bedroom. Empty.

Then his bedroom. Also empty.

Like it or not, she was gone.

"Shit!"

Chapter Thirty-Three

Empty. His chest ached with indecision, then the whirling sound of his Jacuzzi caught his attention. Moving to the bathroom door, he listened to the water running. He took one of those deep breaths to calm his nerves. Damn. He really did have it bad for this girl.

He started to knock then an idea stirred. His body responded to the visions playing in his head, and he practically ran back to the living room to open the champagne and wash some strawberries.

~

The knock at the bathroom door had Cali in a panic for about two seconds. Fear evaporated when Brit stepped in, but modesty took over. She pulled her knees to her chest. Thankful the jets in the tub stirred the water, making it difficult to see everything.

"You're back," she said.

Through the steaminess in the room, he smiled and winked. In his hands, he juggled two flutes of champagne and a plate of strawberries.

"Do you mind if I come in?" He inched closer and set the plate down on the side of the tub and passed her one of the flutes, its contents bubbling along with the Jacuzzi. His gaze lowered to the water, or rather to her under the water. She knew modesty was a moot point when you had agreed to sleep with someone, but this moot point had always been an issue for her. Only child syndrome, she supposed. She pulled her knees a little closer.

Brit ran a finger over her cheek. Picking up a strawberry, he held it to her lips. She chuckled nervously and that caused him to smile. As she sank her teeth into the sweet fruit, Brit sank to the floor and leaned over the tub's edge to press his lips to hers. The kiss tasted of strawberries, champagne and of Brit. Modesty became less of an issue.

Holding the glass in one hand, she curled her other arm around his neck, threading her wet fingers through his hair, dripping water over the back of his shirt. When the kiss ended, he smiled, his gaze putting off more steam than the tub.

"May I join you?" He placed his flute down on the edge of the tub and started unbuttoning his shirt. Okay, she saw a trend here. He asked for permission, but didn't wait for an answer.

Or did he see the answer in her eyes?

She wouldn't have said no. Still, her heart started to race. Not because she didn't want this, but because she wanted it too much—because suddenly she didn't know if she could meet his standards. Something told her that Brit had sex down to an art—that he was a master of seduction.

Sure, she'd almost mastered art. She could stroke color on canvas, sculpt and mold clay, but she was sort of a paint-by-number kind of student when it came to sex. She had read books about it, digested magazine articles about it, hoping to improve her performance and her pleasure. However, the short, unsatisfying fling with Stan told her she needed to buy some more books.

Her gaze refocused on Brit. Maybe what she needed was hands-on experience.

He draped the long sleeve denim shirt over the counter. Catching his white T-shirt by the bottom with his thumbs, he pulled it up, exposing his naked chest. Muscles rippled down his stomach as he slipped the shirt over his head. The T-shirt fluttered to the floor. He kicked his shoes off. His hands eased over his hard abdomen, only to stop at his waist. The top of his snugly fitting jeans snapped open. Slowly, he unzipped, exposing the elastic band of a pair of navy boxers. His gaze told her that each of his moves were intentional and for her pleasure.

To watch.

To enjoy.

Her private show.

And she was turning redder than an over-ripe tomato.

His jeans slipped down his hips. His boxer underwear inched down his thighs. His sex, freed from his shorts, came out to play and made a grand appearance. Hard and heavy, it bounced up and almost touched the treasure trail of hair moving down from his navel. Her heart hit one big thud and stopped. She jerked her gaze back to the flute in her hand.

It was a nice piece of . . . crystal, a tad larger than the average flute. Not that she was an expert on crystals. Or flutes. Or . . .

She heard him chuckle and figured he laughed at her blush.

His foot slipped between her and the back of the tub. He lowered himself in the tub behind her. The water level rose. She scooted forward. Way forward. He curled his arm around her waist and pulled her closer. Close against him. His wet, naked body pressed against her back. She felt his chest, dusted with soft hair, then his abdomen, flat and solid. His legs extended on each side of her, and then she felt his sex, heavy and silky hard, against her lower back.

"You okay with this?" he asked. "Comfortable enough?"

"Yeah." She lifted the glass and sucked in champagne courage. The tingling bubbles fizzed on her tongue.

"Good." He kissed her neck. "You feel wonderful." His palm moved over her bare stomach.

She gulped another sip of champagne, feeling the bubbles race down her throat.

He unclasped her banana clip and her hair fell, tickling her shoulders. Dropping the clip on the floor, he gently turned her face to the side so he could meet her gaze. "Still okay?"

"A little nervous." She nipped at her lower lip.

He grinned and ran a finger down her cheek. "Me, too."

"You don't feel nervous." She shifted slightly where his hardness pressed against her lower back.

He chuckled. "I'm not that nervous." Reaching over, he picked up another strawberry and held it to her lips. "Eat. Drink. Relax. We're not in any hurry."

She bit into the fruit, savoring the burst of flavor—a little tart, a little sweet. "Umm." Her breath caught when she felt his hand glide up to her breasts. His fingers passed over her wet nipples that were tight and so sensitive.

She leaned against him as his touch sent erotic messages to other parts of her body.

Clutching the flute in one hand, she let her other hand fall to his leg. She ran her fingers over his kneecap and followed his leg back under the water to mid-thigh.

Lips against her neck, he moaned. While he continued to tease her nipples with one hand, he reached for the soap with the other. Then his slippery palms glided from one breast to the other. Now she moaned, falling against him. Surrendering.

One of his hands slipped beneath the water to her hip. The touch moved up and down the outer side of her leg. She let her thighs drift apart and waited to feel his hand move over. Instead, he fed her strawberries, made her feed him one, and they sipped champagne, while the warm water bubbled around them, and he seduced her with his slow touches.

At a snail's pace his fingers inched between her legs, gliding over her yet still teasing by not moving to the center. His moist kisses against the back of her neck sent delicious messages down her spine, while his fingers, oh so close, sent even more.

Impatient, she twisted, rose and sat sideways on his lap. The bubbling water waved around them. His hard shaft found its place between her legs, not inside, but when the ridge around his sex pressed against the spot his finger had yet to touch, she dropped the glass. The flute bobbed atop the stirring water, spilling the last sip of bubbly.

Brit caught the glass, set it on the floor then pulled her into his kiss. His mouth covered hers, and they shared air. Their tongues danced and mated and his hips rose and lowered. His sex, cradled between her thighs, moved between her legs, creating a hot desire for more.

Reaching down, she wrapped her hand around him and felt him throb beneath her palm. She shifted, wanting that hardness inside her. Water sloshed around them and his erection found its way to her opening again. Her body cried out to be one, and she started to slide down, to take him inside.

"Bed." His voice sounded deep. The next thing she knew, he had her wrapped in a towel, carrying her out of the steamy room. The chill of bedroom air sent goose bumps over her wet body. He pulled her against his chest—against a wall of male warmth.

Gently, he lay her down on the bed. He took his time, letting his gaze stroke her body. Finally, he lay down beside her, pulling a sheet from the bottom of the bed to cover them. "Cold?"

"A little." She ran her palm over his chest.

Drawing her closer, he dipped down and his mouth took hers. His hands explored, caressed and tempted. And she did her own exploring, sweeping her palm over his chest, and then lower to hold him in her palm again. Moaning, he flipped her over on her back and caught both her hands in his one and held it over her head.

The chill in the air was forgotten as the heat built inside her. He kissed her breasts until she arched her back off the mattress, every nerve in her body begged for release. His free hand moved between her legs again, and she felt his fingers slide into the waiting wetness he'd created.

"Please." She shifted her hips upward.

He inhaled sharply. "Not yet," he whispered, pulling his hand away from the moisture between her legs, as if he understood exactly what she wanted.

"You've got to come first." He slid his fingers down again and took his touch deeper between her legs—dipping in and out.

"Now," she mumbled, and tried to free her hands, but his kiss swallowed her protest and his grip on her wrists tightened ever so lightly.

When his lips pulled back, he released her hands and then ducked under the sheets, and breathed kisses down her breasts, her stomach. Lower. His intentions became clear. Awkwardness shot through her. Oral sex never really worked for her.

She just wasn't good at this. She stared at his sheet-covered body between her legs. "You don't have to." Then his tongue moved against her.

"Relax," he whispered against her thigh.

She reached down and pulled him up by the shoulders. "Seriously, you don't have to."

His head popped out. With the sheet still half draped over his head, he arched a puzzled brow. "You don't like it?"

"It's not . . ." She took a deep breath. "I mean, I've never . . ."

"Never?" He grinned, his eyes sparkled with humor.

She felt her face heat up. "I'm not as experienced as you are. And it's always seemed too . . ."

"Too what?" He was still grinning.

"Just too." She swallowed her embarrassment.

"Give me three minutes. If you don't like it, I'll try something else."

"But . . ."

"No buts. Just try it." He grinned. "I'm good at it." He brought his tongue out and swiped it across his bottom lip.

He slipped his hand down beneath the sheet and his fingers moved over the outside of her lips ever so softly. "I'm really, really good at it."

The swirl of pleasure had her withering. He studied as if waiting for her answer, but again, before she responded, he dipped back down under the covers.

Soft flutter-like kisses moved along the inside of her thigh. She held her breath, waiting for the feel of his tongue, and then he was there.

Not too hard, not too soft, and not in a hurry, he did amazing, amazing things. Her last rational thought was that he hadn't lied. He was really good at this.

Before his three minutes were up, her breath caught with the beginning of an orgasm. And not just any orgasm, but the kind that she'd heard about, but never experienced before. The kind that shook her inside and out. She dropped back on her pillow. She'd never felt like this with sex.

Never.

Never this high. "Oh."

Never this bright. "Oh."

Never with Brit. "Ohhhhh."

As she tried to catch her breath, he kissed his way up her body. When his head appeared from the sheet, he wore a smile and pure male pride glittered in his eyes. "You like?"

She still wasn't able to talk, so she nodded.

He chuckled and moved up beside her, propping up on his elbow. Feeling brave and slightly wanton, and wanting to return the gift he'd just given her, she pushed flat against the mattress. With the sheet still draping over them, she crawled on top and started kiss her way down his body. She arrived just below his navel when he caught her by both her elbows and pulled her up. When she looked up, his eyes were filled with heat.

"Let's save that for another time."

She grinned. "Give me three minutes."

He laughed, but didn't let her go. "Not now. I won't last a second. Later, I'll remind you that you owe me." He pulled her up beside him and ran his hand down the side of her cheek. The humor in his eyes faded into something different, something much more serious. "Thank you."

"For what. You wouldn't let me do it." Right then it hit her that she'd never done this before, never really had fun having sex, never allowed herself to really be present. Before it had been something that happened, and yes, it had been pleasurable, some of the time, but never . . . fun.

He laughed again. "For being here. For reminding me how to laugh. How to sleep." He inhaled. "For reminding me how it feels to be alive."

She smiled, completely understanding his sentiments. "You did the same for me."

Stretching his arm across her to the night stand, he opened a drawer.

He glanced at her, his smile in place. "Not a toilet bowl condom."

Grinning, she watched him open the packet, slide the condom on, then he rolled on top of her. With his arms extended on each side, he kept his weight off her. His biceps bulged, his shoulders looked wide, solid. His hair, blacker when damp, hung across his brow.

His gaze, hungry and ready, met hers. Slowly he pushed his hips against hers. She felt the weight of his sex on her thigh, and the coolness of the condom sent another chill through her. He arched his hips up and resettled between her legs. He hesitated, gazing into her eyes.

She ran her fingers down his neck, to his shoulder and lifted her hips ever so slightly. He pressed deeper, finding his place. Fitting inside her, stretching her, filling her with all kinds of wonderful. "Mmm," she whispered.

"Yes," he said, his voice strained.

His ins and outs started slow, each stroke bringing them closer, each stroke quicker, harder than the last. She moved with him, aware of how their bodies came together, aware of how his chest dipped down and brushed her nipples with his upward strokes, aware of how his lips breathed against hers. Aware of his scent, sandalwood and musk. And sex. Hers. His.

His hips pumped faster. Harder. "Now. Now," he growled.

Everything inside her went bright. She tightened her legs around him, and her clenching orgasm pumped around his.

He made a deep noise against her throat as he pushed deep into her one last time. She threaded her fingers through his hair.

He rolled to his side, holding her close, keeping their bodies joined. "Holy Hell, but that was fantastic," he mumbled, gasping for air.

She stayed in his arms, her cheek against his chest, listening to the thunder of his heart and feeling her own match the beat. Minutes passed before either of them moved.

Finally, he pulled away, leaving her body. His smile came slowly, sweetly. "Seriously, that was amazing."

She nodded. He kissed her, then leaned against the pillows, cuddling her to his chest. Seconds passed. She waited for the awkwardness to hit. Instead came a comfortable silence, or at least until he spoke, "Damn, we really screwed up,"

Cali couldn't fathom how he could call this a mistake only seconds after he'd said how good it had been. Her throat ached and she vowed not to cry. She had loved it.

"What were we thinking?" he continued. "We should have been doing this from the moment we met."

Chapter Thirty-Four

A few hours later, Brit leaned against the headboard a contented man. Cali smiled at him as she tossed away the to-go cartons that had held the fried rice. He didn't like to brag, and he seldom did aloud. But Cali was putty in his hands, his for the taking, and she'd enjoyed every moment of it. He couldn't remember ever seeing her smile so brightly, or seem so relaxed.

They had made love a second time, sat in bed, and ate Chinese food straight from the boxes. Then she had insisted on doing laundry. Now, almost ten o'clock, they had showered and piled back into the bed. Or at least he had. Cali ran around the room as if she couldn't rest until everything was neat.

"Forget that." Brit tackled her back into the bed.

He ran his hand over her hip. She didn't wear any panties, but had insisted on donning one of his dress shirts. He kept unbuttoning it; she kept buttoning it up.

"Hey, look." She pointed to the bedside table.

Brit turned his head and saw Mama Cat sitting beside the phone. "Finally decided to come out, huh?"

The cat's half-gone ear twitched. Cali reached out, and the cat hissed.

"I think she's jealous," Cali said, watching the cat leave.

"I love it when two women fight over me." He kissed her. God, he loved kissing her. "You think you can sleep?" he asked, rolling over and taking her on top of him. He still got a high when he felt her hair spill over his chest.

Her smile brushed against his shoulder. "You wore me out."

"Good." He ran his hand over her hip and tried to think about how to broach the subject of her taking some time off. "You can sleep in tomorrow."

She chuckled. "You call six sleeping in?"

The bomb had to drop. "I don't want you going to work."

As he expected, she stiffened, then sat up. "I have to."

"They can get a sub for a few days." He sat up beside her.

"I want to go to work."

He frowned. "Stan knows you'll be there."

"I don't care." She sat up, ruler straight, her teacher posture. "I've let him chase me out of my apartment. I can't even go to my mom's house, and I need to get her things packed up, so I can put the house on the market. I'm not going to let him keep me from my job."

Brit understood how she felt, but damn it, he couldn't stand the idea that Stan might try to get to her. Off and on the last hour, his gut had pumped acid just thinking that the freak had probably held Cali the way he held her—that the scum had buried himself inside her. Brit had never been jealous. He was now. And while he had to accept that he couldn't change that she'd slept with the asshole, he couldn't accept that the man would even have the pleasure of laying his eyes on her again.

"A few days. A week at the most," he said. "Please."

"No."

The "please" word was losing its power. "It's not safe."

"No." She pulled her knees to her chest and hugged them. "I'm going to work. It's the only normal thing I have in my life. I'm not giving it up. I need that right now."

Brit started to argue, but the blue steel in her eyes told him it was futile. "Okay," he growled. "I'll take you and pick you up. But don't even think about going to lunch."

She nodded. "You need to take me to get my car in the morning."

He let out a deep breath and stretched out on the bed and stared holes in the ceiling.

"Are you mad?" she asked.

"Not at you. At the situation." He brushed his hand down her arm. She scooted over and pillowed her head on his chest. He ran his hand over her back, and neither spoke again for a long time.

"So much has happened this last week," she said, breaking the silence.

"I know." He threaded his fingers through her hair and remembered what she'd said earlier. "I'll help you pack up your mother's things later this week. Do you have a storage place where you want to put them?"

"Not yet."

He heard her swallow. The silence lingered, and he waited, sensing her need to talk.

"Sometimes, I forget she's gone. It's like I'll think of something to tell her or see the phone and think I should give her a call."

"I know." And he did. He felt the same about Keith. He moved his hand to her back, caressing her, comforting her.

She buried her head deeper on his chest.

"Are you still dreaming about her?"

She shifted. "Yeah."

The one-word answer came out with more emotion than it had letters. He rolled over. "Nightmares?"

"No. She just talks to me."

He remembered what she'd told him about the dreams. "About lesbians?" He couldn't help but smile.

The slightest grin played on her lips in return. "She said her hospice nurse was a lesbian."

Brit took Cali's hand in his. "Is she?"

"I think so." She stared at their hands locked together.

The perfect fit. "What else does your mom talk about?" He brushed his thumb over the top of her hand.

"You."

"Me?"

"Yeah, strange huh?" She glanced away.

"What does she say about me?"

"She says our auras have the hots for each other."

"Our auras?" He chuckled.

"Yeah." She glanced at the ceiling. "Dr. Roberts says—"

"Who's Dr. Roberts?" He shifted to his side and brought her face back to him. "What doctor?"

"The psychologist with the Hospice organization. The one I spoke to the other day when I went to the office."

He hadn't known she'd spoken to a psychologist. "What does she say?"

"She says that the dreams are just my own maternal instincts trying to help me out, to keep me from making mistakes."

He tried to understand what she was saying. "So it would be a mistake to let our auras get together?" He didn't like thinking Cali's maternal instincts wanted to keep them, or their auras, apart.

"No. Mama likes you." Cali bit down on her lip. He'd noticed her doing that when she felt nervous. "She tells me others things, too." She sat up again and pulled her knees to her chest. "The night before Stan came to the school, she told me I shouldn't go to lunch. And the night before last, she told me not to stay at the same hotel."

Brit digested what she was saying. "You think it's really her?"

She blinked those big blues. "Do you think I'm crazy?"

Brit sat up beside her. "No. I think your dreams are strange. And I think they're scaring you."

"Yeah, well, Dr. Roberts believes it's just my instinct."

"What do you believe?" Concern threaded through his chest, and not because he thought she was crazy. He didn't like seeing her doubting herself. He'd done his share of doubting these past few weeks, and he knew that hurt.

"She had to be right. I don't believe in ghosts. It's just strange."

He held her closer. "I think losing someone that we care about can do weird things to our minds. I went almost three weeks without sleep. I'd doze, but any time I really fell asleep, Keith's image flashed in my mind. I thought I was losing my mind."

He inhaled. "I was a dickhead to everyone who crossed my path. Or I was until someone pointed it out to me."

She smiled. "You're not a dickhead."

He grinned. "It was the word "little" that you used before dickhead that hurt."

She giggled. "I knew you weren't little."

"Really?" He tossed her back on the mattress and rolled on top of her. "And how did you know?" He pushed his hips against hers, letting her notice it now. But damn, he'd had her twice and was still hard for her.

"You had a condom in your coat."

"Huh?" He rolled off her, but pulled her to his side.

Cali smiled. "In the zipper pocket; an extra large condom."

"No." He shook his head, then remembered. "Yeah, I did, didn't I? Shane did that." He no more said her name when he realized he shouldn't be talking about old girlfriends. "It ended almost two months ago. It wasn't serious."

"What happened?" she asked in a hesitant voice.

"We didn't mesh."

"Mesh?" she asked, and then bit down on her lip. "It's okay. You don't have to tell me." She settled her head on his chest.

But it didn't feel okay. Not to talk about it and not even to keep quiet. As wonderful as tonight had been, he felt as if a lot of questions hung between them. A lot of things left unsaid.

All in good time, Brit thought.

~

Brit woke up with a tingling pain in his arm. Cali's head lay pillowed on the crook of his elbow. He wiggled his fingers, but didn't pull away. A smile spread to his lips as he watched her sleep. Morning light sprayed through the blinds and he welcomed the idea of a new day. Even his concerns about where all this would lead didn't deter the feeling.

Maybe his mood was spurred from the eight hours of sleep he'd gotten for the first time in weeks, maybe it stemmed from the awesome sex last night—or the anticipation that he'd have more this morning. He didn't care. He just wanted to enjoy it.

Welcome back to the living, a voice whispered in his head. But it didn't feel like his life. The feeling that swelled in his chest every time he looked at Cali was brand new. Brand new. And it scared him almost as much as it excited him.

He drew in a breath and got the oddest scent of cigarette smoke.

Cali stirred beside him.

He started to lean down and kiss her when she yelled out, "No!" Then she jerked up and gasped.

"Hey? You okay?"

"Fine." Trembling, she gripped the sheets to her chest.

"Another dream?" He rubbed his shoulder to get some of the feeling back into his arm.

"Yeah." Her gaze skidded about the room as if she expected to see someone there.

Concern stirred his gut. He knew how ugly things could appear in one's mind. He stopped rubbing his own shoulder and touched hers. "You want to talk about it?"

Tears filled her eyes. "No."

"Was this one worse than the others?" he asked, seeing a haunted look in her eyes.

She blinked. "They're just dreams."

~

Two hours later, Cali walked into her classroom. "It won't be blinking. It won't be blinking," she repeated and let her eyes move to the answering machine on her desk. The blinking light made her breath hitch. What had Mom said? "Ask Brit about reading his files and don't, do not tell him about the phone calls until after lunch! Cali, it's really important," her mom kept saying.

Cali leaned against the desk as she recalled the image that had ended the dream. An image of Brit falling to the ground, the front of his shirt soaked in blood. Then she saw Nolan, Stan's friend, holding a gun.

"Don't tell him about the phone calls until after lunch."

Her hands shook. It wasn't true. She glanced again at the blinking light. It couldn't be. It wasn't going to be a message from Stan, she told herself. It wasn't.

Forcing air into her lungs, she pushed the play button.

The voice filled the line. "Cali, it's Stan."

"No!" Dropping in her chair, she gripped the edge of the desk, as Stan's voice pleaded for her to help him. The second message was from him as well, only this time he left a number.

Cali tried to rationalize it, looking at it from Dr. Roberts' viewpoint. She had been worried Stan might call. Hadn't she? And then seeing all those photos in Brit's file, and knowing someone was out there killing cops, made her realize how dangerous his job could be. So maybe she was just hypothesizing. They were just dreams. Oh, jeepers. She didn't believe in ghosts. She didn't believe her mother was really trying to communicate with her, did she?

Of course, she didn't. And Brit needed to know Stan had called. She had to tell him. Yes. She had to.

She found Brit's card in her purse, picked up the phone, and punched in the number. The ring echoed in her ear. She slammed the phone down. Okay. Maybe she did believe in ghosts.

"Oh, hell." She needed to think for a second. Clear her head and then call him.

Chapter Thirty-Five

"You'd better stop it before Adams figures it out," Quarles said as he walked into Brit's office.

"What?" Brit glanced up from cleaning his cluttered desk. Unlike any other morning, today, he didn't mind the broom closet of an office.

"You were humming."

Brit attempted to bite back his smile. "A man can't hum?"

"Not with that chicken-shit grin on his face. The evidence is overwhelming. You got laid last night."

Brit leaned back in his chair, not about to kiss and tell, but he wouldn't deny it either. "I woke up in a good mood."

The humor in Quarles' eyes faded into something serious. "I warned you about getting in too deep."

"Too deep in what?" Adams asked.

Brit and Quarles both stiffened at the sight of the man looming in the doorway. "What's up?" Brit asked.

"The hospital called. You can talk to Garland at nine." He tossed some papers on Brit's desk. "The hotel charge will be posted on Miss McKay's Internet bill by three. I've asked Duke and Mark to back you two up tonight. We'll set you up in two unmarked cars. I figure someone will need to be inside the room, too. You two don't mind pulling a double, do you?"

Brit sat forward, his chair squeaking. "Wouldn't miss it. I want this guy caught." Out of Cali life's forever.

"I'm in." Quarles butted up against Brit's desk.

"Good," Adams said. "Oh, you were right. Humphrey's gun is a match for the one that shot Garland. He might not be the guy who took out Keith and Anderson, but he shot an officer. I want him behind bars or six feet under and don't care which. But I'm not losing another officer. So wear your vests."

Adams tucked his hand into his belt. "If I find out one of you didn't, I'm going to kick ass." He walked out.

Quarles waited a few minutes then turned to Brit. "Wear your vest," he said, tucking his hand into his belt. "Or I'm going to kick ass." Quarles' voice was a dead ringer for Adams'.

Brit laughed. "I didn't know you did impersonations."

"Yeah. You ought to hear me do you."

"Funny," Brit said, his good mood unbreakable.

A tap on the open door brought Brit's gaze up. His smile, and his mood, shattered when he saw Laura, Keith's wife, standing there.

"Laura?" Brit stood. A rain of guilt pelted him. Guilt for not calling her. Guilt for not finding Keith's murderer. Guilt for being alive when his partner and best friend wasn't. Guilt for being happy about being alive.

"Hi." Her smile wasn't as bright as Brit remembered it. "I was in the neighborhood and thought I'd run by."

Brit looked at his new partner. "John Quarles, this is Laura. Keith's wife."

Quarles nodded. "It's a pleasure." They shook hands and then Quarles excused himself.

Motioning for her to sit down, Brit dropped into his own chair. He sought the right words, but none came. "I'm sorry." Guilt fluttered in his chest like a trapped bird. "I've been a piece of shit. I thought about you. I picked up the phone to call you a dozen times."

"But you didn't know what to say." She leaned forward. "It's okay. Really." She found a paperclip on his desk and started twisting it. "I should've come here earlier, but I was hurting so much that I didn't think I could handle seeing your pain."

A deep gush of air left Brit's lungs. "I miss him."

She smiled and twisted the clip, "I accused Keith once a week of having an affair with you. You two acted more like a married couple than Keith and I."

Brit chuckled, but his eyes stung with emotion. "He was a hell of a guy."

"I know. But Keith would be furious if either of us didn't pick ourselves up by our bootstraps. Remember him saying, 'Whine and I'll whack you'?"

Brit stared at the ceiling until his emotions got under control. "If I could just catch the bastard, Laura."

"I want that, too. But it isn't going to bring Keith back. Even if we never know, we still have to move on." She dropped the mangled paperclip on his desk.

"I'm trying." Brit thought about Cali. "How are you?"

A touch of courage filled her eyes. "It will take a while, but I'll be okay. I have a son to take care of."

She stood, and Brit followed suit. She stepped around the desk and hugged him. When she backed up, Brit saw something in Laura, a sweetness, a gentle quality that reminded him of Cali. For the first time, he understood what drove Keith home every night. Laura had been Keith's magic, just like Cali was his.

"How's Keith Junior?" It was amazing how seeing Laura had brought something akin to relief.

"He's great. He's into climbing now. Yesterday, I found him on top of the refrigerator eating the cookies I'd hidden up there. He's with my mother now, so I'd better get back."

Brit smiled. "I'll walk you to your car." As they walked out, Brit thought he heard his cell phone. Whoever it was would leave a message.

~

"Ready? We need to get to Garland." Quarles popped his head into Brit's office as soon as he returned.

"Yeah." Brit picked up his cell phone. "Give me a sec. I missed a call from Cali." He punched in the number. The line rang once and then clicked over to her message machine. He glanced at the time. During class hours, the answering machine automatically picked up.

He left a message, apologizing for missing her call. Then just to assure himself, he found the cell number of Garcia, the security guard.

Brit had spent time this morning with the man, cautioning him about Humphrey and convincing himself that the man would be able to protect Cali. Something about making love to her had made her more his responsibility. Or maybe just plain "his." While it sounded caveman-like, Brit had wanted to toss her over his shoulder, thump his chest and scream out to the world that Cali McKay was his woman.

Garcia picked up. "Hey." Brit told him about the call.

"I haven't seen a thing," the man assured him.

"Do me a favor," Brit said. "Walk to her class, peek in, and tell me she's in her room."

"You got it bad for this girl, don't you?" Garcia chuckled. "Not that I blame you. If I was younger, I'd be chasing you off with a big stick."

"Yeah, I've got it bad." Brit glanced up at Quarles, who looked at the clock and walked out. "You on your way now?" Brit asked Garcia as he started to the door.

They made it to Brit's car before Garcia spoke again. "I'm looking at her now.

She's talking to a student, Sara something. I heard her mom had cancer. Just like Cali to care. You want to talk to her?"

"No," Brit said. "But when class changes, pop in and tell her I called to check on her."

"She'd probably prefer flowers to an old security guard checking in."

Brit smiled. "You're right. I'll have some sent over, too. Thanks."

He followed Quarles to his car and decided to let him drive. After hanging up, Brit called Directory Assistance and got a number for a florist and had a dozen red roses sent to Cali at Height's High School. On the card he had them write, "Just thinking of you."

"Do you know what red roses mean?" Quarles asked, driving toward the hospital.

"Butt out," Brit said and started humming again.

~

Trooper Garland lay in the ICU, only a shade darker than the white sheets.

Garland opened his eyes. A heart monitor sat on a shelf above him, beeping as if marking time. "You the homicide detectives?" the trooper managed to ask, and he moistened his cracked lips with the edge of his tongue.

Brit stepped forward. "Yeah, Brit Lowell and John Quarles."

Garland nodded and looked at the water pitcher.

Brit reached for the large hospital cup and held the straw to the man's parched lips. Garland took a sip. When he swallowed, he flinched in pain. An echo of pain hit Brit's chest.

The constant beeping filled the moment of silence, then Garland spoke. "I've been wracking my brain, trying to find a piece of evidence that might help. But all I got is a general description."

Brit moved closer. "We got a match on the bullet. It's connected to another case."

"The cop killer?" the man asked.

Quarles shook his head. "Not that case. But the guy's wanted in connection to three murders."

"I guess he's pissed I'm not number four." The trooper tried to smile, but it fell flat.

Brit smiled for him. "I bet so." Hesitating, Brit asked, "What did this guy look like?"

"Guys. There were two of them."

"Two?" Quarles' voice radiated the surprise Brit felt.

Garland flinched as if something suddenly hurt. "Yeah. The driver stepped out of the car. I started telling him to get back in when I saw the other guy. The driver was blond, five ten, heavy, two hundred or more. Didn't see the other guy. I don't know which one fired."

Brit digested the information. "Nolan Bright." He looked at Quarles. "Stan and Nolan must be in on this together."

~

Cali stood in her class room chewing on her thumbnail and studied the roses. They'd arrived fifteen minutes ago.

She'd been scared to look at the card. What if they'd been from Stan? They hadn't been. Now she had an hour, her conference period, without conferences, to sit and question the wisdom of waiting to call Brit.

The door to her class squeaked open. Tanya pranced in, smiling when she saw the roses. "Good news, bad news."

"What?" Cali asked.

"Good news." Tanya pointed a finger at Cali. "He enjoyed last night. Bad news is he has zero imagination. Roses are so overdone. He should have found out your favorite flower or at least sent you something original. I got an orchid."

Cali frowned, but refused to let Tanya's opinion dampen her appreciation of Brit's gift. "I think they're sweet."

"You would be that old fashioned." Tanya scooted up to the desk. "I've got ten minutes, so give me the middle of the road version with some juicy details and cut the boring stuff."

"Me?" Cali leaned back in her chair. "What about you? You were late this morning. And you got an orchid. So?"

Tanya smiled. "Okay, I'll go first. Eric came over yesterday after you left. We spent the day biking and having a picnic at the park. Then we went to his place for dinner."

"And?" Cali tried to raise her eyebrow the way Tanya did.

Tanya leaned in. "And I never went home. Let's just say we're no longer as horny as we were."

Cali laughed. "Details."

"Well, it was fabulous. No, it was . . ."

Leaning back in her chair, Cali finished Tanya's sentence. "Mind spinning, out of this world, a little embarrassing, but you'd do it over again a thousand times."

"You too, huh?"

Cali sighed. "Yeah." She bit down on her lip and looked at the clock, wishing it was after lunch so she could call Brit. When she glanced back, Tanya studied her.

"Okay," Tanya said. "You got the I-had-yummy-sex grin, but your Charmin blues are saying something else. What's up?"

Cali blinked her Charmins at her friend. "Nothing."

"Liar." Tanya leaned forward. "Come on. What happened?"

"It's crazy." Cali dropped her elbows on the desk. "Really crazy."

Tanya continued to stare. "I'm going to guess this has something to do with your dreams."

"So you agree. I'm losing my mind."

"No," she snapped. "What happened?"

Cali took a deep breath and decided to spill the beans. Really spill them, just toss them out on the floor. "This morning, in my dreams, Mom told me not to tell Brit about the calls from Stan until after lunch. Then I saw an image of Brit getting shot and one of Nolan's face."

Her friend's mouth fell open. "You didn't tell me that Stan called."

"He hadn't. I didn't know he had. Not until I got here this morning. He called twice and even left a number."

"Oh, shit. That is spooky. What did you do?"

"I called Brit. I was going to tell him because I don't believe that these dreams mean anything. But he didn't answer. And so I hung up and didn't leave a message. I told myself if he called back I would tell him, and if he didn't then I wasn't meant to tell him."

"You didn't call Stan, did you?"

"No. But what am I going to tell Brit? 'Oh, by the way, you know the guy you're trying to catch for killing someone, well, this morning he called and left a number where I could reach him. Sorry I didn't tell you right away but my dead mother told me not to tell you until after lunch.'"

She snatched her banana clip from her hair and started popping it open and closed. "I'm losing it. I swear, I should walk over to the loony ward and have them fit me for a straight jacket."

"You're not crazy." Tanya said. "So Brit hasn't called back?"

"He left a message."

"Okay. You tell him that you tried to call this morning, but he didn't answer. Then you got busy."

"Too busy to call him and tell him something that I know is important to his case?" Cali shook her head. Tears started to sting her eyes. "Everything just feels so mixed up. I read the police file on Stan, and the whole police force thinks that he killed those two guys."

"But you still don't believe it?"

Cali shook her head. "I know he's not a good person. But I don't think he'd kill someone. And it's not just because Mom said it in my dreams. At least I don't think it is."

Stress pinched Cali's stomach. "And Brit said I might have to testify, and I'm going to have to tell the truth, so when they ask me if I think he did it, I'm going to have to say no. And I know Brit's going to flip."

Tanya shook her head. "If everything you told me about Stan is true, if he's looking for the bracelet, I can see why you think Stan didn't kill those guys. It makes sense to believe that he doesn't have the rest of the jewelry. And like you said, the one with the jewelry is probably the one who killed those other two. You're using logic here."

"Logic?" Cali said. "Remember, I'm the girl whose dead mother is haunting her dreams, telling her what's happening in the future. And I must believe it because I didn't call him."

"Hey, I'm Catholic, I grew up talking to dead people, well dead saints, but it's the same thing. Anyway, I'm jealous that you got to talk to someone. Do you know how many candles I've lit and asked for advice? And not one of them has ever spoken a word back to me, awake or asleep."

Cali dropped her face into her palms. "I need a vacation from my life. No, I need my life back to normal."

The door squeaked open, and Cali looked up. Brit stood there—six feet of wonderful. Cali's heart started to race.

Chapter Thirty-Six

Cali met his gaze.

"Hey." He nodded at Tanya but focused on Cali. And she suddenly found it hard to breathe.

Tanya stood from the edge of the desk. "Gotta go."

"Did I come at a bad time?" Brit moved in, watching Tanya skirt out. He tucked one hand in his jeans' pocket and carried a bag in the other.

"No. I was about to call you." She looked at the clock.

He glanced at the flowers. "You got them?" He set the bag on the table. "I brought us lunch. Cheeseburgers."

"Thanks." Cali looked at the roses. "They're beautiful."

"You okay?" Leaning down, he kissed her. Nothing heavy, just sweet. "Am I allowed to do that here?" He glanced back as if to make sure the door was closed. His eyes twinkled, and she saw the heat in his gaze. "Want to join me in the supply closet?"

Nervous, she snatched the clip from her hair and started opening and closing it again. Finally, she just blurted it out. "Stan called."

Brit's facial expression flipped from lover to cop.

Her stomach flipped with it, but it wasn't the good flip this time.

His posture tightened. "When? What did he say?"

She moistened her lips. "I didn't speak with him. He left messages. I tried to call you to tell you."

"That was this morning. And you didn't leave a message." His brow wrinkled. "He called you this morning and you're just now telling me. Did he threaten you?"

She shook her head. "No, he wanted me to call him back."

"You called him?" Suspicion deepened his voice. He held up a hand. "He left a number?"

She nodded. "I didn't erase the messages."

"You should have gotten to me immediately. The moment you received these calls."

He jerked the phone in front of him. "How do I listen to the messages?"

~

Brit pulled into the hotel's parking lot the same time as Quarles. Brit's mind had replayed the messages the freak had left Cali. "Cali, baby. Listen, I'm sorry for scaring you. I love you. You know I love you. Call me. I need your help." He'd left a phone and room number. Brit had called and gotten the hotel's address. Then he'd dialed Quarles to meet him here.

Quarles jumped out of his car. "Duke and Mark are a minute away, too. Let's wait on them before going in. You got a vest in your car?"

Ignoring his partner, Brit took off to the office, pulling his badge out as his feet pumped against the asphalt. As he entered, Brit got a whiff of someone's fast-food lunch and cigarette smoke. He approached the desk and slapped his badge on the counter. "You got a guest in room 103. We're going to need to clear out the two adjoining rooms."

The woman's eyes went big. She dropped her hamburger on its foil wrapper. "Oh, I . . . Wait. Room 103?"

"Yeah." Brit heard Quarles walking in with Duke and Mark.

"The man in room 103 just checked out," the woman said. "Another guy was in looking for him, ten minutes ago."

"Fuck!" Brit swung his hand out, accidently knocking off the woman's hamburger and a crystal bowl filled with jelly beans. The meat, bread, crystal bowl, and colorful candy smacked the wall. The bowl shattered. It became a race to see which hit the white tile floor first, the shards of glass, the multicolored candy, or the dismembered hamburger. The hamburger won.

~

"We'll get him," Quarles said five minutes later, standing by the bed in Stan's former room. "At least we know he's still trying to contact her. He'll show up tonight, and we'll be ready."

Brit cut his gaze around the cheap motel's furnishings. The room didn't offer one clue to where Stan could have gone. They still called CSI for prints. The clerk's description of the man looking for Stan sounded like Nolan Bright. If they'd been five minutes earlier, they would have caught Nolan.

Fifteen and they could have had them both. "Fifteen minutes," Brit growled.

Quarles kept watching Brit as if he might explode. Brit waited for the moment right along with him. Why the hell hadn't Cali contacted him immediately? Part of him defended her, telling himself she'd tried to call him. But damn, why hadn't she left a message, or called him back?

Did she have some perverted loyalty to the bastard? Didn't she want Stan caught? Brit pushed a hand over his face and remembered how she'd pleaded for him to be safe as he'd stormed out of her classroom. But for whose safety had she been more concerned—his or the man who'd vowed his love for her over the phone?

His cell phone chirped, and he snatched it out of his pocket. "Yeah?" His tone matched his mood—dark and threatening.

"Lowell. It's Garcia. I just spotted the truck parked out in the back of the school. I think he's—" The line went dead.

"Damn!" He looked at Quarles. "He's at the school." Brit tore off to his SUV.

"I'll meet you there." Quarles darted to his own truck.

Brit had made trips across Texas that felt shorter than the eight-mile drive to the school. He had to remind himself to breathe. His body throbbed with tension. Images of Cali flashed in his head—of her smile, of her resting her head on his chest.

If Humphrey had put one finger on her, Brit intended to beat the man to a pulp—no guns, no handcuffs, no badges. This would be personal.

Flipping his phone open, driving like a man who dared the devil, Brit hit the redial button.

The line rang. And rang. The knots in Brit's belly tightened. He slung the phone down, and swerved to avoid hitting a car that hadn't heard his sirens.

He drove up to the front of the school. As someone walked out, he snagged the front door, ignoring the stares from teenagers. His gaze cut to the front office, but he rushed past and headed straight to Cali's classroom.

He swung open her door. The noise of five or more conversations pierced his ears. Silence suddenly fell. The students stared at him. Brit scanned the room, desperate to see Cali.

His gaze landed on the empty desk.

"Where's Miss McKay?" he asked.

"She was called to the office," a girl said.

He left, storming down the hall. "She's okay. She's okay." He kept repeating the words like a speech he needed to memorize. His anger at her for not contacting him about Stan's calls took a backseat the moment he thought she could be hurt. Right now, he wanted to see her —hold her. Get her friggin' out of the school before Stan came back.

He slapped open the office door and faced the first woman who looked up from behind the counter. "Where's Cali McKay?"

The woman stepped back and every eye in the room stared at him as if he carried a pitchfork instead of a badge. "Who are you?" another woman said, her tone only an octave short of panic. One thought zipped through his mind—something had happened. Chills ran a course up his spine and down both his arms.

"I'm police." He jerked out his badge. "Where is she?"

"Nurse's office," the woman said. "We've called for an ambulance."

"How bad?" he asked.

"It looked bad."

Brit's heart became a throbbing mass of hurt. "Where is the nurse's office?"

"Four doors down on the left."

He turned and went.

Seconds later, he shoved open the door to the nurse's office. Voices bounced from one of the back rooms. "We've got to stop the bleeding first," someone said.

Then the smell hit him. His gaze dropped to the white tile where a trail of blood led to the voices. "No."

Chapter Thirty-Seven

"I said, don't move," the school nurse snapped. "We've got to stop the bleeding."

Cali stood back as the nurse applied pressure to Roberto Garcia's neck and head wounds. The copper scent of blood filled the cubical-sized room, making her stomach twist with guilt. This was her fault. She'd messed up. If she'd told Brit earlier about the calls, maybe Stan would have been caught and Roberto would be okay.

She heard footsteps and when she turned, Brit came to a halt at the door. His face looked as colorless as the white walls.

"Brit?" Had she wished him here?

In two wide steps, he reached out and touched her arm. "I thought . . ." Relief washed over his expression. He pulled her close. His deep intake of air vibrated through Cali, and she breathed in his scent.

His embrace ended quickly and he looked at Roberto. "What happened?"

"He said Stan caught him in the back of the school. He tried to stop him from leaving. They fought and Roberto fell on some broken glass on the pavement. He cut himself badly."

"Lowell," Roberto ground out, trying to sit up, only to be pressed back down by the nurse.

"I told you to stay still," the nurse said, her voice firm.

Cali moved in closer. "Please listen to her."

"I almost had him," Roberto said. "He was trying to sneak in the back entrance. I had them bring Miss McKay in here just in case he tried to come back."

Cali saw Brit frown at the sight of the blood. "I knew I could count on you."

"It looks worse than it is," the nurse replied, obviously seeing their concern. "But he's going to have plenty of stitches to show off." She turned when her patient tried to sit up again. "Until you stop bleeding, you don't move!"

"I'm fine," Roberto said. "Hell, I've been shot before."

Cali wrung her hands together. "I'm so sorry, Roberto. This is all my fault."

"Hog wash," Roberto said. "You didn't do this."

The nurse removed a bloody cloth she held against Roberto's neck wound. "The bleeding is slowing down."

~

Fifteen minutes later, Brit watched the ambulance drive away with Garcia.

Brit hadn't left Cali's side. She looked like a woman about to shatter into delicate pieces and when she did, he'd be there to catch her.

Quarles, who'd shown up a few minutes ago, stepped up beside him. "What now?"

Brit looked over at Cali then moved a few feet away to talk to his partner in private. "You go to the hospital to get a report. I'm going to get Cali situated at my place before I join you at the surveillance."

The expression on Quarles' face darkened. "If Adams finds out she's staying at your place, he's going to crawl up your ass and camp out for a few days."

"He can roast marshmallows while he's there for all I care. And I'll swear you didn't know a thing about it."

Frustration pinching his brow, Quarles left. Brit spotted Mrs. Jasmine walking up to Cali. He never considered himself an opportunist, but damn if he'd let this one pass.

He hurried to stand beside Cali. "You look as if you could use some time off." He saw Cali cut him a don't-go-there look, but he had his compass set in just that direction. With Garcia at the hospital, Cali was not staying at the school.

If she'd listened to him about not coming to work today, this whole thing wouldn't have happened. And if she'd called right away this morning, Humphrey wouldn't even be an issue.

Focusing on the principal, Brit continued, "Don't you think so, Mrs. Jasmine? Isn't it best all the way around that Cali take some time off?" He felt Cali's baby blues blistering him.

"Maybe we should talk about this in my office?" Mrs. Jasmine started back inside.

As Mrs. Jasmine walked away, Cali gave his elbow a squeeze. "Don't do this," she seethed.

He didn't answer her. The way he figured it, he'd be answering for a lot later because there was no changing his mind. If Cali wouldn't listen to reason, her principal would. And when he got Cali alone, he was going give her a ration of shit for not calling him. No doubt about it, Cali and he were about to have their first "real" fight.

Panic started buzzing in his gut. Normally, this was Brit's bail-out time. The moment any issue arose that invited tempers to flare, Brit called it quits on a relationship. He'd experienced too many domestic battles growing up; he simply refused to be a part of them as an adult. It wasn't that he really believed he'd fight unfair, but why the hell take chances?

But this fight, the one brewing right now, wasn't going to send him running. He'd stay and see it through.

~

"You did that on purpose," Cali said as they left the school fifteen minutes later. A cold wind made her shiver, or was it her anger?

Brit matched her steps, one for one. Clip, clop.

Fury tightened her shoulders and she turned on him. "You knew how I felt about this and you didn't care. I told you last night that I didn't want to stop working and you just overlooked my feelings."

He raked a hand through his hair. "No, you've got that ass-backwards. I care and that's why I overlooked how you felt."

She snatched her keys from her purse. Her hands shook, and tears formed in her eyes. Her knees still felt like worn-out rubber bands.

Letting out a gush of air, he took her chin in his hand, forcing her to look at him. "Cali, try to understand. Humphrey attacked Garcia. Next time, a student or a teacher could get killed. It's not safe for you to be here."

She pushed his hand away, not wanting to understand. She couldn't understand. Not the dreams, not Brit's willingness to go against her wishes.

"You're the one who needs to understand," she said. "You had no right to interfere. None. Zip."

His jaw muscles tightened. "Let me drive you to my house."

"No." Cali leaned against her car and folded her hands over her stomach. The desire to scream, stomp, and to kick a few tires bounced around her head, but sweet Charmin-faced girls didn't do that, so she just leaned against her Honda and tapped her foot to the cadence of anger and panic pulsing inside her.

He stepped close and pulled her against his chest. Even as mad as a cat with its tail on fire, she couldn't push him away.

She breathed in, trying not to be lulled by his scent or the warmth radiating from his shoulders. Finally, anger won over and she pulled back. "I'll drive myself."

"You're too upset to drive. We'll get your car later."

She looked up at him. "I'm very angry with you right now."

He gritted his teeth. "I know you're angry." A cold gust of air ruffled his hair. "And I can accept that because you're not the only one angry. I'm pissed that you didn't call me when you got the call from Humphrey. But let me drive you and we'll talk about this later."

Narrowing his eyes at her, he took the keys from her trembling hands. "Please."

Without keys, she was left with no option but to follow him. The cold cut through her cardigan sweater, but anger still bubbled hot inside her. She got into his SUV and stared out the windshield.

"Seatbelt." He turned the car's heater on.

She buckled in, but didn't look at him. The first half of the drive, neither of them spoke. Then like a shaken soda can, the words spewed out of her. "How could you do this? My work was the last normal thing I have in my life. I need it. I've lost everything else."

"Was Stan normal?" His words came out gritty. "Because you know what? I'm not the bad guy here. I'm the guy who's trying to make sure your ex-loverboy doesn't kill you like he has three other people. And for some reason I'd think you'd be pissed at him instead of me."

She gripped the seat belt, her anger rising. "This isn't about Stan. I told you last night I didn't want to stop teaching. I even explained why it was so important. And you—"

"What does that make me?" He thumped his palm on the steering wheel. "Aren't I normal? Or is Stan your normal?"

"You didn't have a right to interfere in my job."

"I only did it because I don't want to see you or anyone else hurt. I care about you, Cali. I care so damn much that I can't let you put yourself in danger just because you want to feel friggin' normal. And I can't understand why you didn't call me right after—"

"Caring for someone doesn't give you the right to make their choices for them." The impact of her own words turned on Cali.

They sat in silence, staring at the window, then she spoke, "I couldn't make my mother's choices." Tears of frustration rolled down her eyes. "I didn't understand that then, but I do now. People have to make their own choices. I can't make your choices. What if I decided you don't need to be a cop because it's dangerous? There's a nutcase loose killing cops."

He cut his angry gaze toward her. "That's what I do, Cali."

"Yeah, and until about thirty minutes ago, I was a teacher who had a job to go to tomorrow, but thanks to you I've been banned from the school until further notice." Finally feeling as if her point had been made, she stared out the window and dried her tears on her shirt sleeve.

The last five miles were long and silent, except for the lulling sound of his car wheels moving on the pavement and the heater humming warmth. He pulled up in his driveway.

She reached for the door handle, but he caught her arm before she jumped out.

"Cali?" A thousand emotions danced in his eyes. He swallowed as if whatever he had to say was going to cost him a pound of pride. "You're right. I was wrong to do that. What if I call your principal and tell her I'll have a security guard posted at the school? She might change her mind."

"You could try." The lump in Cali's throat doubled. "But Mrs. Jasmine is famous for never changing her mind."

"I'm sorry. When I got to the office and they said they'd called an ambulance, I thought it was you who was hurt. Then I saw the blood."

"You were wrong," she snapped. "Let's just leave it at that." She got out of the SUV and stepped up on the porch. Following her, he unlocked the front door and she walked inside. The silence in the house seemed so loud that if it had a volume switch she'd have turned it down.

He looked at her. "I'll call her right now."

Cali went to the kitchen, not wanting to hear that conversation. In a few minutes, Brit walked in, his expression telling her that he'd hit what the teachers called the Jasmine-scented brick wall. The woman didn't budge when she'd made up her mind. To her credit, she normally made good first-call decisions. Which gave Cali a second of pause. It didn't even take a second for her to see her mistakes.

She had already endangered Roberto's life. Next time, it could be a student. Of course, Mrs. Jasmine had a right to be concerned. Hearing Brit's steps, and not really eager to face him, she dropped her face in her hands.

"I'm sorry," he said. "She wouldn't even let me explain."

Cali moved her hands and looked at him. She was still angry at him, but at this moment she was angrier at herself for overlooking the fact that her feeling "normal" shouldn't come before the safety of others. "You tried," she said.

He pulled a chair over and sat down beside her, so close his knee fit between her legs. "I've got to go to work. There's plenty of food in the fridge. Susan bought groceries. When I come back, you can yell and scream at me. Call me every name in the book. Just know that while I was wrong, I was wrong for the right reasons. I care about you."

She looked at him and realized something else. She hadn't called him about Stan this morning because she had been worried about him. And by not contacting him, she'd prevented him from doing his job. Right or wrong in her decision, she'd done it because she cared. Just like he'd done to her. Her anger melted and guilt stepped in its place.

"I'm not going to scream and yell." She closed her eyes and decided she owed him the same thing he'd given her. "I even understand why you did it. And I'm sorry I didn't call you earlier." She bit down on her lip, still not comfortable telling him about the dream. "I had so much on my mind. The dream I had . . . it upset me."

He brushed a finger over her lip where she'd just nipped. "And you still don't want to talk about it?"

"Not really."

He kissed her, but pulled away before it went from sweet to sexy. "I don't know when I'll be back. But if I'm lucky, maybe I can fix it so you can go to work tomorrow after all."

"You think you'll catch him?" she asked.

"We've set up a hotel room, had it posted on your credit card. Which, by the way, you shouldn't use for a while. And I'm going to drive your car to the hotel. We're parking it in front of the room. If things go well, he'll come looking for you tonight." He pulled away.

"Be careful. I care about you, too." The word 'love' danced on the tip of her tongue, ready to go into the limelight, but she couldn't say it. Too soon. Way too soon.

"I will." He gazed into her eyes as if searching, then smiled. "We did good, didn't we?"

"Good at what?"

"Our first fight. I was angry, and you were angry, but we did okay."

"We've fought before." Cali grinned. "I think that's all we did for a while."

His stared into her eyes. "Yeah, but we haven't fought since we've had sex."

"And only fights after sex count?" she asked, finding that somehow humorous.

He leaned in. "How else are we going to have make-up sex?"

She rolled her eyes. "Men are dogs."

"No, we're just dickheads." He kissed her and stood up. "If you need me, call. And leave a message this time. You got it?" He gave her hand a squeeze.

The radio spurted out Wolowitz's voice. "Hey guys, did you know they got a porn station? I think I'm going to stretch out on this bed and enjoy myself."

It had been four hours since Brit had left Cali and he ached for her. Now he and Quarles sat in an unmarked sedan, staring at the hotel room, waiting. Through the dark parking lot, Brit could barely spot Mark and Luke sitting in a green Toyota. Adams had placed Officer Wolowitz inside the hotel room. Another officer was at the front desk in case trouble broke out in the office. Parked outside the room was Cali's Honda. They hoped Humphrey would see the car and go straight to the only room with the lights on.

Quarles leaned back, making the sedan's seat creak. "You know what puzzles me?"

Brit relaxed on the neck rest and turned to look at his partner. "Women? And why they smell so good—taste so good?"

Laughing, Quarles reached for his bottled water. "No, I've got that mystery figured out. But I think you've got more of a show going on in your head than Wolowitz does on the television."

Brit grinned. "Well, someday you'll have to explain the mystery to me, because women baffle the hell out of me."

"Someday, I will." Quarles stiffened when a car pulled up.

Brit gripped the wheel and studied the driver as the car rolled by. "It's not him," Brit spoke into the radio.

"What puzzles me," Quarles continued, "is why Humphrey didn't do something worse to Garcia or the hotel clerk. Or you, the night at Cali's mom's house."

Brit ran a hand over the steering wheel. He'd wondered about that, too. "Maybe he got rid of the gun."

"The hotel clerk was before Garland's shooting."

"Maybe he didn't want the noise?" Cold air snaked through the vents of the car. Pulling his thin coat a little closer, he missed his leather jacket, and made a mental note to ask Cali for it.

"Okay. So where's the knife he used at the hotel?"

Brit sat up. "Don't tell me you're thinking Humphrey isn't our man."

"No. I'm just hoping like hell that when we snag him, he has both weapons on him."

"He will." Damn it, this conviction had to stick. The message he'd heard on Cali's recorder replayed in his head. The man had told Cali he loved her. Cali wasn't Humphrey's to love. Not that Brit felt up to the challenge. The word "love" generally came with a serious commitment, like marriage. Sure he wanted Cali, wanted her in his life, but—

"Tell me about Susan." Quarles, as if tired of sitting, repositioned himself and his knees popped.

Brit eyed Quarles' profile. The more he got to know his new partner, the less he minded the idea of him and Susan seeing each other. "What do you want to know?"

"Anything, everything." He paused. "She said something that led me to think you two had a stormy childhood."

"I don't think stormy quite describes it."

"So it wasn't that bad, huh?" Quarles sounded relieved.

Brit's inside clinched. If he didn't feel Quarles needed to know for Susan's sake, he'd keep the subject to himself. "It was worse than stormy. Our dad was a drunk. A mean drunk and a part-time criminal. Hell, he was mean even when he was sober. Mom was his doormat. She laid down to clean his shoes on her every chance she got. Susan and I tried to stay invisible. When I got big enough to stand up to him, I stopped being invisible."

Quarles raised an eyebrow. "That must have been hard. I have great, well, a little too worrisome, but good parents. I can't imagine how that would be."

"You live through it. It teaches you things." Things like avoiding serious relationships. Which explained why his feelings for Cali felt like a pair of shoes a couple sizes too small. Could he make this work? Or was he setting both of them up for a world of trouble? .

"Did Susan date a lot?" Quarles asked. "I mean before the blow-up doll freak."

"She had lots of boyfriends before that guy. Things just didn't work out."

"Why not?" Quarles' question came out low.

Brit hesitated, but decided Quarles probably needed to know. "They mostly asked her to marry them."

A pause lingered before Quarles spoke, "Those pieces of shit." Then he half-smiled. "And why was that a problem?"

Brit nodded. "We've seen marriage played out. Actually, thanks to our mom, we've seen many marriages played out. Like I said, if you live through it, you learn from it."

A pair of high-set headlights pulled into the parking lot. Brit leaned against the steering wheel. Air hitched in his chest when he identified the vehicle. The truck rolled by, and Brit recognized the face from the mug shot. He reached for the radio. "It's him."

"We see him," came Duke's voice.

"And just at the good part, too," Wolowitz's voice came on the line. "This chick is stacked."

"Let him get out of the truck," Brit insisted. "He's not getting away this time."

Chapter Thirty-Eight

Cali called Roberto first, needing assurance that he was okay. Then she spoke to Sara's mother. Thankfully, the woman agreed to make an appointment with Dr. Tien. Cali tried to talk the cat into becoming friends again, but all it would do was hiss. Now, with a ham sandwich and chips in tow, she walked into Brit's living room.

Her footsteps echoed in the silence. The house seemed to hold its breath. When the heater clicked on, she actually jumped. Normally, she didn't mind being alone, but as she'd told Brit, nothing felt normal right now.

Looking around at his house, she didn't regret being here—didn't regret that they'd made love, but she did feel as if she'd stepped into someone else's life. Someone who didn't have a mother, a home, a credit card, a car, or a job to go to tomorrow.

Of course, this other person had this great sex life. And maybe when she got her life back, she could keep the sex. Keep Brit. Oh, she really hoped so.

Thoughts of Brit doing police work filled her mind, and she cringed with worry. She pushed the worry back, but said a silent prayer that he would be safe.

Cali heard a car pass by; its headlights slicing through the blinds sent shadows whispering across the wall. The house seemed to hold its breath again. "Great, now I'm scared of ghosts."

She sat down on the brown leather sofa and set her plate on the glass-topped coffee table. "You did this, Mom, thanks."

Her mom didn't answer and whether Cali honestly expected a reply was up for debate. Face it. She hadn't called Brit this morning because a part of her did believe. Which explained why ghostly shadows sent fear bouncing around her empty stomach.

Cali eyed the plate with little interest for a girl on empty. If she believed the dreams, then what else had her mother said? Forgetting the sandwich, she stood and began to pace.

Read the files. Her mom's words sang in her memory.

But why should she read Brit's files? Then she recalled her mom telling her to figure out how she'd known Anderson, the officer who'd been killed. Things about him would probably be in the file. She started to the bedroom to see if the files were still on the dresser. As she moved down the hall, Cali could swear she got a whiff of cigarette smoke. But that couldn't be, could it? Chills tap danced up her spine.

The files were there—as if waiting for her.

Nipping her bottom lip, she picked them up. The picture of Brit's partner fluttered out like an injured butterfly. Goose bumps played a slow song up her arms. She stared at the image, recalling her mother mentioning it in one of the dreams.

Sitting on the bed, she focused on the face and tried not to think about him being dead. A strange sensation welled up. Recognition. Just like with Anderson, she knew the face. Where would she have known them? How? She didn't run in the same circles with cops. Heck, she'd never even been ticketed. Non-bitches didn't break the law, didn't take chances.

She shook her head. No. This had to be a mistake. Her last three years had been surrounded by doctors and nurses, not cops. And when she wasn't with her mom, she was at school or at school functions. She glanced at the image again, expecting the feeling of recognition to fade, but it bit down harder. She knew this man, just as she knew Anderson, but from where?

A shiver chased goose bumps around her body. She inhaled and the smell of cigarette smoke nearly choked her. Immediately, her thoughts went back to this morning's dream. Of seeing Brit, shot and bleeding.

"Please let him be okay."

~

"He's out of the vehicle. Walking toward the room." Brit spoke into the radio. "Ready, Wolowitz? Poe, stay in the office."

"Ready," Wolowitz said.

"You vested?" Quarles asked Brit.

"Yeah," Brit lied. He hated vests. He couldn't move, couldn't breathe, and he didn't intend to let Humphrey get a shot off.

Brit and Quarles got out of the car, their weapons drawn. In the corner of Brit's eye, he spotted Duke and Mark moving in with the same caution.

Time held its breath as they inched up behind Humphrey, standing in front of the door where he thought Cali stayed. The man paused, then knocked. The idiot, Brit thought. Did he actually think that Cali would open the door to him? She wouldn't. She was finished with this creep. Finished.

Humphrey suddenly stopped knocking. He placed a palm on the door, hesitating as if sensing something was amiss. Then taking a step back, he swung around.

~

She stared at the picture of Brit's dead partner again. Where? Where could she have known him from? All she did was go to work, take care of Mom, and maybe attend a school function?

School functions?

"That's it!" Cali jumped off the bed so fast she almost tripped. They were the two cops who had spoken at the quarterly meeting for the At-Risk kids. She'd been late, because she'd taken her mom in for a blood test. So late, she hadn't heard the two speak, but she'd arrived before the ceremony ended and she'd seen them sitting at the speaker's table up front.

She folded her arms over her stomach, feeling lightheaded. Why was knowing this important? Surely, it didn't have to do with their murders.

She looked at the phone on the bedside table. Should she call Brit? Biting down on her lip, she tried to think how she'd put it. It seemed like such trivial information. Or was it? But maybe she shouldn't tell Brit until she knew for certain it had been them. But how could she verify it?

"Tanya." Cali reached for the phone.

"Police. Don't move!" Brit yelled. Humphrey started backing away. Expecting the man to go for his gun, Brit's finger tensed on the trigger.

But Stan didn't reach. Instead he held his hands up. "Don't shoot." He fell to his knees. Then he stretched out on the concrete walk, obviously familiar with the routine.

Quarles glanced at Brit. "This is too easy."

Brit didn't like it either.

~

"Why do you want to know?" Tanya asked.

"I know it sounds crazy," Cali said. "But remember me telling you that I felt like I knew that cop Anderson, the one who came to my place and was later killed?"

"Yeah," Tanya said.

"Well, Mom told me to figure it out. I didn't listen, but now I think I knew him from that meeting. What's really weird is that I think Brit's partner, the other detective that was killed, was there, too."

"Oh, fudge. You don't think that the At-Risk kids are involved in this, do you?" Tanya asked.

Cali slumped against Brit's headboard. "I don't know, but Mom said it would be important."

"Okay," Tanya said, not sounding the least bit put off by Cali's weird confession. Maybe being Catholic really did help some people believe in ghosts. "Let me call around and see if I can find out for sure if it was them. It's late, so it might be tomorrow, but I'll call you ASAP."

"Thanks." Cali looked around the room and wondered if her mom knew she had figured it out.

~

"Damn." Brit hissed after searching the truck again. No gun, no knife, no damn baseball bat. He did find what looked like bloodstains. CSI would go over the truck with a fine tooth comb. Pulling away, Brit could hear Humphrey singing a tune of innocence.

Brit stomped back over to where the handcuffed-Humphrey leaned against the hotel wall. "What about the old man at the jewelry store? I suppose you didn't take part in that either."

Humphrey seemed to choose his words wisely. "I was there. I'll cop to that. But it wasn't me who roughed him up. I even tried to stop them."

"I suppose you didn't beat up any of those old girlfriends either? Or rough up the guy at the last hotel, or the guard at the school. Why, you're just a friggin' angel, aren't you?"

Humphrey's eyes went bright with anger. "I never killed anyone. And those bitches deserved what they got. One came after me with a hammer and the other cheated on me."

"I suppose Cali McKay deserved to get roughed up, too, huh?" Brit gritted his back teeth so hard he thought they would crack.

"I didn't play rough with her. Well, maybe just a bit when she ran from me. But Cali's different," Humphrey snapped. "She's special."

"You're damn right she's different," Brit said.

Humphrey scowled and rose to his feet. "What's that mean?"

Quarles grabbed the man by his arm and held him back.

"You got a thing for my girl?" Humphrey asked.

Quarles gave him another jerk backwards.

But too late. Brit had Humphrey by the shirt and slammed him against the building. "She's not your girl. From what I heard, she kicked your ass out the night you shot the .38 through her door and tried to kill her." It took everything Brit had not to ram his fist into Humphrey's face.

~

Adams was waiting when they got to the police station. The sergeant had called for a report, and when he got the news they'd caught their man, he'd come in.

Duke and Mark took Humphrey down to get him in the system. Brit and Quarles followed Adams to his office to give him the details.

"With no weapon, we're really going to need to speak to his girlfriend," Adams said, looking at Quarles.

"We'll find it," Brit spit out.

Adams glanced at Brit and then back at Quarles. "CSI will go over the truck. I read your report this afternoon about the security guard. You know how to get in touch with McKay, don't you?"

Quarles nodded. "I think I can find her."

"I'll call you with a time tomorrow. Without a weapon for evidence, the DA will want to talk to her."

Brit felt his gut knot.

"Fine." Quarles said, a fine line of worry etched between his brow.

"I don't want anything biting us in the butt on this one," Adams said. "I want to take this guy down."

"Not any more than I do," Brit spouted out.

~

Brit glanced at his watch when he let himself into his house. Midnight. He removed his gun and dropped it on the fireplace mantel. Quarles, Duke, Mark, and the other two officers had gone out for a celebratory beer. Brit, much as Keith had done most nights when he was alive, had bowed out.

He needed to see Cali, to feel her next to him. Maybe then he'd stop second-guessing what he felt, second-guessing what she felt for him, and possibly what she felt for the man he'd put in jail tonight.

Before he left the living room, he felt the familiar brush against his leg. "Hey." Studying the cat, he kneeled. As usual, she backed up when he held out his hand. "Come on." The cat darted away.

Oddly enough, he felt rejected, but he didn't know why. He didn't even like cats. And as soon as things calmed down, he'd find the shelter that didn't put the animals down.

He eased into his bedroom. Looking down at Cali, Brit exhaled as the night's tension evaporated. She rested on her side and hugged a pillow as if she'd needed something to hold when she'd drifted off to sleep. Had she missed him? By damn, he'd missed her.

For several seconds, he just stood there and watched her breathe. He wondered how she was going to react when he told her they'd caught Humphrey. Would she be eager to get back to what she'd called her "normal life?" Would she rush back to her apartment? Where would this leave them? What would she say if he asked her to stay here?

Logic said it was too soon to offer any type of a commitment. But nothing about any of this felt logical. The fact that he wasn't panicking about the idea of a commitment wasn't logical.

Again the thought of Stan Humphrey having ever touched something as sweet as Cali brought a knot of jealousy to his gut. Didn't she know she deserved so much better than that jerk? He shut his eyes when another question bounced back. Did she deserve better than Brit Lowell? He sure as hell didn't have what one would call a good relationship record. Hell, most of his involvements with women couldn't even be called relationships.

He'd liked it that way. And for a damn good reason.

He'd watched his mom and dad and then watched his mom and her four, five or was it six husbands now, do the relationship dance. While his gut churned at the idea that he might be like either one of his parents, the truth was he didn't really know how a normal relationship should go. Hence, his fear of actually getting into one and being horrified that he had more of his parents in him that he wanted to admit.

Closing his eyes, he tried to nudge the thought from his mind. Taking a deep breath, he caught the scent of cigarette smoke. He sniffed his shirt sleeve, then went to grab a shower.

~

Cali woke up when the mattress shifted and she watched a naked Brit slip into bed beside her.

"Hey." His shower-warm body, still moist, came closer. "Do you always sleep in the nude?"

"Don't tell me that's bad manners, because I was hoping you might join me."

Grinning, she touched his face, just to make sure he wasn't a dream. He'd shaved and smelled like soap. "What time is it?"

"Almost one." He ran a hand through her hair.

She remembered what she'd discovered about the two officers, but Tanya hadn't called her back. The idea of telling him something that came unsubstantiated from dreams with her dead mom didn't feel right.

Then she remembered where he'd been and she sat up a bit. "Did you catch Stan?"

He seemed to study her. "Yeah. He came to the hotel just like we thought he would."

A thousand questions ran though her mind. Had Stan confessed to the murders? Had anyone been hurt? But for some reason, she was a tad nervous to ask, afraid he'd read something more into her curiosity.

"Tomorrow you're going to have to go in and answer some questions," he said.

"What kind of questions?" And a thought crossed her mind. "Did someone find out about us?"

"No. The DA just needs to ask a few questions about the bracelet." He paused. "If the subject comes up about us, I expect you to tell the truth."

"I would, but I'm not going to offer the information. The DA shouldn't ask about my personal life, should he?"

"No. But if it comes up, I'm serious, don't lie."

She nodded then pillowed her head on his chest. "I can't believe it's over."

His hand brushed across her back, and he told her about the arrest. When he finished, she lay there, trying to figure out what this meant now. She could go back home. Not too long ago, that had been so important to her. Not now.

He rolled on his side and faced her, his look in his eyes told her whatever he had to say was serious. "Do you think I can become part of your 'normal life'?"

"I was hoping you'd want that." She propped up on her elbow, running her fingers through his wet hair and wondered how big a part of her life he wanted to be. Because the whole relationship hadn't begun in a normal fashion, she didn't know how it was supposed to work now.

"What is it?" he asked as if trying to read her mind.

She grinned. "I thought you promised me make-up sex?" she whispered in his ear.

"Hmm. I think I can do that. But first I'm going to have to get you naked."

Chapter Thirty-Nine

"It's almost time now," her mom said.

Cali looked up. Her mother stood in the doorway, wearing the same navy suit she'd worn in all the dreams.

"Time for what?" Cali asked.

"To pass on. You're going to be okay."

"I am?" Cali tugged at the sheet when she realized she hadn't put on any clothes after she and Brit had made love. Twice. And it had been just as amazing as their first time.

A flock of nerves buzzed around her stomach when she remembered her mom could read her mind.

"It's okay." Her mom grinned. "He's a good man. But you've got to remember that you can't fix him. He's got to fix himself."

"He's not broken," Cali said.

"In his own way, he is. But everyone has their issues to deal with. Like you."

"I've got issues?"

Her mother stepped closer. "You just need to re-find yourself. You lost yourself when

you started taking care of me. But you're making headway. Making friends. Learning to stand up for yourself a little better. You need to start painting again."

"I stand up for myself," Cali said.

"Most of the time. But your nature is to turn the other cheek to avoid conflict. And you've got some conflict coming up. Just remember that a little conflict won't kill you. Sometimes, it even makes you stronger."

Confused, Cali got the feeling her mom was talking about conflict with Brit. "What's going to happen?"

"Just hold your chin up, girl. You have to do what your heart tells you to do. In the end, he'll be forced to respect that."

Cali sat up. "I don't understand."

Her mom walked over and pressed her soft palm on Cali's cheek. "Forward. Move forward." Her smile widened. "I love you. You were the best thing I did in my life."

~

The telephone startled Cali awake. She sat up and felt the tears on her cheeks, and the dream came back to her all at once. Brit rolled over and grabbed the phone, then he looked at her. Concern tightened his brow. She pulled the sheet up to dry her face.

"Hello?" Brit said. "Yeah, just a second." He covered the receiver. "What's wrong?"

"I'm fine," she said. "Who is it?"

He didn't look convinced, but held out the phone. "Tanya."

Cali took a deep breath before answering. "Yes?"

"You were right," Tanya said. "I got Mrs. Chavez this morning. She looked at an old newsletter. It was them. Mike Anderson and Keith Bolts. Originally, it was supposed to be Mike Anderson and some other cop, but he had to cancel at the last minute and Bolts came instead."

Cali bit down on her lip. "Thanks. I'll call you later."

She handed Brit the phone. He hung it up. "What was that about?"

Cali debated on how much to tell him. "I had Tanya check on something."

"Is something wrong?"

"No. Remember how I told you that I thought I knew Officer Anderson?"

He sat up, the sheet slipping down his naked chest. "Yeah."

"Well, last night I realized where I knew him from."

"Where?"

"The same place I knew your partner from."

"Quarles?" He studied her.

"No. Keith Bolts."

His brows rose in small arches over his eyes. "You knew Keith, too?"

She nodded. "I saw them both at a meeting for At-Risk teenagers. They came to speak there in September."

He pushed a hand over his face. "Both of them?"

Now she had to tell him the hard part. "In my dreams, Mom told me that remembering where I met them was important. I think it could be some clue to solving the case."

He half-laughed, half-moaned. "You dreamed you met them?"

"No, I saw them. I had Tanya check to make sure they were really there."

Sitting up, he ran a hand through his hair. "Do the kids go to these presentations?"

She nodded. "It's actually put on for them. They bring in speakers from the community to encourage them."

"Are some of them gang members?" he asked.

She saw from his expression that what she'd said had become important.

She nodded. "I don't know any of them personally, but I know several go to our school. The lady who heads the organization works out of the district office. I would assume she would be the person to talk to."

He jerked the covers back and stood up. He was naked, but didn't seem to care. "This could be it." He swung back around and looked at her in an odd way. "Your mother told you this?"

Cali nodded, trying not to look below his waist, but she couldn't help herself. Goodness, he was beautiful. Had there been a day when she didn't enjoy looking at a man's body?

He leaned down and kissed her. "Can you be ready to get in your car in ten minutes? I want to check this out."

"Yeah. But I have to shower or I'll smell like sex." Suddenly, a big smile started in her chest and met her lips. Brit believed her. That felt good. She let her gaze travel down again. Then she grabbed the sheet, pulled it around her, and waddled into the bathroom.

Brit laughed then said, "I've seen you naked, Cali. I think it was just last night that I came up close and personal with every inch of you."

"Yeah," she called back, feeling her face flush at the memory of how thoroughly they'd both gone over each other. "But if you see it all the time you'll stop appreciating it." She dropped the sheet and stepped into the shower.

"Not in this lifetime, sweetheart," he said and joined her in the shower.

They took a little longer than ten minutes.

~

Once they were out, Brit dressed and called Quarles. "Hey, I've got something I've got to check out this morning."

"I was just about to call you. Adams wants Cali at the precinct at ten. The DA is coming to talk to her."

Brit frowned. He wanted to be there when they questioned her. But he had to check out what Cali had told him. "Okay. But can you be with her? So she won't be alone in case I don't make it back by ten?"

"Sure, but where did you say you were going?"

"I didn't say," Brit answered, not wanting to explain. Hell, how could he explain? Even the fact that he believed Cali left him feeling a little strange. But he did believe her.

~

"Miss McKay, I'm Sergeant Adams, and this is Shane Paxton with the DA's office."

Cali nodded at the heavyset older man and the beautiful redhead beside him. The woman wore a dusty green business suit that came a little too short on one end and a little too low on the other. She glanced at Cali with disinterest. Cali managed to offer the woman a smile. Ms. Paxton didn't feel inclined to return the gesture.

Cali fidgeted with her purse strap. Brit's partner stood beside her as if to offer support. The sergeant motioned to John and looked back at Ms. Paxton. "This is John Quarles. He's new to our department. He's working the case."

Ms. Paxton glanced around, and disappointment seemed to pull at her painted lips. "I thought Brit was working the case."

"Quarles and Brit Lowell are partners." Adams motioned toward the table. "Let's sit down."

Cali didn't miss the fact that the woman had referred to Brit by his first name. Then she remembered Brit mentioning his last girlfriend's name was Shane. Oh, great! Surely, she wasn't about to be interrogated by Brit's old girlfriend.

"What can I do for you?" Cali forced a pleasant tone, but she wanted to finish this conversation before it got started.

"I need to go over your statements to make sure we've got a case against . . ." She looked at the file. "Stan Humphrey."

Cali nodded. "I'm not sure what I can tell you that I haven't already told the police."

"Actually you can tell us a lot." She had a snippy voice that Cali didn't like. The fact that she was beautiful and had probably slept with Brit didn't help.

"Stan Humphrey gave you a diamond bracelet, right?"

Cali forced herself not to frown and she started comparing herself to the sleek redhead. Red had beautiful brown eyes, exotic eyes. And she had at least two inches on Cali, too. Which meant the woman had longer legs. Men liked long legs.

"Yes, I told the police that. And I gave it to Brit . . . Detective Lowell." Cali caught herself making the same mistake the woman had earlier.

The redhead raised a thinly plucked eyebrow. "Did Mr. Humphrey tell you where he got the jewelry?" Now instead of disinterest, the woman gazed at Cali as if she were something the buzzards had abandoned for some better looking road kill.

Cali brushed her fingers along the table's edge. "No. It was a gift and I didn't ask." She chose not to tell her that the piece of jewelry had been slung at her during an argument.

"What kind of business did you think your boyfriend was in, Miss McKay? I'm sorry, I'm assuming he is your boyfriend."

And I'm assuming you were the woman who stuck a condom in the pocket of the man I'm now sleeping with. "We were dating at the time and Mr. Humphrey is a musician."

"And not anymore?"

"No." Cali wrapped her finger around her leather purse strap and stared down at her black slacks and wished she'd worn something less teachery.

"Didn't I read in here that he was living with you?"

"He was staying with me while he found an apartment." How long would she be paying for that mistake?

"Hmm." Ms. Paxton flipped through the pages. "Funny, it seems all these reports were written up by Brit. Did you ever make a report, Mr. Quarles? Or was Brit mostly on the case?"

Unlike Cali, John Quarles seemed completely relaxed. "I'm sure they just haven't gotten filed yet."

The D.A. smiled, but it looked transparent. Then her gaze hit Cali again. "Was Mr. Humphrey doing well in his career?"

Cali tried to imitate John's relaxed composure. "I don't think so."

"So tell me, Miss McKay. If you knew your boyfriend wasn't financially stable, then how did you think he could afford to give you such an extravagant gift?"

Cali stiffened her shoulders at the implied accusation. "I thought the bracelet was fake. Detective Lowell can even tell you that I'd thrown it away. He dug it out of my garbage the day he came looking for it."

The woman looked at John. "I'm surprised Detective Lowell isn't here now to offer her his support." Her brows arched. "He's so good at supporting his female witnesses." She hung her implication out like underwear on a clothesline.

John squared his shoulders, but some of his cool composure slipped and hit the floor. "Brit had some other matters to tend to this morning."

The woman's gaze landed back on Cali. "Tell me. Did you have the opportunity to see the detective this morning?"

Chapter Forty

"Ma'am, I'm with the Hopeful Police, Detective Brit Lowell." He sat down across from Mrs. Chavez in her candle-scented, peach-colored office. Oddly, the middle-aged woman didn't appear surprised to see him.

"Detective Lowell? Your name came up at our last meeting. Mrs. Craft mentioned she was going to ask you to speak to the group at our next quarterly meeting."

"Who?" He leaned forward.

"Tanya Craft. A teacher at Well's High." Mrs. Chavez looked perplexed.

"Yes, Tanya Craft."

"I do hope you'll agree to come. Our programs are set to encourage students to overcome the hurdles that might lead them to dropping out of school."

Brit held up his hand to interrupt. He didn't need the sales pitch on the program—he needed information. "Mrs. Chavez, I'll be more than happy to speak with your group." If you still want me after I try to bust a couple of your future dropouts. "But I'm not here about that."

"Oh, I'm sorry. I just assumed. What can I do for you?"

~

"Did you see Brit this morning?" Mr. Paxton asked Cali again.

"Let's stay on track here," Adams said as if the question had disturbed him as well.

While relieved to be off that hook, the accusation that Cali may have been aware of the robberies still needed to be addressed. She met the woman's glare head on.

Ms. Paxton squared her shoulders and Cali imitated her posture. "I didn't know Stan was robbing jewelry stores, if that's what you're implying."

"I'm simply covering all our bases, Miss McKay. The questions I ask are nothing compared to those Humphrey's lawyer will ask when you're on the stand." The woman tapped her pencil against the table. "So your boyfriend shot at you?"

"Someone shot through my apartment door," Cali replied.

"Someone?" Red leaned closer. Cali swore the woman breathed in as if attempting to catch Brit's scent on her. Somehow she knew. Of course she knew, just like Cali knew. The woman rapped her red fingernails against the file. "According to this report, you said it was your boyfriend."

Cali leaned in, actually hoping the woman got a big whiff of Brit's musk and sandalwood. "Yes, I did say that, but when I came in to file a restraining order against him, I think I mentioned to the other officer that Stan claimed he wasn't the one who shot the gun. I may not have made a big deal about it, because at the time I didn't believe it."

"But you believe him now," the DA said, and the tapping of her nails on the table grew intense. Tap, tap, tap. "Forgive me for being frank, Miss McKay, but for the sake of the case I'd like to know." She paused. "Do you, or do you not think Stan Humphrey is guilty?"

Adams shifted in his seat. "Does it matter what she thinks? She's a fact witness. Can't we stick to the facts?"

The woman twisted to look at the sergeant. "You do your job and let me do mine."

Adams' brows pinched and Red's acute focus shifted back to Cali. It was the kind of direct eye contact that made lumps appear in the target's throat. And Cali's lump started to crowd her tonsils.

Brit's sergeant looked up, and Quarles leaned back in his chair, studying Cali with the same intensity. Three pairs of eyes drilled holes in her. Lying would be so much easier than telling the truth. She knew what they all wanted to hear. They wanted her to say that she believed Stan did it—that he killed the band members, that he shot that cop, but that wasn't what she believed.

Reaching up, she brushed a strand of hair from her cheek. The pause seemed to swell with tension. For just a second, she considered taking the easy way out. It would make them happy. It would make Brit happy. Then she remembered her dream and her mom's words. *Just remember that a little conflict won't kill you. Sometimes, it even makes you stronger.*

~

Brit looked at the woman directly. "So there's no mistake here? It was definitely Keith Bolts and Mike Anderson who spoke."

"Well, yes. As a matter of fact, Tanya called me this morning asking the very same question. Is there something going on that I should know about?"

Brit squared his shoulders. "Yes, Mrs. Chavez, I think something very serious is going on. Have you kept up with the news about the two officers who were shot?"

"I gave up watching the news. It upsets me."

It upset Brit, too. It was meant to upset people, to inform and hopefully encourage them to get involved. He gritted his teeth to keep from voicing his opinion. "The two officers who spoke at your meeting are the two who were shot and killed."

She leaned back in her chair and her olive color washed white. "You think someone with At-Risk is involved with this?"

"Yes. That's exactly what I think." He splayed his hands out on her desk. "And this is what I'll be needing—a list of every student in the program. Any background information you have on them, such as involvement in drugs or gangs, and especially of those who attended the last meeting."

"That's a lot of kids, Detective."

He didn't blink. "And I know you're already considering how quickly you can get those to me. And by quick, I don't mean tomorrow. So I'll just wait here while you pull that info together."

She stood and fidgeted with some papers on her desk. "Dios Mio, I seriously hope you're wrong about this."

Brit didn't say it, but he seriously hoped he was right. Finding Keith and Anderson's killer meant more than anything to him. An image of Cali, wrapped in a sheet, waddling to the bathroom, trying not to expose her backside, filled his mind. Okay, finding the killer meant more than almost anything. It didn't even matter that she talked to her dead mother in her dreams. But, hell, considering where this lead came from, he loved her dead mother, too.

Then it hit him, right between the eyes, but mostly in his heart. He loved Cali. The thought came with a certainty that he couldn't deny. What's more, he didn't want to.

~

An hour later, Brit danced out of his car to the precinct with a list of fifty teens. He figured by the time they narrowed it down to those who fit the descriptions Rina gave, he'd only have fifteen or twenty. But damn. They could have Keith's murderer locked away by this time next week. Even sooner.

As Brit made it up the stairs, he saw Quarles storming out. The man didn't look happy, but Brit figured he'd change that with his news. The whole precinct would celebrate.

Brit hurried his pace.

"Guess what I got," he said.

"What?" Quarles asked.

"Keith's and Anderson's case. Big tip. And it panned out."

Quarles' eyes did light up. "What did you get?"

"Both Keith and Anderson spoke last September at an At-Risk program for possible dropouts. And at least 50 percent of these kids are gang-related."

Quarles' eyes widened. "How did we miss this? I personally went through all their public appearances."

"The woman in charge said that at the last minute the cop who was supposed to appear with Anderson had something come up. Keith was added at the last minute. I figure they never felt compelled to change it on the paperwork. "

"Yeah," Quarles said and Brit could see the man's mind turning. "We'll need a list of the kids involved."

Brit thumped the file he held in his hand. "Got it. I'm on my way to run the records and see which ones have priors."

They headed for the door, a new bounce to Quarles' step. "Where did you get this tip?"

Brit decided on a partial truth. "Cali."

Quarles stopped and his brow furrowed. "Cali?"

"She volunteered at that meeting. Last week, she told me she was trying to piece together why Anderson seemed so familiar. He was there at her place, remember? Then she saw a picture of Keith and recognized him too. Last night, she figured it out."

"Fine. But I'd advise you that when you're repeating this to Adams, leave Cali's name out of it."

"Why?" Brit got a bad feeling. "Did the questioning go badly?"

"That would be putting it mildly."

"What happened? Is Cali okay?"

Quarles folded his arms over his chest. "First the DA came on like a bitch on wheels. She–"

"She? Shit! Please don't tell me it was Shane Paxton."

Quarles gave him a cutting look. "Yeah. Adams told me you two were an item. Anyway, it was as if she had this sixth sense that you and Cali were getting it on between the sheets."

"That woman is a trained Doberman. She could chew Cali up and spit her out. Is Cali okay?"

"Cali? You're worried about Cali? You should worry about your ass and mine. By the time the meeting was over, that Doberman had pretty much convinced Adams that we'd done a half-ass job on the case. She frowned upon the little issue of us not having a murder weapon. Then she laid out some serious implications that you may have overstepped boundaries with the witness. But the crap really hit the fan when Cali, your sweet little lady friend, made it pretty clear which side of the fence she was on."

"What do you mean?" Brit rolled the papers in his hand into a tight tube.

"She basically corroborated everything Humphrey has been saying since we brought him in. You'd think Cali and Humphrey had compared notes and had their stories straight."

"What?" Every bit of happiness that had filled his chest now squeezed out of his lungs.

"Humphrey claimed he didn't shoot Cali's door that night. And Cali just seemed to remember that Humphrey told her he wasn't the one to shoot. Then Paxton came right out and asked if she thought Humphrey was guilty of murder. The girl didn't blink. She said, 'No, I don't think he'd kill anyone.' She went on to say the man was kind to the elderly, and she didn't see him killing his friends. Right now, she's down there trying to see Humphrey. She's obviously still got the hots for him. Sorry, I know you don't want to hear that."

Brit struggled to breathe. "She's trying to see him?"

"Yeah," Quarles said.

The last piece of info fell on Brit like sharp rocks. He shot up the rest of the steps and stormed into the building. For every step he took forward, he took one back to his past. How had he let himself be fooled again? Hadn't he seen it in the beginning? Hadn't he known it? Cali McKay was his mother's clone. They always went back to the guy who mistreated them.

He stormed downstairs to the holding tanks. He found Cali in the waiting room, sitting in a metal chair, twirling her purse strap around her fingers. He didn't speak to her when she raised her gaze. Instead, he took her by the elbow and led her into one of the small visiting rooms.

He flung the door closed, slamming his palm on the wall so hard that pain shot up his arm. "What the fuck are you doing?" He saw her flinch, but was too angry to care.

"What?" She looked up at him with those huge innocent orbs of blue.

"Do you still love him?" Hadn't he asked his mother the same question?

Cali blinked those eyes at him. Oh yeah, he'd bought his mother's "poor me" looks for years. How many times had he stepped between her and his father—even taken the blows for her? For what? She always let the old man move back in.

"Answer me, damn it!" He took a step closer. She took a step back. He moved in, a man with a mission, a man with a broken heart. "You love him."

She shook her head. "No. I need to talk to him. I need to make sure that I'm right. If I have to testify then—"

"For him or against him?" When she didn't seem to understand what he was asking her, he explained. "Are you going to be testifying for him or against him, Cali?"

"I'm going to tell the truth." She had tears in her eyes.

He refused to acknowledge them, refused to let them affect him. He'd played this game with his mother, he wasn't about to play it with her. "What the hell is wrong with you? Wait, you don't have to tell me. I had it right in the beginning. You're just like my mom."

"I can't fix you," she said.

"Good. Because I don't want to attempt to fix you either!'

Her hot blue eyes tightened to thin slits, but pain rivaled with anger for top emotion. "I'm leaving."

She said the words with such certainty, that it hit his gut like a bullet, but that's what he wanted. Wasn't it? As he watched her walk out, the pain he'd seen in her eyes echoed tenfold in his chest.

~

Cali left. She didn't have the strength to confront Stan now. Oh later, she intended to do it. She needed to be sure she was right about his inability to commit murder. She didn't care what Brit thought.

She didn't care.

She didn't.

So why did it feel as if she was dying inside?

She drove to her mother's house, shaking so badly her hands hardly stayed on the wheel.

~

Once inside, she shut and locked the door. She went to her mother's room, threw herself down on the hospital bed where her mother had died less than two weeks ago. Wrapping her hands around a pillow that still smelled like her mother, Cali sobbed.

Mom was right. She couldn't fix Brit. And remembering the things he'd said, Cali hurt so badly, she wasn't sure she even cared if he fixed himself.

Chapter Forty-One

Two days later, Brit stood over Rina Newman's shoulder and waited with bated breath for her answer. He'd worked nonstop for the past forty-eight hours, chasing down leads, compiling photo lineups, and doing whatever it took to catch Keith and Anderson's killer.

"That's him," Rina said, pointing to one of the photographs. "He was the one waiting in the car."

Quarles slapped a hand on Brit's back. His partner hadn't backed down either. For every hour Brit worked, Quarles had stood beside him. Both of them were running on empty. Only fast food and bad coffee kept them on their feet. Sleep had been something he'd left behind. Brit picked up the photograph and looked at the back to see where the kid lived and went to school. It was ten A.M. The school would be the first place to hit. Wells High.

Brit gritted his teeth. With the whole damn district, why did the teen have to go there? The idea of running into Cali sent acid burning through another layer of his stomach.

But the only thing that would hurt more than seeing Cali right now would be not catching Keith's killer. "Come on," he said to Quarles, who was already on the phone calling for backup.

They didn't meet resistance. Mrs. Jasmine called the boy to the office, and they escorted him out. Of course, the paperwork they'd slapped on her desk didn't leave her any option.

On the way out, Brit stopped by the main office to tell someone to call the boy's parents and let them know where they were taking him. When he turned to leave, he saw Tanya, standing on the other side of the hall. She started toward him, her attitude adding a bounce to her steps.

He considered ducking out. He'd already been privy to her smart mouth, and he didn't care to hear it again, but some sort of masochist emotion kept his feet planted to the hall floor.

Her eyes shot daggers at him when she came to a halt. "The only thing that keeps me from ripping your heart out and feeding it to the roaches in the science lab is knowing that, sooner or later, you're going to realize that you were wrong—and stupid. One of these days, you'll know what you lost. Thank God, even people as sweet as Cali have limits and you crossed hers. And that, Mr. Little Dickhead, brings me a hell of a lot of pleasure." She walked off, so damn sure of herself.

Brit turned and left with the same certainty to his gait. He was doing the right thing.

~

An hour later, Brit sat at his desk, waiting to hear if the kid's lawyer and the DA hashed out a deal. Images of Cali kept flashing in his head. His chest hadn't stopped hurting. He wasn't sure it would.

Brit rolled a pencil on his desk, if he wasn't hoping they might get some info on Keith's killer, he'd go out and get dog drunk—drunk like his old man used to get. So drunk that he fell flat on his face and could sleep.

"You look miserable," a feminine voice asked.

Brit looked up to see Shane Paxton pressing against the doorjamb. He should really learn to shut his door to keep the trash from blowing in. Biting back the harsh comments he'd like to toss at her, he answered. "Did we get anything from the kid?"

"I didn't catch that case." She moved in, seductively. "I'm here because I got news on the Humphrey case."

Brit looked down at the pencil caught between his fingers and snapped it in two. "What do you have?"

She stopped at the edge of his desk and propped her hip on top. "You really are banging the witness, aren't you?"

Brit pointed to the door with half a pencil. "Is that your news? You just came here to start shit? Take that up with Adams. Or Internal Affairs if you want, I don't give a damn."

She let out a deep breath. "I didn't come here to throw stones. I came to tell you the news. I'll admit I'm shocked, but your little teacher was right about everything."

Brit leaned forward. "What?"

"Nolan Bright's brother got snagged in Arkansas for drugs. He asked to cut a deal for giving them something on another murder and a

Texas cop shooting. He pretty much gave the same story Humphrey told us. Humphrey's only crime is robbery and being a sleazeball."

All the ugly things he'd thrown at Cali started echoing in his head. Brit let out a bitter-tasting gulp of air, but he didn't speak. Hell, what could he say? Cali had been right.

Was she telling the truth about her feelings for Stan, too?

Right then, he recalled Cali's friend Tanya's words. Sooner or later you're going to realize that you were wrong—and stupid. One of these days, you'll know what you lost.

Shane continued, "I suppose I was a little hard on her. I'm a tad upset that we didn't make it."

"Make it? We were about sex, Shane. That's what you said you wanted. That's what I wanted."

"But it was good sex."

Not that good. But he kept himself from saying it. What he'd had with Cali had been good. But he'd lost it. No, he hadn't lost it. He'd thrown it away because . . . because he was as fucked up as his parents. "You should probably leave."

"Is it just about sex with her, too? Or is it more? She's such a vanilla-looking girl. Does she really do it for you?"

"You know, in this tiny little room, I didn't think I'd have to show you where the door is?"

Shane leaned in as if hoping the sight of her cleavage would make him go weak. Wrong. Now, there was nothing about this woman he wanted, liked, or admired.

She ran her tongue across her lips. "If you call me later, I'll dress up like a teacher. Get a ruler." She leaned in.

Brit backed up and stared her dead in the eyes so she'd know he meant what he was about to say. "Go find someone else to screw, Shane. I'm not your fuck toy."

Shane looked verbally slapped. "Anyone ever tell you that you're a jerk?"

He watched her leave and his chest ached where his heart used to be. Not a jerk, he thought, but a dickhead. Standing, he didn't know where he was going. He just couldn't sit here and wait. Snatching his thin, useless coat from the chair, and headed out. He'd lost his leather jacket and his heart. He was going to miss his jacket. His heart was another matter. He recalled how hurt Cali had looked when he said all those terrible things to her.

"Just like dear ol' dad," he muttered.

He didn't deserve a heart. He sure as hell didn't deserve her.

Once outside, the damp, cold hit and he made up his mind. As soon as he caught Keith's killer, he'd go to Mexico. Three weeks of warm weather and good tequila, and he might be able to forget.

~

An hour later, Cali sat down in the metal chair and looked at Stan through the glass. He hadn't shaven, his hair hung even longer, dirtier, but he seemed thrilled to see her. She studied him and wondered how she could have convinced herself she'd been attracted to him. He pointed to the phone. Cali picked it up on her side of the partition as Stan picked it up on his.

"Hey, babe," he said and his lips spread in a come-on smile.

Cali didn't smile back. "I'm not your babe."

"Ahh, sweetie. You love me and you know it. That's why you came."

Cali squared her shoulders. "No. I don't love you. I never loved you. It may sound callous, but I only got involved with you because my mom was dying and I was scared."

"Yeah, and I was there for you, too. So now you've got to be here for me."

She shook her head, finding it difficult to speak.

"No," she said. "You weren't there for me. You never even asked about my mom. You broke into my apartment, you broke into my car, you broke into my mom's house. And I'm not here for you."

She pressed her hand on the cold metal table. "However, I told the DA that I didn't think you killed those guys, but now I want to hear it from you."

"I didn't kill them." He leaned forward. "I didn't even hit the old man. I asked them to stop. And I even took the bat and hit the wall, hoping he'd do what they said and not hit him anymore."

She looked into Stan's violet eyes and believed him. Even villains had soft spots. Stan cared about the elderly.

"I need your help," he said. "And you're going to help me. You owe it to me because if you hadn't called the police, I'd be free."

She shook her head and kept shaking it. "I don't owe you anything. I can't fix you. As a matter of fact, I'm out of the fix-it business. Good luck, Stan."

He looked shocked, then he looked angry. "I don't need fixing. I need a really good lawyer. I know you got some money from your mom."

Cali sat up straighter. "You're on your own."

"You bitch!" he snapped.

She almost hung up, but then brought the phone back to her mouth. "I'm working on it."

~

Brit was sitting in the bar, staring at his first whiskey, when his cell rang. He didn't check the number, but he prayed it was news about Keith's killer.

"Yeah?" he snapped.

"We got a name and address," Quarles said. "The warrant is being drawn up as we speak. We're going in."

He flipped the cell closed, dropped a ten on the counter by his untouched drink and took off.

When he got back to the station, everyone was geared up. Adams tossed him a vest. "Put it on or you don't come."

Brit put it on.

On the drive over, they filled him in. The suspect in Keith's murder, Moses Johnson, was barely eighteen and already head of the new gang. He'd earned his position because he'd been the willing tough guy who took out two cops. But tough guy lived with his eighty-six year old grandma in a low-income neighborhood.

Brit prayed he had a chance to prove to the kid what tough was.

At least twelve officers unloaded from the two vans. It took them five minutes to get the place surrounded. The house, once white, had paint peeling off its siding. The yard hadn't seen a mower in months. The porch steps were concrete and had weeds growing from the cracks. If it wasn't for the lawn chair on the porch, and the two cars parked in the driveway, one of which was registered to their suspect, the place would have looked abandoned.

Brit, positioned at the side of the porch, covered the side window and had eyes on the porch in case Moses came out fighting. Quarles and Adams were stationed at the back. Duke and Mark, with two officers backing them, took the lead. It was a position Brit had wanted, but Adams refused to give him.

Brit watched Duke and Mark step up on the porch, their guns drawn. The other two officers moved up and bracketed the door. Brit held his breath. Stomach knotted, he waited for them to make their presence known. Brit's palms began to sweat, the vest heavy on his shoulders. He held tight to his own gun.

We're going to get him, Keith. We're going to get him.

~

Cali walked into her apartment. Memories of Brit when he'd helped her clean up filled her heart and she let go of a deep breath.

Her home phone had several messages on it. The blinking yellow light seemed to flash at the same rate as her heart. And with each beat, it hurt.

Her gaze caught on the lamp, the heavy ceramic that was cracked, and she knew if she could see inside her chest, her heart would probably look worse.

She sat on the sofa and pushed the button to see the numbers of those who'd called her. Most of them were listed as unknown. She almost hit the button to listen, but decided against it. If it was Brit, she didn't want to hear it.

Or did she?

A new wash of tears filled her eyes as she pushed the button. None of them were Brit.

He hadn't called to beg for her forgiveness. Though why she wanted him to, she didn't know, especially since she didn't even know if she wanted to forgive him.

Or did she?

You can't fix him.

Her mom's words filled her head and she cried harder.

A knock came at the door. Brushing her tears back, she remembered that Tanya had insisted on coming by. She'd tried to tell her no, but Tanya didn't take no for an answer.

Cali walked to the door, opened the lock, and hadn't gotten her hand on the knob, when someone shoved the door open.

Knocked to the floor, Cali saw the knife and screamed. As she scooted back, scrubbing her butt over the carpet, she managed to focus on the person wielding the weapon over her.

Nolan Bright.

"Where's your boyfriend, Bitch?"

~

"Police! Open the door," Duke shouted.

The door came open and Brit saw an elderly woman standing in the doorway.

He heard Duke spouting out orders. Brit's heart pounded in his ears, and he didn't hear the conversation, but he saw the old lady nod her head, and then her shoulders seemed to slump in defeat as she stepped outside.

Another officer took her by the arm and moved her off the porch as Duke, Mark, and three other officers stormed the house.

It took everything Brit had not to follow them inside. He wanted to be there when the guy resisted. Wanted his own personal revenge.

He inhaled and the air reeked of cigarette smoke. A vision of Cali filled his head. Pushing the image back, he concentrated on what he was doing. On what he was supposed to be doing. Taking down Keith's killer.

Brit heard a commotion come from the back. He heard Quarles yell out and Brit took off. No way in hell was he going to lose another partner!

Before he got to the back, he heard the shots. He'd barely cut the corner of the house when the bullet knocked him flat on his ass. The pain took him down the rest of the way.

~

"What do you want?" Cali asked and slowly got to her feet, backing up until her legs hit the end table.

"Where the hell is Stan?" Nolan asked and took a step closer, holding his knife out.

Her heart began to pound and the sound of it seemed to echo in her ears. She started to answer him, to tell him the truth, but something stopped her. "What do you want with him?"

"Unfinished business," he snapped. His eyes looked glassy. Wild. He looked dirty. Everything from his stringy blond hair to his light gray shirt with stains running down the front needed a good washing. "Now talk or die."

Her breath caught. Was this it? Was she really going to die like this?

"He's . . . not here."

"I know that, bitch. Where is he?" He took another step closer.

She got the crazy feeling that as long she had something he wanted—information—then he wouldn't attack. But once he got it . . .

He'd already killed three people; instinct told her he wouldn't mind making it four.

"Start talking!" he seethed.

She glanced at the door, left ajar. Could she get past him quickly enough?

She had to try, didn't she? Heart pounding, adrenalin flowing through her veins, she was poised to run, when the door swung open.

"Cali?" Tanya stood in the open door. Her eyes widened when she saw Nolan and his knife.

Nolan turned.

"Run!" Cali screamed. Not thinking, just acting, she reached for the broken ceramic lamp and swung it hard, harder than she knew she could, right at Nolan Bright's head.

She heard the sound of it hitting his skull, but didn't care. Then she bolted to the door and prayed she made it in time.

Chapter Forty-Two

"Man down! Man down!"

Brit heard the words. And in some distant part of his brain, he knew they were talking about him. But he didn't want to be the man down, so he tried to stand up.

"Stay down! We got him."

It took Brit a minute to realize it was Quarles talking—another minute to realize that his partner was running his hands over his shoulders. Damn, he liked the guy, but not like that. He swatted at his hands.

"The vest caught it, you lucky bastard." Quarles smiled. "But I know it still hurts like hell, doesn't it?"

Brit pushed Quarles back and jackknifed up. He didn't hurt. Well, he did, but not bad enough to lay on the ground while his partner ran his hand over him. He balanced himself on his two weak legs, but his lungs still weren't completely functioning. He scanned the backyard to make sure Quarles hadn't been lying. Then he stepped forward, needing to see for himself the son of a bitch who'd killed his partner and tried to kill him was in custody.

"Easy," Quarles said.

Brit saw Adams yank the cuffed suspect from the ground. Brit started forward again, but Quarles grabbed him by the arm.

"Don't do it."

Brit's gaze took in the dark-haired suspect, wearing jeans and a school jersey. He might be eighteen, but he didn't look a day over fifteen, and he probably didn't weigh a hundred and twenty pounds soaking wet. He was just a kid.

Which probably explained why Keith and Anderson hadn't had any defensive wounds on them. The boy didn't look like a threat.

But he was. He'd taken lives. Innocent lives. Brit curled his fist up tight. He thought about Keith's son and hoped like hell that Keith Jr. was an old man before this punk ever saw freedom.

Fifteen minutes later, the suspect had been carted away and the crowd was beginning to thin. Brit spotted Adams walking over, a huge frown on his face.

Brit had refused medical attention, and no doubt the man was pissed and planned to jump Brit's ass about it.

As soon as Adams got close, Brit spoke up. "Get that look off your face old man. I'm fine. It's just a bruise."

Adams hesitated before speaking. "It's not that. Nolan Bright got to Cali McKay. We got a couple of units heading to her apartment now."

~

Three cops were parked in front of Cali's apartment when Brit brought the unmarked police van to a sudden stop. He spotted a couple of paramedics shutting the back of an ambulance and bolted out of the van.

"Who you got?" He ran up to them, his chest so tight he thought it would crack.

When they didn't answer right away, he flashed his badge. "I asked you a question."

One man held up his hand. "Calm down. We got the perp."

"Cali McKay?" Saying her name brought a wave of pain to his heart.

"She's in the apartment giving a statement. She's fine."

He heard a car screech to a halt behind him. Looking back, he saw Quarles and Adams getting out. But he didn't wait; he took off, taking the steps two at a time, just wanting to see her for himself.

The officer holding fort at the door recognized him, and shifted back to let him inside.

He took one step inside and then stopped. She sat on the sofa. No blood. No signs of injury, not physically, anyway. Emotionally was another matter.

Just the way she wrapped her arms around herself told him how upset she was. She needed someone to hold her.

The image took him back to when he'd first seen her. She wasn't wearing a Mickey Mouse nightshirt, but she looked just as vulnerable, just as devastated. A victim.

"A hell of a girl there." Officer Logan, Mike Anderson's old partner, stepped beside Brit. "She took the guy out."

"How bad?" Brit asked.

"Nothing serious. He's just unconscious."

"Then someone needs to finish the job." And Brit would love to volunteer for the job.

Brit noticed Tanya, Cali's friend, sitting in the chair. Her gaze met his and she frowned at him.

He looked away from her and back to Cali.

"She's not hurt, is she?" he asked Logan just to be sure.

"Just shaken up."

Cali bit down on her lip and he saw a sheen of tears in her eyes. And just like that, he remembered what an ass he'd been to her in the beginning. He remembered with clarity the awful things he'd said to her when he'd caught her trying to visit Humphrey.

Then she looked over toward the door, toward him. The hurt and anguish he saw in her eyes made him catch his breath. Knowing he'd been partly responsible for putting it there sent a bolt of regret echoing in his chest.

A hell of a girl. Logan's words rang in his head. And she deserved a hell of a guy. She deserved someone so much better than him. Not someone who carried the baggage from his dysfunctional childhood—doomed to screw up any relationship he had. Unable to breathe, but telling himself it was the right thing to do, he turned and left.

~

"Is that everything, ma'am?" the moving guy asked.

Cali turned around, her gaze taking in her mother's living room. "Yes. The sofa stays."

"Okay. We'll be here tomorrow with the things from the apartment."

Smiling took effort, but she managed. "Thanks." She watched him leave. It was Monday and instead of returning to work, she'd taken the week off to finish getting her mother's house emptied and her things from the apartment ready to move in.

She hadn't thought she'd ever want to live here—in the Cancer House. But after what happened at her apartment, she hadn't wanted to stay there, either. So she'd come here. And once she recovered from her four-hour cry, she'd started remembering things. Good things—like how she and her mom had laughed over dinners, how they spent evenings, each of them with a good book in their hands. Or watching old Burt Reynolds movies.

Yes, her mom had died here, but she'd also lived here. Cali needed to remember those good times. Cancer had taken away her mom—Cali wasn't going to let it take away her memories or the home her mother had loved.

She still felt as if a part of her was missing, as if someone had come in the dead of night and surgically removed an important limb— an arm or a foot. She continued walking, pretending it was still there, but she kept tripping, stumbling over the pain that hit so hard at certain moments she couldn't breathe.

She told herself the thing missing was her mom and not Brit. But she lied. She missed them both. The difference was that her mom had died. The other had left on his accord. Brit had just walked out. Walked out without even talking to her. Hadn't he seen how much she needed him? That had hurt even worse than the things he'd said to her the last time they argued.

However, she refused to dwell on it. Forward. She needed to move forward. That's what her mother said and that was what Cali intended to do.

She went to the table where she had laid out the paint chips last night. Tanya had offered to come over tonight and help her paint. Cali had chosen pale yellows for the walls, and next week the carpet would be removed and hardwood floors installed.

Walking into one of the extra bedrooms, Cali remembered her mom telling her that the room would make a good art studio. She'd been right.

The large windows allowed in a lot of light, making it a perfect place to paint.

Tomorrow, Cali planned to go to the art supply store and buy paint and canvases. Forward. She would survive. Hadn't her mama said she'd be okay?

Last night, Cali had prayed she'd dream about her mom, but she hadn't. She'd dreamed about Brit. She didn't dwell on it. Instead, she made plans.

Next week, she'd return to teaching and spend her evenings either working on the house or reconnecting with some part of herself she'd lost when her mother got cancer. Funny how the memory of her mom getting cancer brought back memories of Marty.

It took thinking about Marty and his dream job which had ended their relationship, to realize that her own dream of being an artist hadn't vanished. It had only been sleeping. So during her time off for Thanksgiving, Cali would try to reconnect with her old dream.

Normal. Life would never be like it was. But she'd find a new normal, because the old one didn't exist anymore.

As good as it had felt to face Stan, and even to fight and win against Nolan Bright, Cali had decided she didn't want to be a bitch, after all. She just needed to be stronger and more selective of whom she allowed into her life. That meant no more dickheads. Even little dickheads.

She'd already signed up to work at the shelter on Thanksgiving Day. Yesterday, she'd visited Sara and her mother, too, and offered to help any way she could. The woman was scheduled for a mastectomy in two weeks. Doctor Tien had reviewed the test results and recommended she do more than just a lumpectomy. Cali figured if she spent time helping others, she wouldn't have so much time to feel sorry for herself. Pity parties just weren't her thing.

She'd also made another appointment to talk to Dr. Roberts. Her mother had said Cali had issues. Maybe it was high time she understood those issues a little better. Maybe then, she wouldn't have to work so hard to forget Brit.

Forward. She was moving forward.

Chapter Forty-Three

The week after Thanksgiving, two weeks since she'd moved into her mom's house, Cali stood back as Tanya studied her first two paintings. Until now, she hadn't had the guts to show them to anyone.

"I'm speechless." Tanya's brown eyes grew large.

"Are they that bad?" Cali asked.

"Please." Tanya rolled her eyes. "This is no time for modesty, girlfriend. These are marvelous."

"You think?" Cali smiled. The images were of couples—one of them dancing on a crowded dance floor. The other was of a man and a woman soaking in a Jacuzzi. She'd used a washed watercolor treatment to give them almost an impressionistic appearance. They were traditional in style, but contemporary in subject.

Cali didn't fool herself. She knew where the images had come from, but she didn't care. Oh, she cared, but this was art therapy. Maybe if she painted enough scenes of herself and Brit, she'd get them out of her head.

Sure, she admitted she'd come a long way. She still missed her mom. She still missed Brit. But she'd gotten down to painting her toenails only once every other day instead of the six daily coats of polish she'd been doing.

And she no longer cried when she replayed his messages on her machine. Okay, she still cried, but not like before. He'd left the first message less than a week after the whole episode went down. "Hey, it's Dickhead. I miss you so badly I can't breathe. I can't sleep. I can't think. The tequila isn't working. Call me if I stand a snowball's chance in hell."

She hadn't returned the called. Since then, he'd called two more times and almost repeated the same message.

"You know what?" Tanya said. "I'm going to show these to Tiffany at the gallery. I'll bet my right tit that she's going to sign you up on the spot."

Cali's answer gushed out. "No. I mean, I just want to paint for a while. You know, get my feet wet again. Besides, I don't want to sell these."

Tanya looked at the painting again and her mouth fell open. "Oh, God. These are—"

"It's just art therapy," Cali insisted, but her tears formed and gave everything in the room an impressionist appearance.

Tanya hugged her. And in the embrace, Cali felt their shared pain. Eric had called it quits two days ago when an old girlfriend had moved back into town. Tanya swore she hadn't been in love with him, just lust.

Cali wished she could say the same. Of all the things she missed about Brit, it wasn't sex. It was feeling a part of someone, feeling as if she were important to someone. It was feeling connected. It was his smile, the way laughing with him had felt like she'd discovered some new toy. Okay, she lied—she missed the sex a little, too.

"Oh, Cali. Has he called again?"

Cali wiped the tears from her face. "Not since last week."

"Have you erased them yet?" Tanya knew her too well.

Cali sniffled. "Not yet, but I'm close."

Tanya let out a huffy breath. "Oh, fudge. I didn't think I'd ever say this, but maybe you should call him."

Cali straightened one of the paintings on the easel. "No."

"Why?" Tanya asked. "You obviously love the dickhead."

Cali shrugged. "Yeah, but he's the one who left."

"But he's been calling you."

She shook her head. "My mom said I couldn't fix Brit. And I'm not sure if he walked in that door right now, that I wouldn't attack him with a twelve pack of fix-it glue. I'm not even sure I'd know if he managed to fix himself."

She looked away from the painting because suddenly it hurt too much to see the emotion captured on the canvas. The fact that her work was good enough to show emotion did make the artist inside of her happy, but it still hurt.

"I've got two more sketched out," Cali said and squared her shoulders. "I'm moving forward." Even Dr. Roberts agreed. Cali needed to think only of herself for a while. She wiped a few more tears from her eyes. "Forward."

~

Quarles waved as Brit stepped out of the Customs area. Brit had extended his stay in Mexico for another week, which gave him four weeks in Cancun. He'd hoped time, the beach, the sun, and the tequila would heal the wounds. No luck.

Wearing a smile, Quarles took one of his bags and gave him a thump on the back. "Welcome home, stranger."

Brit stretched his shoulders. "Thanks. How is everything?"

"Damn good. Except Adams is going to crawl your ass for thinking you can just call up and leave a message saying you won't be back for another week."

Flashing a grin, Brit asked, "So what else is new?"

"Well, Homicide is back in our own building. We're mold-free. I found homes for all your kittens, except Mama Bitch. I've already taken her back to your house. Your sister is moving back to Hopeful and, oh, yeah, Rina decided to quit hooking and went back home to her folks in Tennessee."

Brit studied him. "And I'm supposed to assume that you have something to do with this?"

"It wasn't me. Rina checked herself into rehab and I think this time it worked for her."

"I didn't mean Rina," Brit said.

"Oh, you mean Susan." He grinned. "I damn well hope I had something to do with it."

"Does she need a place to hang her hat?" he asked.

"Nope." His friend's chest seemed to puff out.

"She's moving in with our mom?" Brit's suspicions grew.

"Nope," Quarles said, sounding rather proud.

Brit eyed his friend and partner, and prepared himself. "With you?"

"Yeah." Quarles smiled like a man who'd won the lottery.

Brit debated how he felt, then voiced his concern. "And you don't think this is kind of soon?"

"No. Since you've been gone, she's been here more than she's been in Austin. We've gotten close. Real close."

He eyed Quarles. "Remember, my threat still stands."

Quarles laughed. "I love your sister. I'm not going to hurt her."

They drove straight to Brit's place. Quarles talked about work and about Susan. Brit half-ass listened. Once home, he dropped his suitcases and went into the kitchen. Mama Cat came to the threshold of the laundry room and peered out.

Brit edged a little closer, but she darted back inside.

"Be careful," Quarles said. "She's scratched me every time I've even tried to get close to her. She hates people."

"She doesn't hate people. She's just scared." Brit opened the fridge. His sister had bought groceries again. He got himself and Quarles a beer and they settled at the kitchen table.

"So?" Quarles asked. "You over her?"

Looking at the beer, Brit started to deny he had anything to get over. He ran his finger along the condensation of the bottle, then he answered, "As much as I'll ever be." He paused. "Have you heard from her at all?" Hope still vibrated in his chest, but he fought it.

Quarles shook his head. "Rumor has it that you were hard on her."

The bitter pill hung up on Brit's tonsils. "Yeah, I'm pretty much an asshole. I come by it naturally."

"If it makes you feel any better, I'd probably have reacted the same way if I'd found her trying to see her ex."

It didn't make him feel better, but Brit nodded. "Any news on Nolan Bright?"

"DA thinks the case if rock solid. I'm hearing whispers of them asking for the death penalty."

Brit nodded, and just stared at his beer.

"Do you love her?" Quarles downed a sip of beer.

Brit stood up and opened the fridge. "You want a sandwich?"

"Do you love her?" Quarles asked again.

Emotionally flinching, Brit shut the fridge. "No, I just spent four weeks in Mexico staring at the damn phone, praying she'd call because I don't feel a damn thing. What do you think?"

"Then for God sakes, fight for her."

Brit's frustration level climbed, but it was toward himself and not him. "You don't understand."

"What do I not understand?" Quarles hunkered back in the chair.

Brit ran a hand over his face, unwilling to put the truth into words. "I called her every week. She didn't call me back."

"Hey, a few weeks ago, your sister stopped taking my calls. You want to know what I did?"

Brit scowled. "I told you not to hurt her."

"I didn't do anything. She just got scared because I said I loved her. But the point isn't that. The point is that when she didn't answer my calls, I got in my truck and drove three hours to see her in Austin. She's that important to me."

"Well, Mexico to Houston is a little farther than Houston to Austin."

"What? The tequila fry your brain? You're not in Mexico anymore."

Brit raked a chair across the floor, but didn't sit down. "It would be wrong."

"Why?"

Dropping his ass in the chair, he closed his eyes, wishing he'd stayed in Mexico. "I messed up. I said terrible things to her. I hurt her. She deserves someone who can get it right."

Quarles stared. "Sounds like you're trying to get it right. And as for what you said, well, that's what apologies and expensive jewelry are for. Look, I'm just saying that if you love her, fight for her."

That damn hope stirred again. "How? She doesn't want me."

"Well, I'd start by going to see her. Then I'd suggest you be a real man and put your tail between your legs and beg. Get down on your knees if you have to."

Brit crossed his arms over his chest. "Beg, huh?"

"How do you think I got Susan to open the door when I got to Austin? Did you know your sister was that stubborn? But damn, if I don't love every stubborn inch of that woman."

~

Brit went to bed as soon as Quarles left. Sleep had been a rare commodity in Brit's life, but he always tried. He lay there, staring at the ceiling and thinking about Cali—about all the things he should have done differently. One word kept playing over in his head. Beg. He closed his eyes, exhausted, and prayed for sleep.

A thump on the bed brought his eyes open. Standing next to him was Mama Cat. She let out a deep meow.

"Yeah, I'm back," he said.

She dipped her head and took another step closer.

"You know I don't like you, right?" He held out his hand.

She meowed again as if to say, "Yeah, and I don't like you either." Then she bumped his hand with her head. She actually let him touch her.

Brit smiled and ran his fingers over her chin. "Admit you missed me, and I'll admit that I thought about you, too."

She purred and brushed up against his hand again.

"Okay, here's the deal, you can stay. But if you tell anyone we actually like each other, I'm taking you to the shelter."

The cat meowed and then leapt off the bed. Brit lay back down. Beg? His eyes drifted shut.

"Do you want to talk about Cali?" a female voice asked.

Brit shot straight up. A middle-aged woman—red hair, big blue eyes, dangling a cigarette between her fingers and wearing a navy business suit—sat at the foot of his bed.

"Who the hell are you?" Brit wiped his eyes.

"If it waddles like a duck, quacks like a duck, it's probably a duck."

"So you're a duck?" He raked another hand over his face. This had to be a dream. He had locked his door, hadn't he?

"No. And neither are you." She inhaled a puff of smoke and let it out slowly. "That's a big part of why you're so scared."

"What am I scared of?" he tossed out, now pretty certain this was a dream.

"Why, love, of course. But you're not like him. Or her." A row of about six gold bracelets jiggled on her arm. "You got a good heart. Sure, you're hard-headed, but you play fair more than most people do. And you care a hell of a lot more than most. You're a softy."

Confusion settled in his gut. "What are you talking . . .? Who are you?"

"You're no duck, Brit Lowell. You speak before you think, I'll give you that, but my daughter isn't milquetoast either."

"Daughter?"

"You want to be forgiven. Then you best learn to forgive. It's part of the fixing process."

A ringing noise sounded as his mind began piecing together the question. "Are you Cali's mom?"

Brit suddenly woke up to the sound of the ringing phone. He looked at the phone then back at the foot of the bed. No woman. He inhaled. Air scented with cigarette smoke hitched in his lungs. He snatched the phone, his heart thumping. Had he just seen a ghost?

"Hello?"

"Brit? It's your mom."

He continued to look around the room.

"I know your voice, Mom. Is something wrong?" Had Frank or Fred or whatever his name was hurt her? His chest gripped with concern.

"No. Yes. I'd love to see my son."

His first impulse was to come up with some excuse, but he heard the woman voice from his dream. *You want to be forgiven? You best learn to forgive.*

He gritted his teeth, then said, "Can you make some coffee? Strong coffee. And I'll be there in about an hour."

~

345

Later that day, after an almost pleasant visit with his mom, Brit knocked on Cali's door, holding a bag in his trembling hands. A man about Brit's age—a good looking guy, maybe too good looking— opened the door and Brit's stomach dropped.

Was this why she hadn't called him back? Was he too late?

Jealously rolled over Brit's heart. Pride made him want to walk away, love kept his feet planted in front of the door. Beg.

"Is Cali here?" His voice rang hoarse. When the man's brows creased, Brit continued, "I'm not leaving until I see her."

"But—"

"There are no buts. I love her, even though I was stupid about it." Damn, this hurt and the thought of this man with the woman he loved just about chewed up his insides. "I'm not a duck." Shit! Had he said that aloud?

"You smoking something, buddy?" the man asked.

"Just let me see her." Brit stepped forward.

The man's posture grew defensive. "Look, you've got—"

"I know, I got a set of balls to show up here after I screwed up. But I'm not walking away. I'm fighting for her. And if that means you and I go to fist city, right now, right here, I'm fine with it."

"Fighting for who?" A woman appeared at the door, holding a bowl of soup. She glanced at the man standing next to her. "Are you seeing someone else?"

"No," he said. "I swear. This idiot is talking about ducks and some chick named Cali."

"I told you if you ever did that again, I was leaving," the woman said, sounding angry.

"But I didn't do anything."

"Cali doesn't live here?" Brit asked, as the couple started to throw verbal punches.

"Who's he seeing?" The woman stopped screaming long enough to ask Brit. "Is it that bimbo at the gym? It is, isn't it?" She turned to leave, but decided it wasn't enough and she swung back around and slung the bowl of soup at the man. Only half the soup missed the man and landed on Brit. Not that he didn't deserve it.

He looked down at the bits of alphabet pasta clinging to his jacket, then at the number on the door to make sure. "You guys just moved in here, didn't you?"

The man knocked bits of carrots off his face and frowned at Brit.

Brit shrugged. "Sorry. My mistake. My girlfriend used to live here." He said it loud, hoping the woman could hear.

The woman popped back at the door. "So he isn't . . . ?"

"No," Brit said. Then before the man decided to take Brit up on his trip to fist city, he shot down the apartment's steps, trying to think of the quickest way to find Cali.

When the idea came, he wished it hadn't, but he started his car, and headed that way. Five minutes later, stepping up to Tanya's door, he prepared himself to get an earful. But as long as that earful included Cali's address, it would be worth the verbal beating.

~

Tanya answered his knock with her purse and keys in her hands. A spark of satisfaction lit her eyes. Lucky for him, she didn't try to rip his heart out and feed it to the roaches.

She shook her head as if she considered him pathetic. And she was right. Standing before her was one heartbroken guy wearing alphabet soup.

He swallowed. "Go ahead. I deserve some of your lip."

She raised an eyebrow. "Give me one reason why I should tell you where she is."

Relief swelled in his chest. "How about two? Because I love her. And because I think she loves me or else you'd already be dismembering my body and feeding it to the roaches." God, he hoped he was right.

She propped a hand on her hip and then her gaze tightened. "Are you wearing alphabet soup?"

"Where can I find Cali?"

She rolled her eyes. "Try her mother's house."

He smiled. "I owe you big time."

"Pay backs are hell," Tanya called as he ran off.

~

Brit parked beside Cali's Honda in the drive and knocked on the glass storm door. December cold cut through his windbreaker, but he still sweated.

"Come in," Cali called from inside. "I'm just trying to finish up."

Brit's heart raced. Damn, he'd missed hearing the soft timber of her voice. Missed her. He opened the door, and looked around. The place was different. It looked like Cali. Soft colors, organized bookshelves. And it smelled like her. He inhaled the scent like a starving man coming home for dinner. And that's what he was, starving. Starving for her.

"I opened some wine." Her voice came from a back bedroom.

Had Tanya called her? Was she expecting him? Did that mean he had a chance? His level of hope inched up.

I'm not a duck. He repeated to calm his nerves. He loved her. And he'd spend the rest of life proving that to her if she'd let him.

Her voice rang out again. "Pour the wine and bring me one."

He spotted the bottle and two glasses on a table. He set the bag down. His hands shook as he poured the wine.

"I can't wait for you to see how this painting came out," she called out again. "I think it's my best one."

Cali was painting again. Fighting a case of serious angst, he followed her voice down the hall to the third bedroom.

She stood with her back to him. Her shoulder shifted ever so slightly as she brushed paint on a canvas. Her blond hair shimmered down her back, and the wispy strands caught the evening sun spilling through the uncovered windows. She wore a fitted white T-shirt and a pair of gray sweats. On her backside were smeared paint prints where she'd wiped her hands.

"I was about to call to see what was keeping you." She still didn't turn around.

Disappointment flickered in his gut when he realized that Cali didn't know it was him. "Cali?" he whispered her name.

Her hand stopped making the tiny brush strokes. Her back stiffened. Brit took a deep breath.

Chapter Forty-Four

Brit's heart felt like it doubled over. "Please don't ask me to leave."

She dropped her brush in a cup at the edge of the easel and, slowly, as if it cost her to do so, she faced him.

He wanted to touch her so badly his hands shook. Instead, he handed her a glass of wine before he spilled it.

She took it and then cleaned her other hand on the bottom of her sweats. "I thought you were Tanya."

Brit's gaze fell to the painting—two people in bed, nude, in a lover's embrace. Then he noted the cat in the painting, perched up on the nightstand beside the bed. His breath caught when he saw the cat had a missing ear. He looked at Cali, and her blush told him he was right. "It's us."

She pushed a strand of hair from her cheek. "Let's go in there." She moved past him and waited at the door.

He didn't follow. His gaze moved around. They were everywhere —five, six, seven of them. Painted images. Each one took him back to a moment in time. His and Cali's time. Captured emotions bounced off the canvases and filled his chest until he thought he might explode.

He didn't know what to say.

The soft patter of her bare feet on the wood floor making tracks down the hall filled his ears, but he stayed in the studio. He attempted to gather his thoughts, to enjoy Cali's work, and to let the hope now flourishing in his chest chase away the God-awful fear that she wouldn't care anymore. He knew differently now. She cared. Which meant he still had a chance.

Turning, he walked back into the living room. She stood by a window looking out onto the backyard. Slowly, she faced him, but stood silent.

He stopped a few feet away from her. "I've missed you so damn much."

Seemingly unimpressed with his confession, she looked away.

He forced words out of his mouth. "I was wrong."

"Yes, you were." Spoken so quietly, her words seemed to float in the air.

"I'll do whatever it takes to get you to forgive me." The pause grew heavy. "I know you still care or you wouldn't be painting us."

She stared down at her bare feet. He followed her gaze to her toenails, red-tipped and perfect like the rest of her. When she didn't answer, he realized she didn't plan on making this easy for him. He didn't blame her. He didn't deserve easy.

He deserved hell. But it had been hell. "I spent four weeks in Mexico waiting by the phone. Praying you'd call."

She kept her eyes downward. "You left without even speaking to me."

He tried to think of a way to pretty up the truth he needed to tell her, but the truth wasn't pretty. "My father beat my mother, Cali. I saw it. I got in the middle of it. I hated him. Then he died, and I thought things were going to be good." His palms itched with nerves. He'd never told anyone this.

Silence fell like soft rain. "But Mom, she brought home someone else just like Dad. Every time I stood up for her, but she chose them over me."

He took a sip of wine because his next words hung in his throat. "When I met you, I assumed you were like her."

She studied her wine glass, not speaking, but listening. It was more than he'd thought she'd give him. "When I found out that you didn't think Stan was guilty, it felt just like those times with my mom."

He inhaled, wanting to say it all, needing to say it all. "I realize now that I was less afraid of you being like my mom, than I was afraid of me being like my dad. Or maybe just being like both of them. I've always felt relationship impaired. That's why I left with even talking to you. I felt you deserved better." His voice cracked and his pride took a beating when his eyes began to sting.

"And now," she asked in almost a whisper.

"Now, I spent a lot of time this last month thinking about who I am and who I'm not."

She looked up.

He continued. "I don't want to be like them. I don't have to repeat their mistakes."

She nipped down on her bottom lip. Was she going to ask him to leave?

"I'll beg. I'll do whatever it takes." Tears filled his eyes, but his pride could be damned. This was bigger than pride.

She set her glass on the table.

"I love you." The words he'd never told a woman came out. His breath hitched in his throat. He set his wine down beside hers. "I love your laugh and the way you blush when you say sex. I love watching you eat all proper like. I love that you seldom cuss and that you bite your lip when you're nervous. I love that you're so nice to everyone you meet. I love you. All of you. Every single thing about you."

She took a step closer. Did that mean something?

Her blue eyes washed with emotion. Her next step brought her against him. She didn't say a word. She didn't repeat the words he needed to hear, but she rested her cheek against his chest. Was this good-bye or welcome home? He was so damn scared. But he couldn't help but wrap his hands around her back, and bury his face into her hair. He would take this moment for however long it lasted. He savored the feel of her against him. She felt so right in his arms. So right in his life. Was having forever too much to ask?

"Your mother," he said, finding it hard to admit. "She . . . I had a dream."

Cali raised her head and rested her chin on his chest as she gazed into his eyes. "You dreamed about her?"

He nodded and noticed she had a little piece of soup pasta, an O and P on her cheek. He reached up and knocked them off. "She told me, when it wobbled like a duck and quacked like a duck, it was duck. She said I wasn't a duck. I think what she meant was that I'm not like my dad. I'm . . . I'm a softy."

A smile touched her lips. "Sounds like Mom." Emotion filled her eyes again.

A knot of fear formed in his throat.

She looked at his chest. "Why do you have alphabet soup all over you?"

"Oh, I almost got in fight with a guy I thought was your new boyfriend." He just stared at her. It was heaven looking at her. His chest filled with a light, bubbly feeling.

"I don't have a boyfriend."

He smiled. "I know, I found out."

"What?" she asked.

God, being with her felt so damn good. He wanted to laugh, to pick her up and swirl in her his arms. "I went to your old apartment and he answered the door."

And he threw soup on you?" she asked.

"No, his wife or girlfriend did. Well, she threw it on him because she thought he was cheating on her again. And I was standing by him."

She chuckled. "That's crazy."

"Yeah, it pretty much was."

She continued to look up at him. "I hope you explained."

He nodded. "I did."

She knocked a few more letters from his coat. Then she met his gaze. "I love you, too."

He let go of a deep breath that he hadn't even realized he'd been holding. "Damn, for a minute there, I didn't think you were going to say it."

He pulled her into his arms and kissed her. And she never flinched. Even when the kiss ended they stood there, holding on to each other.

"Oh." With one hand, he reached for the bag he'd left on the table. The other he kept around her. It might be a while before he let her go.

"What is it?" She laughed when she pulled out the sweater she'd left at his office nearly two months ago. "I guess this means you want your leather jacket back."

He smiled. "As long as I have you, you can keep it."

A teasing glint lit her eyes. "What if I keep both you and the jacket and let you borrow it occasionally?"

"Excellent plan," he said. "But I have to warn you. If you keep my jacket, I'll be hanging around a long time. I'm talking commitments and official documents and all that stuff."

She smiled. "Are you asking me to marry you?"

"No, I was planning on asking you that question with much more flare, a ring, some flowers."

"Really?" she grinned.

"Yeah, but if I was asking would you—"

"Yes!" she said with enthusiasm. "I'd say yes."

*Read on for an exciting preview
of the second book in Christie Craig's
Hotter in Texas series,*
Blame It on Texas!
*Available from Forever
in September 2013!!*

Chapter One

"Why are you so sad, *Tio*?"

Tyler Lopez looked down at his six-year-old niece. Her brown eyes were so warm they could . . . They could persuade a grown man to make a complete idiot out of himself.

Pinching the red ball rubber-banded to his face, Tyler dropped his clown-suited ass on the picnic bench beside the birthday girl. When the real clown canceled late last night, his sister, Samantha had called him in desperation. *Anna will be so disappointed.* Tyler adored all his nieces and nephews, but there was something about Anna—quiet and a bookworm like himself—that made her his favorite. And that made the thought of disappointing her impossible.

"I'm a clown. Clowns aren't sad." He looked out at the twenty or so family members mingling together at the other picnic tables in his sister's backyard. Two of his brothers were pointing and laughing at him. If Anna wasn't sitting there, he'd have shot them the bird. The Texas humidity, still almost unbearable in September, made the clown suit cling to his arms and . . .

"Da . . . dang it!" he muttered and reached down and caught the little orange kitten who had mistaken his leg for a climbing post. Bringing the spirited, blood-drawing feline on top of the table, he knew he couldn't complain too loudly or Anna's mother would be over here to give him hell. Especially since, he'd given the kitten to his niece last month as an early birthday present. And according to his sister, the animal was a reincarnated demon. Hence the kitten's name, Damian.

"Some clowns are sad," Anna said. She closed the book she'd been reading and gave Damian a purr-inducing scratch behind the ear.

"Not this clown." He told himself it wasn't a lie. Tyler gave the cat an under-chin rub. That led to the kitten jumping into Tyler's lap and curling up. No doubt the feline remembered who'd snatched him up from the middle of I-10 before he got smeared on the freeway. And he'd better remember it—Tyler had almost become an oil spot in the road himself in the process.

"You remember my friend, Austin?" Tyler asked Anna. "Well, this is his suit and he specifically told me it was a happy clown." Austin, one of the partners at their private detective agency, had purchased the costume to do an undercover gig. As fate would have it, he hadn't gotten around to tossing it out yet.

"But when you walked in, Mama told *Tia* Lola, 'Here comes the sad man behind the clown face.'"

Tyler inwardly flinched, but continued to smile. It was something he'd gotten good at doing—putting up a front. A skill he'd mastered during his year and a half in prison.

"Do you believe everything your mama says?" he asked in a teasing voice to hide his frustration. He loved his seven siblings, but a big family came with a big price. Having them poke around in his personal business was part of that price.

"I do." Anna's dark brown pigtails, tied with bright red ribbons, bounced around her face as she bobbed her head up and down. "Mama doesn't lie. She says it's a sin."

Okay, that hadn't been the right thing to say. "I think she was just joking."

"She wasn't laughing. Then *Tia* Lola said you were sad because you missed Lisa."

Tyler's chest tightened. He didn't miss Lisa. How could he miss someone who turned her back on him when he needed her the most? Someone who—

"And then," Anna continued, "Leo walked into the room and said it was probably because you picked up a bar of soap in prison." Her tiny brows pulled in confusion at the same time Tyler's gut pulled with fury. "I don't understand that,, *Tio.* "

"Leo's full of . . ." Tyler caught himself just in time.

"Full of what?" Anna asked, a half-smile pulling at her lips.

Tyler's gaze shot to the piñata hanging above the tree. "Full of candy."

Anna snickered. "Mama said he was full of shit."

Tyler grinned. "Well, like you just said, your mama doesn't lie. But . . . we all have . . . excrement in our insides."

"Excrement?" He could see the child figuring out the word's meaning and filing it away in her knowledge-hungry brain. "That's gross."

"I agree." Tyler's smile came easier.

"Almost as gross as how babies are made," she said.

That little announcement came out of left field and Tyler's jaw fell open.

Anna stared at him with the same face she'd made at dinner a few weeks ago when her mom made her eat a bite of broccoli. "I read a book about it."

"What book?" he managed to ask.

"The one mama bought me after I told her I didn't believe the stork brought my baby brother."

"Oh," he said, not sure what else to say. But his smile lingered as he thought about his sister dealing with her inquisitive daughter. He smiled until he saw Anna's full-of-shit stepfather walk out of the patio door and snag a beer from one of the coolers.

Leo Medina, his twin sister's second husband, was a jerkwad, right up there with Anna's deadbeat daddy. While Tyler tried to overlook his sister's ghastly taste in husbands, ignoring Leo was hard. And for damn good reasons, too—or suspected reasons.

"Did you and Lisa want to have a baby?" Anna asked.

Tyler swallowed, searching for words. "We . . . we weren't married."

She made another funny face. "I'm not getting married."

"Me either," he told her honestly. After living with the result of his parents' dysfunctional relationship, he'd always had reservations. Lisa had made him throw caution to the wind. Unfortunately that wind blew up a hell of a lot of heartache.

"I liked Lisa," Anna said. "She was pretty. She told me I was going to get to be the flower girl in her wedding. Why are you and her not getting married anymore? Is it because you think making babies is gross, too?"

He nearly swallowed his tongue. "Lisa married someone else."

"Maybe if you told her you were sorry, she would get a divorce like Mama did with my daddy. Then Lisa could marry you."

Sorry for what? For being framed for a crime he didn't commit? "I don't think so."

"Saying you're sorry works. It worked on Mom when Leo hit her. And she was mad."

Tyler felt like his blood pressure shot up a good twenty points. He hadn't needed another reason to dislike Leo, but damn if he didn't have one. "Leo hit your mom?"

"Yeah, but he said he was sorry. So if you apologize to Lisa—"

"Excuse me, Anna, but I need to . . . I have to do something." He passed Anna her cat and gave the girl's pigtail a teasing yank, hoping his rage didn't show through his painted clown face.

"Okay." The innocence on her face was the opposite of everything Tyler felt.

He stood up and looked around for Samantha. When he spotted his twin sister setting food out on a table, he realized her large sunglasses meant something other than protection from the glare. It meant protecting her son-of-bitch husband.

Moving in, Tyler caught her by the arm. "We need to talk."

"I'm getting the food out," she protested. Her long black hair shifted around her shoulders. While they shared their light olive skin and dark hair—both inherited from their Hispanic mother—Anna had also taken her mom's petite build. Tyler's six foot frame came directly from his father. He hoped to God it was the only trait he'd inherited from the SOB.

"Food can wait." He pulled off his multi-colored wig, and his red ball nose, and walked her inside the house, guided her past the kitchen and didn't stop until they stood in the enclosed laundry room that smelled like clean clothes.

"What the hell is up with you?" She snapped her hands on her hips. The action reminded him of their mom that if this wasn't so damn serious, he might have been distracted. While his mother had been dead for four years, he still missed her.

"Take your sunglasses off, Sis."

"What?"

"You heard me."

She frowned. Carefully, he removed the shades. He held his breath, afraid of how bad it was. Thankfully, it wasn't as bad as he feared. As an ex-cop, he'd seen women so battered that he'd puked. But it was his childhood memories that were the worst. Sam hadn't just inherited their mother's build and coloring; she'd inherited their mother's knack for choosing losers. Staring into his twin's face, there was no mistaking the light bruise under her left eye. Then he remembered she'd missed the family's mandatory Sunday breakfast last week. The bruise had had time to fade, which meant it must have been nasty when it was fresh.

He touched his sister's cheek under the evidence. "Leo do this?"

"No," she snapped, proving her daughter wrong. Sam did lie. She just wasn't good at it.

But holy hell, why did she put up with this crap? The answer rolled over him like an overloaded concrete truck. Because their no-good father had treated their mom the same way. Tyler had studied it in college.

Statistically, the odds of her choosing men just like dear ol' Dad were great. The odds of him becoming his dad were greater. And considering the rage he felt now for Leo, the odds might be right.

He turned to leave and Sam caught his arm. "Don't do it, Tyler. I beg you."

He gently cupped her face in his palm. "If you knew someone was hurting me, would you stand by and let it happen?"

"No but . . ." Tears filled her eyes. "He was drunk."

"Isn't that what they said about dear ol' Dad?"

"Please," she muttered.

"I love you, Sam. I know you're going to be pissed at me, but he needs to know he can't do this."

He didn't stay around long enough to hear her pleas. That would have broken his heart, and Tyler wasn't sure his heart could take any more breaking. So, he plopped his wig and rubber nose back on, and shuffled his clown ass out to teach his brother-in-law a lesson about hitting girls.

~

Hesitating in the kitchen for a minute to collect himself, Tyler stepped outside. He went to the cooler, figuring Leo wouldn't be too far from the alcohol. He pulled out two beers, uncapped one and drank half of it in one swig, then looked around for Leo. He spotted him chatting with Tyler's oldest brother's wife. And damn if he didn't see the man eye his sister-in-law's breasts, when she wasn't looking.

"Leo?" Tyler held up the two beers as if to say, "Come join me." When Tyler saw the man coming, he stepped through the backyard gate and moved between Sam's house and the neighbor's. He heard the gate shift behind him.

"What's up?" Leo asked.

Setting the two beers on top of an air conditioner that hummed as it cooled his sister's house, Tyler faced Leo, who stood so close that the man's beer-laden breath filled Tyler's airspace. He didn't waste any time getting to the point. "You hit her."

Leo stepped back or he started to. "It was just a tap." Before his left foot landed, Tyler's fist landed on the man's nose and knocked him flat on his ass.

"Christ!" Leo reached for his nose.

"It was just a tap," Tyler growled but knew Leo's nose had to be hurting like hell, because Tyler's fist did. And he saw his knuckles bleeding where he'd obviously loosened a couple of teeth.

"You fucking jailbird clown! You broke my nose!"

The jailbird word that almost did Tyler in.

Leo started to get up, no doubt to give what he'd gotten, and Tyler almost let him. Almost chose to let go and enjoy this. But taking a deep breath, he pulled his emotions back and moved in to tower over his slimeball of a brother-in-law.

"Don't do it, Leo. If you get up, I'm going to hit you again. I know you think you want to hit me back. It's only fair, right? But it wasn't fair when you hit Sam. And I'm not planning on fighting fair now."

He rubbed his fist in his other hand and continued, "If you get up, and if you even get one punch in, I'm going to yell for my four brothers and when I tell them what you did, every one of them will help me beat your ass to a pulp. Consider yourself lucky you faced only me this time."

Leo wiped his bloody nose and stared up with hatred in his eyes. But the man was smarter than Tyler gave him credit for. He didn't get up.

A damn shame, too. Tyler ached to get in a few more punches, and he would if he ever proved that Leo had something to do with Tyler's prints showing up at the staged crime scene. Prints on a glass that was the same pattern his sister had owned at the time. Someone had to have helped the drug lord asshole who had framed him and his partners, Dallas and Austin. Right now, Leo was Tyler's prime suspect. However, considering Tyler had been unjustly accused, he wasn't accusing anyone until he had proof.

"Oh," he added, "if I see one bruise, one little bruise, on my sister, I won't come alone next time." Pulling off the red rubber nose, he tossed it at Leo. "Since I broke yours, have this one."

~

"Spiders. Definitely spiders."

"Don't forget snakes."

"Trust me, it's clowns." Zoe Adams removed her waitress apron and added her two cents to the conversation the other waitresses of Cookie's Cafe were having on their biggest fears. She plopped down on one of the stools lining the breakfast counter, and pulled out her tips to count. She hoped she had enough to pay the rent. Looking up at the other diner employees, she added, "And considering my regular gig is that of kindergarten teacher, I've had to face that fear more times than I care to admit."

"I'd take a clown over a spider any day," said Jamie. Like Zoe, she was in her mid-twenties.

"I can step on a spider," Zoe said, looking at the other waitresses. "Clowns are too big for my size sixes." She held up her foot. "I don't know what it is, but I see one and it's like I hear scary music and my mind starts flashing *Friday the 13th* images." In truth, clowns weren't her biggest fear. Small, dark places scared Zoe more than anything. Not that she'd share that with the ladies at Cookie's, or anyone else for that matter.

Some things Zoe didn't talk about. Especially the things she didn't understand. And lately her life was filled with a lot of those things. Crazy how watching an episode of the TV series *Unsolved Mystery Hunters* had turned her life upside down, and brought her from Alabama to Texas in search of the truth.

"Flying roaches. I hate 'em," Dixie Talbot said, joining in on the conversation. In her sixties, Dixie was the matriarchal cook, waitress, and part-owner of Cookie's Café. "Years ago, I stood right over there by Booth Two and one of those nasty creatures flew into my shirt."

Zoe stopped counting her money and laughed. "Yeah, Fred told me about the striptease you pulled, too."

"Honey, he'd better be glad that roach flew off my right boob once the top came off or I swear to everything holy I'd have been standing there naked as a jay bird."

"Was that the day he proposed to you?" Zoe asked.

They laughed. It was the laughter, the camaraderie of Dixie and the other diner employees that kept Zoe from looking for a higher paying gig while she was here. God knew she could use the money. Kindergarten teachers didn't rake in the big bucks.

Oh, it was enough to get by, but not enough to fund this research trip to Miller, Texas when she had to pay for two apartments. Not to mention the entire month off from work—a month she only got because the principal had been friends with her mom. But more than money, Zoe needed companionship. Since her mama died two years ago, and especially for the last year since her live-in boyfriend had decided he'd rather date a stripper than a kindergarten teacher, Zoe had spent too much time alone.

And lonely.

Hey, maybe she should get Dixie to teach her a few moves. Not that Zoe wanted Chris back. Nope. For four years, she'd given her heart and soul to that man. She'd already had names picked out for the two kids they'd give life to, thinking any day he'd pop the question. And he had popped one. It just wasn't the question she'd expected. *"Do you mind if I bring home my stripper girlfriend to live here until you can find another place?"*

Okay, he hadn't actually worded it like that, but he might as well have. He'd taken Zoe's heart, and returned it, along with her self-esteem, in a big mangled mess. Not so much of a mess that she hadn't reminded him that she'd been the one to rent the apartment, and he could just grab his stuff and get the hell out. Oh, he'd accused her being so unfair. Didn't she realize it wasn't his fault he'd fallen in love with someone else?

What she understood was that she'd been played for a fool—paying most of the bills, being his personal housecleaner, trying to be the perfect housewife. Even a year later, it still stung like a paper cut right across her heart.

Zoe's cell rang. Considering she'd gotten all of two calls in the four weeks she'd been in Texas—one from her principal back in Alabama confirming she'd be at work on September 25th, and the other a wrong number—a call was a big thing. Zoe checked the number. Unknown Caller.

"Hello?" Zoe answered. While she hated it, there was a part of her that hoped it would be Chris, wanting her back, telling her he'd screwed up. Not that she'd take him back, but it would be nice to know he missed her.

She heard someone breathing, but nothing else. "Hello?"

"Leave," the whispery voice said.

~ ~ ~

Step into the world of Shadow Falls,
a camp that helps teens tap into their
special . . . talents. Once you visit,
you'll never forget it and
you'll never, ever be the same.

Visit the Shadow Falls Series Facebook page
for excerpts, bonue materials and more!
www.facebook.com/ShadowFallsSeries

Read on for a preview
of the first book in the series,
Born at Midnight

Chapter One

"This isn't funny!" her father yelled.

No, it wasn't, Kylie Galen thought as she leaned into the refrigerator to find something to drink. In fact, it was so not funny she wished she could crawl in beside the mustard and moldy hotdogs, shut the door, and not hear the angry voices spewing from the living room.

Her parents were at it again.

Not that it would go on much longer, she thought as the mist of the fridge seeped out the door.

Today was the day.

Kylie's throat tightened. She swallowed a lump of raw emotion and refused to cry.

Today had to be the suckiest day of her life. And she'd had some pretty sucky days lately, too. Acquiring a stalker, Trey breaking up with her, and her parents announcing their divorce— yup, sucky pretty much covered it. It was no wonder her night terrors had returned full force.

"What have you done with my underwear?" Her father's growl spilled into the kitchen, snuck under the refrigerator door and bounced around the moldy hotdogs.

His underwear? Kylie pressed a cold diet soda can to her forehead.

"Why would I do anything with your underwear?" her mother asked in her oh-so nonchalant voice. That was her mom alright, nonchalant. Cold as ice.

Kylie's gaze shot out the kitchen window to the patio where she'd seen her mom earlier. There, a pair of her dad's tighty-whities dangled half out of the smoldering grill.

Just great. Her mother had barbequed her father's shorts. That's it. Kylie was never eating anything cooked on that grill again.

Fighting tears, she shoved the diet soda back on the rack, shut the fridge, and moved into the doorway. Maybe if they saw her, they'd stop acting like juveniles and let her be the kid again.

Her dad stood in the middle of the room, a pair of underwear clutched in his fist. Her mom sat on the sofa, calmly sipping hot tea.

"You need psychological help," her father yelled at her mom.

Two points for her dad, Kylie thought. Her mom did need help. So why was Kylie the one who had to sit on a shrink's sofa two days a week?

Why was her dad—the man everyone swore Kylie had wrapped around her little finger—going to move out today, and leave her behind?

She didn't blame her dad for wanting to leave her mom, AKA the Ice Queen. But why wasn't he taking Kylie with him? Another lump rose in her throat.

Dad swung around and saw her, then shot back into the bedroom, obviously to pack the rest of his things—minus his underwear, which at this moment sent up smoke signals from the backyard grill.

Kylie stood there, staring at her mom, who sat reading over work files as if it was any other day.

The framed photographs of Kylie and her father that hung over the sofa caught her attention and tears stung her eyes. The pictures had been taken on their annual father and daughter trips.

"You've got to do something," Kylie pleaded.

"Do what?" her mom asked.

"Change his mind. Tell him you're sorry you grilled his shorts." That you're sorry you've got ice water running through your veins. "I don't give a flip what you do, just don't let him go."

"You don't understand." And just like that, her mom, void of any emotion, shifted her attention back to her papers.

Right then, her dad, suitcase in his hand, shot through the living room. Kylie went after him and followed him out the door into Houston's stifling afternoon heat.

"Take me with you," she begged, not caring if he saw her tears. Maybe the tears would help. There'd been a time when crying got her whatever she wanted from him. "I don't eat much," she sniffled, giving humor a shot.

He shook his head but, unlike her mom, at least he had emotion in his eyes. "You don't understand."

You don't understand. "Why do y'all always say that? I'm sixteen years old. If I don't understand, then explain it to me. Tell me the big secret and get it over with."

He stared down at his feet as if this was a test and he'd penned the answers on the toes of his shoes. Sighing, he looked up. "Your mom . . . she needs you."

"Needs me? Are you kidding? She doesn't even want me." And neither do you. The realization caused Kylie's breath to catch in her lungs. He really didn't want her.

She wiped a tear from her cheek and that's when she saw him again. Not her dad, but Soldier Dude, aka her very own stalker. Standing across the street, he wore the same army duds as before. He looked as if he'd just walked out of one of those Gulf War movies her mom loved. Only instead of shooting at things or being blown up, he stood frozen in one spot, and stared right at Kylie with sad, yet very scary eyes.

She'd noticed him stalking her a few weeks ago. He'd never spoken to her and she hadn't spoken to him. But the day she pointed him out to her mom, and Mom hadn't seen him . . . well, that's when Kylie's world slid off its axis. Her mom thought she was making it up to get attention, or worse. With the worse being that Kylie was losing her grip on reality. Sure, the night terrors that had tormented her when she was a kid had returned, worse than ever. Her mom said the shrink could help her work through them but how could she do that when Kylie didn't even remember them? She only knew they were bad. Bad enough to have her wake up screaming.

Kylie wanted to scream now. Wanted to scream for her dad to turn around and look—to prove that she hadn't lost her mind. At the very least, maybe if her dad actually saw her stalker, her parents would let her off from seeing the shrink. It wasn't fair.

But life wasn't fair, as her mom had reminded her more than once.

Nevertheless, when Kylie looked back, he was gone. Not Soldier Dude, but her dad. She turned toward the driveway and saw him shoving his suitcase in the backseat of his red convertible Mustang. Mom had never liked that car, but dad loved it.

Kylie ran to the car. "I'll make Grandma talk to Mom. She'll fix . . ." No sooner had the words escaped Kylie's lips than she remembered the other major sucky event she'd had plopped into her life.

She couldn't run to Grandma to fix her problems anymore. Because Grandma was dead. Gone. The vision of Nana lying cold in the casket filled Kylie's head and another lump crawled up her throat.

Her dad's expression morphed into parental concern, the same look that had landed Kylie at the shrink's office three weeks ago.

"I'm fine. I just forgot." Because remembering hurt too much. She felt a lone tear roll down her cheek.

Dad moved in and hugged her. The embrace lasted even longer than his usual hugs, but it ended too soon. How could she let him go? How could he leave her?

His arm dropped from around her and he physically set her back. "I'm just a phone call away, Pumpkin."

Swiping at her tears, hating her watery weakness, she watched her dad's red convertible get smaller as it buzzed down the street. Wanting to be alone in her room, she started to run inside. Then she remembered and looked back across the street to see if Soldier Dude had pulled his usual disappearing act.

Nope. He was still there, staring, stalking. Scaring the bejeebies out of her and making her angry at the same time. He was the reason she had to see a shrink.

Then Mrs. Baker, her elderly neighbor toddled out to get her mail. She smiled at Kylie but not once did the old librarian glance at Soldier Dude taking up residence on her front lawn, even when he stood less than two feet from her.

Weird.

So weird it sent an unnatural chill tiptoeing down Kylie's spine, the same kind of chill Kylie had gotten at Nana's funeral.

What the hell was going on?

Chapter Two

An hour later, Kylie walked down the stairs with her backpack and purse over her shoulder.

Her mom met her in the entryway. "Are you okay?"

How could I be okay? "I'll live," Kylie answered. More than she could say about Grandma. Right then, Kylie had a vision of the bright blue eye shadow the funeral home had put on her grandmother. Why didn't you take that off of me? Kylie could almost hear Nana asking.

Weirded out by the thought, Kylie looked back at her mother.

Her mom stared at Kylie's backpack and her worry wrinkle appeared between her eyes. "Where are you going?" she asked.

"You said I could spend the night with Sara. Or were you too busy grilling Dad's shorts to remember?"

Her mom ignored the grilled-shorts comment. "What are you two going to do tonight?"

"Mark Jameson is having an end of school party." Not that Kylie felt like celebrating the event. Thanks to Trey dumping her and her parents divorcing, Kylie's whole summer was headed for the toilet. And the way things were going, someone was going to walk by and flush it.

"Are his parents going to be there?" Mom raised one dark eyebrow.

Kylie flinched emotionally, but physically didn't blink. "Aren't they always?"

Okay, so she lied. Normally she didn't go to Mark Jameson's parties for that very reason, but blast it, look where being good had gotten her. She deserved to have some fun, didn't she?

Besides, hadn't her mom lied when her dad asked about his underwear?

"What if you have another dream?" Her mom touched Kylie's arm.

A quick touch. That's all Kylie ever got from her mom these days. No long hugs like her dad gave. No mother/daughter trips. Just aloofness and quick touches. Even when Nana, her mom's mom, died,

Kylie's mom hadn't hugged her and Kylie had really needed a hug then. But it had been her dad who'd pulled her into his arms and let her smear mascara on his suit coat. And now Dad and all his suit coats were gone.

Drawing in a gulp of oxygen, Kylie clutched her purse. "I warned Sara I might wake up screaming bloody murder. She said she'd stake me in the heart with a wooden cross and make me go back to bed."

"Maybe you should hide the stakes before you go to sleep." Her mother attempted to smile.

"I will." For one brief second, Kylie worried about leaving her mom alone on the day her dad had left. But who was she kidding? Her mom would be fine. Nothing ever bothered the Ice Queen.

Before walking out, Kylie peered out the window to make sure she wouldn't be assaulted by a guy wearing army duds.

Deeming the yard to be free of stalkers, Kylie ran out the door, hoping that tonight's party would help her forget just how badly her life sucked.

~

"Here. You don't have to drink it, just hold it." Sara Jetton pushed a beer into Kylie's hands, and ran off.

Sharing elbow room with at least thirty kids, all packed into Mark Jameson's living room and talking at once, Kylie clutched the ice cold bottle. Glancing around at the crowd, she recognized most of them from school. The doorbell rang again. Obviously, this was the place to be tonight. And according to every other kid at her high school, it was. Jameson, a senior whose parents never seemed to care what he did, held some of the wildest parties in town.

Ten minutes later, Sara still MIA, the party shifted into full swing. Too bad Kylie didn't feel like swinging along with them. She frowned at the bottle in her hand.

Someone bumped into her shoulder, causing the beer to splash on her chest and run down in the V of her white blouse. "Crap."

"Oh, I'm so sorry," the responsible bumper said.

Kylie looked up into John's soft brown eyes and tried to smile. Hey, being nice to a cute guy, who'd been asking about her at school made trying to smile easy. But the fact that John had been friends with Trey kept the thrill down to a minimum.

"It's okay," she said.

"I'll get you another." As if nervous, he shot off.

"It's really okay," Kylie called after him, but between the music and the hum of voices, he didn't hear her.

The doorbell rang again. A few kids shifted around and gave Kylie a view of the door. More specifically, the shift gave her a view of Trey walking inside. Beside him—or she should say plastered against him—sashayed his new slutty girlfriend.

"Great." She swung around, wishing she could teleport herself to Tahiti or back home would be even better—especially if her dad would be there.

Through a back window, she spotted Sara on the patio and Kylie darted outside to join her.

Sara looked up. She must have read the panic on Kylie's face, because she came running over to her. "What happened?"

"Trey and his screw toy are here."

Sara frowned. "So, you look hot. Go flirt with some guys and make him sorry."

Kylie rolled her eyes. "I don't want to stay here and watch Trey and what's her name making out."

"Were they already making out?" Sara asked.

"Not yet, but get one beer in Trey and all he'll think about is getting into a girl's panties. I know because I used to be the girl in the panties."

"Chill." Sara pointed back at the table. "Gary brought margaritas. Have one and you'll feel fine."

Kylie bit her lip to keep from screaming that she wouldn't feel fine. Her life had toilet-bound stamped all over it.

"Hey," Sara nudged her. "We both know all you'd have to do to get Trey back is to grab him and take him upstairs. He's still crazy about you. He found me before I left school today and asked about you."

"Did you know he was going to be here?" Betrayal started unraveling the little sanity she had left.

"Not for sure. But chill."

Chill? Kylie stared at her best friend and realized how different they'd become these last six months. It wasn't just Sara's need to party or the fact that she'd given up virginhood. Okay, so maybe it was those two things, but it seemed like more.

More as in Kylie had a sneaking suspicion that Sara longed to rush Kylie to join the partying-non-virgin ranks. Could Kylie help it if beer tasted like dog piss to her? Or if the idea of having sex didn't appeal?

Okay, that was a lie, sex appealed to her. When she and Trey had made out, Kylie had been tempted, really tempted, but then Kylie remembered her and Sara talking about how the first time should be special.

Then she recalled how Sara had given in to Brad's 'needs'—Brad who was the love of Sara's life—yet, within two weeks of giving in, the love of Sara's life had dumped her. What was so special about that?

Since then, Sara had dated four other guys, and she'd slept with two of them. Now, Sara had stopped talking about sex being special.

"Look, I know you're worried about your parents," Sara said. "But that's why you need to just let loose and have some fun." Sara tucked her long, brown hair behind her ear. "I'm getting you a margarita and you're going to love it."

Sara darted off to the table by the group of people. Kylie started to follow but her gaze slapped against Soldier Dude, looking as scary and weird as ever, standing by the group of margarita drinkers.

Kylie shot around, prepared to bolt, but she smacked right into a guy's chest, and darn it if more beer didn't jump out of the bottle and fall right between her boobs. "Great. My boobs are going to smell like a brewery."

"Every guy's dream," the husky male voice said. "But I'm sorry."

She recognized Trey's voice before she did his broad shoulders or his unique masculine scent. Preparing herself for the pain that seeing him would cause, she raised her gaze. "It's okay, John's already done it once."

She tried not to stare at the way Trey's sandy brown hair fell against his brow, or the way his green eyes seemed to lure her closer, or the way his mouth tempted her to lean in and press her lips to his.

"So it's true." He frowned.

"What's true?" she asked.

"That you and John have hooked up."

Kylie considered lying. The thought that it would hurt him appealed to her. It appealed to her so much that it reminded her of the stupid games her parents played lately. Oh, no, she would not stoop to their 'grown-up' level.

"I haven't hooked up with anyone." She turned to leave.

He caught her. His touch, the feel of his warm hand on her elbow, sent waves of pain right to her heart. And standing this close, his clean, masculine scent filled her airways. Oh God, she loved his smell.

"I heard about your grandma," he said. "And Sara told me about your parents getting a divorce. I'm so sorry, Kylie."

Tears threatened to crawl up her throat. Kylie was seconds away from falling against his warm chest and begging him to hold her. Nothing ever felt better than Trey's arms around her, but then she saw the girl, Trey's screw toy, walk outside, carrying two beers. In less than five minutes, Trey would be trying to get in her panties. And from the too low-cut blouse and too short skirt the girl wore, it appeared he wouldn't have to try too hard.

"Thanks," Kylie muttered and went to join Sara. Luckily, Soldier Dude had decided Margaritas weren't his thing after all and left.

"Here." Sara took the beer from Kylie's hand and replaced it with a margarita.

The frosty felt unnaturally cold. Kylie leaned in and whispered, "Did you see a strange guy here a minute ago? Dressed in some funky army outfit?"

Sara's eyebrows did their wild, wiggly thing. "How much of that beer did you drink?" Her laughter filled the night air.

Kylie wrapped her hands tighter around the cold glass, but worried she seriously might be losing her mind. Adding alcohol to the situation didn't seem like a good idea.

An hour later, when three Houston cops walked into the backyard and had everyone line up at the back gate, Kylie still had the same untouched margarita clutched in her hands.

"Come on, kids," one of the cops said. "The sooner we move you to the precinct, the sooner we can get your parents to come get you." That was when Kylie knew for certain that her life really had been toilet bound—and someone had just flushed.

~

"Where's Dad?" Kylie asked her mom when she stepped into the room at the police station. "I called Dad."

I'm a phone call away, Pumpkin. Hadn't he told her that? So why wasn't he here to get Pumpkin?

Her mom's green eyes tightened. "He called me."

"I wanted Dad," Kylie insisted. No, she needed her dad, she thought and her vision clouded with tears. She needed a hug, needed someone who would understand.

"You don't get what you want, especially when . . . My God, Kylie, how could you do this?"

Kylie swiped the tears from her face. "I didn't do anything. Didn't they tell you? I walked a straight line. Touched my nose and even said my ABCs backwards. I didn't do anything."

"They found drugs there," her mother snapped.

"I wasn't doing drugs."

"But do you know what they didn't find there, young lady?" Her mother pointed a finger at her. "Any parents. You lied to me."

"Maybe I'm just too much like you," Kylie said, still reeling at the thought that her dad hadn't shown up. He'd known how upset she'd been. Why hadn't he come?

"What does that mean, Kylie?"

"You told dad you didn't know what happened to his underwear. But you'd just flame-broiled his shorts on the grill."

Guilt filled her mother's eyes and she shook her head. "Dr. Day is right."

"What does my shrink have to do with tonight?" Kylie asked. "Don't tell me you called her. God, Mom, if you dare bring her down here where all my friends—"

"No, she's not here. But it's not just about tonight." She inhaled. "I can't do this alone."

"Do what alone?" Kylie asked and she got this bad feeling in her stomach.

"I'm signing you up for a summer camp."

"What summer camp?" Kylie clutched her purse to her chest. "No, I don't want to go to any camp."

"It's not about what you want." Her mom motioned for Kylie to walk out the door. "It's about what you need. It's a camp for kids with problems."

"Problems? Are you freaking nuts? I don't have any problems," Kylie insisted. Well, not any a camp could fix. Somehow she suspected going to camp wouldn't bring Dad home, it wouldn't make Soldier Dude disappear, and it wouldn't win Trey back.

"No problems? Really, then why am I at the police station at almost midnight picking up my sixteen-year-old daughter? You're going to the camp. I'm signing you up tomorrow. This isn't up for debate."

I'm not going. She kept telling herself that as they walked out of the police station.

Her mother might be bat-shit crazy, but not her dad. He simply wouldn't let her mom send her off to a camp filled with a bunch of juvenile delinquents. He wouldn't.

Would he?

Chapter Three

Three days later, Kylie, suitcase in hand, stood in the YMCA parking lot where several of the camp buses picked up the juvenile delinquents. She freaking couldn't believe she was here.

Her mom was really doing it.

And her dad was really letting her mom do it.

Kylie, who'd never drunk more than two sips of beer, who'd never smoked one cigarette, let alone any pot, was about to be shipped off to some camp for troubled kids.

Her mom reached out and touched Kylie's arm. "I think they're calling you."

Could her mom get rid of her any faster? Kylie pulled away from her touch, so angry, so hurt she didn't know how to act anymore. She'd begged, she'd pleaded, and she'd cried, but nothing worked. She was about to head off to camp. She hated it but there was nothing she could do.

Not offering her mom one word, and swearing not to cry in front of the dozens of other kids, Kylie stiffened her back, and took off to the bus behind the woman holding the sign that read: Shadow Falls Camp.

Jeez. What kind of hell hole was she being sent to?

When Kylie stepped on the bus, the eight or nine kids already there raised their heads and stared at her. She felt an odd kind of stirring in her chest and she got those weird chills again. Never, not in all sixteen years of her life, had she wanted to turn and run away as much as she did now.

She forced herself not to bolt, then she met the gazes of . . . Oh, Lordie, can you say freaks?

One girl had her hair dyed three different colors—pink, lime green and jet black. Another girl wore nothing but black—black lipstick, black eye shadow, black pants and a black long-sleeve shirt. Hadn't the Goth look gone out of style? Where was this girl getting her fashion tips? Hadn't she read that colors were in? That blue was the new black?

And then there was the boy sitting almost at the front of the bus. He had both his eyebrows pierced. Kylie leaned down to peer out the window to see if she could still see her mother. Surely, if her mom took a look at these guys, she'd know Kylie didn't belong here.

"Take your seat," someone said and stepped behind her.

Kylie turned around and saw the bus driver. While Kylie hadn't noticed it earlier, she realized even the bus driver looked a little freakish. Her purple tinted gray hair sat high on her head like a football helmet. Not that Kylie could blame her for teasing her hair up a few inches, the woman was short. Elf short. Kylie glanced down at her feet, half expecting to see a pair of pointed green boots. No green shoes.

Then her gaze shot to the front to the bus. How was the woman going to drive the bus?

"Come on," the woman said. "I have to have you kids there by lunch, so move it along."

Since everyone but Kylie had taken their seats, she supposed the woman meant her. She took a step farther into the bus, feeling as if her life would never, ever be the same.

"You can sit by me," someone said. The boy had curly blond hair, even blonder than Kylie's, but his eyes peering at her were so dark they looked black. He patted the empty seat beside him. Kylie tried not to stare, but something about the dark/light combination felt off. Then he wiggled his eyebrows, as if . . . as if her sitting beside him meant they might make out or something.

"That's okay." Kylie took a few steps, pulling her suitcase behind her. Her luggage caught on the row of seats where the blond boy sat and Kylie looked back to free it.

Her gaze met his and her breath caught. Blond boy now had . . . green eyes. Bright, very bright green eyes. How was that even possible?

She swallowed and looked at his hands, thinking that maybe he had a contact case out and had changed his lenses. No case.

He wiggled his brows again, and when she realized she was staring at him, she yanked her suitcase free.

Shaking off the chill, she moved on to the row of seats she'd chosen as her own. Before she turned to sit down, she noticed another boy in the back. Sitting by himself, he had light brown hair, parted to the side and hanging just above his dark brows and green eyes. Normal green eyes, but the dusty blue t-shirt he wore made them more noticeable.

He nodded at her. Nothing too weird, thank God. At least there was one normal person on the bus besides her.

Sitting down, she gave blond guy another glance. But he wasn't looking at her, so she couldn't see if his eye color had gone weird again. But that's when she noticed the girl with three different hair colors had something in her hands.

Kylie's breath caught again. The girl had a toad. Not a frog—a frog she could have probably handled—but a toad. A huge honking toad. What kind of a girl dyed her hair three different colors and carried a toad with her to camp? God, maybe it was one of those drug toads, the ones people licked to get high. She'd heard about them on some stupid crime show on TV but had always thought they'd made it up. She didn't know which was worse: licking a toad to get high or carrying a toad around just to be weird.

Pulling her suitcase up on the seat next to her just so no one would feel the need to join her, Kylie let out a deep sigh and looked out the window. The bus was moving, although Kylie still didn't see how the bus driver managed to reach the gas pedals.

"Do you know what they call us?" The voice came from the seat where toad girl sat.

Kylie didn't think she was talking to her, but she turned her head that way, anyway. Because the girl looked directly at her, Kylie figured she might be wrong.

"Who calls us?" Kylie asked, trying not to sound too friendly or too bitchy. The last thing she wanted was to piss these freaks off.

"The kids who go to the other camps. There's like six camps in the three-mile radius in Fallen." Using both hands she pulled her multi-colored hair back and held it there for a few seconds.

That's when Kylie noticed the girl had lost her toad. And Kylie didn't see a cage or anything where she could have tucked it away.

Great. She would probably have some freak's humongous drug toad hopping into her lap before she knew it. Not that toads totally scared her or anything. She just didn't want it jumping on her.

"They call us boneheads," the girl said.

"Why?" Kylie pulled her feet up in the seat just in case a toad hopped by.

"The camp used to be called Bone Creek Camp," the girl answered. "Because of the dinosaur bones found there."

"Ha," said the blond boy. "They also call us boners."

A few laughs echoed from the other seats. "Why is that funny?" the girl wearing all black asked in a tone so deadly serious that Kylie shivered.

"You don't know what a boner is?" Blond Boy asked. "If you'll come sit beside me, I'll show you." When he turned around, Kylie got another look at his eyes. Holy mother of pearls. They were gold. A striking feline gold. Contacts, Kylie realized. He had to be wearing some kind of weird contacts that were doing that.

Goth girl stood up as if to join the blond guy.

"Don't do it," Toad Girl, without her toad, said and stood up. Moving out into the aisle, she whispered something in the Goth girl's ear.

"Gross." Goth Girl slammed back in her seat. Then she looked over at the blond boy, and pointed a black-painted fingernail at him. "You don't want to piss me off. I eat things bigger than you in the dead of night."

"Did someone say something about the dead of night?" a voice came from the back of the bus.

Kylie turned to see who'd spoken.

Another girl, one Kylie hadn't known was there, popped up from the seat. She had jet black hair and wore sunglasses almost the same color as her hair. What made her look so abnormal was her complexion. Pasty. As in pasty white.

"Do you know why they renamed the camp Shadow Falls?" Toad Girl asked.

"No," someone answered from the front of the bus.

"Because of the Native American legend that says at dusk, if you stand beneath the falls on the property, you can see the shadows of death angels dancing."

Dancing death angels? What was wrong with these people?

Kylie swung around in her seat. Was this some nightmare? Maybe part of her night terrors? She pushed deeper in her cushioned seat and tried to focus on waking herself up from the dreams the way Dr. Day had shown her.

Focus. Focus. She took in deep breaths, in through the nose, out the mouth—all the while silently chanting, It's just a dream, it isn't real, it isn't real.

Either she wasn't asleep or her and her focus had gotten on the wrong bus, and darn if she didn't wish she'd followed it onto a different bus. Still not wanting to believe her eyes, she gazed around at the others. Blond Boy looked at her, and his eyes were black again.

Creepy. Was none of this coming across completely off the normal chart to anyone else in the bus?

Turning in her seat again, she looked back at the boy she'd dubbed the most normal. His soft green eyes, eyes that reminded her of Trey's, met hers, and he shrugged. She didn't exactly know what the shrug meant, but he didn't appear all that weirded out by everything. Which in some small way, made him as weird as the others.

Kylie swung back around and grabbed her phone from her purse and started texting Sara. Help! Stuck on a bus with freaks. Total, complete freaks.

Kylie got a text message back from Sara almost immediately. No, you help me. I think I'm pregnant.

About the Author

Award-winning author Christie Craig grew up in Alabama, where she caught lightning bugs, ran barefoot, and regularly rescued potential princes, in the form of bullfrogs, from her brothers. Today, she's still fascinated with lightning bugs, mostly wears shoes, but has turned her focus to rescuing mammals and hasn't kissed a frog in years. She now lives in Texas with her four rescued cats, one dog—who has a bad habit of eating furniture—a son, and a prince of a husband who swears he's not, and never was, a frog.

If Christie isn't writing, she's reading, sipping wine, or just enjoying laughter with her friends and family. As a freelance writer, Christie has over 3,000 national credits, as well as three works of nonfiction, including the humorous self-help/relationship book, *Wild, Wicked & Wanton: 101 Ways to Love Like You're in a Romance Novel*. Christie writes humorous romances novels for Grand Central, as well as paranormal young adult romances under the pen name C. C. Hunter. Contact Christie—she loves hearing from readers—or learn more about her and her work through her website, www.christie-craig.com.